BETWEEN SILK AND WOOL

A novel of
HOLLAND
and the
SECOND WORLD WAR

LENA SCHOLMAN

This is a work of fiction. Names, characters, places and incidents are either the product of the author's imagination or are used fictitiously, and any resemblance to actual persons, living or dead, business establishments, events or locales is entirely coincidental.

Copyright © 2022 by Lena Scholman
All rights reserved.

No part of this book may be reproduced in any form or by any electronic or mechanical means, including information storage and retrieval systems, without written permission from the author, except for the use of brief quotations in a book review.

Cover Design by Kim Collins 4x5design.com

The Westerbork Serenade (Public Domain) was written by Nol van Wesel and Max Kannewasser. May they rest in peace.

LIBRARY CATALOGING-IN-PUBLICATION DATA

Names: Scholman, Lena, author.
Title: Between Silk and Wool: a novel/Lena Scholman.
Identifiers: ISBN 978-1-7780188-1-7 (ebook)
ISBN 978-1-7780188-0-0 (print) | ISBN 978-1-7780188-2-4 (hardcover)

For Wayne
with all my love

UNIFORM AT NIGHT

The German barge has been anchored in the canal all winter, its massive berth hiding the dockyard from view. A man waits nervously in the shadows, unaccustomed to the uniform he donned an hour earlier. It scratches his skin and does nothing to keep out the wind. He thinks back to the last words the men said to him before he walked out into the night: *Bullets are precious*.

The man in uniform sees the civilian approaching from a distance, his gait brisk, as though he expects to settle matters quickly and return home for dinner.

"Heil Hitler!"

"Heil Hitler!" the uniform answers. Coughs. "You've brought something?"

His accent isn't perfect, but the civilian, who quickly hands over a piece of paper from his pocket, doesn't seem to notice.

There's nothing he can do now; and this is the part the uniform hates. He always hopes they change their minds, but they don't. He scans the list, tucks it into his belt and hands the civilian his payment.

As the man reaches to accept the envelope and turns to leave, the uniform swings his baton and knocks the civilian out.

A woman screams into the night.

The uniform looks up, but the street is empty.

Quickly, he retrieves the money, relieving the civilian of his valuables. He looks at the poor sod and a wave of sympathy wells up inside him. But it has to be done. Westerbork haunts him. The uniform crouches down, checks once more over his shoulder, and rolls the man towards the edge of the pier, pushing the limp body into the canal.

Sometimes the cold revivifies; a man might briefly struggle before disappearing beneath the black waters. This one sinks.

He tears off the ill-fitting uniform, shivers in his clothes, and looks one last time at the open water beside the barge, where the body will be found in the morning.

I'm sorry, he whispers. And he is, he truly is.

In the distance, he hears sirens. But they're not coming for him. He squints beyond the docks, and sees smoke billowing from the woods surrounding the village.

The forest is on fire.

PART I

SPRING 1940

NEUTRAL, AS BEFORE

1

BRUMMELO, GELDERLAND

MAY 1940

I'd inherited two things from my mother—her Singer sewing machine and her flat chest. Nonetheless, with a few well-placed darts, I hoped to improve on what nature had given me. One pretty blue blouse likely wouldn't be enough to stir Carl's attention, but it was a start. Biting off a loose thread, I held up the fabric, inspecting my clever alterations. Behind me, my sister Loti snored softly, her heart-shaped face even more beautiful while she slept. She took after Papa's sisters, blond and voluptuous, like a film star from America.

Before the Germans came there was no shortage of boys who wanted to walk her to school. Afterwards, like so many things, they disappeared like crayfish under rocks.

It was almost midnight. The machine whirred and hummed while my foot gently coaxed the pedal up and down in a steady rhythm. The lamp was burning low when Papa knocked on the bedroom door. The scent of his pipe filled the air.

"Why on earth are you still awake? You have school tomorrow."

I offered up a guilty smile. Loti and I obeyed Papa without question. Ever since Mama died in the sanatorium ten years earlier, he'd always known what was best for us. And I should have been asleep hours ago.

"I lost track of time," I said, because that was easier than admitting my stubborn vanity.

He looked from me to the machine and shook his head, as though waking from a dream.

"Why are *you* still awake, Papa?"

He'd gone out earlier that evening to another meeting. There were deep furrows between his eyes and lately he didn't want to answer any of my questions.

He rubbed his chin and sighed.

"Hard times ahead, *Muisje*," he said, kissing the top of my head. He only called me Hilde at church or in the market. At home, I was his little mouse. Small-boned, with brown hair that was neither a striking chestnut or golden blond, my appearance was unremarkable, like a tiny creature that skirts the kitchen searching for crumbs.

"The flower seller was greasing his rifle yesterday," I said, trying to gauge his response. The air in the market had subtly shifted from tulips and bread to bleach and oil. It was as though we were meant to inhale the warning: *get ready.*

Papa looked at his watch. "In this house it's my job to worry..." He lifted the quilt beside my sister and nodded towards the bed. "...And your job to go to sleep. Goodnight." He waited until I was under the covers and then turned down the lantern.

"I love you," I whispered.

Years later when I remembered how the invasion loomed over us that night, I don't recall feeling afraid. I trusted nothing bad would happen because Papa was paying attention. In my lifetime I would make hundreds of blouses, even one made famous by a certain ballerina who spent the war in Arnhem, but that silly blue one remained unfinished, forgotten like the fog that rises off the canals in the morning.

. . .

THE NEXT DAY as I walked down the Nonnenstraat, once again late for school, Carl came running towards me. He stopped in front of the newsstand, across from his family's bakery.

"There's no school today, sleepyhead," he said. "Miss Reinhart has sent everyone home."

"Is she sick?"

He shook his head, leading me by the elbow to a crowd of people scanning the newspapers.

"German spies captured in Utrecht…" I read the headlines slowly.

Carl stared at the canal. The cables creaked as the bridge slowly lifted up, though there wasn't a barge in sight.

"The army is preparing for invasion." His usually calm face wrinkled with uncertainty. He lifted his hand to shield his eyes from the sun and scanned the skies.

We'd been at peace for over a century. Papa swore Holland would remain neutral as before. But when Carl looked back at me, I shivered despite the day's warmth.

"I'll walk you home." He took my hand in his, squeezing it protectively, all the while glancing at the sky as if something would drop out of it.

I was too stunned to speak.

Carl De Boer had been my best friend since the first day I set foot in school after Mama died. The teacher's eyes were wet with tears and none of the other children quite knew what to say, so they turned away, as if I might contaminate them and make their mothers ill, too. All but Carl. He patted the bench beside him. The following day, he brought a woolen teddy bear and shoved it towards me. "I've still got my mother," he mumbled. It was hard to say when I went from loving him to being *in love* with him — somewhere between the first signs of polio in his six-year-old body and his indiscreet habit of copying my homework as soon as he was well enough to return to school. Either way, here we were, fourteen years old, our country the next Nazi target. It was no time for romantic fantasies. And yet his warm hand was holding mine.

Two blocks from Papa's greenhouse, we came across Mayor

Schueller, Brummelo's recently elected mayor. He stood facing the Nonnenstraat with a crow bar in his hand, sweat pouring down his forehead and the trunk of his fancy Adler full of wood.

Carl ventured closer. "You're taking down the road signs!"

"That's right. I could use a hand if you two aren't busy."

"Mayor Schueller," I said. "How are people supposed to know where they're going?"

He wiped his brow. "People from around here know which way to go."

I considered him for a moment. Mayor Schueller had bought sprouts at our stand for years, but his mother had been German. What if...?

"We don't want to make it easy for outsiders, is that it, sir?" Carl said.

"*Intruders*," Mayor Schueller corrected. He stared at the two of us for a moment and then violently spat on the ground.

What reason did I have to distrust him?

Before I could change my mind, I went and stood behind him. "I'll hold the ladder for you, sir."

PAPA HAD NAILED thick wool blankets to the windowpanes to protect us from the enemy, but a million blackout covers weren't enough to save us. Holland fell after little more than a week of fighting. The *Luftwaffe* spared our village but rained incendiary bombs on the centre of Rotterdam, killing over eight hundred civilians. After we heard General Winkelman had surrendered and the queen had escaped to London, Papa retreated to the greenhouse and stayed there for hours. He thought we didn't see him crying, leaning against his potting bench, but we knew our Papa well enough. I wasn't sure if he wept because he'd been so wrong, or because we'd been so badly crushed, but either way, defeat sank into the slant of his shoulders as he smoked his pipe. He looked worse than when Mama was taken away, when the infection in her tooth spread to her brain. Grief returned to his deep blue eyes, telling me how scared I should have been. I couldn't imagine what could be worse than the empty hospital bed in the Apeldoorn Women's Hospital. But he could.

I promised myself to be a good daughter. Whatever happened next, we'd be alright as long as we stuck together.

I waited for him to reassure us, but he stayed in his garden. Finally, I couldn't take it anymore. I decided to tiptoe upstairs and see for myself what the world looked like now that we were occupied. I slipped my hand under the heavy blanket covering the window only to discover the streets were completely empty. Coloured papers had been dropped from the skies, the first of hundreds of edicts that would slowly transform our lives. I wanted to sneak out and read them, but I'd promised myself to behave. A promise I was already regretting.

I missed the sunshine on my face. I missed walking along the canal with Carl and gossiping with his mother in the bakery. (Mevrouw De Boer had a subscription to Vogue magazine and saved the old copies for me.) As the days went by, Loti and I helped Papa in the greenhouse, but he forbade us from venturing out onto the Nonnenstraat. Our only news came from the wireless, and none of it was encouraging. Every afternoon Papa went out only to quickly disappear down to the cellar upon his return.

"What's he doing?" I asked Loti.

"Counting supplies."

"Again?"

He'd ticked off the potato barrels and preserves in his neat ledger book on the kitchen table numerous times. Yet he'd emerge from the dark in dirty coveralls, mumbling to himself and going through his notebook over and over. I opened his book one day and saw he had two columns. One was clearly for food, but the other was a mystery to me.

"Papa," I asked him. "What's this?"

He grabbed the ledger from me. "It's none of your concern, Muisje."

"Maybe I could help?"

A sad smile appeared on his face. "Try not to be so nosy. And whatever you do, don't tell anyone about the food in the cellar. Do you understand?"

It seemed important that I agree with him just then, so I nodded, though Papa had never been secretive like this before.

As we tried to fall asleep one night about a week after the official surrender, we heard a low rumble echoing on the cobblestone along the Nonnenstraat. Loti and I inched closer to one another.

Suddenly, Papa burst into our room. "Girls! Quick! Back to the cellar!"

"But Papa, there's no siren," I said.

"Never mind. Follow me." He gathered our quilts and we hurried down the stairs behind him. In the cellar he'd laid down an old carpet to keep us from the damp. On the street outside, we heard muffled shouting, a man on a loudspeaker, an engine revving and then... silence.

"Can we go back to bed now?" Loti yawned.

Papa shook his head. "We'll sleep here tonight."

My sister didn't bother arguing and soon after, drifted off. As for me, I kept trying to imagine our town. Who was out there? What were they doing? I was too anxious to give into slumber.

Papa smiled gently. "Some things never change, do they?"

He got up, opened the hatch and went in search of his pipe. When he returned, he carried a thick book under his arm. Turning up the lantern, he beckoned me close. I rested my head on his shoulder.

"I'm too old for stories."

"I was afraid of that, Muisje."

"What's going to happen?"

"We make the best of things, as we've always done."

He made it sound so simple. He put his arm around my shoulders and cleared his throat. "Let's not speak of this anymore."

He held out the familiar book, *Java Ho*. Papa hadn't enjoyed his time as a marine, he didn't see the point in empire building, preferring to grow potatoes in his little plot, but he loved Asia. Reading about the South Pacific made him feel warm. I closed my eyes and his baritone voice recalled the tropical isles, the brave captain and the exploding brandy kegs. My eyelids grew heavy, and the next thing I knew, it was morning and the Nazis had come to Brummelo.

I SAW them for the first time when the bells on the Catholic Basilica chimed nine o'clock. The soldiers wandered through the market, as though it was a perfectly ordinary thing to do. We stared at them while they bought herring and lounged under the plane trees, like men in hunting gear, ready to venture into the Veluwe forest in search of wild boar.

A shadow stood in front of our stall, blocking my view.

"A serious one, *ja?*"

The captain himself reached forward to shake hands with Papa. "Captain Wolfgang von Hahn. I congratulate you on your fine produce."

Papa stared at the gold epaulettes on the captain's jacket. Loti and I shrank behind him.

"Carry on with your gardens."

How dare he speak to Papa in that condescending tone. As if we needed *his* permission to plant and harvest! Just when I thought Papa might make a face, turn towards me and roll his eyes or even just mutter *scheisse* in his comical German accent, he cleared his throat and called the captain back.

"Herr captain. Try the radishes. Picked fresh this morning."

My cheeks burned. How could he?

"Thank you!" The captain helped himself to an entire bunch and strode off to his subordinates, offering up the bright red vegetables. One young officer looked over his shoulder towards our stand. He couldn't have been much older than twenty. White-blond hair stuck out from underneath his helmet like feathers. Oh God, please don't come over here.

Too late. He'd already spotted Loti rearranging the asparagus, and like everyone else, he was drawn in for a closer look.

He crossed the square in less than a minute. "Delicious, sir," he tried to maintain the façade of interest in my father's vegetables.

Papa looked up.

"Is it true the soldiers are staying at the school?" Loti asked.

The officer nodded. "Not for long. Once we're billeted, the schools will reopen."

"That's good news," Papa said. "I don't want my daughters' education to suffer."

The officer looked over his shoulder towards the school. "Of course. Schools will open once the appropriate teachers are in place."

"What's wrong with our old ones?" I blurted out.

Papa opened his eyes wide and slowly shook his head. "Hilde…"

The German shrugged. "Perhaps nothing. As long as they pass the captain's approval."

My heart sank. Some of the older boys called our teacher, Miss Reinhart, 'the communist' behind her back, but if she heard them, she didn't care. She'd shown us on the map how Hitler's army was seizing other countries, telling us about a dangerous book he'd written that nobody seemed to worry about. *This is the high-water mark*, she'd said. *And this* — she'd waved her arm above her head — *is where we are right now*. No one had listened. The bell had rung and we'd escaped her warnings for another day.

"What's your name, son?" Papa asked, eager to change the subject.

At that moment I looked towards the bakery and saw Carl step onto the street. His limp, barely noticeable most days, stood in stark contrast to the rigid goose steps of the soldiers. Though he saw me, he didn't wave. A look of confusion crossed his face as he took in the German lingering at our stall.

The officer's name was Frid. His smile revealed a gap between his teeth, which made him appear harmless, until his gun glinted in the sunshine. Until his gaze rested a moment too long on Loti when Papa turned his back.

We didn't sell much that morning.

Papa removed his cap and ran his fingers through his hair. "Well, girls, we might as well head back and pickle this asparagus."

The streets were quiet again. I wanted to stop at the bakery but Papa was determined to steer us home. Once we arrived at Number

Eleven, Papa lit his pipe, Loti filled the sink and I started on dinner. On the radio Queen Wilhelmina implored us to quietly resist the occupiers.

"See Papa? We can't give them our food. We must stand up to them!"

He puffed away, wearily shaking his head at me. "You know nothing about war, daughter. There's no resistance without blood."

I stared at him blankly.

"If the captain or any other soldier, speaks to you, you must both defer to them. Do you understand?"

Loti nodded, but I disagreed. I peeled the potatoes so quickly I shaved the skin off one of my knuckles. I reached for a cloth before Papa noticed. Nevertheless, he looked up and saw the abandoned knife and red seeping through my bandage.

"Muisje. Holland has fallen. We must make the best of things."

I turned towards the sink and in a flash saw my mother standing in front of me.

I'm five years old and she's wearing her favourite yellow dress, dancing to Louis Armstrong on the radio. When she catches me staring, she laughs. "Well now, Muisje. Are you going to just stand there, or are you going to join in?"

We ate the evening meal in silence, while Krupp trucks rolled down the street outside our front door.

We must make the best of things.

As far as Papa knew, we canned a dozen jars of asparagus. He carefully added to his ledger and carried the preserves to the cellar. What was the harm of setting aside the thirteenth jar in the back of my wardrobe, behind the bolts of fabric leftover from Mama? I didn't know what compelled me to do it. Many years later I would look back and wonder what instinct drove us to do the things we did. I have so many excuses.

THAT NIGHT, I went to bed and curled against Loti's warm body. We lay in the darkness listening to the strange new sounds of patrols.

Sometimes I imagined I heard a motorcycle idling in front of the greenhouse, but I couldn't be certain.

"The Germans are ugly, aren't they?" I knew Loti wasn't sleeping yet. I could always tell when her breathing changed. "Loti?"

"If you say so," she murmured.

Now I was wide awake. "Don't tell me you think that feather-head *Mof* is handsome?"

"Go to sleep, Hilde," Loti sounded older, impatient, scared.

Despite our proximity, she felt far away. I reached for her hand in the dark, promising myself that whatever happened, I would not lose her. Just by pressing her fingers against mine, I thought I'd keep her safe.

I should have squeezed harder.

2

The sun rose pink and mauve over the horizon, casting cool shadows from the turrets onto Soelenkasteel's manicured lawn below. Astrid tied her thick brown hair into a bun and quietly stole away to the stables so as not to wake her children. She needed time alone.

Peaceful, she thought, as the horses looked up at her expectantly. She searched their faces in the dim light, wondering if they sensed her apprehension. The young gelding whinnied, and Astrid caressed his glossy flank.

"I'll take care of you now, little one." Closing her eyes, she nuzzled the horse's neck. The sound of a pitchfork being tossed into the hay made her jump.

"I've already fed them, Lady Astrid. Everything's ready." A short, thin man appeared in the doorway. He fumbled with a ring of keys in his hands.

"What are *you* doing in my stables?" She hated surprises.

Kurt Schueller, former jockey, recently elected mayor, fixed his gaze upon her and smiled. Tanned and boyish, with strawberry blond hair that needed trimming, he was a wiry flirt forever punching above his weight. "There aren't too many people around here and the girls were getting hungry."

Astrid huffed. "Yes, well…my stablemaster found his reservist's uniform last month and his unit was sent to patrol the border."

Schueller sighed.

"Exactly. We both know how that went."

"You haven't heard from him since?"

Astrid shook her head. Most of her staff had left, save for her cook, Eva, the gardener and two of the younger maids. Even the governess had left, claiming her family needed her. Here was a woman who'd been in Astrid's employ for years and knew how to handle impulsive fourteen-year old Katrine and her shy younger brother, Hans. Astrid had offered more money, but her pride stopped her from begging — a decision she was beginning to question as the weeks went on.

Schueller broke her reverie. "I need to show you something."

He turned into the storeroom where the tack hung from the rafters. Taking a key from the ring, he opened a door hidden by the feedbags. A narrow shelf revealed bottles of muscle liniment, and tucked behind, the unmistakable sheen of gunmetal. Two hunting rifles, a pistol and half a dozen boxes of bullets lay hidden away in the dust. Astrid's eyes widened.

"All weapons must be turned in…" Astrid said, her voice a whisper. Where did this all come from and how did Schueller know about it if she didn't?

"It's concealed well enough. We could pretend we never saw it," Schueller said. "I thought your husband would have told you." His voice trailed off.

There had been no word from Batavia. It wasn't only Astrid who wondered if her children would ever see their father again; the servants had been whispering for years about Jan Stenger's eccentricities.

"I must have forgotten," she said, looking away. Swiftly, she pocketed a pistol and some cartridges. Just in case.

I can take care of myself. I definitely don't need help from you, of all people.

They walked together back up to the castle, her new acquisition a comforting weight in her pocket.

"Could you shoot a lame horse if you had to?" he asked.

Astrid looked at him in surprise. "What?"

"If there was no one else around, could you do it?"

She glanced back at the paddocks. She never ate *rookvlees*—horse meat—she forbade it in her household. Jan had thought her aversion melodramatic, but he was from the city. To him, a horse was a commodity, like soap or cooking oil. The fifteen year age difference was only one of a thousand little things that separated them.

"I've hunted grouse since I was six years old," she said, straightening her spine. "Of course I know how to shoot a gun."

Schueller nodded, but he didn't look convinced.

Astrid watched him drive away in his fancy car. The truth was, she could shoot anything. Anything but a horse.

"It's been months and we haven't heard a thing," Katrine complained later that day. "Do we even know if Father's *trying* to get home?"

Balancing a bucket of grain on her hip, her daughter looked to her for answers Astrid did not have. A woman could only write so many letters. There were no replies to her pleas for money, no sympathetic acknowledgement that she was running the estate completely on her own.

Her shoulders ached from mucking out the stalls. Hans worked twice as fast as his sister, and kept his mouth shut. The governess hadn't left on account of him, that much was certain.

"It's never been easy to cross the ocean. The entire world seems to have slowed to a halt, and your father is caught in that—"

"If *you* would just let us go into the village, we could see for ourselves what's really going on," Katrine muttered.

Astrid sighed, picked up the pitchfork and lined the pregnant mare's stall with fresh straw. Soon the horse would foal and she had to be ready. She missed the stablemaster very much right then, but she'd given up hope the poor fellow would return. What would become of them now? How would the children get a proper education? How would she pay the staff? Staring at her blistered hands, she wondered how long until they became calloused.

Her thoughts were interrupted by the arrival of Eva, the cook.

"I brought you some coffee and warm bread, Mevrouw. You're all working so hard." She overturned a crate and covered it with a checkered tablecloth. "It's ten o'clock. Time for a break."

Her son smiled. "Some things never change."

"If you learn how to rest, you'll learn how to work," Eva said. "And you are a good worker, sir, helping your mother until the men come back."

Hans blushed. He was every servant's favourite, always had been.

"What is it like in the village, Eva?" Katrine demanded. "Is it true there's one German for every ten Dutchmen?"

"Darling, where do you get these ridiculous notions?" Astrid said.

Eva shook her head. "When I went to see about the mail, I noticed a regiment setting up in the public school. They've been delivering edicts door-to-door. They were polite enough, but—"

Astrid quickly downed her coffee. "Yes, well. I'm sure we'll see them soon enough. I have business to attend to in the village." She looked at her daughter. "Once I've determined whether it's safe, you may accompany me."

"Mevrouw," Eva said, averting her eyes. "There's one more thing. You received a letter today."

"For heaven's sakes, why didn't you say so right away? We've been waiting for word from Batavia—"

Eva held the letter towards Astrid. "It's not from Meneer Stenger, Mevrouw." The elderly cook trembled. "And I don't have a good feeling about it."

Astrid examined the envelope. Her heart sank at the swastika insignia. Hurriedly she opened the letter and began reading. When she'd finished, she took a deep breath.

I can't do this.

She forced a tight smile and with all the nonchalance she could muster, folded the letter back up and tucked it into her pocket. "Well then…children. Please finish up in here. My presence is required immediately at the Stadhuis. I'll see you for luncheon." Astrid stood up to leave.

"What's going on?" Katrine said.

"It appears we're to receive some unexpected guests—"

"Guests? Oh my. I'll have to get to work then," Eva said.

"No, Eva. It's not like that." Astrid shook her head in disbelief.

I can't do this.

"Soelenkasteel has been selected by the local captain to house some of the officers."

Katrine's hand flew to her mouth. "What? Mother! We can't have them here."

"We don't have a choice," Hans said. "Do we?"

Astrid reached for her son and gently smoothed his hair from his eyes. She must be brave in front of her children. "I'm sure something more suitable can be arranged."

With that, she waved goodbye and headed up the path towards Soelenkasteel. She paused to look at it from the stone wall of the garden. Ivy covered the sections that had been rebuilt after the Napoleonic Wars, but the scars remained. She placed her palm on the limestone and felt its reassuring solidity. It was made to withstand invaders. Could she?

Astrid dressed in her finest riding attire and prepared Philomena, her best mount.

"Send me, Mevrouw," Eva offered. "There are long lines everywhere."

Astrid shook her head.

I must do this.

SHE RODE into the village along the footpath through the woods and tied Philomena up under the shade of an old plane tree. She made her way onto the *Hoofdstraat* where the dry goods shopkeeper was waving his hands in the air, breaking up the crowd.

"There's no more tea here! Come back next week, maybe we'll have some then."

Astrid studied the faces of those who'd been queued up for some time. They began to grumble, sending dirty glances down the street towards the soldiers lounging in the café. Were these the same men who would soon come to Soelenkasteel? What a horrid thought!

For now, she must have money. She joined the line at the bank and waited. It was cool inside, and she was grateful for the quiet. She was almost at the teller when a sound like a swarm of millions of bees sent everyone to the ground.

The customers screamed. What was happening? The fighting was over, wasn't it? The glass crystals of the chandelier rattled. Outside on the street, a child wailed.

"I'll bet it's the RAF," someone muttered. "A bit late."

The droning ceased and slowly people began to collect themselves up off the ground. A long-faced man peered into the street but was roughly pushed back in by a soldier.

"*Achtung!* Everyone stays put. That's an order!"

What were Katrine and Hans doing at the castle? Hans would be with the horses, but Katrine? Astrid had forbidden her to leave the grounds but that meant nothing if she was restless. She glanced around at the other patrons. Men in wrinkled suits checked their watches and housewives dabbed their faces with handkerchiefs, everyone resigned to a long wait. Tentatively, Astrid approached the wicket, tapping her boot on the marble floor until a teller reappeared.

"Is it possible to withdraw funds now?"

The teller's face was pinched and tired. "There's a daily limit."

Astrid wondered if this woman had heard the queen's speech encouraging citizens to quietly resist the occupiers. A minimum withdrawal wasn't going to do. Just as she was about to argue, other patrons began grumbling behind her.

"Just take what she can give you today, Mevrouw."

"Come on, we'll be out on the streets again soon, keep it movin'."

And then from somewhere behind her, Kurt Schueller whispered, "If you need cash, you could always sell Philomena."

Astrid spun around, locked eyes with him and gave him a curt nod. "Mayor."

He knew she'd never sell Philomena. The golden palomino was her one sure source of income. As long as people were still racing thoroughbreds.

Grumbling, she signed for the small stack of guilders, placed them securely in her purse and took a seat on a bench by the wall to wait for the all clear. Kurt Schueller plunked himself down opposite her. A lifetime ago, they'd been friends — of sorts.

To her left a young girl about Katrine's age sat on the bench smiling in Schueller's direction. Astrid stared at her dress. It was an original cut — a diagonal seam from the shoulders with a pin-tucked bust. She'd seen something like it in the latest Vogue magazine. It was hardly the kind of thing she'd expected to find in Brummelo.

"What do you think of the new mayor?" the girl asked.

"You know him?" Astrid said, surprised.

"My older sister just got a job at the Stadhuis." Her blue eyes had a faraway look to them. "Working for the mayor, of course."

Astrid nodded absently. How long was she going to be stuck here?

"I'm Hilde." The girl with the big blue eyes and unkempt hair stuck out her hand. "Hilde Zontag."

Astrid hesitated. Out of the corner of her eye she saw Kurt Schueller put down his book. He was such an obvious eavesdropper.

"Hilde! You've met Brummelo's enigmatic chatelaine! I bet she has a few gowns you could repair up at the castle, don't you, Mevrouw?" Schueller's eyes sparkled under heavy brows.

His presence was so unsettling. Astrid remembered the Queen's Cup at the Veluwe's Royal Lodewijk Racetracks before the children were born. They'd chatted amiably only hours before he was hauled away in handcuffs. She heard the rumours, but before she'd made up her mind what to believe — did he *mean* to harm her horse? — her parents had married her off to a man fifteen years her senior, whose fortune would restore their own. After that, at barely twenty she had Katrine and didn't have time to worry about the goings on at the racetracks anymore.

"I don't see myself putting on evening gowns in the near future, though I do love your dress *jongedame*." Astrid smiled benevolently at the girl and turned back to Schueller. "What I really need right now is advice about my horses. Perhaps you could help?"

The door burst open before he could answer.

"The danger has passed. It's safe in the streets again." A middle-aged German, with piercing blue eyes under hooded lids held the door. It was a chivalrous gesture, but no one thanked him.

He smiled towards Hilde. "Hello again, Miss Asparagus."

Hilde ignored him and slipped through the door, hurrying towards a stall in the square. The officer rocked on his heels. "I have a daughter her age at home."

Schueller stood up. "Mevrouw, this is Captain Wolfgang Von Hahn. Captain, Lady Astrid Van Soelen."

The captain stared at Astrid, as though he were trying to solve a problem. Slowly, she realized he was the author of the requisition. A trickle of perspiration ran down her spine.

"Lady Astrid...of Soelenkasteel, the castle by the forest! Yes, yes. I shall see you in a few days. We expect to have all the men settled in various residences by next Tuesday."

Next Tuesday. That hardly gave her any time...

He turned to go, but Astrid grasped his arm impulsively. He started at her touch.

"Captain..." Astrid held her head up, trying not to care that the other patrons were glaring at her. Let them stare. They didn't have her debts. They might be content with the daily limit, but how was she supposed to run a household like hers on a pittance?

She lowered her voice. "Perhaps you can assist me, Herr Captain. There are new regulations about withdrawals, but my staff need their wages, and now we must get your rooms ready." She lowered her eyes. "You understand, sir?"

The captain's face broke into a smile and he wasted no time cutting to the front of the line. Astrid filled her wallet with the extra guilders and minutes later strode outside to untie her restless horse.

Schueller strolled past smoking a fat cigar, for all appearances simply watching the world go by.

"Well played, Mevrouw, well played."

"I couldn't care less about the Germans, Schueller. But my children..." She paused. "They cannot spend their days mucking out horse stalls. I simply must find a new governess for them."

"Do you plan on sticking your head in the sand whenever it suits you?"

If she could manage such a thing, that was precisely what she would do. She had no desire to get involved with the captain or anyone else. Astrid mounted her horse and looked towards the four turrets of her castle rising above the pine trees in the distance.

"It's called *neutrality*."

"Ah, yes. Wonderful strategy." He snorted, a look of disgust crossing his face.

She stared back at the jockey. "Are we on the same team this time, Mayor?"

If it is indeed a game.

She didn't like his lack of decorum, she didn't like his smile and she didn't trust his loyalties, especially now. But he was resourceful, and if she couldn't manage neutrality all the time, his connections had to count for something.

He took a long puff of his cigar and continued watching her.

"Mayor Schueller?"

He patted Philomena's glossy neck. "I'm not sure *you* know which team you're on yet, Mevrouw."

"I do not take sides. I'm only looking out for the best interests of the children. And our home."

"I see."

She sighed. Soelenkasteel had stood through Habsburg rule, Spanish imperial conquests, the Eighty Years' War and centuries of religious conflict. Its walls had weathered many battles; certainly this would be but one more.

"I am not a complicated woman. Men create chaos and women clean up the mess."

"And if the rules change?" he said.

Astrid thought of the old rumours of Schueller's ruthlessness at the tracks. "*You'll* be ready I suppose?"

"I was born to bend the rules, Mevrouw." He said this without his usual cockeyed smile. "Especially if the rules are no good to begin with."

Astrid scowled. "They're coming to Soelenkasteel."

"So I heard. Lucky you."

His gaze was starting to make her uncomfortable. "I should go."

Schueller moved his hand from Philomena's neck to Astrid's knee. "They'll *take* your horses and send them to the front lines if you don't act fast. Let me help you negotiate a loan agreement. Maybe you can keep them close."

They'd requisitioned cars, bicycles and schools. Why hadn't she anticipated they'd take the livestock, too?

"I wouldn't know where to start. I have a pregnant mare I could use a hand with soon. The foal will be a big one. I bred her with Nuage."

"Aha! Practically royal pedigree."

Astrid shrugged. "Will you be lurking around my stables again if I need you?"

"Oh, my little ostrich." He winked. "I already took what I needed from your barns." He smiled at her alarmed expression and smacked Philomena on the rump, sending Astrid lurching forward towards her home.

"Send someone when the contractions start!"

ASTRID WAS ON HER KNEES, holding the delicate cups from the blue and white Limoges tea service her grandmother had received as a wedding gift from the Crown Prince. Instinct told her to pack everything. The captain would arrive the following afternoon with four officers. Eva and Katrine had the silverware half boxed up when Astrid abruptly changed her mind.

"Wait," she said. "They'll expect us to use it. We mustn't show that we've let our standards slip. Take it out again and arrange it in the sideboard."

"What if they break our family heirlooms?" Katrine said.

Why should they think she was making room for them? There had to be a way to keep what was theirs.

"There are more valuable items we can hide. Keep one of everything for regular service. Start with the crystal and china, I'll do my jewellery."

"Where will we put it all?" Katrine asked.

Where indeed? The stables? Yes. She knew just the spot. But she'd keep it to herself.

"I'll take care of that, darling."

The less they knew the better.

The Horch town car rumbled through the gates the following morning. Astrid had been pacing her balcony since breakfast and felt almost relieved when they finally arrived.

The captain stood with four other officers, admiring the large fountain that occupied the central garden around the laneway. He had his back to her and for once didn't seem to be in any rush. She recognized one of the officers, a young man with white-blond hair who'd acted as an intermediary communicating the captain's arrival. The others stood at ease beside their superior, surveying the view of the pine forest. A large Alsatian nosed around the yard and one of the soldiers slipped it a snack from his pocket. Astrid was seized by a pang of sympathy for them. They were so young. A change of clothing and they could be tourists enjoying an afternoon in the Veluwe. But no. Their uniforms confirmed these men were no sightseers.

Astrid swallowed a sigh. "Captain."

He turned. "Mevrouw. Lovely home. The gables remind me of the manor houses in Lübeck or Potsdam. Our countries were once united kingdoms, you know."

She knew the important families of Europe, but in no way did the borders of another century make her feel any kinship towards this man. Instantly she despised his proprietary gaze.

He spoke in a mélange of Dutch-German that Astrid mostly understood.

"It's a privilege to preserve my family's ancestral home, captain." There was no need to tell him she was also a pragmatist; she'd married a man of her father's choosing for the sake of the estate. As she watched the captain take in the castle towers and the heavy wooden doors, she guessed he was prone to nostalgia, too.

"Are you from Lübeck?"

"No…Dresden. I was stationed in Lübeck for training."

Training to invade Holland, Astrid thought bitterly. Aloud she asked if the officers wanted tea. To her surprise, they'd brought provisions. The officer with the platinum hair, Frid, handed Astrid a small box containing tea, biscuits, jam and a small tin of sugar—all staples the stores were out of. She tried not to show what a small thrill it gave her to see these simple items again. Turning, she motioned the Germans to follow her into the foyer.

"Eva," Astrid called out. "Please prepare tea. I will take our"—the word caught in her throat—"*guests* to their quarters."

The cook slipped away with a nod. Astrid waved at Katrine and Hans, who were lingering on the landing, to join her. Hans walked slowly down the elegant marble staircase, measuring each footfall carefully, averting his eyes from the gaze of the young soldiers who would soon sleep one floor above him. Katrine squared her shoulders, lifted her chin and breezed down behind her brother, taking in each German with open curiosity.

Astrid was unsure of the protocol for introductions under such circumstances. Various governesses had tried to teach them proper decorum. But there was nothing in the etiquette manuals for how to greet soldiers requisitioning one's home. On the streets, most townspeople ignored the Germans. They treated them as though they were invisible, and Astrid had to admit she admired their stubborn silence. And yet. Here they were in her home. Finally, the captain broke the tension.

"We are cousins, Germans and Dutchmen. *Ja?*" He stuck out his hand and introduced the others.

Astrid felt prompted to introduce her children in return. Shyly, Hans shook hands and fell back into her shadow. When Katrine spotted the dog, she caressed his silky ears. Animals knew no borders.

"And your husband?" the captain inquired, squinting around at the closed doors along the empty hallways. "This home is registered to Meneer Jan Stenger, *ja?*"

Astrid led them to the dining room. "Indeed. My husband imports silks, brocades, velvets and satin from the islands." She fingered the bright palm designs of the heavy curtains. "His travel back to Europe from Batavia has been…impeded by present circumstance."

"I see," he said, joining Astrid by the window and surveying the view of the gardens. He grunted approval at the neat rows of potatoes, carrots, onion and kale.

"Show us the rest of the castle, Mevrouw," he said, his tone suddenly less friendly.

"Very well. Follow me please."

He instructed his men to enjoy their tea and bring in their trunks. "I shall select my quarters now."

Select his quarters? After a moment, she left her children with the soldiers. Looking over her shoulder she wondered if they'd sit in silence or cobble together a conversation of sorts. Which would she prefer?

She led the captain up the stairs and stood on the landing. Though electricity was installed after the last war, the corridors were still not well lit and Astrid hated how the heavy wool carpet muffled their footsteps; she liked to know when people were coming or going. A castle was meant to echo a little. The intimacy of the hallway seemed oppressive to her in the company of this brusque foreigner.

Five bedroom suites dominated the second floor. Only a month ago servants occupied the third. Astrid marched down the hallway and continued up another flight of stairs. The garret bedrooms all shared the same slanted ceilings and general draughtiness. But the beds were solid and the washstands serviceable. Astrid looked upon the quarters the governess had so recently vacated and was seized by a wave of loss.

The captain assessed the rooms and shook his head. "Show me the other rooms."

The hallway narrowed again.

"In the family wing?" she asked, horrified.

"Naturally." He brushed by her and stomped down to the second floor. She caught up to him in the hallway.

"Open these doors."

Astrid's hands shook as she fumbled for the keys to open each of the five bedrooms. She tried to keep her face neutral as she followed one step behind him. He began in the spare bedroom at the far end. No one had stayed there in years, and the furniture was covered in white sheets and dust. He strode through the children's rooms and Astrid's suite, where he picked up a silver-framed family portrait from her desk, examining it for a long moment before casting it aside and proceeding to the end of the hallway—Jan's velvet-papered suite. He rocked on his tiptoes in front of the French doors that led onto a small balcony, his hands clasped behind his back.

"Perfect. I like to follow the progress in the garden. The boys can stay upstairs, but this is more to my liking." He puffed out his chest.

How dare he? She suddenly felt the weight of Jan's abandonment. How could she ignore the captain if he slept so close? She ran her finger along the banister and inspected a thin layer of dust. Taking a handkerchief from her skirts she rubbed the wood vigorously as though she could save her home by polishing it to death. The gleaming veneer gave her no satisfaction. Instead, Schueller's warning sprang to mind.

Which team are you on?

She must forget the captain's insult, and any others, showing nothing but indifference. She would drink German tea and hold her head higher than the humiliation she felt. If it meant her children would be safe, she would do whatever it took. Wriggling a key off the ring, she thrust it towards the captain in a magnanimous gesture.

"*Welkomen*, Captain."

3

A name is all one has in the end, but Benjamin Rosenblum wasn't a sentimentalist. His name, *their* name, would put them in danger. It was time to leave. He hated to argue, especially with his uncle, a gentle man who fed the pigeons in the Dam Square every morning. But on this wager, Benjamin was certain he'd gambled on the winning side.

"It's not legal," Nathan protested. "And it's robbery besides. How can a bit of ink on paper cost so much?"

But he hadn't seen the man at work like Benjamin had. The talented forger, a commercial artist whose name Benjamin's contact refused to share, worked in a dark backroom behind a steel door with four deadbolts. Benjamin reminded his uncle of the troubles in Berlin —the Night of Broken Glass.

Nathan Rosenblum took off his spectacles and stared at him, a deep searching gaze that held older memories of upheaval and goodbyes. "Can you be sure it will work?"

Certainty wasn't Benjamin's strong suit. For the better part of the last thirty years he had operated on instinct. A new name mightn't be enough to keep them safe, but it was a start.

"This is the best way I know how to protect you," Benjamin said softly. He sat down across from Nathan's workbench and switched off his lamp. "Enough for tonight."

Suddenly his uncle laughed, deep worry lines disappearing. "What a *putz*! I suppose I should be grateful. It's not as if those scrawny muscles of yours could protect me."

Benjamin held up a bicep and scowled. "Sinewy, not scrawny."

Nathan rolled his eyes and they laughed, breaking the tension for a moment. His uncle always teased him about his schoolboy hands. Where Nathan's fingers bore the marks of decades spent shaping rocks into precious gems, Benjamin rarely held anything heavier than a textbook. He'd taken up rowing on the Amstel River once to impress a girl, and had come home complaining of callouses. His uncle had scolded him for chasing skirts when he ought to have been pursuing tenure at Amsterdam's Free University.

Back then—was it only a few months ago?—Benjamin thought he had time. But first Austria, then Czechoslovakia, Poland…and before they knew it Holland, Luxembourg, Belgium and France. The fresh-faced youngsters who'd lined the seats of his Introduction to Economics course had gradually disappeared into volunteer regiments. If it weren't for the seizures that had plagued him as a child, he would have been marching alongside them.

Before the occupation, he sipped coffee in the River Quarter cafés, listening as German Jews recounted the violence in Berlin. At first, Benjamin made plans to go to England. He could afford two passages to Liverpool. But the ports were blown up to protect the British, and their ship never sailed. His uncle believed it was the Almighty's will—they were not meant to leave.

In the city, his friends had debated endlessly about the experimental farm, the *Werkdorp*, and whether they should abandon their floundering businesses, learn agriculture and find their way to Palestine.

"Benji," his friend Saul once teased. "Ever milked a cow?"

They had laughed to cover up their fears. Benjamin's colleagues and students were neither farmers nor fighters. And now they were trapped without the means or connections to secure visas and leave for America like their wealthier friends had done. The Almighty's will, Benjamin hoped, was that his desperate letter, sent a fortnight ago, might reach an old friend who might be in a position to help.

If Amsterdam turned into another Berlin, Benjamin Rosenblum couldn't protect his elderly uncle. He was no hero, but he wasn't a fool, either. In the quiet despair in other men's eyes he saw danger on the horizon. It was time to move. The Exodus that coursed through his blood propelled him to leave the city behind.

By the time he'd marked his students' final papers, he'd no longer be Benjamin Rosenblum. He stared at his new passport and turned it over in his hand.

Benjamin Van Laar. It was a typical Dutch name. Neutral, poetic even. Until he could find a way for them to leave, perhaps a new name could help them blend in. His uncle's familiar refrain echoed in his mind.

Be'ezrát hashém—if God willed it to be so.

Was that a blessing or a curse?

BENJAMIN STOOD on the bustling platform beside his uncle Nathan, their shoulders lightly touching. Neither man spoke. They'd argued for weeks; now, exhausted and out of words, they counted down the minutes until the train pulled into the station. It was early, the city not yet awake.

"I'm not sure about this," Nathan said miserably. "I promised your parents I'd look after you. The Jewish Council is hopeful..."

Benjamin swallowed a sigh. His uncle had thrown his lot in with the Council—a dubious set of civil servants trying to make the best of an untenable situation.

"Uncle," he turned away from the tracks and faced the old man. Nathan thought him stubborn, pigheaded. Benjamin thought his uncle was blinded by the assurances of an aging rabbi who reasoned the synagogue was secure only because it hadn't been firebombed. Yet.

"I'll find work on a farm and bring you back food and money. It's *my* turn to take care of you." Benjamin forced a smile.

His post at the university had been taken, and the city was flooded with intellectuals from Austria and Germany. Like Herr Blum, who'd lost his right eye during the riots in Berlin. Or Frau Henkle, whose three sons went missing from their accounting firm one morning. It was only a matter of time until the same happened in Amsterdam. He'd once thought his career would give him stability, but he'd quickly learned that nothing was guaranteed. A degree was worthless if the institutions burned to the ground.

"You didn't raise me to be a lazybones."

"I'd rather you lazy and safe than industrious and far away. I shall miss you."

"I'll write as soon as I'm settled."

The train whistled into the station. Around them people picked up their suitcases and began to say goodbye. How many others carried with them the guilt of leaving?

"May the Almighty lead you in peace, direct your steps in peace, support you in peace…"

"I will reach my destination in life, joy and peace. Be well, uncle." Benjamin finished the prayer, kissed Nathan on both cheeks and stepped onto his train.

As he made his way down the rows he looked out the window and saw tears streaming down Nathan's wrinkled face. His lips were moving, and though Benjamin couldn't hear, he knew the murmured prayer by heart.

"…Return to me in peace."

BRUMMELO, Benjamin decided, was the kind of town people mostly travelled through while making their way towards more important destinations. Apeldoorn or Arnhem, perhaps. It wasn't an end point, though not because it lacked charm. Tucked into the Veluwe Forest, its medieval square was bordered by the Town Hall, a Catholic basilica and a Reformed Church. The streets fanned out towards shipping canals, a large bridge and the railway yards. Benjamin only knew of its existence at all because of an episode years earlier that his uncle ruefully referred to as his *delinquent adventure*.

As the train travelled east, Benjamin leaned against the cool glass window and closed his eyes. He remembered the idealism of his student years, a naïveté so blinding it landed him in jail. As though it were only yesterday, he recalled the bunk beds and the strange, wiry roommate who immediately stood up to introduce himself.

"Kurt Schueller." The short man had stuck out his hand to shake Benjamin's as the metal door clanged shut behind him. "So…what did you do?"

Do? She was a friend in need.

"I helped a young woman. She didn't want to marry the person her parents had chosen."

Schueller raised an eyebrow. "Ah, so you're a kidnapper."

Benjamin laughed. "I tried to barter her jewellery for her so she could go to South Africa."

"So you're a thief?"

"Worse. Her father showed up at the dealer's."

"And here you are." Schueller whistled. "She must have been gorgeous. What did they charge you with?"

"Fraud, mischief, extortion…"

Schueller assessed him. "So basically you're an idiot?"

"Guilty as charged."

They'd laughed so hard the guards yelled at them to shut up or else.

As the train travelled through Apeldoorn, a porter walked down the aisle offering snacks to the passengers. Benjamin shook his head no and buried his nose into his well-worn Agatha Christie novel. His stint in prison was so long ago; he was just a kid in many ways, guilty of delusions of heroism. But as he went on to his doctoral studies and found his place in the world of economics and academia, Schueller's story had stayed with him. He put down his book and stared at the scenery rushing past, recalling the night Schueller told him why *he* was locked up.

ONCE A PRIZE-WINNING JOCKEY, Kurt Schueller had retired from competition and turned his hand to breeding. And then the Depression struck. He'd put all he had into one horse and made a few risky gambles on the side. He was set to win the National Championship, when along came a rival. A golden palomino bred by an aristocrat. One look at that horse and Schueller knew he was in trouble. When the groom stepped out of the competition's stall for a break, he seized his chance and slipped the mare a sedative.

Schueller swore he only wanted to take her out of one race. *Just enough to dull her senses you see.* But her foot caught, and the beast stumbled, crushing her handler against the stable wall, breaking the man's collarbone and humerus. When Benjamin asked if he'd confessed, Schueller had slowly nodded.

The aristocrat had seen him go into the paddock. She wasn't the kind of woman you could lie to, Schueller explained.

So you also struggle with beautiful women? Benjamin had teased.

On that, he remembered Schueller was silent.

They spent their days walking the yard and talking. When Benjamin's uncle brought a lawyer to visit him, he asked the man to take on Schueller's case, too. Cowboys, he'd thought then, shouldn't be locked up. The lawyer was a German Jew from the same region as Schueller's mother, and he knew his way around a courtroom. When they walked free, Schueller thanked Benjamin and told him to visit the Veluwe someday. Benjamin couldn't imagine ever wanting to go to some backwoods village then. And now, here he was.

When at last the train trundled into the small station, he looked out the window and recognized the energetic jockey immediately.

"Benji!" Kurt Schueller boomed. "Welcome!"

He noted his friend's fine clothes and elegant car. Schueller loaded his suitcase into the trunk and they were off. As they drove towards Schueller's home, Benjamin finally exhaled. Amsterdam was behind him. He was starting over. The village was picturesque, something from a children's storybook. The cottages that lined the canal were neat and tidy red brick, with flowers spilling from window boxes on every level. It hardly seemed like an occupied village at all, until they rounded the corner. Schueller pointed out the main square and Benjamin saw the flags hanging from the Town Hall.

"That's the *Stadhuis*, where I work. Unfortunately, it's also where the Germans have set up a command post."

Benjamin made a mental note to avoid the square. Schueller pointed out the various churches that anchored the Hoofdstraat. Moments later, he turned onto a quieter road. A factory stood on one side of the canal and across the bridge, behind an elegant privet hedge, was Schueller's home.

"Here we are. Come inside and have a drink."

Benjamin followed Schueller into a newly built, modern home. It was bright, airy and completely the opposite of his apartment in the city. Schueller cut up some bread and cheese and poured two large tumblers of *jenever*.

"Now. Let's not waste any time. Tell me about yourself, Meneer…?"

Benjamin took his new identification from his jacket pocket and passed it to Schueller. "Van Laar. Benjamin Van Laar."

Schueller scanned it. "Nice work. Did you use this on the train?"

Benjamin shook his head. "No. There were no controls today, but I'd planned on using my old card until I arrived here."

"Where is this old card?" Schueller asked.

Benjamin reached into his trouser pocket. "Here."

Schueller studied the two documents. "You should get rid of this." Then, he looked at Benjamin very seriously. "Are you ready to become Benjamin Van Laar? A schoolteacher?"

Benjamin nodded.

"Fine. Tell me about yourself, Meneer Van Laar. Where are you from?"

Benjamin cleared his throat. "I was born near Enschede…"

"But of course you have no memories of that town because your parents moved to Amsterdam when you were little." Schueller dug a thick cigar from a box on the counter and the room filled with smoke.

"...I received my teacher's diploma from the University of Amsterdam."

Schueller smiled knowingly, and exhaled a thin puff of smoke. "Ah! Your diploma. The one your mother had framed and which you hung behind your desk at the high school where you taught in Rotterdam."

"Before it was bombed," Benjamin added. He wondered how many men and women would add invented histories to the burned shell of that unfortunate city in the months to come.

"And what street was that school on?" Schueller persisted.

"It was near the boulevard, 88 *Beilenstraat*. The girls entered from the courtyard garden and the boys from the street. It was a beautiful Renaissance building." Benjamin remembered old photographs he'd studied, of buildings now in ruin. There was a flowering tree in front of the school. He committed the tree to memory, a detail he felt compelled to include.

"It's where I met my wife," he added. Wouldn't that be something? He imagined the soft scent of a woman wafting through the apartment above Nathan's shop.

Schueller raised an eyebrow and puffed away on his cigar.

"Wife? Your card says unmarried."

"She died in childbirth, along with the child," Benjamin said hastily, losing the thread of his story.

"At home, or in hospital?"

Benjamin paused.

"Too slow!" Schueller banged his fist on the table, sending sparks from the end of his cigar across the table. "The less information you give, the less you have to make up. Don't give them the chance to catch you in a lie."

Benjamin nodded.

Schueller tossed his old ID into the fire. As the flames licked the paper, he became Benjamin Van Laar, a schoolteacher from Rotterdam. Simple.

He'd figure it out. Perhaps there were colleagues he'd need to invent. But Schueller was right. He was a man without a family now. He must concentrate on how best to be invisible and useful. And a much better liar.

"You look pale." Schueller extinguished his cigar.

"I just need some air." A name was not all one had in the end. Nathan had their name, but Benjamin had a chance, and he intended to take it.

Schueller threw him an old cap. "Why didn't you say so? Come on, *Maat*. Let's go for a ride."

4

I didn't recognize the man who stepped out of the mayor's car. The Adler, the only motorized vehicle in the market, stood out amongst the wagons and bicycles. Standing beside the mayor, the man appeared very tall, with curly dark hair and bright green eyes. I was sure I'd never seen him before, but something about the cautious look on his face made me want to call out, *cheer up!* or even the forbidden "OSO!"—*Orange Shall Overcome*. Instead, I just smiled and said, "We have fresh sprouts."

The stranger gave me a faint smile.

"Good morning, little lady!" Mayor Schueller grinned. "Very well. Show us these sprouts you're so proud of."

Papa appeared behind me, bearing a wooden crate of the tightly furled greens. "Good morning."

"Morning, Meneer Zontag. Say, have you joined the National Socialists Farmers' Union yet?" Mayor Schueller asked, producing a shiny black and red pin from his pocket. The party initials in one corner, and in the centre, the red, white and blue Dutch flag with a lion. Anton Mussert's Dutch party of traitors.

Naturally, Papa shook his head.

"They say it may get harder for those who don't sign up." Mayor

Schueller smiled in my direction and indicated he'd take a basket of sprouts.

I wondered why he kept the pin in his pocket, and not on his lapel. On what occasion did he wear it?

Papa looked over his shoulder to see who might be listening and dropped his voice. "The Germans have no use for that party, they're funny that way. They have…" He paused. "A code of honour, despite…" He gestured around the square, shaking his head. "I can't see the advantage of joining up. Loti has a good job thanks to you, Mayor, and Hilde and I are managing just as we are. We'll carry on for now."

This answer seemed to satisfy Mayor Schueller. Yet only an hour before, Papa had told Meneer Krusselbrink, the local veterinarian, that he might join up in the next week or so. Was he lying to the mayor or was he really unsure what he should do?

As though he'd just remembered his companion, the mayor turned to introduce the stranger at his side. "This is my friend, Benjamin Van Laar. He's from Rotterdam."

Rotterdam! That explained the stranger's sad eyes. The poor man. Brummelo had quite a few refugees from the devastated cities lately, especially from South Holland.

"Welcome to Gelderland," Papa said, nodding sympathetically.

The stranger tipped his cap.

"Meneer Van Laar was a teacher…" Mayor Schueller began.

I gave up eavesdropping and burst in. "Will you be teaching here at the school?"

Meneer Van Laar considered my question. "Are all the students so curious?"

I blushed but he smiled and twin dimples appeared on his cheeks. They disappeared too quickly.

"Alas, I'll take any kind of work at the moment."

"We must all make the best of things," Papa encouraged. "Perhaps Mayor Schueller knows of some opportunities?"

Mayor Schueller shrugged. "I keep my ear to the ground."

All around them the empty market merchants were packing up for the day, without having earned more than a few pennies. Weary peddlers trundled towards home, their carts heavy with unsold goods.

Papa continued. "We've heard that when the school reopens, the new staff must pledge allegiance to the Germans. If you want a teaching job, Meneer Van Laar, you might need a pin like Mayor Schueller's."

Papa's jaw moved back and forth, and I sensed he was considering whether to add something further. But just then, a young woman rode into the square, and all eyes turned towards her, or more precisely, towards the majestic horse underneath her. She tossed her thick, blond braid over her shoulder and searched the stalls until her eyes settled upon our customers.

"Mayor Schueller!" she called out in an urgent voice. "Could you come to the castle at once?"

"I've never been able to resist a lady's summons!" Mayor Schueller winked at us and turned back towards his car. His companion slid in beside him, like a shadow. And then, with a roar of the engine, they were gone and the square was quiet again.

I'd glimpsed Lady Astrid's daughter a handful of times over the years. She used to come into the village accompanied by a harried governess. At school they'd nicknamed her 'the princess' but there was something about her, underneath her mask of propriety, that made me wonder if she wasn't quite someone else altogether when her chaperone's back was turned. Her gaze was beguiling, mischievous even. But what did it matter? We were never going to cross paths. She lived in a castle learning to be a lady, whatever that entailed, and I lived on the Nonnenstraat and sold sprouts in the market square.

"What are you daydreaming about?" asked Papa.

"I never thought I'd say this, but I miss school."

"I thought so." He sat down and lit his pipe staring at the patrons at the *koffiehaus* across the square.

German soldiers now occupied the room where the upper classes normally dined, forcing Brummelo's wealthy onto the terrace with the labourers. The doctor's wife, a proud woman, sipped her coffee with her back to a painter, who sat with his apprentice, white speckles on his forearms.

"What would your teacher say if she were here observing a scene like this, Muisje?"

I smiled at Papa. The rumour was Miss Reinhart had been fired for her communist beliefs, but Papa knew I admired her. I think he respected her, too, because she challenged me. *Who cares about verzuiling—the class system?* I'd once said. *You should,* she'd answered. *Without equality, we cannot build a modern country.* I'd written her words in my notebook, in the margins beside my carefully practised future signature: *Hilde De Boer.* I wasn't sure which scribbles were sillier.

Now that Papa mentioned her, I missed my teacher's voice. I wanted to know what she thought of the Germans, of the affiliations people kept in their pockets or displayed on their lapels. That she would have an opinion I had no doubt.

Papa squeezed my arm gently. "You need to go back to school. You have a mind like your mother. I can almost hear the wheels turning."

His forehead creased with the familiar sadness that overtook him from time to time when he remembered her. The market was empty but still he scanned the square.

I put my hand over his. "Papa. I don't think we're going to have any more customers today."

"That may well be so, Muisje. Let's pack up."

He looked towards the school, where Frid, the soldier with the gap tooth, directed the soldiers moving supplies. Papa shook his head, as though arguing with himself, and then smiled at me, his eyes sparkling, the way they did when he'd solved a problem, when he was on the cusp of happiness. My heart sank.

I didn't want Frid to be the answer to any of our problems.

5

Sweat trickled down Astrid's spine as she spoke softly to the labouring mare. It had been more than thirteen years since there had been a breech birth at Soelenkasteel. Normally a foal was birthed in thirty minutes and the mares laboured alone. Hans was beside her, quiet as usual, but watchful. They would lose the mare unless they got help soon. The horse's eyes were glazed over from exertion; over an hour ago she'd lowered her swollen belly to the ground to prepare to push. The mare's head lay in the straw as the foal's rump pushed against her cervix.

Finally, Astrid heard the roar of Schueller's Adler six-cylinder in the lane. The engine shuddered to a stop and moments later the mayor rushed into the barn followed by a man Astrid didn't recognize. The two men stood together in the stall but the sight of the sideways foal stretching the mare's flanks made Schueller forget introductions.

He tore off his blazer and rolled up his shirt sleeves. "Tranquilizers?"

"Won't it hurt the foal?" she asked.

Schueller's face was grim. "We have to risk it."

Astrid drew the needles. Schueller would try to shift the foal into position while the mare was sedated. She didn't think it would work but said nothing. She passed over the syringes and Schueller jabbed two into the horse's rump. Within moments, the mare's breathing slowed and the shuddering of her flanks subsided. Schueller knelt down beside her.

Katrine returned on her horse and joined them, staring at Schueller and his companion. "I'm trading this pony for an automobile," she muttered as she tossed her tack aside.

"We must work quickly and gently. If we tear the placenta, the foal will drown and we may lose the mother as well. When I say push,"—Schueller indicated the foal's torso—"gently apply pressure here."

Astrid held her breath as though she were the one labouring.

The mare's contractions slowed, and between each one, Schueller and Astrid attempted to gently rotate the foal. At first, nothing happened. It remained stubbornly misaligned with the birth canal. Astrid's forearms burned.

"Mother, do you need anything?" Hans asked.

Oh my sweet boy. She shook her head, looking up at the sunshine streaming through the barn boards, the hazy lines of dust in the hayloft. This mare would not die on her watch; she was a fighter, capable and strong, just like Astrid. That's what she needed her children to witness.

Schueller had more mundane desires.

"I'd kill for a coffee if you've got any," Schueller said to Hans. Turning to Astrid he whispered, "The *moffen* keep you stocked up, no?"

"They do." Astrid sat up and straightened herself out. She stared at the stranger standing beside Katrine. He was a tall, thin man with unusually bright eyes. For a moment, his intelligent face distracted her from the crisis at hand.

"I beg your pardon. We've not been properly introduced."

He held out a smooth, elegant hand. "Benjamin Van Laar. I'm an old friend of Mayor Schueller's."

"So, bad news then."

The stranger chuckled and dimples appeared on either side of his smile.

Schueller stood up. "Hans, take Meneer Van Laar on a tour of the grounds while we deal with this."

Hans nodded and led the stranger towards the castle.

Katrine lingered behind. "Let me take over from you, Mother."

"I'm not sure—"

Astrid's daughter squeezed in beside Schueller and placed her slender hands on the mare's flanks. Astrid spoke softly into the horse's ear. She stroked her neck and whispered words of comfort and encouragement. When the next contraction rolled through the mare, Katrine pushed harder than Astrid had dared. The foal rotated slightly.

Schueller cheered. "That's right! Like that! Good!" Perspiration poured off his face and his shirt clung to his taut, sinewy muscles.

As the contractions increased, they redoubled their efforts. A quarter hour passed and Astrid saw that miraculously the foal was slowly shifting position. Still the mare's shallow breathing frightened her. How long until the tranquilizer wore off? By Schueller's grim expression she guessed he was concerned too.

"If you had to choose…" he said between gritted teeth, avoiding Astrid's gaze. "Mare or foal?"

The past or the future?

Astrid put her face on the mare's silky neck, now wet, and breathed in her familiar smell. "Mare."

Schueller nodded. "Katrine, a bit harder this next time."

When the mare's flanks tightened and relaxed, both Schueller and Katrine grunted as they dug in with their palms. The mare exhaled noisily.

"Again!" Schueller commanded. In unison, they kneaded the tender flesh until at last the foal was turned. Astrid continued to whisper into the mare's ears.

"Now," Schueller announced. "Nature runs its course." He rolled back on his haunches and stretched his neck.

As the effects of the tranquilizer wore off, Astrid stayed close. At first, she couldn't see the foal moving and she despaired. But then the small bump gently pulsed. She reached out, and sure enough, the foal was still alive.

"Now what? We just *wait?*" Katrine cried.

Schueller nodded. "She'll know what to do once the sedative wears off." He covered the mare in a heavy blanket.

Astrid rose and went to the pump. She filled two buckets with water and handed one to Schueller. Side by side they washed up as best they could.

Katrine found towels and draped them over Astrid and Schueller. "Here comes your friend."

Hans and Benjamin returned with a thermos and some *boterkoek* from Eva. They sat on straw bales in the dimly lit passage. Schueller hopped down to help himself to a big slice of the buttery cake.

"Now," he said, his mouth full, "introductions."

Astrid smiled at the crumbs on his chin. How did he ever become mayor?

"Lady Astrid. Meet Benjamin Van Laar. He's a teacher from Rotterdam," Schueller explained.

Astrid looked from Benjamin to Schueller. She poured some coffee and offered a cup to the stranger. "What brings you to the Veluwe, Meneer Van Laar?"

Benjamin cleared his throat and told them about the bombs that fell on his school and neighbourhood. "I thought I'd head west and look for farm work until things settle down."

"I suggested he stay with me for a while," Schueller said.

Astrid nodded. Farms in the East were flooded as a last-minute defense measure, sacrificed for battles that never happened. Tragic, certainly, but what did it have to do with her?

"Mother," Hans spoke softly. "Meneer Van Laar is a *teacher*."

Astrid put her cup down and considered the stranger. A hush fell over the stable. It was clear to her now why Schueller had brought his friend along. She caught Schueller's eye and he raised his eyebrows innocently. Farm work! She bet the stranger couldn't tell wheat from weeds.

The mare whinnied and panted behind the wall. Schueller downed his coffee and went to check on her.

"Two feet poking out…sac looks healthy," he reported.

Astrid stood and went to watch. She wanted to comfort the mare again but Schueller shook his head. "No distractions. If the foal gets stuck, I'll give a tug at the end. Patience."

Benjamin Van Laar hung back with Hans and Katrine. Astrid watched him from the corner of her eye. Hans was asking him questions about Rotterdam, wondering if he'd been conscripted in the defense forces, but Meneer Van Laar had never been in the military, he explained. Seizures. She'd assumed he and Schueller knew one another from a royal regiment. Astrid looked back at the foal forcing its way into the world.

"Come on, old girl. You can do this." Astrid clasped her hands together.

She wasn't particularly given to superstition, but in that moment, watching Benjamin Van Laar and her children, and her beloved mare struggling to give birth, she decided that if the beast survived, she'd take it as a sign: the stranger could stay.

Schueller moved back into the stall and crouched down at the mare's rear. He swore, rolled up his sleeves again and reached into the horse to untangle a leg. The mare shrieked and the rest of the foal shot out in a bloody mess. The uterus hung outside the mare's body and she dropped her head onto the straw in exhaustion. Astrid retrieved the iodine and sponged Schueller's hands and arms. He carefully scooped up the battered womb and slowly pushed it back into the mare's stretched out cavity. Next, he washed and stitched her bleeding vagina. Still, the foal lay motionless on the ground.

The teacher was very pale. This wasn't a man who spent time with animals. Or blood.

Katrine kicked the stable wall angrily. "All that and it's not even going to move?" She knelt beside it to check for signs of life.

Astrid held her breath. At least they hadn't lost the mare. Yet.

Benjamin crept into the small space beside Katrine. He leaned over the waxy foal, whispering softly before gently touching its forehead, like a priest giving last rites.

What on earth?

The foal shuddered.

Schueller turned, wide-eyed, and yelled at Katrine to fetch another blanket. They covered the foal and rubbed it gently. When it made a quiet cry, the mother lifted her head and exhaled a soft groan in reply. Schueller looked at Benjamin and together they lifted the foal and placed her close to the mother's head. Astrid sent Hans to get fresh water with honey for the foal.

"Are they going to be alright?" Hans asked.

Astrid shook her head, disbelieving.

She got up and began to feed the other horses. Her bun had fallen out and her hair clung to her neck. How long until she could take a bath? She was filthy.

Schueller followed her to the other end of the barn. "Can you help him?"

She put down her bucket and looked up towards Soelenkasteel. The castle full of Nazis. "Who *is* he? And don't tell me he's just some teacher."

Schueller had the decency to look slightly guilty. "I'll admit, we share a rough patch of history, me and Benji."

Astrid narrowed her eyes. "Oh, come on. Don't tell me he's a gambler or some seedy fellow from the tracks."

Schueller shook his head. "No. But we did once share a cell at the men's prison in Vught."

Astrid's mouth dropped open. He was teasing her, taking advantage of her fragile state of mind. And then she realized he was serious.

"For heaven's sakes, Kurt. I'm actually relieved." She laughed nervously. "For a moment I thought you'd brought me a Jew."

Schueller coughed. "Mevrouw, you have Nazis living here. As if I would suggest such a thing to my little ostrich."

Astrid smiled wryly. "He looks Spanish. Or Portuguese."

"You see? I knew you liked the tall, dark, handsome types."

"Very funny. So what? I hire this…this *criminal* to educate the children?"

"*Reformed* criminal. With an honours degree from the University of Amsterdam."

"My last governess was educated at La Sorbonne," Astrid said drily.

"And where is Mademoiselle now?" Schueller turned to her and lowered his voice. "Let him live in the stablemaster's cottage. No sense leaving the staff quarters empty."

'I don't know—"

"He speaks a little German," Schueller added. "That may come in handy."

"*You* speak German, what do I need him for?" she protested.

"I'm going away for a while," he said.

"Where?"

"Berlin."

Astrid narrowed her eyes. "What for?"

"Never mind. In the meantime, don't sell any of the horses until I return."

"I'm not sure I have a choice. Have you seen the latest edict?"

"If they are in the employ of the *Wehrmacht* and you're caring for them, we can figure out a way to loan them out. The Germans will pay for the grain and we'll take care of them on their behalf."

"You've thought it all through."

"The mayor must have the inside track." Kurt smiled at her. She wrinkled her nose. He also needed a bath.

Hans called out to them. "Mother! Mayor Schueller, come look!"

They returned to the stable. The mare had risen to her legs and the foal was standing shakily, suckling.

Astrid started laughing. She hugged her children. Katrine was crying but Hans just smiled broadly. She kissed their heads and looked up, locking eyes with Benjamin Van Laar.

"Meneer Van Laar. Won't you stay for dinner? I should like to discuss something with you."

Why should her children lose their chance at a proper education, just because some lunatic with a moustache thought he was the next Napoleon?

The man gave her a strange smile, as though he were relieved and surprised all at once. "It would be my pleasure, Mevrouw."

6

June and July passed like a quick-tempered summer storm. The days faded into one another with only the sounds of wagon wheels on Market Day and church bells on Sundays marking the passage of time. When she wasn't at choir practice, Loti ripped glossy prints of Johnny Weissmuller from magazines and pinned them around our bedroom. While all the other girls at youth group had moved on to Deanna Durbin and Robert Stack, Loti remained loyal to Tarzan. In a way, I also loved Tarzan. At least, I liked the idea of walking around barefoot all the time. In the midst of my lazy daydreaming, a familiar tune drifted up the stairs from the kitchen below. *Het Wilhemus*—the national anthem—was blaring from the radio! I ran down the stairs and saw Loti and Papa sitting together by the window.

"*Koninginnedag!*" The Queen's Day. I'd almost forgotten. The usual parade and market had been cancelled months ago and I hadn't thought about it since. I ran to the garden to cut a small bouquet to put on the front steps, like I did every year.

But Papa held me back, pointing out the window.

"Honouring the queen is treasonous," he said in a low voice.

Shards of ceramic scattered the street, surrounded by dirt and trampled blooms. Two young soldiers strode down the street. When they spotted more orange chrysanthemums they stomped on them as though the orange blooms were afire—threatening embers in a dry field of grass.

I turned back to stare glumly at Papa. Under my breath I cursed *de besetting*—the occupation. It was ruining everything.

Papa lit his pipe. "There is *one* tradition they plan to respect."

I helped myself to the hard, black bread Loti had laid out and poured a cup of watery tea. "What's that?"

"School starts again tomorrow."

I almost choked. "What?"

Loti smiled mischievously. "That's what you get for saying you were bored." Then, whispering in my ear. "Now you can give Carl those love letters you've been writing all summer."

I ignored her. "I can't go to school tomorrow."

Papa frowned. "Can't?"

I lifted my leg and placed my foot on Papa's lap. "I need new shoes."

He let out a low whistle at the sight of my blisters. "Why didn't you tell me, Muisje?"

Because you'll worry, and when you worry you do crazy things like letting Loti go for walks with that German...

"I hoped I could go barefoot forever."

Finally, the hint of a smile.

I'd spent weeks walking along the canals collecting kindling for the colder months ahead, my too-small shoes flung over my shoulder.

"My little gypsy," he said, turning his attention back to the crushed flowers along the Nonnenstraat. "Do you want to go to school in your *klompen*? Tomorrow you'll wear Loti's church boots, and after school stop by the Loewensteins." Papa got up and counted out some coins for the shoemaker from the coffee tin on the shelf.

Who would be standing in front of the blackboard in the morning? Would Carl be there? If he wasn't, would I run into him after school? After all, the shoemaker's shop *was* next door to the De Boer's bakery.

"Long live the queen," I said, planting my foot back on the ground.

Papa snorted. "Long live your new shoes. Pray they last longer than this bloody war."

THE STRANGER STOOD at the front of the classroom with his shoulders pulled back, textbook in hand, watching each of us file into the rows of neatly rearranged desks. His spectacles were too large for his face, as though he'd received them from someone else. His clothing, too, had the appearance of having been roughly taken in to fit his slender frame. Too bad we didn't get Mayor Schueller's green-eyed friend from Rotterdam. He seemed a much nicer teacher than this unsmiling fellow.

"I'm Meneer Paul, your new teacher—"

Piet Van Noord, a gangly teenager in the back row, interrupted. "Where's Miss Reinhart?" A murmur spread across the room.

The colour rose beneath Meneer Paul's collar. He cleared his throat several times before responding.

"The *Reichkommissar* has selected new educators. My family and I," the teacher said, nodding towards two children sitting to his left, "have just moved here from Hengelo."

I turned to see who'd shown up for class and was dismayed that Carl wasn't there. His usual crowd was sprawled in seats made for smaller children. From their defiant expressions I saw that they'd sized up Meneer Paul, and decided that unlike with Miss Reinhart, they might get away with slouching and speaking out of turn.

The new teacher called on each row to select a textbook from the desk at the front of the room and sign their names on a list. The students jostled along, joking with one another until the teacher banged on the desk.

"Silence!"

I stared at the wall behind Meneer Paul. Where the Dutch flag once hung, a Nazi flag now covered the peeling paint. Queen Wilhelmina had also been replaced by an unsmiling photograph of Hitler. I hated the man with the moustache! Meneer Paul sported a similar style, but the fine hair on his upper lip was so light his moustache was only perceptible up close.

The spine of the textbook was damaged and some of the pages had been removed. Meneer Paul asked us to copy the lesson from the blackboard. Again, the boys groaned. Miss Reinhart always began the daily lessons with a lively discussion.

The first words Meneer Paul printed were *farmer, bread, student, school and church*—in Dutch. Then, in impeccable cursive, he wrote the same five words in German. Turning towards the class he clasped his thin hands together.

"You will learn five new words a day in German. By Friday, you'll have twenty-five new words. By Christmas, you shall be reading in a new language!"

None of us returned the teacher's smile. We looked down at the floor. What was the point of learning German if no one wanted to speak it? It was hard enough getting some of the students to leave their dialects at the doorstep. Trying to decipher the new words, I didn't hear Carl sneak into the back row. His presence didn't escape Meneer Paul.

"*Jongen*? Come here at once! Why so late?"

Carl stood and walked to the front, and Meneer Paul's eyes widened when he noticed Carl's limp. I don't think I imagined the flash of sympathy that crossed his face—most adults recognized the ravages of polio and treated Carl gently.

"All the bicycles have been taken and I had to manage with the old *Bakfiets* delivery bicycle." He paused. "It's not the most efficient, sir."

He stood so close I caught the yeasty scent of the bakery on Carl's clothes. I kept my head down but continued to eavesdrop. One of the peculiarities of village life was that Protestants bought their bread from the protestant bakery and Catholics from the catholic bakery. It didn't matter that the flour came from the same mill, the customs were as old as the printing press. Children usually went to separate schools, too, but while Papa faithfully bought bread from the protestant bakery on the other side of the canal he stopped short of sending us to the protestant school. Rather, we went to the village school instead of taking the bus to the next town. *I like to keep my girls safe.*

I can't remember when I let go of Papa's hand, how old I was when I told him I could walk alone, but I'll never forget the first time I bought bread at the De Boer bakery instead of crossing the canal. I'd lingered after school to play marbles and before I knew it, the church bell rang. I was late and the catholic bakery was so close. I quickly gathered my drawstring velvet bag and ran inside the shop. Carl's mother, Mevrouw De Boer, smiled at me, and called me by name. I was surprised she even knew who I was. *Carl dear*, she'd called out, *your friend is here.*

"What can I get you?" He smiled, and as he passed me the loaf of rye, his fingers touched mine. I couldn't help thinking he lingered a moment longer than necessary. Martin Luther and John Calvin could roll in their graves all they wanted. I would buy our bread here as often as possible.

Papa couldn't taste the difference between Meester's and De Boer's rye. But I knew better.

I looked up to see what the new teacher would say next to Carl, but he appeared at a loss for words. It was, after all, the Dutch Nazis who'd hired him and had rounded up all the cars and bicycles in the first place.

Meneer Paul wiped his forehead with a handkerchief that needed laundering. He indicated a seat beside me for Carl. These were the moments I knew for certain God loved me. I was glad I'd spent some time on my hair that morning.

He settled in, opened a textbook. "What did I miss?"

"We're learning German," I whispered.

He rolled his eyes.

"Where are your neighbours?" Carl always arrived to class with the Loewenstein children tagging along behind him.

"They've been acting strange lately," he said with a sigh. "Hannah and Ari didn't want to come to school."

"And miss out on meeting this charming man?" I nodded towards the front of the room.

Carl raised an eyebrow.

Our new teacher delivered an impromptu geography test, followed by a short break before launching into a lecture about the Visigoths. The youngest pupils looked as bewildered as I felt.

As I struggled to write down some of the main points, I felt a soft *swoosh* of air as a volley of crumpled paper balls landed on the floor at my feet. Carl bent down to unfold one and read it underneath his book. His face betrayed nothing as he shoved it in the desk and continued working. Surreptitiously he kicked the other paper balls away from his desk, but not before Meneer Paul came and towered over us. He stooped down, picked up the papers and smoothed them flat. I held my breath.

"So… we have an artist among us," the teacher's voice dropped to a lower timbre.

No one said a word. We wouldn't even look at one another.

"The technical skill is impressive," he continued. "Unfortunately, the illustrator is deluded if he feels *this* is the future of the Netherlands."

He turned the image towards the classroom and strode up and down the aisles, showing a caricature of Hitler and Meneer Paul headed to Germany with hobo sticks and tattered clothes.

"You see, what this generation needs are citizens of principle and ambition, ready to modernize the nation. You've been so accustomed to cowards leading you, it's difficult to recognize strength and power, but…in time you will see the wisdom of the *Führer's* vision to enfold the Low Countries into the *Vaterland*."

Meneer Paul ripped the caricature in half. "This," he scoffed, "represents the sad illusions of people who refused to join their *friends* when asked, and then dared to hope for rescue when Germany's might was at the doorstep!"

The boys in the back row struggled to hide their indignation. Van Noord's face grew red with anger.

"The Netherlands needs the moral fortitude of the *Reich*. It can rise from the ashes of generations of misguided policy and become part of a great empire once again—"

Van Noord spoke up once more. "Good luck with that!"

"I suppose you believe the people have options?" the teacher replied in an icy tone.

Carl shifted in his seat beside me. He spread his palms and very lightly slapped the desk three times, followed by three taps of his fingers. He repeated this slow, palm-lap rhythm then glanced sideways, as if to say, *care to join me?*

I froze. This wasn't like him at all.

All around me, one by one, my classmates worked themselves into a giddy frenzy, slap-tapping the subversive OSO—*Orange Shall Overcome*—in a crude version of Morse code. Meneer Paul's children looked around, confused, as though they'd missed the instructions to a strange music lesson.

Finally, the nazi-approved substitute caught on.

"That's enough!" he shouted, his mouth pinched in a rictus of fury.

But they refused. Now almost the entire class had joined in and was successfully working in unison. I wondered what Miss Reinhart would think if she could have heard it. Our former teacher would be proud to know they hadn't forgotten her, or the queen. Still, I held my hands together and kept staring at Carl.

Meneer Paul raised his voice again. "I *said* enough!"

They stared past him. Carl looked as though he were in a trance, as though his single purpose was to defy this imposter.

The man stomped his foot and turned to his desk. He flung open the top drawer, seized a black whip and snapped it hard against the desk.

At once the entire class quieted.

He took a deep breath. "It's difficult for me to know who the talented, albeit deluded, artist is." He paused. "Just as I cannot say for certain who began this abominable tapping."

He wiped his brow and glowered at the class. "But in order to learn, we must have a disciplined environment. This will *not* happen again."

Van Noord stood up. "My father says if you lay a hand on me or my brothers, you'll be sorry."

Meneer Paul narrowed his eyes. "Is that so?"

Now Van Noord looked uncertain. He nodded anyway.

Meneer Paul picked up the whip in one hand and the class list in another. "Then choose a number, Van Noord."

The colour rose in the boy's face. The fool was trapped. "Three."

Meneer Paul consulted his list. "Colijn, Gert."

All eyes swung towards the unfortunate small-boned boy in first form. Meneer Paul looked disappointed that his fury should find an outlet in such a defenseless creature. He sighed and summoned the boy to the coat hall and closed the door. The whip snapped back and connected with a *smack* against Gert Colijn's bare skin. A howl escaped the child's lips and echoed through the thin glass door. Carl stirred beside me. The class listened as Meneer Paul whipped the innocent boy again. Another scream pierced the stale air of the classroom.

Carl stood up and headed towards the coatroom. Van Noord leapt up.

"Should we take him down?" he asked eagerly.

Carl shook his head. He opened the door, and through the crack I saw him push Gert Colijn out of the way and turn his back to Meneer Paul. The door swung shut. I imagined the look on Meneer Paul's face as he realized the offender had come to replace the scapegoat. The thrashing that followed was enthusiastic, but we didn't hear a sound from Carl. Moments later, the teacher, perspiring, returned to his desk and lit a cigarette. His eyes had a far-off look, as though he weren't really in the classroom at all. And then he seemed to remember his own children, still sitting perfectly still in the front row. His face crumpled, and though he spoke to the whole class, he looked only at them.

"*Ja*," he said softly now. When he whispered to his children, for a moment German became a beautiful language. "*Ja*...that is enough. Class dismissed."

I fled the classroom and gulped in the fresh air of the courtyard. I looked around for a few girls to walk with along the Hoofdstraat, but everyone had scattered. Just then, I heard a sniffle and turned to see

Carl consoling Gert Colijn, on a bench under a gnarly old tree. I knelt in front of the boy.

"Hello, *schatje*..." I reached into my skirt pocket and produced a small, sugar-coated black licorice and placed it in his hands. "Can I walk you home?"

The boy took the candy and sucked it noisily. His eyes were full of fear and confusion.

"Let's walk together," Carl suggested.

I hesitated for a moment. I'd been hoping for a chance to walk with him for weeks, waiting for him to come find me near the canals and bring me some old magazines. I knew that other girls, through elaborate schemes of letters passed and glances exchanged, were somehow able to make boys understand their feelings. I didn't know how to tell him I adored him but that what he'd done was supremely idiotic. Maybe this was something mothers taught their daughters. No wonder I had no clue. He looked at me expectantly.

"Okay," I relented. No one was going to teach me this. I might as well figure it out on my own.

We fell in step together and slowly walked towards the Hoofdstraat while I gathered my thoughts. After a few minutes we passed my church and arrived at Gert's house, a small brick cottage with freshly painted front windows. The boy looked scared again.

"Mama will cry when she sees the marks," he whispered. "She's been so sad since Papa was sent away..."

I bent down in front of Gert and looked into his eyes.

"*Jongen*...listen. What happened in class today won't ever happen again, do you understand?"

I promised myself to protect him, and the others. I wasn't sure how, but my heart swelled with a defensive instinct. I was pretty sure Carl wasn't about to get whipped every day, either.

Gert nodded, opened the front door and disappeared into a dark, quiet house.

Carl and I continued on.

"What I did today was stupid." He looked at me sideways.

"*Ja*...the queen said *passive* resistance."

"So, do you have some kind of passive plan to protect all the Gert Colijns?" Carl stopped to rest his bad leg.

"Not really, but I don't plan on provoking a Nazi teacher, either."

I sat on the stone wall of the graveyard garden. Carl leaned against it and I realized his backside was sore by the way he moved gingerly and winced every so often. He took a crinkled pouch from his pocket and silently rolled two small cigarettes. He offered me one, eyebrow raised as though my acceptance were a test.

"You have no plan, Hilde, none of us do."

He lit his own and then held a match to mine. I tried to inhale like a movie star in a silent film, glamorous and sad all at once. Mostly, I tried not to cough.

"When you were a little boy, you knew you would walk again," I said.

"Yeah."

"But you didn't know how."

"True…"

"I don't know how to fight back, but I know that we have to. We can't just make the best of things. That feels like giving up."

I waited for him to say something, to agree with me. Instead, he was distracted. Across the street towards the bustling square, diagonal to our spot in the shade, I noticed a familiar red dress. Outside the *koffiehaus*, Frid stood with his hand cupped gently under my sister's elbow. No one could miss the tenderness of his protective gesture. Loti was oblivious to her graveyard audience.

Carl's expression hardened. "Or you *could* just make the best of things. Looks like the Zontag girls do have a plan."

I shook my head.

"Is she working for them?"

"She's helping Mayor Schueller at the Stadhuis."

Carl's face darkened. "Things are going to get harder. The moffen will have better food, coffee…" He exhaled a puff of smoke. "…Cigarettes. Maybe it's not such a bad idea to get yourself a German boyfriend, too."

My hand flew out and connected with his cheek before I could stop myself.

I forgot about Carl's bad leg, the red welts on his back…everything except his hurtful words.

We stood and stared at one another for a few moments, the silence of the garden filling the air between us. He touched his cheek gingerly, and before I could say anything, he turned and headed towards the bakery.

He deserved that. I wished I could take the moment back—not to apologize, but to find the courage to admit the truth.

I'll never want anyone but you.

7

Benjamin took a deep breath and knocked on the ornate mahogany doors of the library. Two weeks had passed since the dramatic foaling. Today he'd begin lessons with the children. The castle was quiet but he knew the household was awake from the smell of bacon wafting up from the kitchen. He knocked again and tried the brass knob. It opened.

It took a moment for his eyes to adjust. Dark exotic wood, probably from the Cape, covered the walls from floor to ceiling. Rows of books were framed by Rococo carvings that would have lent a certain playfulness to the room, were the embellishments not balanced by sombre emerald walls. He opened the heavy shutters to let some light in. Dust sprinkled down from between the slats, making him cough. There was a shabby gracefulness here that made him wistful for the halls of the university. He loved the permanence of old institutions, the comforting sense that both innovation and discovery could happen behind old stone walls. He once felt he belonged there, now he wondered if he'd ever belong anywhere.

Checking his watch, he sat down at the table with his notes. The last time he'd stood in front of students he'd been a professor of economics while the National Socialists were gaining support by criticizing the emergency price controls of agricultural goods. Patiently he'd tried to outline theories of supply, demand, trade and taxation. But urban young people didn't understand the stakes of an agricultural crisis. He guessed the farmers surrounding Soelenkasteel had a keener sense of bad legislation, as it was their herds that shrunk in value. Someday people would wonder how the Nazis became so powerful. No one would believe how an accumulation of seemingly mundane grievances could lead to so much evil. He rubbed his fingers over his forehead. *What a mess.*

"Sir, are you alright?"

How had the boy slipped in so quietly?

"Fine...fine." Benjamin tried to arrange his face into a reassuring smile. "How are you, Master Hans?"

"Just Hans, Meneer Van Laar. Mother wants to know how you're finding the cottage?"

"You can tell her I slept very well, thanks. I read through the notes from the governess, and—"

Katrine appeared from around the corner and stood beside her brother on the threshold.

"Oh, don't tell me we're to have more boring lessons like before! I thought you were a *real* teacher." Katrine strode across the room and plunked down at the table.

Benjamin wasn't used to interruptions. The girl stared at him while her brother sat down, looked at an empty notebook and fidgeted with his pen.

"You'd better shake my hand," Benjamin said seriously.

Katrine's eyebrows rose. "Pardon me?"

"Just to make sure I'm real," he teased. "What if I'm a ghost?"

She cracked a smile. "That's not what I meant. Hans, tell him what I mean."

Hans looked up. "Our former governess began the morning with drills, sir. She said it woke us up."

"Humph! More like it sent us into a bored stupor! Please don't be like her, I can't bear doing tables every morning."

Benjamin had an idea. "Do you have a newspaper, Miss Katrine?"

"Of course. Mother is always looking for the latest news out of Asia. What do we need a newspaper for?"

"Please see if you can find it. I'll explain in a minute."

Katrine strode out of the library and hollered for the cook. Benjamin smiled at Hans.

"So, what do you think? Does reviewing tables wake up *your* mind?"

Hans shrugged. "It takes me longer than my sister to remember things. She's not as strange as she seems, but she gets bored waiting."

Benjamin passed a sheet of word problems across the table to the boy. "See if these wake up your mind. I'm going to discuss the news with your sister and then we'll come together again."

"Do I have to sit here?" Hans asked.

"Where do you normally like to sit?"

Hans grinned, a slow, shy smile. He glanced over his shoulder and whispered, "Away from her."

Benjamin nodded towards a smaller desk by the window and Hans got to work just as his sister reappeared.

"It's wrinkled and smudged, but all the pages are here."

Benjamin spread out the paper and scanned it. *De Volkskrant*, the catholic daily. He was a Catholic now; he should know what the Catholics cared about. He'd start by reading their newspapers. But would they even publish a scrap of honest news?

"Choose an article, read it twice, and tell me what you think about it," Benjamin directed. He watched her face for a reaction.

She stared at him for a moment. "Is there some kind of test afterwards?"

He shook his head. "No test. A conversation."

"Could be worse." She shrugged and then muttered under breath. "Mother wanted to send me away to finishing school before you arrived."

After several minutes, she stopped. "How much do you want me to read?"

"Until you find something that wakes up your mind," he said

simply. He left her alone and looked over Hans' work. Before long, she interrupted him again.

"This is interesting," she pointed to the headline *President of Supreme Court Urged to Resign*.

Benjamin sighed. He scanned the article Katrine had turned towards him. He'd expected something like this. Lodewijk Ernst Visser had been his professor a decade earlier and had risen to the top. Now his star was falling.

"Why is this interesting to you?" Benjamin had expected Katrine to gravitate towards something frivolous, like the curlicued high heels that were all the rage in Paris, but she'd ignored the fashion pages and had been drawn to a photograph of an old man with intelligent eyes.

Katrine huffed. "Whose laws are judges supposed to uphold? The queen's or the Germans'?"

"Well done. Your brain is awake." Benjamin passed the article from Katrine to her younger brother. "And I suspect this judge is struggling with precisely that same question."

Katrine sighed. "If he tries to uphold the Constitution, Seyss-Inquart, that Austrian turncoat, will replace him."

Benjamin marvelled at how quickly this young girl's mind worked. Her brother finished the article and sat quietly.

"He's stuck," Hans said at last.

"Stuck?" said Katrine. "At least he's not trapped on some far-flung tropical island like Papa."

Hans ignored his sister. "If he resigns, what then?"

"Maybe he'll try to get to England," Katrine suggested.

Benjamin blinked at the word *England*. He stared down at the newspaper and swallowed a lump in his throat. He'd pushed aside thoughts of his uncle Nathan alone in their apartment. He had to steer this discussion to a close.

He opened a German grammar primer.

"Sir, we're supposed to be learning French, not German," Katrine said, her voice polite but with an edge of petulance, a blended intonation that marked her as an aristocrat.

"It is the classical tradition to learn French, but these are different times, Miss Katrine." He pointed to the newspaper. "Montaigne, Molière and Rimbaud will have to wait."

"Will we study Goethe and Mann?" Katrine got up to scan the leather-bound titles of the books without waiting for an answer.

Benjamin shook his head. "What you need is the ability to converse. Once the two of you have discovered the utility of speaking German, I release you to appreciate Germany's fine literature."

Katrine sat back down and stuck out her chin. "Alright. How do you say *wipe your boots, you dirty moffen, our carpets are getting ruined!*"

Hans laughed and then quickly looked over his shoulder towards the heavy doors. "Katrine. Watch your mouth."

Benjamin envied the girl's naïve impetuousness. The luxury of having an opinion was closed to him now, and he wondered how long he would be muzzled, biting his tongue for his own good. A child might be forgiven a slip of the lip. Or not.

He cleared his throat and began an introduction to German pronunciation, vocabulary and a few primary verbs. Afterwards, they practised questions and answers on one another. Benjamin pretended to be a shopkeeper and made Hans and Katrine ask for the goods they needed. When Katrine butchered the pronunciation and said 'I come me appled for,' the three of them burst out laughing.

"Time for a break. Come back here in a half an hour." Benjamin stood up and stretched. He planned to wander back to the stablemaster's cottage the maids had prepared for him, but on the way past the mill he spotted Lady Astrid struggling to hang up a load of sheets in the garden. She wore men's trousers cinched at the waist and an oxford blouse halfway buttoned. An elegant silk scarf circled her thin neck. The peculiar outfit made him smile.

"Can I help, Mevrouw?"

The sheets were twisted and heavy with damp.

"I left these out in the rain," she said. Her face was flushed with exertion.

"Here." He took one end of a flat sheet and held it. "Now twist and walk towards me. Wring out the water before you hang it again."

She followed his instructions. "You probably think I've never done this before."

"You're not the first person to hang the wash out when the clouds are dark," he said gently.

"I didn't even think to look at the sky," she said. "But the laundress quit and went to work at the factory."

She twisted the sheet until she was in front of him. She smelled like lavender.

"To think one could aspire to more than a life of laundering," he deadpanned.

"Ridiculous."

"Absolutely."

They laughed, and he helped her drape the cotton sheets over the line and secure them so they didn't blow off in the wind.

"Thank you, Meneer Van Laar."

He nodded.

"How are the lessons going?"

He smiled. "Your children are very clever, Mevrouw."

She was, he thought, holding back a smile. "It's almost luncheon. Will you join us? Eva is preparing *boerenkool*."

Benjamin hesitated. "That's very kind. I have cheese and bread in the cottage—"

"I know, but perhaps it is time for you to meet our..." She hesitated. "Our *guests*. We don't eat together as a rule," Astrid explained, "but as we're a bit short on coal this week, we can't keep the oven warm all day," Astrid explained.

"That's very...practical, Mevrouw. Thank you for the invitation."

He tried to hide the tremor in his hands. Although his stomach was empty, he wasn't hungry anymore.

THE CAPTAIN and his subordinates rose from their seats when Astrid walked into the dining room with Meneer Van Laar and the children. The courtesy was at turns amusing and irritating and Astrid wondered if her face betrayed the conflict she felt inside. Eva had lit the fire in the hearth, but nevertheless a chill seeped through her linen shift. She shivered from the draft.

"Mevrouw," said the captain. His men nodded towards them, their eyes flitting from the family to the steaming pots Eva had laid out in the middle of the table.

"Gentlemen, allow me to introduce the children's tutor, Meneer Van Laar," Astrid said.

Meneer Van Laar bowed his head slightly, and in flawless German, wished them a pleasant meal.

"Are you German, sir?" the captain asked.

"I grew up close to the border," Benjamin answered.

Astrid indicated they should sit, and showed Meneer Van Laar his place opposite her. As was her custom since Jan had left, she led a blessing. When she said 'Amen,' Meneer Van Laar crossed himself—backwards. Her eyes lingered on him for a moment and then she nodded to Eva to serve the food. The cook lifted the silver spoon and served the captain two heaping servings of mashed potatoes mixed with sausage and bright green kale. By the time Astrid was served, the portions were half the size, but she didn't care. She couldn't afford to spend money on fancy cuts of meat now. If keeping Soelenkasteel in the black meant eating like peasants, so be it.

The Germans conversed in hushed tones Astrid couldn't follow, but she heard the word *fallschirm* repeated over and over. The captain ate quickly and excused himself from the table to retreat to his chambers—Jan's chambers—for the afternoon. The remaining officers eyed the tureen hungrily. Eva returned to the table to refill their glasses.

"May I please have some more potatoes?" Hans asked.

"Hans, we must first offer seconds to our guests. Gentlemen?" Astrid looked down the table towards the officers.

The youngest—Frid—responded. "Thank you, Mevrouw. Please allow your son to have it."

"*Ja*, soon we will need his muscles to help us. Eat up!" Another officer smiled in Hans' direction.

Astrid tried to breathe deeply. The very suggestion of her son aiding the Germans! If they ever tried to take him away from her she'd...

"Mevrouw!" Schueller waltzed into the dining room wearing a three-piece suit and a violet silk cravat. "I knocked until my knuckles hurt and finally just let myself in. What happened to your butler?" Without waiting for an answer, he looked greedily at the table. "Anything left over for your favourite horseman?"

"Mayor Schueller. You've made it home safely from your travels. To what do I owe the pleasure of this unexpected visit?" Astrid hoped her voice sounded calm. She was still getting used to seeing him more regularly after years of keeping her distance. He shook hands with the officers and sat himself down at the other end of the table. Eva sighed, gave Hans an apologetic smile and served the last portion of potatoes and kale to the mayor.

"The captain didn't tell you? We have a meeting this afternoon to discuss how Soelenkasteel's horses can serve the transport needs of the *Reichskommissariat Niederlande*."

Astrid swallowed. She'd forgotten, or more accurately, she'd put the thought of her finest animals being ripped away out of her mind. Denial was a kind of survival, wasn't it? She doubted it would serve her well in the long run.

"Shall I bring coffee to the library for your meeting, Mevrouw?" Eva asked.

"You still have coffee? Real coffee?" Schueller lowered his voice and grinned mischievously. "I almost wish I had some Germans living with me."

The men at the other end of the table eyed him suspiciously as they rose to leave.

Astrid ignored him. "Yes, please, Eva. Children, off you go to study."

"How did the lessons go, Benji?" Schueller inquired, patting a large Alsatian who lolled by the fire.

"Lady Astrid's children are very bright," Van Laar answered, smiling in her direction.

"He's teaching them *German*," Astrid muttered.

Schueller ate the last bite of his lunch and stole Astrid's linen napkin to dab his lips. "You'll thank him later. The Germans aren't leaving anytime soon, Mevrouw. You want to hold onto to your castle? Your horses? It's not such a bad idea to figure out how to live with them."

"In victory one deserves champagne, in defeat one needs it," Van Laar added.

"Who said that?" Astrid asked.

"Napoleon," Van Laar answered. "I think what he meant is that we have to find our little sips of sweetness to endure what's ahead."

"Are you a philosophical person, Meneer Van Laar?" Astrid said.

He shook his head. "Not usually. But Schueller inspires a certain *je ne sais quoi*..." Van Laar smiled. "Thank you for lunch. Good afternoon and good luck."

Astrid watched the teacher walk out of the room and turned back to Schueller.

"So, tell me, what did you learn in Berlin? Can I possibly hope to hold on to Soelenkasteel?"

Schueller grinned. "You're not going to like this, my little ostrich, because if you want to hold on to anything, you'll have to play the game."

Astrid stared at the mayor and slowly nodded, ignoring the tiny flicker of doubt that rose in her mind. Was this really worth it?

ASTRID MEANT TO help Eva in the garden after lunch, since the gardener still had not returned, but she'd forgotten her straw hat on the balcony that morning. When she went to retrieve it, she heard the captain's voice drift out from the window of Jan's quarters. She stood on the threshold to listen, just for a moment.

"Lady Astrid is fortunate to have you negotiate on her behalf, Mayor."

There was a silence before Schueller answered. Astrid smelled cigarette smoke and heard the voices draw nearer. They'd moved onto

Jan's balcony and were leaning over the railing to admire the expanse of forest. She shifted further into her chambers.

"The War Office will wire the money to you Thursday," the captain said. He was drinking Jan's sherry, she noticed. What nerve! He must have raided the armoire. Schueller's hands were empty.

Schueller spoke again. "Hans and I will load the wagons and take the munitions to the warehouse on Saturday. It will take us about four or five trips from the train station to the canal, but we'll have it done by dinnertime."

Astrid's hand flew to cover her mouth. Hans?

"What does Lady Astrid think about her precious son assisting in the transports?"

"She prefers to have him concentrate on his studies—"

"Surely the boy doesn't have lessons on Saturdays."

Astrid hadn't heard a word about Hans working with Schueller. As soon as she had the chance, she'd tell him exactly what she thought of his plans to use her son.

Across the garden, through the gate, Astrid watched Benjamin Van Laar pull weeds from the path that led to his cottage on the edge of the grounds. Katrine appeared with her books and sat down on the bench beside him.

"Teacher *and* gardener, eh?" the captain said.

"He's from Rotterdam. He's starting over."

The captain was quiet for a moment. "Don't blame me. General Winkelman could have surrendered sooner."

Astrid peeked around the doorframe. Schueller finished his cigarette and flicked the butt over the balcony. Astrid followed his gaze to where Katrine tucked a few herbs in her notebook. Meneer Van Laar stopped pulling weeds, looked up and smiled at Katrine. In jest, he offered her a bouquet of wilted dandelions.

"There's something off about him," Astrid heard the captain say. "But never mind. The *Organisation Todt* will soon need more labourers. Building the *Atlantikwall* will be more important than tutoring a couple of spoiled aristocrats in the countryside."

Schueller turned away from the captain and caught sight of Astrid.

She shrunk back, but it was too late. When he spoke next, his voice was louder.

"But there are exemptions to the *Arbeitseinsatz, ja*? Especially for food production. Lady Astrid has ten hectares here and the ground is fertile—"

"What do you care what happens to this woman or her servants? You seem like the kind of man who knows how to protect his own interests."

"I've known her for many years." Schueller leaned towards the captain. "This place means everything to her—"

The captain sneered. "And what does she mean to you?"

Astrid held her breath. She'd been wondering the same thing since their reunion in the bank last spring. Why help her now, after so many years? Down below, Katrine and Meneer Van Laar were laughing. Schueller didn't answer the question.

"Women always prefer the tall ones, don't they?" the captain muttered. "But it's all the same lying down." He clapped Schueller on the back. "Isn't it?"

Schueller stared at Astrid as he replied. "I'll come back Thursday."

"Ah yes, for your fee. You know, we pay for other things, too. We could use someone with your background. You'd earn more than you do brokering loads from the train station."

"I'll think of ways I might be of service." Schueller turned and left the captain alone on the balcony. Moments later, he doubled back and slipped into Astrid's chambers, holding a finger to his lips. She closed the door to her balcony and sat down by the fire.

"What's in it for you in all this?" she asked, keeping her voice low.

Schueller took a deep breath. "Do you trust me?"

"I don't have many options," Astrid admitted.

"We were friends once."

"And then you ruined my chances of independence."

He looked genuinely confused. "How?"

Not wanting to remember, Astrid took a deep breath. "I'd made a deal with my parents. If my horse won at the Royal, I could keep the winnings and build up our stables," Astrid sighed. "Because of you, I had to get married instead."

Schueller grew quiet.

"So here I am once again out of options." Astrid closed her eyes. "When were you going to tell me about Hans?"

Schueller sighed. "He knows the horses best. You heard the captain—they'll be rounding up men and boys to work in Germany. But…if we work *with* them, on our terms, I can keep Hans close."

Astrid frowned. "Why bother with all this effort for my sake?"

"Other than trying to make amends?"

"Ha. Why do I not believe that's your first priority?"

He looked hurt. "I've changed, Astrid. I still like making money, but I won't hurt anyone to do it. I swear."

She sighed. "Promise me Hans will be safe."

"I promise." He reached out his hand towards her.

"My son does all the work around here while his sister—"

"Lurks around stalking her tutor?" He laughed.

"Something like that. Speaking of spies…I didn't know what the officers were whispering about at lunch, *fallschrim* this, *fallschrim* that…so I looked up the word. Tell me, are there really English airmen hiding in the woods?"

"I've only heard rumours, but obviously the moffen are worried. If you see anything, any signs of people in the barns or any other outbuildings, tell me right away."

"What are you going to do?"

Schueller cocked his head to the side. "I said you could trust me."

Because I have no choice.

She'd found an ally, but he was as slippery as an eel.

8

When Papa left early one morning to call on Reverend Van Veen, I seized my chance to creep into his bedroom and search through the pockets of his coveralls. Nothing. If he'd received a work summons, he'd taken it with him to seek the pastor's advice. Unless...

A paper poked out of the Bible on his bedside. Gingerly, I tiptoed across the room and slid it out. It was simple card with the ominous swastika stamp. Hands shaking, I lifted out the paper and scanned it rapidly. *All men aged 18-50 must report to the Employment Office. The Office will determine the suitability of candidates for labour in Germany.* Abruptly, I stood up and looked at the faded map of Europe on Papa's bedroom wall. From our village to the German border was only about a hundred kilometres.

I remembered Piet Van Noord and his friends, their usual bravado replaced by worry.

"They don't need Dutchmen on the *farms*, they need them in the factories...in the cities," Piet had said. "But the cities aren't safe, which is why our mothers are terrified. The English don't bomb farms, they bomb factories."

I sat back down on the bed. Papa couldn't leave us. If something happened to him, what would become of Loti and me? Surely there was a proviso that would allow him to stay and take care of us. I heard my sister's footfall on the stairs and hastily stuffed the notice into my vest.

"Hilde?" Loti entered Papa's bedroom and narrowed her eyes. "What are you doing in here?"

"I…I wanted to look something up on the map," I said.

Loti's eyebrow arched slightly. She turned and glanced at the faded map. After a moment, she traced the Nederijn River southeast into the Rhine.

Curious, I went and stood beside her. "What are *you* looking for?"

"Duisberg. This is where Frid comes from," Loti said. "His mother and sisters are working in an industrial plant."

I hadn't imagined Frid as someone who belonged to a family. He was a soldier, and not one of ours. If I'd thought of him at all, it was that I resented the time Loti spent with him and not me. Because of him, Carl was polite, but his hands no longer lingered on mine when I went to buy bread. We'd hardly exchanged more than two words since the day I'd slapped him, both of us uncomfortable and awkward, neither willing to apologize. Most days I walked home from school on my own.

"Have you had breakfast?" Loti asked.

"Not yet—I made porridge but it tastes like water." I started off towards the kitchen and she followed.

"Add some salt."

"There's none left. There are cloves and a bit of cinnamon, but I wanted to save that for the Christmas party."

Loti grumbled but I knew she agreed with me. We sat down and ate quietly with only the ticking of the grandfather clock breaking the silence. I glanced at my sister while she ate. She was the prettiest girl on the Nonnenstraat, maybe in the whole neighbourhood. That morning she'd put on a bit of rouge, which meant she'd be meeting Frid later on.

"What made you pick him?" I blurted out.

Loti gave me a wry smile. "He's decent, Hilde. You should see some of the others that come into the Stadhuis—"

"Decent! *Decent?* You can do so much better than decent."

Decent was how the bicycle repairman described affordable tires. It wasn't what I'd hoped for my lovely sister. The most decent German in the world would never be good enough for her. Maybe I wouldn't have been so harsh if we weren't at war, but we were.

"We have to make the best of things."

I stared at her. I bit my lip to stop from saying the one thing I promised I wouldn't. *What would Mama say?*

Instead, I let out a loud sigh. "Of all the boys—"

"*What* boys Hilde?" Loti snapped. "In case you haven't noticed, there are no boys. They've disappeared into thin air since the summer. And now that the Germans are recruiting workers from the West—"

"So you know all about the *Arbeitseinsatz*—the summons?"

"That's what I'm trying to tell you. I'd love a Dutch boyfriend but all the young men are being sent away…"

"Not just the young men…they want to send Papa too!"

At this, Loti paled. "What are you talking about?"

I retrieved the summons from my vest and slammed it on the table.

"Oh God, no—"

"We've got to do something. We must convince that ugly captain that we need Papa here—"

"They won't care about that, we're old enough to manage." Loti bit her lip. "What we have to do is show the Employment Office that Papa provides an indispensable service. That's our only hope."

"What indispensable service is Papa providing?" I asked.

Loti took my hand and led me out the back door. We stood looking out at the enormous garden and the four small greenhouses.

"Brummelo has been designated a rest post for German soldiers on furlough from the front. All those soldiers need to eat—"

"And why should we be the ones to feed the enemy?" I protested.

"Do you want Papa to go to Germany or do you want keep our family together?"

I looked down at the summons between us.

"Papa can grow food, and you can help him deliver it. Both of you will be safe if you take care of the garden."

"What about you?"

She waved a pale hand in the air. "Since the Germans moved into town, there's three times the paperwork at the Stadhuis. Don't worry about me."

If we sold our produce to the Germans, what would our regular customers eat? What would *we* eat? I didn't like this solution, but I imagined Papa whistling as he worked, carefree and maybe even happy. Would it be worth it if we could be happy? What other choices did we have?

Loti opened her purse and took out three ration cards and placed them in my hands.

"What's this?" I was sure we'd already used up our allotment, and I should know since I was the one who stood in line for everything. What else was she hiding?

"Go down to Eyk's general store and see if you can get some more salt."

"But how did you get—" I looked at the cards, confused.

Loti shook her head. "Don't ask so many questions, Muisje. For the love of God, stop asking questions and just get us some salt. Please."

THE QUEUE WOUND its way from underneath the red awning of the general store to around the corner past the blacksmith's shop. Although it hadn't yet begun to rain, the sky was dark, and my face felt damp from the mist. The warmth emanating from the forge provided some temporary relief from the cold, but I wondered how much longer I'd have to wait. Several neighbours in the line were familiar faces. The shoemaker's wife was a few feet ahead, wrapped in a fashionable shawl that looked much warmer than the thin raincoat I'd chosen. As though she sensed me staring, she turned around and waved.

When I'd looked in the mirror before leaving the house, I'd been pleased with my smart attire. An hour into queuing up and I was sorely regretting my vanity. The new boots Mevrouw Loewenstein had sold me at the beginning of the school year had tiny elegant heels, but now my back ached and I had no idea how slowly this procession would move. Even my *klompen* would have been better than the boots I'd chosen. The plump woman ahead of me wore the kind of sturdy lace-up oxfords I should have bought.

I must have been grumbling aloud, for the woman turned slightly and smiled.

"November is so chilly, isn't it?"

I nodded. "Soon we'll be skating down the canals again."

"When I was your age, my father set up an *appleflappen* stand on the canal and we drank warm milk in a little hut by the bridge."

I imagined the warm, oily dough and the hot morsels of apple. "Did he pass down the family recipe to you?"

The woman laughed. "And many more. I'm the cook up at the castle. But there's not much oil for fancy treats right now. It's rations for the lot of us."

It surprised me to imagine they were running low on supplies at the castle, too

"My picky sister won't eat her porridge without a bit of salt," I muttered.

"Ooh. I can sympathize." The older woman smiled again and I realized we were finally inching our way towards the front of the line.

At last, we were inside the general store. The proprietor, Meneer Eyk, looked haggard. His skin was flushed and the collar of his white shirt grimy. Not long ago the same man would pause to chat with his customers, adding extra scoops of this or that to their brown paper bags with a wink and a smile. I felt badly for his changed circumstances.

I was almost at the register when a commotion broke out.

"I'm sorry ma'am. We can't serve you anymore." The shop owner spoke in a hushed voice, but everyone stopped chatting and his attempted whispers were for naught.

"Why ever not? My ration cards are in perfect order…"

"Mevrouw Loewenstein, please don't fuss. Look at the sign."

I followed the proprietor's pointed finger to a hand-printed notice on the shop's window: *"Joden Niet Gewenst."* Jews Not Welcome.

Mevrouw Loewenstein's face reddened.

"I'm your *neighbour*. Since when are we suddenly undesirable customers? My money's as good as anyone else's. For heaven's sakes, you're wearing shoes my husband made especially for your crooked feet!"

Her voice rose a couple of notes higher with every accusation.

"I've been in line for forty minutes in the cold." Mevrouw Loewenstein wasn't quite yelling, but every part of her body was shaking with rage.

Not one of the bystanders said a word.

"Who put that despicable sign in your window?" Mevrouw Loewenstein finally asked.

Meneer Eyk just shook his head. "There isn't enough for the Dutch *and* the Jews."

A few people in line began to grumble. "Go down to the docks and make a few trades there," someone muttered.

"You people always find money somewhere," another added.

I turned and glared. How dare they?

"That's ridiculous. I was born in this town! What right do you have to tell me I'm not Dutch?"

The bells on the door of the shop tinkled and two German soldiers walked in, tipping their caps to the owner. The lineup quieted once again. Mevrouw Lowenstein wrapped her shawl tighter and glared at Meneer Eyk. The soldiers sat in the back of the shop at a table and took out a deck of cards. From the shadows, Meneer Eyk's wife appeared and brought them coffee. An impatient murmur rose from the other customers.

Meneer Eyk cleared his throat. "I would be happy to serve the next customer." He stared through Mevrouw Loewenstein as though she were a ghost. She refused to move, and the next customer was forced to make her transaction in the shadow of the shoemaker's angry wife.

Meneer Eyk became increasingly agitated. I worried the soldiers would come and drag her away if she didn't leave.

"Hold my spot, will you please?" I implored the friendly cook.

She nodded.

Leaving my basket behind, I slid up beside Mevrouw Loewenstein. Gently, I touched her arm.

"What do you need, Mevrouw Loewenstein?"

Her eyes widened and filled with tears. She leaned in towards me and whispered her order. Moments later, she slipped out the door, as though she'd never been there at all. Meneer Eyk's shoulders sagged. I returned to my place in line. A woman behind me whispered *good riddance*. I gritted my teeth. How would *she* feel to be singled out and humiliated? Angry words gathered on the tip of my tongue, but I remained silent.

Finally, it was my turn at the polished counter.

"Hello, little lady. I haven't seen you in a while. What can I get for you?"

"Molasses, dried peas and a pound of cornmeal please."

Meneer Eyk smiled wearily and slipped a tiny extra scoop of cornmeal into my bag. Gathering the items in my basket I nodded a curt thank you. Back on the sidewalk, I reached out and tore down the offending sign and shoved it in my pocket. Everyone was too busy looking over their shoulders at the Germans drinking coffee in the back corner to notice me. Pulling my hood up against the wind and rain, I made my way down the street towards the shoemakers' shop. The windows had been crudely boarded up. Mevrouw Loewenstein pulled me inside and locked the door. Her eyes were red. I emptied my basket onto the table beside Meneer Loewenstein's workbench.

"Why are they treating you so badly?" I asked.

Mevrouw Loewenstein shrugged. "Hitler isn't the first tyrant to want to get rid of us. It's been a rough couple of years. When people suffer, politicians need something—or someone, to blame."

I'd ask Papa to explain it to me later. He could help me understand. For now, there was at least one thing I could do.

"Give me your ration cards, Mevrouw Loewenstein. I'll buy your food for you."

She wiped away her tears. "You are a sweet girl, Hilde, but who knows how long we'll even get ration cards. In any case, hopefully we won't be here much longer. My cousins in America are trying to help. Meneer Loewenstein has an appointment in Amsterdam with the Jewish Council to get us on a special list to leave."

"I haven't seen Ari or Hannah in school. Are they alright?"

At the mention of the children, Mevrouw Loewenstein pursed her lips.

"They're safe."

I wanted to ask more, but Mevrouw Loewenstein was no longer in the mood to share confidences. That's when I remembered Loti's salt. In all the excitement, I'd forgotten to get some.

"Why the frown, Hilde?"

"I was so angry, I forgot my sister's salt."

Mevrouw Loewenstein laughed. It was such a pure, tinkling giggle. "You'd better learn to control your temper or you'll end up in hot water."

"Throw some potatoes in and we'll have *stumpot!*" I wanted to hear Mevrouw Loewenstein's laugh again. Instead, she disappeared into the back of the shop and returned with a package.

"Not only are we getting shut out of the stores, we haven't had any customers here. My husband is afraid looters will come and damage the house, hence the planks." Mevrouw Loewenstein sighed heavily.

"Take these boots home, Hilde. They'll do better for the winter months than the ones you chose in August." She winked. "I probably shouldn't have sold them to you in the first place, but I have a weakness for pretty things, too."

Tears pricked my eyes. I didn't deserve her generosity. I had no way to pay her for the boots, and she knew it.

"Thank you, Mevrouw Loewenstein."

"We have to make the best of things, don't we, love?"

I nodded, but I didn't agree. I did not agree at all.

. . .

WHAT HAD BEEN a cold mist earlier turned into a downpour. I should have run home, but being next door to Carl's house, I couldn't resist waiting to see if he might return from deliveries anytime soon. He hadn't been in school lately either, probably because he didn't relish Herr Paul's lectures.

A light was on at the De Boer's bakery but the front door was shut and the closed sign propped in the window. I convinced myself that the idea to slip around back and ask if I could trade some salt from his mother had nothing to do with Carl. I just didn't want to disappoint Loti. I'd head back home afterwards.

The De Boer's garden was small. The *Bakfiets*, the clunky delivery bicycle that Carl manoeuvred through the village, rested against a stone wall. I opened the gate and stepped inside. From the corner of my eye, I thought I saw someone abruptly draw the curtains tight. It was early in the day to be closing shutters and blinds.

I approached the thick door and rapped my cold, red knuckles against its polished surface.

Waiting, I put my ear against the door, and listened to what sounded like chairs scraping against the floor. I tried to peer through a gap in the blackout curtains. Maybe no one had heard me knock because of the rain.

"Hello! Anyone home? It's Hilde. I've come to ask a…"

Mevrouw De Boer opened the door and, glancing around the garden, quickly beckoned me inside.

It took a moment for my eyes to adjust to the darkness of the parlour. What was once a cozy room now felt strangely sombre, and it wasn't just the thick drapes pulled tight. A lamp glowed in the corner and a fire crackled in the hearth, but otherwise the atmosphere was anything but homey. I removed my kerchief and surveyed the room. Carl sat by the fire and gave me a strange half smile.

"Hello," he said, standing to greet me.

A half-finished game of canasta and a dozen teacups littered the coffee table in the middle of the room. I swore I could smell spicy men's cologne, an unfamiliar scent in this house. I tore my eyes away from the table and smiled sweetly at Mevrouw De Boer.

"I got stuck in a downpour on my way home from Eyk's general store. There was a disturbance, and in the end I didn't get what I went for..."

Carl crossed his arms. "Why are you here?"

"I'm sorry to have interrupted..." I gestured at the teapot. "I wondered if I could trade some ration cards for salt."

"Oh, dear girl," Carl's mother clucked. "You're soaked right through. Give me your coat and sit by the fire for a moment. Carl, hang this up for her, will you? I'll see about the salt."

I obeyed, rubbing my hands back and forth in front of the fire in a feeble attempt to warm up.

"How's Paul?" Carl asked.

"You missed an important test yesterday."

"My father was called up this week. He's been sent to work near Cologne." He put my coat on a hanger and hung it from the beams above the fireplace. "No more school for me, for now. I have to help my mother."

I was stunned. "I'm sorry. I had no idea." No wonder he looked so tired. He'd probably been up since before dawn.

Carl shrugged and pulled at a soggy paper protruding from my coat pocket.

Don't!

"What's this?" He unfolded the poster I'd torn down on my way out of Eyk's general store.

"It was hanging outside the store," I mumbled.

"You can't just rip those things down!" he said.

Mevrouw De Boer came back into the room with two packets of salt and an elegant maroon coat. "This belonged to me once, but it doesn't fit properly anymore. I know you have a gift with a needle and thread—maybe you can give it a new life? For now, it will keep you dry on your way home. You won't even need an umbrella with this hood... what's the matter, Carl? You look upset."

"He's angry with me for taking this down." I grabbed the poster from Carl and showed it to her.

"That was a stupid thing to do," he muttered. "Impulsive."

"I'll remember that, *Morse Code*," I whispered.

His hard gaze softened, and he put his hands up in a gesture of surrender.

"Stupid or brave?" Mevrouw De Boer asked.

I ignored them both for a moment, mesmerized by the coat Mevrouw De Boer was offering to me. It was an English style, beautifully lined and adorned with fashionable epaulettes. I didn't know what to say. On the one hand, Mevrouw De Boer was giving me a beautiful gift. On the other hand, I got the distinct impression she wanted me to leave. Certainly, she wasn't offering a cup of tea and magazines today.

She pressed the salt into my hands and waved away my ration cards. "Sometimes..." Her eyes darted towards the back of the room near the stairs. "...It's best not to draw attention, Hilde. We can do the right thing quietly. Do you understand?"

"I think so." I stood up, confused, and slipped on the new coat. My old one still dripped beside the fire, making a puddle on the floor.

"I'll drop it off tomorrow," Carl said. "After mass."

I nodded and said goodbye. It was cold and I wanted to go home and sit by the radio with Papa, but when I stepped back into the alley I spotted Mayor Schueller's Adler further down the lane. What business did he have with the De Boers? And if he *was* there, why was he hiding in the kitchen? I shivered, despite my new coat, but I couldn't go home yet. What exactly had I interrupted? I had to know.

The church bells chimed four o'clock, the echoing gongs taunting me while I waited in the doorway of the chapel, my eyes on the bakery. Maybe Mayor Schueller was trying to help Carl's father get an exemption, like the one Loti hoped to secure for Papa. But that theory didn't explain the extra teacups on the table...

The bakery door clanged shut, startling me from my reverie. A large, ruddy-haired man emerged, a loaf of bread wrapped in brown paper tucked under his arm. He looked over his shoulder and began walking towards the square. I inhaled sharply. Reverend Van Veen. Never in a million years would our conservative, upstanding pastor spend the afternoon playing canasta. Moments later, a woman stepped onto the street. I squinted. She looked familiar, but a dark hat cast a shadow across her face. She strode along the sidewalk purposefully, shifting a bulky carpet bag from one hand to the other. I'd know that bag anywhere! Miss Reinhart.

So why would a Protestant minister, a Communist teacher and Mayor Schueller spend the afternoon playing cards in the back parlour of De Boer's bakery? I needed to walk and clear my jumbled thoughts.

Papa liked Schueller. He believed one day the short, wiry man in the fancy car would become a member of parliament. Certainly he bought plenty of vegetables and never haggled over the price, like most customers. But I couldn't figure him out. He conversed with German officers in the café with ease, as though their presence at the Stadhuis wasn't a bother at all.

I was almost at the bridge when I heard the sound of a motorcycle. Only the Germans rode motorcycles these days, and I didn't relish an encounter with a soldier on my own. But the engine slowed and I couldn't ignore the man trailing me.

"Hello, Hilde. You've got your hands full, want a lift? I'm headed to your place," Frid said.

My trepidation dissolved into annoyance. I'd wasted the afternoon hiding in doorways and now I'd missed my chance to have Loti to myself.

Frid extended a hand. "Hold on to my belt. Here we go."

I'd never been on a motorcycle before. I held onto Frid with one arm and my new boots with the other. Closing my eyes, I imagined he was Carl. *Oh God, don't let Carl come onto the street and see me now.*

My teeth chattered. I was chilled to the bone despite my new dry coat.

"You alright back there?" Frid asked.

"Yes," I answered. But in truth my forehead was burning. He *was* decent. But that didn't change the fact he was also a Nazi.

"I'll tell you something, Hilde. I love your sister, but I don't want to live here for the rest of my life."

We arrived at Number Eleven.

"When things settle down there, I'd like to take her to live in Spain. Somewhere on the coast. Instead of all this fog and rain—sunshine and warmth."

"I don't mind the rain," I muttered. I didn't want to go into my warm cottage just then. When Mevrouw De Boer's eyes darted towards the stairs in her parlour, I spotted a little door I hadn't seen before, and I just knew I wasn't alone. Some actions weren't merely stupid or brave, but simply a quiet 'yes' to a neighbour in need. In a village where I thought I knew everyone, I finally found the ones who believed that making the best of things would never be enough.

I only had to convince them to set out a cup of tea for me, too.

9

Fall quietly gave way to winter that first year of the occupation in the Veluwe. The dwindling birdsong in the woods was the same, the crisp bite in the air still familiar to those who knew the forest like Astrid. The morning of the first frost she quietly got dressed in worn riding britches, pulled on an old sweater, and, seeing the white-tipped lawn, added Jan's wool blazer. She crept out of the castle before sunrise, before Eva was stirring in the kitchen, and shivered in the early morning darkness. She stashed her pistol in a leather satchel with an old tin can and a box of bullets hidden underneath her shirt.

Hurrying to the stables, she saddled up Philomena as the mare snorted and nuzzled her. Astrid caressed the horse's silky neck, wishing they could spend the entire day together. An hour would have to do. They left the barn and headed to the *Posbank*, the rippling hills where the sandy heath gave way to deep pine groves.

Once the familiar path opened between the trees, she encouraged Philomena to gallop. She held on tightly and hoped no fox or rabbit would dart across their path—neither she nor Philomena could afford to break a leg. But she needn't have worried. The heath was quiet and dark, and they were alone. The hills around them made Brummelo seem far away. For a moment Astrid could almost forget the occupation beyond the evergreens.

The path gave way to a clearing where Astrid dismounted and tied Philomena to an old fir. Opening the ammunition box, she loaded the pistol. Thank goodness for Schueller, who'd given her a refresher.

You do know how to fire a gun, don't you, Mevrouw?

Of course I do. I'm a fifth generation Van Soelen. I've shot a wild boar from the saddle. She hadn't admitted that she'd missed, because she resented the insinuation she was helpless. A little rusty, true, but with a bit of practice...

Once she'd loaded the gun, she took the old tin and placed it on a rotted fencepost. She'd try at ten paces and then back up. Her first shot rang out in the darkness, and from the trees overhead a flock of crows protested. The tin remained upright; the bullets sailed into the trees. She tried again, and again, and still the tin remained stubbornly erect. What was she doing wrong?

While Astrid studied her target, Philomena pulled away from the tree trunk, her velvet ears drawn back. Something was moving in the brush. Astrid's eyes had adjusted to the semi-darkness but she couldn't make out what was approaching. Her hands grew clammy around the gun. She gripped it tighter.

"Hello?" a baritone voice called out to her from the shadows. The accent was foreign. A Brit?

"Who's there?" Astrid held her pistol out, challenging the stranger.

"Thank goodness you're here! Have you brought me a change of clothes?" A young man stepped into the clearing.

He couldn't have been more than twenty, Astrid decided.

"I wasn't expecting anyone so soon, but I'm glad to see the women also in training. Everyone together against the Krauts, eh?"

She lowered her weapon. Astrid's English wasn't strong at the best of times, but the man in front of her had such a heavy regional accent, she could only make out about half of what he was saying. His eyes were so eager she was almost sorry to disappoint him.

She untied Philomena quickly and shook her head. "I'm not the person you were hoping for."

The man ran towards her. "Please ma'am, I've been out here for three days. I've buried the parachute—I just need to get out of this uniform."

"I'm sorry, I can't help you." She didn't want to get involved with this fellow any more than she wanted to be involved with the captain.

In one swift movement, she mounted the horse and quickly snapped the reins.

When she'd put about fifty paces between them, she began to sweat. An image of Hans crossed her mind. What if he were ever caught up in such a mess? She slowed to a canter. Her mind was a confusion of voices. *You have to play the game. You can't be an ostrich all the time.* Before she could change her mind, she yanked off Jan's leather-buttoned wool blazer. Turning Philomena around, she approached the dejected airman.

"Put this on. I know someone who might be able to help you, but don't venture into the village on your own, it's too dangerous."

"Thank you, ma'am. I knew you'd turn around. That's why I didn't swallow this yet. They only give us one, see, so I'm saving it for a real emergency." He dangled a small canister in front of his face.

Oh good heavens.

He chuckled and slipped his one precious pill back into his pocket. "Say, did you rip out the labels in this fancy coat?"

Astrid stared at him, confused. "I beg your pardon?"

"Last fellow they caught had a suit with dry cleaning tags in the pocket. They tracked down the suit's owner—poor sod—and his family hasn't heard from him since."

"There's no name in that jacket," she said, trying to remember when Jan had purchased it. He'd had it for as long as she'd known him.

"That's swell!" He reached up and shook her hand. "Thanks again, you're a real lady, I can tell."

He began to walk away, then turned and pointed at Astrid's target. "You almost had it on the last round," he said. "But you know what your problem is?"

Astrid shrugged. She was freezing now.

"You're trying to hit a can of biscuits. Use your imagination. Defend yourself against the *enemy!*"

There was one bullet left in the pistol. She really needed to get back to the stables. A thin band of light was creeping up on the horizon. The captain would soon be up, drinking coffee and peeling a boiled egg at the dining room table, every day making himself more at home at Soelenkasteel.

Taking the gun from the satchel, she pictured the captain, his sideways glances and proprietary airs. She took aim and fired.

The tin toppled from the fence and crashed to the ground.

———

AT A LITTLE PAST SIX, Benjamin waited for Hans and Katrine in the library for their evening lesson. He'd read the newspapers from cover to cover already. Even without the construction of Luftwaffe bases throughout the country, things were getting worse for his friends. He'd stayed on longer than intended, vowing he'd return to check on his uncle, but for now only sending what little money he could. Jewish doctors and lawyers still had a few practices open in the larger cities, but across the country they were being forced to register and pay a guilder for special yellow identification cards. What was more humiliating—pretending to be someone else or paying to be who you really were?

He left the library and looked down from the landing. Where were the children? The afternoon chores should be finished by now. He thought of Moses, Joseph, Esther. A single Jew could blend into Egypt or Babylon, sleeping with the enemy, but thousands? His papers had passed the muster of the first work summons, and he'd received the coveted exemption—thanks to his attachment to Soelenkasteel and its special status in service of the Reich. But he wasn't naïve enough to believe he'd be safe forever. Even Schueller had mused aloud that Benjamin would be better off if he were he missing a hand. Benjamin wasn't sure he'd been entirely joking.

Katrine and Hans appeared in the front hall, their faces wet from their post-chore wash-up.

"Meneer Van Laar! We've received word from Papa!" cried Katrine.

Her eyes shone as she waved a thin blue envelope in front of him and ran up the stairs to where he waited.

"Come into the library and tell me your news. Eva's lit a fire."

Katrine sunk into an overstuffed velvet armchair in front of the crackling logs and sighed.

"Mother thought he was dead, because it has been so long since we've received any news." Katrine took the letter from the envelope and smoothed it out in front of her. "But I *knew* he was still alive—I just knew it."

"So why isn't he here, with us?" Hans asked, his voice cool. He sat on a leather ottoman facing his sister.

Katrine exhaled loudly.

"My brother thinks it's simple to get on a boat and come home during a war. He doesn't understand, as Papa clearly states in his letter, that there *are* no boats and the Chinese overseers at the factory are worried about a Japanese invasion."

"And your father isn't worried about such things?" Benjamin asked, looking from Hans to Katrine. He thought of Astrid then. He would risk an ocean of submarines if he had such a beautiful wife waiting at home. Something was missing from this story, he was certain of it. Moreover, he thought the postal service between Indonesia and Europe had been completely severed. Meneer Stenger must have some interesting connections indeed.

"I'm sure he is. Without the factory, we'd be completely bankrupt," Katrine said.

Hans got up. "That's not true. We're managing by breeding the finer dams. With Mayor Schueller's advice we've held our own."

"Mayor Schueller isn't our *father*." Katrine tossed a thick braid over her shoulder. "I forgot my notebook in all the excitement. I'll be right back." She tucked the letter into her pocket and left.

"Hans? Are you alright?" Benjamin inquired.

"My sister has always been Father's favourite, the princess…you get the picture."

"I see."

Hans glanced at the door and dropped his voice. "Father would always get our hopes up, promising to be here for our birthdays or telling us he'd bring us home a new bicycle. But something always got in the way."

"And your mother?"

Hans shrugged. "Mother is pragmatic."

"Where is she now?"

"In the kitchen. Father sent all kinds of spices—cinnamon, cloves, nutmeg, cardamom and ginger. She and Eva are dreaming of the *speculaas* they can make."

"Hmmm, here's a question for you then. What did the gingerbread man say when his house burned down?"

Hans stared at him, confused.

"Darn it all! That cost a lot of dough!"

Hans rolled his eyes and the mood shifted. Benjamin thought the boy even chuckled a little.

"Mother should trade the spices. We need to stockpile medicine for the horses."

Benjamin smiled at the boy, so wise and worldly for his age. He was overcome with a desire to protect him from growing up too quickly. Nathan had tried so hard to preserve *his* childhood after his parents' death, and though he couldn't undo the heartbreak, he'd created a safe cocoon for Benjamin despite everything. Surveying the warm library, Benjamin wondered if he could somehow do the same for Hans and Katrine. He took a deep breath. Refuge in study? Why not? He opened his folder and passed Hans the daily review.

But there was no time to begin. The sound of shouting drifted upstairs from the foyer and they threw down their notebooks and ran down the stairs.

Astrid noticed the smell first. The air was filled with the stench of wet ash and sweat. The captain's face was covered in black soot. His officers looked wet, cold and dirty. Even Frid, the most cheerful of the men, was unsmiling as they stripped off their uniforms and left them in a pile underneath the oil portrait of Astrid's ancestors.

"Captain?" Astrid asked.

Eva rushed from the kitchen to stand beside her.

"Call a servant to launder these uniforms immediately!" he shouted, pumping his fist in the air.

The men eyed him warily, shivering in their wet trousers and boots.

Astrid turned and went into the kitchen. She pumped the water, soaked a towel and returned to the hall, handing the cloth to the captain and motioning for him to wipe his face.

The captain's shoulders slumped. He wiped his forehead and the cloth turned black. "There's almost nothing left," he said.

"What happened?" Astrid asked.

"There was a fire in the storage facility next to the Stadhuis," Frid said. "A young private was filing registrations in the basement and became trapped…" His face crumpled.

Another officer interjected. "We couldn't put it out in time. The hoses were difficult to hook up and the building was so old, it burned like a haystack."

Astrid wondered if the fire brigade even had petrol for the truck. Were the volunteers at home or had they been sent to Germany, too? By the looks on the faces of the men, they were asking the same questions. The captain instructed them to go to bed, and they shuffled upstairs ignoring the curious gazes of Van Laar, Hans and Katrine.

"Everything is alright children. You may continue with Meneer Van Laar." Astrid nodded to the tutor, who fixed his green eyes on her. There was something in his gaze that made her think he didn't want to leave her alone. He put his arm around the children protectively, and led them away, glancing back at her twice before turning into the library.

"What shall you do, now?" she asked the captain.

He sat down wearily. "We'd finished all the livestock registrations and were preparing to phase in the new identity cards. Now we won't be able to issue the *Persoonsbewijs* until the New Year."

She meant, what would he do about his dead soldier.

The captain rubbed a filthy hand over his forehead, forgetting himself for a moment. "My men will go door-to-door with the assistance of the *Schutzstaffel* officers stationed in Rheden. We'll count the livestock ourselves if we have to."

Astrid said nothing but imagined many people would quickly butcher their own meat for Christmas in the meantime.

"I wanted to go home," the captain whispered to himself, so softly Astrid barely heard him.

"Will you be taking a leave?" The thought of having the castle to herself was almost too much to hope for.

"Had things gone according to plan, yes. But now…" He struggled for a moment to retain his authorial tone. "Mevrouw. We will need all the horses on Saturday." The captain rose abruptly.

Astrid bristled. "I'm sure they can be readied for transport. I'll have Hans bring them to the station…"

"Not the station," The captain was curt. "To the Lyceum. The men will ride through the village and on to the church."

Astrid was confused. "A parade?"

"A procession." The captain spoke slowly, making an effort to control his emotions. "I promised his mother he'd be home for Christmas. He was only seventeen."

Seventeen. Just a boy.

Astrid folded her hands in her lap and looked at the closed doors of the library, behind which her own children were safe. She thought of the letter she'd write to her husband.

Dear Jan,
The children are safe. I would have preferred to ignore the Germans' presence, but as this is impossible, I find I must adapt…

She thought of what she couldn't write.

There's another man here. I'm trying to ignore him. Forgive me—I cannot.

The morning of the funeral, a thin glaze of ice covered the canals. A military chaplain from Apeldoorn arrived in a black Horch with an entourage of officers. The flag flew at half-mast at the Stadhuis, and Schueller quietly encouraged Astrid and the children to attend. *A little goodwill goes a long way,* he'd advised.

The ceremony was short, with only a brief homily. Astrid, Hans and Katrine followed a small crowd of villagers to the churchyard where the simple coffin was lowered into the frozen ground. After the final blessing, Frid stepped forward and whispered to the chaplain. The old man nodded and Frid slipped a harmonica from his jacket and began to play a familiar hymn. After several moments, the captain joined in and soon all the Germans sang together. Astrid felt tears pricking her eyes when their voices cracked ever so slightly, stumbling over the final words *"Now as here on earth we wander, then through all eternity."*

They stood in silence, and then the captain remembered himself. Straightening his back, he barked instructions. Shots rang out followed by a loud rendition of the German anthem, *Deutschland Über Alles.* Astrid felt her sympathy evaporate as the soldiers' faces hardened and their resolve once more masked the tenderness she'd witnessed only moments before.

"Let's go home," she said to Hans and Katrine. She pulled her silk scarf tighter and motioned for their carriage.

"Mevrouw?" The baker's wife stopped her. Her son stood beside her, a boy Astrid had sponsored years earlier, when his family couldn't afford the polio clinic. He'd grown handsome and strong despite his slight limp.

Astrid nodded at the pair. "Good morning."

"Eva mentioned you received a shipment from Batavia. I was hoping to make *pepernoten* but I'm out of spices…It's been difficult since my husband was sent to Germany."

"I see." Astrid had hoped to sell to someone with deeper pockets.

"I could bring you what you need," Katrine blurted out. "We're happy to help, aren't we, Mother?"

Katrine grinned at the baker's son and tossed her braid over her shoulder flirtatiously. Astrid gritted her teeth, and in her mind continued her reply to Jan's letter.

> *Your daughter, who will next month turn fifteen, should now be preparing for her debutante season. Instead, she's riding into the village like a common delivery girl. The war is turning each of us into peasants, hawking this and that just to survive.*

Mevrouw De Boer's son smiled at Katrine. "Thank you."

> *It's imperative she learn some proper manners, so she can meet a decent young gentleman and settle down. The tutor I've secured is quite clever, and even if he exudes a certain bohemian aura, I believe he's a positive influence on the children.*

Astrid stepped into the carriage and Katrine slid onto the bench beside her. The crowd in the graveyard dispersed.

> *Of course, I'd like to lock her up in the castle, keep her safe, let the war pass and hope for the best. However, I fear that may not be possible. She has your wanderlust. I wish you'd come home; she listens to you. I feel her slipping away.*

Katrine hummed quietly beside her, lost in her own thoughts. Astrid reached over and held her daughter's hand. Could she just let her be a normal girl?

"Mother?" Katrine's blue eyes shone.

"Yes?"

"Shall I take the spices in the morning?"

Astrid pursed her lips. Send Hans. Send Eva. Send anyone.

"Or perhaps, after my lessons with Meneer Van Laar?" Katrine persisted.

Astrid thought of the dresses she'd wanted to have made for Katrine, for elegant parties at the manor houses of Ruurlo, Middachten and Rosendaal. She'd imagined the invitations, the flowers, the food. Now all the estates were either occupied by Germans, abandoned or boarded up. The life she imagined for her daughter was in the past. As the carriage wound its way back to Soelenkasteel, the potholes in the road grew deeper. Astrid's girdle dug into her waist and her apprehension swelled.

"Why don't we all go together?" Hans suggested. "Tomorrow is the first day of the Christmas Market."

"Mother, can we?"

Astrid closed her eyes. She saw herself wandering the stalls of Christmas Markets as a child, the scent of appleflappen and roasted peanuts in the air. She remembered a small stall where an old man carved ornaments out of olive wood, and a nativity scene her father bought. Where was it now? She wondered if the stalls, like everything else, would only be a shadow of what they'd once been.

"Alright. After your morning lessons. I'll take you both out for lunch and you can share your father's gift with the baker."

Thank you for sending the spices, Jan.
You have no idea how things have changed.

10

It didn't matter that it was only an hour. I loved my father, and would do most anything for him—anything but this. I took a deep breath. "There are plenty of girls who would be perfect to lead the parade. Let the younger ones have a turn."

Papa puffed on his pipe and stared at me. His gentle smile wavered. He wouldn't force me, but I could tell by the way he chewed on the end of his pipe that he didn't relish the thought of telling the captain his daughter had rebuffed his invitation. Why should I lead the *Nationale Jeugdstorm* through the streets, ahead of the annual *Sinterklaas* float? The captain had gone so far as to have Frid deliver a Hitler Youth uniform to our house. The starched light blue shirt, navy skirt and stiff tie sat folded on the coffee table, untouched.

"It's hard to believe we'll even have a parade, after the death of that young soldier," Papa said. "With all the rumours that it wasn't an accident."

I thought this over. My friends at school had different opinions about the dead soldier. Those whose fathers were working in Germany said little about it, but some of the more outspoken ones, like Piet van Noord, said the Germans were getting what they deserved. Even when some of the girls pointed out the poor fellow was only a few years older than us, he didn't back down.

Papa rubbed his forehead, as though trying to push the tension away with his thumb.

"If it wasn't an accident, there will be trouble ahead," he said, agitated.

I tried a new tack. "I know you only want the best for us, but can't you understand how carrying their flag through the town will be humiliating for me?"

Wearing this uniform would only confirm Carl's suspicions about my family and push him further away.

Papa closed his eyes. "I wish it were our flag you were waving back and forth, but what can I say to the captain?"

"But Papa, I'm not even a member," I muttered.

"The captain just wants the world to see how civilized this occupation is!"

"How does stuffing me into uniform show the world anything?"

"They'll capture a photograph of a beautiful young Dutch girl and use that to prove how life continues on as before."

My retort caught in my throat upon hearing my father call me beautiful. Loti was the beautiful one. I was just plain Hilde, little mouse.

"They'll call me a traitor," I whispered.

"That's because silly school girls don't know the difference between surviving and starving," he said. "Besides, I'll be right behind you. If anyone says anything, I'll step down from the float and send those nasty buggers off to Spain with a lump of coal!"

"What do you mean, you'll be right behind me?"

Papa put his pipe in the ashtray and smiled. "Say hello to this year's Sinterklaas."

ASTRID DID NOT WANT to go into the village. Usually she relished the chance to wear her mother's mink shawl over her fine winter suit, but she didn't feel the same excitement she normally did when she dressed that morning. She'd scrimped together the funds to sponsor the usual hospital float but was annoyed that her own horses were being used to pull the carriages. The captain was deaf to her protests. Even Schueller hadn't been able to find a better solution when she'd protested the idea. *Traditions maintain stability,* he'd said, as though that settled everything.

"Mother?" Hans's voice interrupted her thoughts. He stood with Katrine, apart from the crowds, beckoning her to follow him.

As patrons of the parade, Astrid and her family always had a special spot on the dais, sheltered from the wind and sitting a little higher than the makeshift bleachers that lined the sidewalk. The sun was peeking out from the clouds and Astrid felt momentarily cheered as an alderman spotted her and ushered her to a reserved seat. Maybe it wouldn't be so bad. She sat on the upholstered bench amongst a few other prominent citizens—the owner of the Officer's Club, a doctor and a few others she didn't recognize—and waited for the parade to begin. Children lined the rails below as their parents milled around chatting and admiring the decorations. There were fewer lights and banners than usual, but for the little ones, someone had made an attempt at festivity.

From a distance, the drumming of a marching band pounded a lively number. Katrine and Hans left to wander down the street and get a better look at the musicians. Astrid pulled her shawl closer and leaned back against the seat, content to remain in the booth.

Meneer Van Laar appeared from the sidewalk, holding a bag of roasted peanuts. "May I join you?"

Astrid nodded. She'd been surprised he'd wanted to come into the village today since he usually preferred the quiet of the stablemaster's cottage, but she welcomed the company of someone she could at least have an intelligent conversation with.

"Nice up here." He smiled and offered up his warm treat.

She held out a gloved hand. "I haven't had these in years."

He laughed. "I can see that." He lifted his hand to her cheek. "May I?"

Astrid frowned.

He brushed off a peanut skin. "Now you can face your subjects properly."

"I'm no queen," Astrid said.

"No? But you have a nice throne..."

His dimples reappeared. Trouble.

"Meneer Van Laar, are you making fun of me?"

"Never. You are the lady of the house." His green eyes twinkled. "Unless you are taking a break?"

"I am not," she replied.

He raised his eyebrows at her. "You may want to consider it someday. It's good for your health."

Another couple entered the dais. The woman was excessively perfumed, and her husband wore a military overcoat with the insignia of the National Socialists. Meneer Van Laar moved towards Astrid to make room. He sat closer, their legs touching. Removing a silver case from his pocket, he held out a cigarette. She shook her head. Meneer Van Laar lit up, leaned back and inhaled deeply. Astrid stole a glance at him from the corner of her eye. He had long, dark lashes. It was strange to be so close to him, and yet she welcomed the warmth of another person to ward off the chill of the frozen ground. She turned her face towards the sun and closed her eyes for a moment.

The first float to pass by was sponsored by the railway union. It was a carriage built to resemble a locomotive. Small children hung out from cardboard windows, waving wildly to the crowd, searching for their friends and pulling a cord to release a loud whistle. Meneer Van Laar winced at the high-pitched sound.

"What made you decide to come into town today?" Astrid said.

"After a while you get to feel caged up," he replied.

"And now, are you enjoying your freedom?"

"Enormously." His smile turned into a frown as he looked down the street. "But I don't think she is."

Astrid followed his gaze. A lone girl marched ahead of three rows of youngsters in matching uniforms, carrying a red banner close to her chest, as though to hide it. In contrast to the enthusiastic reception of the railway float, this procession was met with silence and even a few scowls from the crowd.

"Poor girl," Astrid said.

"They should really work on their recruitment efforts," Meneer Van Laar whispered. "Not much of a flag bearer, is she?"

"I recognize her. We met in the bank once. Her father has the greenhouses at the end of the Nonnenstraat. The Germans love the wholesome peasant nonsense."

"You don't find peasants wholesome?"

"I think glorifying any one group over another is a recipe for disaster."

"For an aristocrat, you're quite the egalitarian. Are you certain you're not a closet Communist, Mevrouw?"

There he went teasing again. It had been a long time since someone had concentrated so much effort just to ruffle her. She felt flattered, and slightly confused. Meneer Van Laar wasn't even thirty years old.

In the distance, carolers approached. The crowd quieted to listen to the familiar songs, joining in for a verse or two as they passed by.

"I prefer the older hymns myself," Astrid remarked.

Meneer Van Laar said nothing, instead he hummed along to the chorus of "O Tannebaum."

"Mother!" Katrine cried out from the crowd below. "Here he comes!"

Astrid looked and saw the familiar spry figure of the mayor dancing through the streets, his face painted black, wearing a velvet robe and carrying a sack. Three or four other young boys trailed behind, their faces covered in black masks. They walked alongside the Sinterklaas float, holding giant oars in one hand and pretending to row in a ship from Spain. In their other hand, they carried bags of treats. Schueller looked up, waved at Astrid and winked.

"Have you been good, Mevrouw?" he shouted above the little children's heads.

Astrid gave a curt nod. Schueller's blackened face and bright red lips unsettled her. As a child she'd been frightened by *Zwarte Piet*,

Sinterklaas' assistant, and his list of naughty children. When her father had encouraged her to sit on Sinterklaas' knee at Christmas parties, she'd refused, unsettled by the disguises. Meneer Van Laar shifted on the bench beside her, his discomfort equally palpable.

"I can tell by the look on your face you find Zwarte Piet as odd as I do," he muttered.

Astrid pulled her mink tighter around her shoulders. "Indeed I do."

"Caricatures seem innocent but they leave deep impressions, especially on children," he remarked.

Meanwhile, Schueller gleefully tossed *kruidnoten* cookies at them. The children grew more animated as Sinterklaas approached, and began to sing a familiar little rhyme about Sinterklaas filling their shoes with treats.

> *Sinterklaas, kapoentje*
> *Gooi wat in mijn schoentje*
> *Gooi wat in mijn laarsje*
> *Dank U Sinterklaasje*

No sooner had they belted out their plea for treats, than the older children sang it anew, with louder, more insistent voices. *RAF Kapoenje...*

Astrid glanced at Meneer Van Laar to see if he caught the shift in lyrics. He leaned forward to hear better, while the adults pretended not to notice the cheeky variation.

RAF Little Capon, throw something in my little shoe, throw bombs at the Krauts, but scatter candy in Holland!

The NSB man pushed past his wife and brusquely forced his way out of the dais and into the melee. He raised his fist in the general direction of the kids, but they stuffed their mouths with cookies and feigned innocence. An uneasy murmur ran through the crowd. Astrid looked again for her own children and caught sight of Hans bending down to collect scattered treats from the sidewalk. Pepernoten cookies dotted the pavement in translucent green bags. Astrid got up from the bench, hurried out of the booth and picked one up. When she opened it, alongside the sweets, a small pamphlet fell out. In bold typography, the words written across the front page were impossible to miss: *RESIST!*

When the parade reached the burned-out storage building next to the Stadhuis, a soldier collected my flag. At last I was free! I'd agreed to meet Papa and Loti in the pancake house afterwards, but that was before I'd noticed my former teacher give one of the young Zwarte Piets a bag of treats and slink away from the square. My family would have to wait. I dashed down a narrow lane in pursuit of Rosaura Reinhart.

"Miss Reinhart!"

She didn't slow, didn't look back. I called out again and quickened my pace.

"Miss! It's me, Hilde Zontag." I broke into a run and followed her down a narrow alley.

Miss Reinhart quickly climbed up the steps to a three-story apartment, before abruptly turning to glare at me. "What do you want, Hilde?"

I pulled myself up to full height. "I want to help."

Her eyes gave nothing away. "With?"

I retrieved a rolled-up paper from the green bag in my pocket.

Miss Reinhart's eyes flickered. "I've never seen that before."

"Miss, I saw you with the pepernoten today and I noticed you leaving De Boer's bakery last week. Don't say you're not up to something."

Her shoulders sagged. She glanced around the street below, hesitated, and reluctantly waved me into her apartment. It was as cold inside as out. The gas had been turned off and the windows were covered in a layer of frost. Surveying the sparse surroundings, I shivered.

"Did you read it?" Miss Reinhart asked, taking off her hat and hanging her coat on a hook by the dormant radiator.

I shook my head. I'd only glanced at the first sentence before stuffing *De Nieusbrief* deep into my pockets.

"You're young, Hilde. Perhaps you can think of ways to quietly resist—"

"That's just it! I can't. Do you think I wanted to wear this ridiculous uniform and march through the streets today? Everyone treats me like a child, but I want to do something. Please."

She bit her lip. "Your mother would never have made you carry that flag."

That was news to me. "You knew my mother?"

Miss Reinhart nodded. "Of course. Everyone knew Monica. You look just like her."

I stared after my teacher as she disappeared into the kitchen, rattled around for a minute, and came back with a small package in her arms.

"You know they say I'm a Communist?"

I nodded.

"I can't stay here in Brummelo much longer. But...someone has to continue my work..." She opened the parcel and I reached out and touched the thin papers.

I squinted at the blurry print. "The flame will flare up from the spark?"

"That's our motto. We are the most organized of the resistance groups right now. We have the infrastructure to bring people together, those who want to resist."

"Like me."

Miss Reinhart sighed. "I admire your sincerity, but you're young. Have you considered the consequences?"

"You mean that we're becoming Germans and every day more of our neighbours are humiliated by unfair rules?"

"If you join our little cell, if you get caught...you could go to jail or worse."

I was quiet for a moment. "I don't want to cooperate with them."

"Even if you were to quietly adapt to the changes—"

"Why are you trying to talk me out of this? I don't want to *adapt* to curfew, ration cards, military patrols or violent German teachers—"

"The teacher is violent?"

I nodded. "He is."

"But you're not afraid of him."

It wasn't a question.

"I don't want to be like every terrified person out there…"

Maybe Miss Reinhart understood. At least she was nodding her head. "A lot of people are very scared. Fear makes them act in ways we can't understand."

I thought of Papa and winced, feeling disloyal but not enough to let this go.

"…I don't want to simply make the best of things. Nothing will change if we do that. I want something more." I took a deep breath and pointed to her parcel. "So why don't you tell me what to do with these?"

Miss Reinhart held up her hands and a smile gradually spread across her face.

"You're a pest, you know that?"

I took the compliment.

"Fine. Leave these where people can read them. And make sure no one sees you. If you are caught…"

She didn't need to finish her sentence. I knew what would happen if Papa—or anyone—discovered what I was about to do. I tucked the bundle away safely in my satchel. I wasn't so concerned about Papa just then. Finally, I had something that would prove I wasn't the girl in the *Jeugdstorm* uniform. I left the apartment and headed towards the restaurant, walking briskly and rehearsing excuses as I jostled through the departing crowd. I pushed open the door, heard it clang shut behind me and squinted through the haze of smoke.

In the middle of the room Papa sat at the head of a long table, still wearing the white beard and pointed hat of his Sinterklaas costume. All around him were our neighbours and friends, enjoying a pitcher of beer as though the war had paused for a moment. Mayor Schueller was there, too, with his friend the aristocrat and her family.

But then everything in the room slowed down and blurred as I caught sight of Carl. *My* Carl, who I'd longed to see relaxed, whose smile had to be cajoled more often than not, was clutching his side, doubled over with laughter at some witty remark the Van Soelen girl had just uttered. Before anyone noticed my presence, I turned and ran out the back door, colliding with the green-eyed teacher from Rotterdam.

"Pardon me," he said. He looked at me for a moment, recognition dawning on him. "I saw you in the parade."

I felt my face flush. How could I defend myself? Everyone had seen the uniform. Would they always remember me as the girl in the *Jeugstorm* parade? I looked down at the cobblestone.

"Are you coming in for a pancake?" he asked, his voice gentle.

I met his gaze and shook my head. "I've had enough Sinterklaas for one day."

His face broke into a smile. "That makes two of us."

I clutched the satchel full of *nieuwsbriefs* close. I wanted to open the flap and show him, *this* is who I am, not that girl you saw earlier. But of course, that was impossible. If I was going to do this, I had to learn how to be content with people thinking the worst of me while I tried to do my best.

I could do that. I could learn. But gazing through the steamy windows of the pancake house at Carl, I wondered how much it would cost.

11

Benjamin sat alone at the small desk in the stablemaster's cottage, facing the snow-covered pines outside his window. A year earlier, he'd been pacing the *Nieuwe Keizersgracht*, waiting for the ink to dry on an English name, ready to leave the country. If he'd gone when he had the chance, he'd already have a new life in London, far from the River Quarter and the violent raids that now separated him more than ever from his uncle.

A knock on the door interrupted his brooding. He wasn't expecting anyone. Warily he approached and saw a thin man rubbing his hands together on the threshold. Benjamin hurried to usher Schueller inside. The mayor kicked the snow from his boots and slid into a chair. "How are you, Benji?"

Benjamin picked up the newspaper, his hand trembling slightly. "The news from Amsterdam is horrific."

"I heard about it on the radio." Schueller scanned the headlines, sat back and took a cigarette from his case, offering one to Benjamin.

"They're calling the residents of the Jewish Quarter 'rebels'..." Benjamin said, accepting one of the fine cigarettes Schueller always managed to procure.

Schueller nodded. "It's surrounded by barbed wire. Non-Jews are no longer permitted inside."

"What are they planning to do, create a ghetto like in Warsaw and Łódź?"

Schueller shrugged. "I'm going to see what I can find out. I don't trust this rubbish." He gestured dismissively at the newspaper in Benjamin's hands.

"What do you mean *you're going?*" Benjamin asked. "You've only just returned from Berlin."

Schueller nodded. "There's an excellent business opportunity to sire Lady Astrid's stallion Hercules with a dam in Utrecht. I'm taking Hans along. We'll be home in a couple of days. Until then, I'll keep my ear to the ground for what's really happening in Amsterdam."

"Hans is very young."

"The more he learns about the breeding business, the more he can help his mother, and believe me, she needs all the help she can get. Jan Stenger isn't coming home anytime soon."

"That's the husband?"

Schueller nodded. "The children look like him but they both have more personality in their baby finger than their father has in his whole being. I never warmed to the man; he wasn't from around here."

Benjamin thought this had more to do with Schueller's affection for Lady Astrid than anything else but he kept his theory to himself.

If Schueller were taking Hans, Benjamin would be left to conduct lessons with Katrine on her own, a thought he didn't relish. The girl bored easily and was inclined to interrogate him on his personal life. He'd have to come up with something to keep her occupied. He'd find a thick book for her to read, or introduce the Präteritum tense. Meanwhile, he still had other questions.

"Have you been able to get in touch with my uncle?"

"Aha! You didn't think I came here just to moan over the newspaper reports, did you?" Schueller held out a thin envelope and smiled. "Go on, have a read."

Benjamin tore open the letter.

Dear Nephew,

How wonderful to receive your letter and the money you sent. I'm grateful that you are safe. As you suggest, it would be good for me to also enjoy some country air. Alas, at the moment, it isn't possible. We shall meet again, but please don't think of coming here. You would find the neighbourhood unbearably changed.

Yours,

Uncle Nathan

He folded up the letter.

"What does he say?" Schueller asked.

"He's trapped." Benjamin ran his hands through his hair. "I should have insisted he come with me last summer."

Schueller put out his cigarette, angrily mashing it into the ashtray. "Stop punishing yourself. This isn't your fault."

Could he risk it and go back for him? Force his uncle into hiding? Nathanial Rosenblum was a proud man; assuming the identity of a Catholic would be impossible for him. If not impossible, beyond his wildest imaginings.

―――

The castle was quiet, but Astrid felt anything but peaceful. She paced back and forth on her balcony, kicking at the fresh snow. In the two days since Hans and Schueller had left, the entire country had ground to a halt as people took to the streets in a nation-wide strike. Each time a vehicle came up the lane, she would leap from her chaise, hoping it was Hans and Schueller, but it was only more German soldiers, coming and going.

Despite the snow falling around her, Astrid felt feverish. She stared across the garden, past the outer walls towards the stables. Was she a complete fool to trust Schueller? With her horses? With her *son*? The captain and his men were patrolling the railway to put down any further riots stemming from the strike—maybe that's what was keeping Hans and Schueller. If they encountered trouble, surely Schueller could talk his way out of it. Wearily, she turned from the balcony and went back inside. Finding a candle, she hastened down the hall to Katrine. Her daughter was seated at her vanity, brushing out her hair.

"Mother?"

"I came to say goodnight," Astrid said, stroking her daughter's shoulder.

"Your hands are cold as ice. Where have you been?"

"I needed a bit of fresh air, that's all." She took hold of her daughter's hair and began to braid it. Only the governesses had managed to tame her thick mane over the years. Astrid had forgotten the weight and texture of it; it was as soft as a silken rope.

"Could you have a word with Meneer Van Laar, Mother?"

Astrid startled. "Is anything the matter?"

"I'm bored out of my mind. These last few days he's been giving me piles of research to do while he sits and pores over the newspapers," Katrine explained. "He's obsessed with the *razzias*."

Astrid tied the end of Katrine's hair with a ribbon and kissed her daughter on the top of her head. She'd lived behind the safe walls of Soelenkasteel, protected from the world. And she would for as long as Astrid could continue to appease the Germans. But it wouldn't do for her children to be completely naïve to the troubles outside the estate.

"Have you learned anything useful from all this research?"

"I've learned that I hate history and economics."

Astrid swallowed a sigh. She wanted her children to retain their innocence, but she abhorred the vapid opinions—born of ignorance and inexperience—she'd often overheard around elegant dinner tables in the homes of the upper class. She wanted her children to be educated in the true sense of the word. A bit of history, an understanding of economics, a sense of wonder for the natural world…it was good for a young woman to be filled with knowledge. Astrid was pleased with all Katrine had learned from Van Laar, and yet to placate the girl she promised to have a word with him.

"Don't forget to lock your door," Astrid said, as she rose to leave. "*Both* locks."

She could have waited until morning, but something pulled her downstairs. Taking a lantern, she found her scarf and wool coat and quietly headed over to the stablemaster's cottage.

Meneer Van Laar answered the door in his undershirt and trousers. His face was half covered in foamy soap.

"Lady Astrid? Is something the matter?" He was looking past her, his green eyes momentarily fearful.

She stood in the doorway and took in his lean muscles and broad shoulders. He wore a gold chain around his neck she'd never noticed before. Behind him, his shirts hung over the fire, droplets of water making a hissing sound on the cast iron.

"Might I come in, Meneer Van Laar?" she asked.

He stepped aside and indicated a chair. "Give me a moment, Mevrouw. I'm almost done."

Astrid mindlessly twisted the signet ring on her baby finger while Meneer Van Laar finished shaving. His stubble was so dark it was almost blue under his skin. A spicy, musky scent filled the tiny room. He dipped a cloth into a bowl of water and quickly wiped his face.

"Is the captain back?" he asked, sitting opposite her.

"Not yet," she answered. "Nor are Schueller and Hans."

He had missed a spot of soap under his ear. Without thinking, she leaned across the table and wiped it away. She blushed and quickly withdrew her hand. The warmth of his skin stirred her unexpectedly.

He smiled and reached for a sweater. "I can see that you're worried, but Hans has a good head on his shoulders. Schueller told me how much he appreciates an extra set of hands."

Astrid nodded. "But I have no way of knowing where they are… with the strike."

"Schueller will take care of Hans. And Hercules, too. He loves that horse."

"Hmmm." *He likes money, like any of us*, she thought.

As though reading her mind, Meneer Van Laar said, "He's changed, Mevrouw. He's your partner, not your rival."

"Are people really who they say they are?"

Meneer Van Laar's smile disappeared. "Did you come here to talk about Schueller, or was there something else?"

"How are the lessons going with Katrine? She mentioned that you've been upset by the news this last little while…"

"That's war. Some days, the news is more dispiriting than others. But…" he shrugged. "I apologize, Mevrouw. I don't mean to neglect my duties."

"I'm sure you haven't neglected a thing. I didn't wish to imply you were in any way unprofessional. I was…curious."

He looked at her. "Curious?"

Astrid took a deep breath. "They say men have been taken to work camps in the east…"

Meneer Van Laar shook his head vehemently.

"You don't believe that?" Astrid asked.

"Mevrouw…"

"Please, from now on. When the children aren't here, just call me Astrid."

Meneer Van Laar raised an eyebrow.

How could she explain that she was forgetting herself completely? How could she admit to this unusual stranger that anyone she might have called a friend had long since left the country and the last person to call her by her name was thousands of miles away?

"If one needs to speak frankly, one should have the confidence to use first names."

"Then you must call me Benjamin."

"Alright, Benjamin. What makes you think those men *aren't* headed to work camps?"

"The Germans don't round up men in suits for work camps. They don't send men without boots, either." He sighed. "And they certainly don't break the arms of men needed in fields and factories. Those men are never coming home, Astrid."

Hearing her name, spoken with such gravitas and intimacy, softened something hard and tight inside her chest. *Don't get involved.* She stared at his serious expression. The fate of the men in the newspapers was personal to him. Very personal.

"You're not...a teacher...from Rotterdam, are you, Benjamin?"

He looked at her for a long time, long enough for Astrid to understand his answer before he gave it, waiting to see if he could trust her. She leaned forward. He slowly shook his head.

"But you can understand how much it would mean to me if we continue to say I am."

12

Slipping into the shoemaker's shop, I looked over my shoulder cautiously, but the Nonnenstraat was quiet. The bell on the door jingled and echoed over the empty display shelves.

"Mevrouw Loewenstein? It's Hilde. I've brought you some food…" I stopped at the sight of the children playing on the floor. I hadn't seen Ari and Hannah for ages and they'd grown in the months their desks had sat empty at school. Mevrouw Loewenstein emerged from the backroom, her husband behind her.

"Good morning, Hilde," she said, her eyes red-rimmed and tired.

"What have you got there, dear?" Meneer Loewenstein peeked into my basket and smiled at the array of preserves. I didn't think Papa would notice a few pears and beans missing, thanks to a few edits I'd made in his ledger book.

His voice cracked when he spoke again. "This is so kind of you."

I noticed the suitcase beside boxes of unsold merchandise. "How was your trip?"

"The situation in Amsterdam is very tense," he said.

I nodded. I'd seen the newspaper reports about the strike and the brutal retaliations. "I'm glad you're home safe."

"For now," he exhaled. "They want all Dutch Jews to register with the Jewish Council. There are thirty-five pages of questions about assets, family members…" Meneer Loewenstein shook his head.

I'd never heard of a Jewish Council. Papa hadn't mentioned anything like it and he followed the news as though his life depended on it. "Can they help you?"

"Oh, Hilde. You don't want to hear all this miserable business," Mevrouw Loewenstein said. "Let's talk of something else. Did you see the dress Ava Gardner was wearing on this month's cover? The red velvet dress with the pleats?"

Maybe last year I would have been distracted by the mention of a new Vogue magazine. Part of me wanted to pore over the latest designs with her, and I was sad we couldn't. I loved Ava Gardner. But unless Ava Gardner could help the Loewensteins, she didn't matter right now.

"Your troubles are my troubles."

Meneer Loewenstein turned to his wife. "She's just like Monica."

Mevrouw Loewenstein nodded. "She even sounds like her. Stubborn."

I felt a warm sensation in my chest. "So tell me about this council."

Meneer Loewenstein shrugged.

"Across Europe, Jewish elders have organized as intermediaries between the Nazis and the Jewish communities. In Amsterdam, the Council believes compliance is the safest way to manage the…aggressions."

Mevrouw Loewenstein shook her head.

"Did *you* register, Meneer Loewenstein?" I asked.

"This cartothèque…it's voluntary." He rubbed his eyes and sighed. "For now."

Mevrouw Loewenstein leaned against the counter and stared past me towards the empty displays. "We'd feel safer in Belgium or France, or another country where religion isn't indicated."

"Modern day Inquisition." Meneer Loewenstein muttered as he sat down beside his children on the floor, helping them build a precarious wooden tower.

I wanted to cry then, for the tender way Meneer Loewenstein

traced his fingers along his son's spine, at once lost in a daydream and overwhelmed by anxiety. What kind of father would he be if he didn't have to worry about the danger outside his doorstep?

"We'll wait and see. Many of the German Jews who've sought refuge in the Netherlands are also refusing to register. What do they know that we don't?" Mevrouw Loewenstein said. "Would it be wiser if the children were not registered at all?"

A stranger stepped into the store. Meneer Loewenstein rose immediately to greet him with a vigorous handshake. The man wore a long trench coat and a woollen hat in the Russian style. He spoke with Meneer Loewenstein in hushed tones. I strained to listen, but only caught *urgent* and *now*.

"Could you mind the children dear? My wife and I need to step out for an hour or so."

"Of course." I took off my coat. "My father's not expecting me until supper."

I knelt down and took Meneer Loewenstein's spot on the floor and tried to fortify the precarious tower with the children. We played quietly for a while, until Ari asked if I wanted to see their fort.

"No! Ari, it's a *secret*, remember?" Little Hannah began to chew her fingernails.

"I'm very good at keeping secrets," I said.

The dark-eyed siblings exchanged serious glances and looked back at the front door worriedly. I got up, slid the deadbolt shut and closed the curtains tight.

"She's not a bad one, Hannah. Let's show her," Ari said.

Hannah nodded reluctantly, got up and grasped my hand. They led me to the back of a storeroom to a closet door.

"At first, you must crouch down..." Ari explained, eager to impress, his impish grin inviting me in.

The closet was dark and cramped, but I could see how a child would enjoy playing there.

"...But then you push here—" Ari leaned into the wall and it moved. The look on my face made Hannah burst into giggles. I followed the children into a secret room. Hannah pushed the door closed behind us and Ari lit a lantern. There was a mattress, a pile of blankets and a few books.

"This is wonderful," I said sincerely. I picked up a worn copy of *Treasure Island*.

"Can you read to us?" Hannah asked shyly. "Mother hasn't had much time lately, making plans for the move."

Move?

"Of course. Show me where your mother left off."

I opened a dog-eared page and was halfway through the seventh chapter when voices penetrated through a smaller door I hadn't noticed on the far wall.

"Uh oh, now we must be quiet." Hannah curled into a ball beside me.

Ari sighed and laid his head on a pillow. I closed my eyes and leaned my head against the wall. Carl was speaking with his mother! The De Boer's kitchen must be directly on the other side of the door. A kettle whistled and then I heard the clatter of cups and spoons. No wonder the little hideaway smelled of bread.

Another person entered the kitchen.

"Mevrouw De Boer, let me take that."

Ari smiled and whispered, "That's the leader."

I strained to hear better.

I closed my eyes again to concentrate on the strands of conversation. The room was filling up and soon there were too many voices to keep track of. The people gathered on the other side of the wall were worried.

"Five hundred men, Rosaura!"

"He's angry," Ari said. "Again."

Mayor Schueller was angry. I'd know his growl anywhere. What was going on?

"We couldn't stand by and do nothing!" said my former teacher in her gravelly voice.

Every week I'd been collecting bundles she left for me by the gate of our canal plot and doing my best to distribute them. I wished I could get them from her apartment so we could chat for a moment, but she warned me against being seen with her. *Remember, this is dangerous, Hilde.* In spite of her warnings, I hadn't come close to getting caught. Everyone had enough to worry about without paying me any mind.

There was a low murmur of discord. Though united in their grief over the retaliations for the nation-wide strike, they were far from unanimous about what to do next.

Another familiar voice, one I listened to each Sunday, summed up what I supposed the entire group was thinking.

"For every act of sabotage or rebellion, there will be swift and deadly repercussions." Reverend Van Veen cleared his throat. "Nine hundred were killed in the bombing of Rotterdam…" He paused. "And now nine hundred and twenty-five more are dead."

Hannah began to cry beside me. I held her close to muffle the arguing. But my soothing words were no use—Hannah was inconsolable. Her quiet tears turned into wracking sobs. And on the other side of the wall, silence fell.

The hidden door to the De Boer's kitchen opened and Carl stuck his head inside.

He froze at the sight of me with the children.

"What are *you* doing here?"

"It's okay. She's a good one," Ari said. "Mother likes her. She brings us food."

Carl looked back and forth between Ari and me. The tension in his face was so painful I wanted to reach out and touch him.

Mevrouw De Boer was beside her son, staring with concern at Hannah.

"Children, you know this is a secret room. You weren't supposed to tell anyone." Her scolding was serious, but gentle. She reached out to embrace little Hannah and the child's sobbing subsided.

I decided now was as good a time as ever to introduce myself to the rest of the room. I stood up, brushed off my skirt and walked into the kitchen.

"Presumably you've heard our conversation." Mayor Schueller stood with his hands on his hips, frowning.

I nodded and smiled weakly at the people gathered. The air was stuffy and for all their polite nods, I wondered for a moment if *I* was in danger. Miss Reinhart broke the spell.

"She's been helping me deliver nieuwsbriefs since Christmas," she admitted, avoiding Schueller's shocked expression. "With a face like that, she flies under the radar. We can trust Hilde."

The room remained silent, except for Schueller, who paced the floor. "You don't make those decisions, Rosaura, *I* do. That's how this works."

"Hilde," Reverend Van Veen began. "The queen has called for all of us to quietly resist as we're able—"

"But we feel a higher calling, a riskier calling. This group isn't for the weak," Mayor Schueller interjected.

"…Or the impulsive," added Mevrouw De Boer.

"I want to help."

Mayor Schueller plunked himself down on a hard, wooden chair, crossed one leg over the other and lit a cigarette. The others waited for him to make a decision.

"If we accept you, you cannot breathe one word of this to your father," he said, exhaling slowly. "Or your sister."

I stared back at him, willing myself not to blink.

"Your father respects German efficiency," Reverend Van Veen remarked.

"Ha! He's profiting from them! He's already bought seeds to feed the enemy," another man objected. "I vote *no*."

"He's doing his best to survive," I explained. "He hasn't joined the NSB or taken advantage in any way. He's a good man." I paused. I couldn't deny what they'd observed. Papa *did* admire the organization and coordination of the Germans. He quizzed Frid on their movements and the logistics required to house and feed their troops and wondered at the level of synchronisation that contributed to such military might. I wanted desperately to help, to prove my allegiance, but I had to defend Papa, too.

"You're right, Reverend. Papa loves order, because after Mama died…everything just became chaos."

Carl's gaze softened and my voice caught. "He just doesn't want to lose more than he already has. He's trying to make the best of things." And Loti, too, I realized. But now wasn't the moment to mention Frid.

The room grew quiet. Miss Reinhart wiped away a tear.

"Hilde." It was Reverend Van Veen again. "No one disputes your father is an upstanding man, a good father. But how would he react to his youngest daughter delivering illegal newspapers? Your precious life is at stake, jongedame." He glared at Miss Reinhart as he spoke those last words.

Mayor Schueller's warnings weighed on me, and suddenly I felt tired. My own father was willing to sacrifice his reputation so we'd always have food. Would he disown me if I betrayed him by ignoring his cautions and aligning myself with this ragtag band? Silence returned to the room.

Carl spoke up. "I'll walk Hilde home. Maybe we don't need to make a decision today."

The group nodded in agreement and Miss Reinhart smiled weakly in my direction. The Loewenstein children snuggled with Mevrouw De Boer. I guessed she'd make sure to reunite them with their parents later. Carl offered his arm as we stepped outside.

We walked in silence in the rain, neither one of us sure of what to say.

Carl stopped in front of the café. "I didn't know you were feeding the Loewensteins."

"You're not the only one with secrets. I keep trying to tell you I'm not like—"

Carl shook his head. "Loti. I know. I'm sorry."

We passed over the stone bridge, heading towards the old windmill. When the rain stopped we sat under the willows near the canal. Carl rubbed his bad leg for a moment and then reached out and took my hand.

"I'm sorry I doubted you. One minute you're ripping down Nazi propaganda, the next you're leading their parade."

Whatever I wanted to say in reply was lost because he leaned forward and kissed me softly on the lips.

Somehow I recovered from the shock of his touch. "Left to my own devices, I can be a bit impulsive. You'd probably say foolish."

"But?"

I thought of Papa, alone in his armchair, worriedly smoking his pipe, the ledger his only comfort.

"Sometimes I have to obey him." Isn't that what anyone would do to keep their family together?

He nodded. "I think I knew that…"

I put my fingers to his lips and kissed him again. "I've missed you."

He smiled. "Mother makes me keep up with my lessons after deliveries, and it's terrible without anyone to copy."

I punched him gently on the arm. "You never needed to copy me."

"No, but it was a good excuse to get closer to you."

I rested my head on his shoulder and sighed. "You know, after the Sinterklaas parade, I was worried you'd begun to fancy the Van Soelen girl when I saw you laughing with her in the café."

Carl looked confused. "I remember her—Katrine—a real joker. Where were you? Your father was waiting for you."

I was embarrassed to admit how easily I became jealous, so I made up an excuse. "I had to shed that horrible uniform."

He was quiet. "It's a good disguise if you ever need one."

"That's what Miss Reinhart said. But I'd rather just be me. I'm not a very good actress."

He swept a blond fringe of hair away from his face and grew suddenly serious.

"Why do you think I don't want you involved in this? I'd never forgive myself if something happened to you."

I put my arm around his waist, and he pulled me closer, so that my lips brushed his neck.

"And I'll never forgive you if you keep pushing me away. Let me in."

PART II

FALL 1941

EIGHT MONTHS LATER

13

The morning of her thirty-fifth birthday Astrid asked Eva not to make a fuss. Any extra money she'd spend on the horses. What did it matter if she went without a party just this once? Next year will be better, she told herself as she rushed out to the laneway where Hans had rigged up the old carriage. The banker had sent word he needed to speak with her urgently.

"Darling," she protested. "I can just as easily ride Philomena on my own."

"I know, Mother, but Meneer Van Laar wanted to go to town, so I thought we might as well join you."

"Surely you don't want to be alone on your birthday?" Katrine said, claiming a seat for herself.

That was exactly what Astrid wanted for her birthday, but she said nothing.

When they were halfway to the village Benjamin asked, "How would you like to celebrate your birthday? If we weren't at war, I mean."

Astrid closed her eyes. "Cake," she answered.

"Oh, Mother, remember last year's lemon cake with custard filling?" Katrine said.

"I was recalling a toffee cake with mocha-cream icing," Astrid said.

"You're making me hungry," Benjamin said, smiling. "So that's it, eat cake and what else? Have a nap?"

"Sounds heavenly," Astrid said, feeling herself relax against the cushions.

"Mother, remember we used to go for long rides on the dunes after your birthday dinners?" Katrine said.

Astrid nodded. Her husband had done birthdays well, spoiling her with gifts to make up for his long absences. But that was long ago. When the war was over she'd celebrate properly once again. A tent in the garden, a band playing the latest songs, gauzy dresses and frivolous heels that sunk into the grass…Who would she'd invite to such a grand affair? Would the upper classes return when the war was over? Looking across the carriage at Benjamin, she wondered if he liked to dance or if he was the type to step on a lady's toes. She shook away the thought. No point getting lost in daydreams.

HANS TIED up the horses and carriage and wandered off with Benjamin and Katrine on some mysterious birthday errand while Astrid headed into the bank. Apparently they planned to ignore her "no fuss" rule. It wasn't busy that morning, and as soon as she entered the manager came running up to her.

"Mevrouw. Please come into my office. We must speak at once."

She followed him into a small room and he shut the door behind her. "What's all this secrecy? Is something the matter?"

He nodded. "Meneer Stenger has been transferring funds from abroad for years, yes?"

"Usually every two or three months," Astrid confirmed.

The manager nodded. "Many Dutch Nationals in Indonesia are sending money abroad to Australia or England. The remittances are slowing to a trickle. I fear a Japanese attack is imminent."

"Surely the Royal Dutch East Indies Army can guard the industry on the islands?"

He scratched his head. "Hopefully we'll get some help from the

Brits to protect the oil reserves, but for everything else, I'm not sure Mevrouw. The foreign newspapers suggest many Indonesians would welcome the Japanese."

"Nonsense. Meneer Stenger's family has been working in Indonesia for hundreds of years. His employees are like family to him."

The bank manager pulled at his cravat and cleared his throat. "May I assume you haven't heard from your husband?"

Astrid shook her head. "We've been completely cut off."

"Fortunately, I can give you some news, though it's lacking in personal endearments." He slid a folder across the desk.

Her eyes widened. "What's this?"

"It's a lump sum remittance. The note from the Java Bank indicates that this represents the closing balance of the company's cash holdings. I'm no detective, Lady Astrid, but this leads me to believe your husband is abandoning his assets abroad and trying to leave the East Indies."

Astrid shook her head in disbelief. She always thought he would he stay and fight for the factory, the warehouses and his friends. What would she tell the children? The banker was mumbling something about Dutchmen heading to Australia. Was that where he'd gone?

"I can see you're in shock. Might I propose some safe investments for now?"

She nodded. "Of course. I appreciate your concern."

Astrid half listened to the manager's advice, trying to look interested. She had her own list of investments, improvements she could make to the stables. In the end, she asked him to deposit the money into the estate's account and promised to discuss the portfolio more the following week.

"I do wish him well, wherever he is, for your sake, Mevrouw."

A pang of guilt swept over her. She didn't miss her husband the way other women missed theirs; she hadn't chosen him in the first place. Still, he was the children's father, and she knew he loved Katrine and Hans, in his way. It would be cruel for them to wonder about Jan forever. She'd make an effort to find out whatever she could.

"Indeed. Let us hope for his safe return. Good day, sir."

AstRID RUBBED the lovely cream Benjamin and the children had purchased for her into her dry skin. She'd always had soft skin until now. Spending her days in the barn or the wash house had transformed her hands into the rough, cracked hands of a servant. It was a frivolous gift, but just holding the little jar pleased her immensely. She would use it sparingly. Who knew when the money would run out? She put on her silk scarf and headed down for dinner, where she listlessly moved the food on her plate around.

"Everything alright, Mevrouw?" the captain asked, his mouth full of cabbage, tendrils of sauerkraut dripping over his lips.

"Quite, thank you," she lied, refusing to be drawn into any kind of disclosure. She needed time alone, to think through what to do next. When his plate was clear, she excused herself.

The captain rose to block the door and put his thick fingers on her arm. "Before you go…there's a small matter I'd like to discuss with you."

"Now?"

"The *Reichskommissar's* wife is a horsewoman like you," he said, steering Astrid back towards the table.

She sat down, shaking off his grip. "So I've heard."

"Her favourites are the broodmares you're so fond of—"

"What are you getting at, Captain?" Astrid snapped.

His face registered shock at her tone. "Mevrouw…" he said, a warning in his voice.

"I apologize. I have quite a lot on my mind today."

"I see. Then I'll get to the point. Gertrud Seyss-Inquart is an elegant lady, and seeks elegant horses for her riding pleasure, and for entertaining…"

Dread wrapped itself around her like a heavy winter shawl. "Surely she can procure a suitable mount from the farms surrounding The Hague?"

The captain pursed his lips. "I think it would be good for you to get away from Soelenkasteel for a while, have a bit of fun." He smiled then, and Astrid's heart sank.

"I don't understand," she said, holding onto the edge of the table to steady her nerves.

"The Reichskommissar and his wife are hosting a ball for many of South Holland's upper class at Clingendael Manor. Perhaps you've visited before?"

"My husband imported many of the oriental features in the gardens," Astrid replied. *A lifetime ago.*

"Yes, well. I've made arrangements for Mayor Schueller to take four of your finest broodmares as a gift to Frau Seyss-Inquart. She is expecting you at the reception; I'm sure she'll want to thank you for your generous expression of support."

Astrid ignored the menacing tone of the captain's voice and caught his subordinates staring at her. She lifted her chin and took a deep breath.

"One has to admire your efficiency, Captain." She needed air, she needed to talk to Schueller and find out how much he knew of this plan. With a curt nod, she made her escape.

He rose and followed her into the hall.

"Mevrouw," he said, placing a sweaty palm on the small of her back. "I almost forgot. Happy Birthday. Please accept a small token."

He slipped a tiny box into her hand. She was too stunned to say a word. Opening the box, she uncovered a small, carved wooden horse. The detail was exquisite. It was an exact replica of Philomena.

"Frid carved it. He was an artist before the war."

"It's beautiful," she said. Then she remembered the invitation to Clingendael, the beautiful royal mansion now occupied by Nazis. Would this trinket be the only horse she had left in the end?

"Thank you, Captain." Before he could say another word, she hurried up the stairs and disappeared into her chambers.

. . .

"Whose side are you on, Kurt?" Astrid stood at the entrance to his garage, arms crossed over her chest.

He rolled out from beneath the Adler, covered in grease, wrench in hand. "He was going to send them either way. I figured if we accompanied them, at least they'd make it there safely and we could attend a party or two while we're at it."

"What on earth makes you think I want to get dressed up and dine with Nazis?" Astrid said.

"I didn't say you *wanted* to dine with Nazis, but I know you love caviar, and you must admit, it's been a while."

"I don't want to lose my best horses for a handful of canapés!"

"My darling ostrich, the homes of the nobility are being expropriated one by one across the country," Schueller explained.

"I know, I know…"

"You said you would do whatever it took to keep Soelenkasteel. As long as we continue to provide valuable services, your castle is safe." Schueller sat up and looked her in the eyes. "Your *family* is safe."

Astrid shifted uncomfortably. "And if I said, *that's enough*?"

"You'll be out of a home, out of money, and I daresay you can't afford to lose anymore income."

She sighed. He was right. "I have news and I need your advice."

"I love to feel needed. Tell me more."

She sat on the grass beside the car and told him about Jan's deposit. He let out a low whistle.

"Can it get any worse in Batavia?"

"I'd say you're lucky he transferred the money while he had the chance." Schueller's expression was grim.

She massaged her temples, trying to think. "If I agree to this ball, when would we leave?"

"It's scheduled for the thirteenth of December."

That gave her less than a month. She'd ride her team every day, brush them down every night and whisper a promise into their silky ears. *I'll find you when this is over.*

But like everyone else, Astrid didn't know when *over* might be.

14

Here's another truth: if the war had started when I was twenty-four instead of fourteen, things might have been different for me. Had I children, a business, a partner—maybe I wouldn't have done the things I did. But we don't get to choose whether we are born into castles or cottages, or the families that raise us in the best way they know how. It has taken me a lifetime to accept this. Indeed, I'm not sure I ever will.

———

IN LATE NOVEMBER 1941, I carried a basket full of illegal papers hidden under skeins of yarn, ready for distribution. Who wrote them, who printed them, I didn't know—and Miss Reinhart told me not to go digging. "Do your part and stay quiet. The less each of us knows, the safer we all are." My job was simply to tuck the leaflets into as many mailboxes as possible, which was easier before the snow had fallen. Now every time I looked behind me, all I saw were incriminating footprints. The freedom to be foolish perhaps. Though I'd rehearsed my story a hundred times—Hilde Zontag, wool peddler—I still darted between houses looking over my shoulder, paranoia making me work quickly.

Why didn't I stay in my warm cottage on the Nonnenstraat working out new designs on my Singer sewing machine? This would have been the sensible thing to do. But Carl didn't care about clothes. He *was* impressed I could deliver so many nieuwsbriefs in such a short time. I didn't admit how scared I was whenever a mailbox clanged shut too loudly.

Schueller had cautioned us months ago to stay away from the neighbourhood around the train station. The Germans stored their military vehicles in sheds around the marshes and gathered in a beer hall not far from where I stood. Still, it was early. Once I'd reached the last house bordering the park, I planned to go straight home. I hadn't ventured beyond the train station, but I had about a dozen leaflets left. Surely I could leave a few in the row houses there; it would only add a few more minutes to my circuit.

Walking quickly down the sidewalk I dropped a leaflet in the first mailbox I saw. It was almost too quiet on the street. For a moment I wondered if this section of town had been evacuated for some reason. I continued up the street deciding whether to turn left or right when I heard the distinct sound of military boots crunching on the cold snow behind me.

"Halt!"

Slowly I turned to face a German soldier approaching. I crumpled the papers in my hand and pushed them into my basket.

"What are you doing?" he asked.

"Collecting trash, sir," I stammered. "And deadwood for kindling."

He didn't look convinced. "Here?"

Desperately I reached under a nearby hedge for a handful of sticks, dropping them atop my wool. Before I could stop him he thrust his hand into the bag and grabbed the crumpled leaflets. Carefully, he smoothed one out and scanned it.

"Where did you get this?" he demanded.

"They are littered along the train tracks," I lied. "Excellent fire starter, sir."

"This is illegal propaganda. You could go to jail for having this in your possession."

I tried to sound as young as possible. "I had no idea. I just need enough wood to start a fire for dinner. There's always rubbish around the tracks, it's the best place to come."

He considered my story. "Most children go to the woods for kindling."

"We used to, but the woods have been fenced off. The signs forbid us from entering and cutting down the trees." I took a deep breath. "The villagers think the forest is mined."

He rolled his eyes. "We would never do that. There are no dangers in the forest. But you'd best be careful around here—there are saboteurs tinkering with the railways."

"I'm not a saboteur, sir."

He looked at the nieuwsbrief and back at me. "No...I can see that. You don't have a permit to sell your goods, so you've tried going door-to-door. That's it, isn't it? Show me your papers, please, jongedame."

I reached into my pocket and retrieved my identification card. As he studied the picture and address, it occurred to me that there might be an easier way out of my predicament.

"Sir, do you know my sister Loti? She works at the Stadhuis."

His face brightened. "Of course! Frid's girl. You must be Meneer Zontag's other daughter!"

I nodded.

"You shouldn't loiter around here. We've had trouble with the trade unionists who live in the marshes." The German looked up at the row houses suspiciously. "Not as helpful as your old man, this lot."

My heart sank.

"Give me that garbage right away. I must report it to the captain. We'll find out who's responsible for these lies."

This was my chance. "With your permission, I'll be heading home then, sir."

Before he could ask me another question, I quickly turned and walked as fast as I could. I would keep this little adventure to myself.

. . .

THE FOLLOWING DAY, I stepped onto the sidewalk outside of school and saw Schueller in the middle of a crowd, holding court on the sidewalk. I approached the group and waited until he saw me.

"Good afternoon, Miss Zontag. Can I have a word with you in a moment?"

"Certainly, Mayor Schueller."

I sat down on a bench and eavesdropped for a few minutes. The townsfolk were angry because the co-op had been taken over by the Germans. He promised they would be looked after; he'd meet with the farmer's association that evening. No, he couldn't guarantee they'd receive the same prices, but they'd have food, he assured them. Schueller managed to placate a few, but others stormed off unhappily. Things were getting worse for the average family, and Mayor Schueller's influence only reached so far. At least, that's what Papa said.

"How was Meneer Paul today?" Schueller asked when the last complainant left.

"The usual. The virtues of the master race, the glorious future of the Reich..."

He shook his head. "That good, eh? I'm glad my school days are over."

We fell in step with one another and headed towards the Nonnenstraat.

"What was it you wanted to talk about, sir?" I asked, trying to keep my voice as casual as possible. Had he found out about my close call yesterday?

We walked slowly around the block, the scent of midday soup wafting out onto the street from the tidy brick cottages.

"Hilde, I'd like you to come to Soelenkasteel with me this afternoon. Lady Astrid needs a seamstress."

"Me? You must be joking. I just fool around...a little mending."

"Ah. You are modest. I saw that coat when Mevrouw De Boer wore it. You've transformed it. Not only your coat but Loti's dresses, too. Women who meet her can't help but comment on the modern cut."

I stared at him in surprise. "Really? Which women?"

He waved his hand in the air dismissively. "Who cares? You've never been out to the castle, have you? It feels a bit like a third-rate hotel now, but you can still see the grandeur underneath the Nazi flags hanging in the foyer."

We were to have a meeting in the bakery's back room about food distribution that afternoon. Was Mayor Schueller trying to get rid of me for some reason?

"Why don't you have lunch with us, Mayor? Then you can ask my father if I can accompany you later."

"Very well." Then, as though it were an afterthought, he added, "Have you distributed all the nieuwsbriefs?"

"I finished my rounds yesterday," I answered, neglecting to mention the Germans had the last dozen in their possession.

"And you were cautious?"

"Of course, sir." I hated keeping secrets but I didn't want to be reprimanded, or worse, expelled.

We arrived at our cottage and he lowered his voice. "Good. Remember—follow the rules, stick to the plan and everyone will be safe."

I had to smile at that. For a moment, he sounded just like Papa.

"She's not learning anything useful in school anymore," Papa grumbled as he passed Schueller the bread.

Loti winked at me across the table. Papa's complaints about school were becoming a familiar refrain.

"Papa has been teaching me accounting fundamentals and would much rather I learn a trade than study more history or geography." I smiled half-heartedly.

Mayor Schueller seized his opportunity. "I agree with you one hundred percent Meneer Zontag. Young people need practical skills for the future." He smiled at me sideways, a small assurance he was on my side. "Why, with a bit of support, Hilde could easily open her own alterations shop. A skilled seamstress is a valuable trade—"

"With all due respect, Mayor Schueller," Papa interrupted. "Most women can sew on a button in a time of crisis."

"*Most* women, yes. But Lady Astrid Van Soelen is not your average woman," said Schueller.

Papa blinked. "They want Hilde at the castle?"

"Her reputation precedes her. I'm headed to the stables this afternoon. I could easily give her a ride."

Loti got up and washed her bowl at the sink. "Oh, Papa. Let her go. Or, let her quit school and give me a hand at the Stadhuis. We're swamped and could use another girl at reception." She kissed Papa on the cheek and found her coat. "We've always taken Hilde's talent for granted, Papa. Not just anyone can take apart a wool coat and turn it into a pair of coveralls in two evenings."

Papa smiled at me then. "They are the best coveralls I've ever had."

I blushed at his sudden praise. "I know, Papa."

Loti was triumphant. "Nice of you to join us for lunch, Mayor Schueller. I have to get back to the Stadhuis now. Papa, I have choir tonight so I'll be home late. *Doi!*"

A smile played upon Schueller's lips. Like most men, he was enchanted by Loti's friendly manner and natural beauty. I felt sorry for him that women didn't often turn their heads in his direction. They mostly looked over his head.

"If you want to go, you may. Mayor Schueller, you'll bring her home again?"

"I'll be back for dinner," I promised, gently kicking Schueller's foot under the table. I'd return *after* our cell meeting at the De Boers. There was no way I was missing out, just because some aristocrat needed a new dress.

SCHUELLER WALKED QUICKLY through the grand house and up the stairs to Lady Astrid's private chambers, while I ran to keep up. Once we arrived on the landing, he disappeared, saying he was going to chat with Meneer Van Laar in the library. I wasn't sure I'd be able to find my way back out on my own.

I opened the door to find Lady Astrid and her daughter, Katrine, sitting on matching velvet chairs. They exuded the same impatient manner, although Lady Astrid leaned forward and Katrine sank back into the cushions, a bored expression on her face. An array of gowns was laid out on Lady Astrid's enormous bed. The fabric smelled of cedar and lavender. Rich peoples' clothes.

"Hello again Hilde," Lady Astrid greeted me. "Tell me what you think. I've always loved the red one, but I've worn it many times already."

"And *I* think she's too pale for the red one. Besides, she'll blend in with the decorations if she wears it. It's almost Christmas!" Katrine argued.

I fingered each gown. The fabrics were exceptionally beautiful, but the cut of the gowns was out-of-date. Lady Astrid would look like someone's poor cousin if she wore any of them.

"I have a suit that will suffice for travelling but I require something for a ball." Lady Astrid's voice was soft, as though she was temporarily lost in memory.

"Do you have the Saturday newspaper, Mevrouw?" I asked.

Mother and daughter looked at one another quizzically.

"There's one in the library," Katrine said. She stood up and slipped out, eyeing me curiously.

"How old are you, jongedame?" Lady Astrid asked when we were alone.

"Fifteen."

"Katrine's age," Astrid observed ruefully. "Her governesses could never get her to focus on domestic arts. I daresay she can't thread a needle."

"I'm sure she has other talents."

"Let's hope so," Lady Astrid murmured.

I lifted up a pale yellow gown and ran my hands along the bodice.

"That's a summer dress," Lady Astrid said.

"The fabric is quite substantial," I said.

"True. I rarely wore it because it was so heavy."

Katrine returned with the newspaper. "Here you are."

I left the gowns and scanned the newspaper until I found the Paris Fashion pages on Lady Astrid's desk. Finding the advertisement I remembered, I held the image up towards Lady Astrid.

"What do you think, Mevrouw?"

"It's beautiful, but I have nothing like it."

"I could take the fur from that coat over there and make a little bolero, and line the skirt with the material from the green gown, because it's the most out-of-date…"

Katrine stifled a laugh.

"…And finally, I'd make a thick belt to tie it all together. It would be modern, elegant and one of a kind."

Lady Astrid and her daughter were silent. I wondered if I'd gone too far. We were at war. Perhaps it was too extravagant. Minor repairs to the red dress might suffice. I felt warm now, waiting for an answer. Finally, Lady Astrid spoke.

"Jongedame, Mayor Schueller and I leave in a week."

It wasn't a lot of time. If only I didn't have to go to school. What if the money I brought home convinced Papa the job was worth missing a few classes? I'd had more than enough of Meneer Paul and his nationalistic exhortations anyway.

"I can refurbish this gown for ten guilders, Mevrouw." I hoped I sounded confident.

Lady Astrid stiffened. "That's a month's rent from the tenant's cottage."

It was also the price Papa would now earn for two hundred eggs at the co-op, ever since it had been absorbed by the Germans.

"Oh Mother, you can afford it! Just say yes!" Katrine went to the bed and held up the yellow silk gown.

Lady Astrid threw up her arms. "Alright. Give it to Coco Chanel here and let's hope for the best."

I smiled at that. She wasn't as stiff as I'd first thought. "I won't let you down, Mevrouw."

I bundled the gowns into an extra-large suitcase and heaved it off the bed.

"Katrine, can you please escort this young lady to the library? Mayor Schueller will take her back to the village."

I felt like I should curtsy, but unsure of the exact protocol I managed a polite nod and took my leave. Once in the hallway, I let out a sigh of relief.

"Would you like a little tour of the castle?" Katrine asked.

I hesitated.

"Leave that there. It only takes a few minutes. Mayor Schueller and our tutor tend to have rather long-winded conversations..."

Katrine pulled me along the hallway and down the stairs. On the main floor she pointed out the severe-looking portraits—her great-grandparents—and then hustled me into the kitchen. Eva, the cook, turned around to see who'd barged in.

"Oh, it's just you, Miss Katrine. Who's this? You look familiar, jongedame."

I shook her hand. "We met in the queues. I'm Hilde Zontag."

"Of course. Our gardener bought seedlings from your father for years. What brings you to the castle?"

"Hilde is some kind of genius seamstress. She's getting Mother's gowns ready for Clingendael," Katrine said.

Clingendael? Lady Astrid was going to The Hague? I felt dizzy.

"Lady Astrid's husband used to bring in seamstresses from Apeldoorn, but with the war, those luxuries are no longer possible," Eva said.

I nodded. The kitchen was immense. Along one wall, large sinks and drainboards stood under brick foundation walls. A large stone fireplace heated the room and an iron grate kept the sparks from the long wooden tables and boilerplates. Herbs hung alongside copper pans from the ceiling, no doubt from the fall harvest.

"Are you hungry, dear?" the cook asked.

"No, thank you," I replied.

"Good, because we don't have much extra. The moffen eat it all," Katrine said.

The cook shot her a reproachful stare. I wondered if she always talked like this.

Katrine waved goodbye and we left the kitchen for the dining hall. I marveled at the high ceilings and the intricate carved paneling. Fine drapery and a warm oriental carpet contrasted with the opulence of a shimmering chandelier and immense mahogany dining table. We were heading out of the parlour when I heard soldiers' voices coming from the front entrance. I froze mid-step.

"Don't worry. Eventually you get used to them," Katrine whispered.

I didn't think I'd ever get used to them anywhere, least of all in my home. She steered me towards the staircase, and two officers turned and nodded at us. Katrine greeted them in smooth German. I couldn't speak at all. Standing before me was the officer from the marshes.

"Jongedame. We meet again. Are you selling your wool here?"

His companion looked at me quizzically.

"No sir. I'm doing some alterations for Lady Astrid."

"Ah. I see."

The officer turned to his companion and explained in German about the nieuwsbriefs. I only caught bits and pieces, but thankfully, the other officer was uninterested in the fire-making endeavours of a young village girl. Still, he lit a cigarette and gave me a once-over as he exhaled.

"Don't touch those leaflets. They could cause trouble for your family."

Katrine's fingers dug into my arm as she steered me away and took leave of the officers.

We climbed the steps two at a time and arrived breathless at the library. I wanted to get out of there and back to the village. But before I could knock on the door to get Mayor Schueller, Katrine spun me around to face her.

"I want you to explain what Officer Werner took from you yesterday."

"It was nothing."

Katrine crossed her arms. "Those moffen may believe your sweet innocent face and your lame kindling story, but I don't."

My protests died on my lips. She continued to stare at me, her bright blue eyes swirling with energy. I hated being cornered and vowed to admit nothing to Katrine, someone I barely knew. Someone who wasn't careful with her words. Miss Reinhart would never forgive me.

"You can trust me. What were you *really* doing in the marshes?"

I heard chairs moving behind the library doors.

Mayor Schueller appeared with Meneer Van Laar behind him. "Ready to go?"

I nodded and picked up the heavy suitcase. The sooner the better.

"I look forward to seeing you again soon," Katrine said. "So we can get to know one another a little more."

I straightened my spine. "I'll see you next week when I deliver the gown. *Tot ziens.*"

No one could see my hands trembling as I gripped the suitcase and held on tight. Though if anyone had placed their hand on my heart, they would have felt it pounding against my chest, a steady beat of rising trepidation.

15

Paper chains, juniper boughs and candlelight formed a festive cocoon around Astrid, Benjamin and the children while they finished a last round of *Klaverjassen*. To forget their uninvited guests they'd retreated to the comfort of the library. Though she'd grown up playing bridge, Astrid had to admit she preferred the card game Benjamin had taught them. In fact, she often won, but tonight she was distracted by the loud conversation floating upstairs from the drawing room where the officers were unwinding. The captain was on patrol that evening, and in his absence the men relaxed.

"Mother, it's your turn!" Katrine said impatiently.

Unlike Jan, who always winked if he was winning, Benjamin kept a poker face and she had no idea whether they should call the next trick or not. Astrid laid down a queen. Benjamin's placid smile did not waver. But Katrine's did.

She smacked down her cards in triumph. "We win! The candy is ours, Hans!"

Hans' face remained serious. He folded his cards on the table and leaned back in his chair. "Something's happening," he said quietly.

"Mother's lost her nerve, that's what. Or she's letting us win because she doesn't care for the sugar hearts anyway." Katrine popped leftover *strooigoed* into her mouth.

"Shhh," Hans put his finger to his lips.

Astrid closed her eyes and listened. Downstairs, the Germans had turned up the volume on the radio, and the unmistakable notes of Beethoven's fifth symphony came over the airwaves.

"BBC," Benjamin whispered."It must be serious if they're tuning into the enemy broadcasts."

He tilted his head to catch what was happening, but it was no use. He stood up, opened the door, and they abandoned their cards and followed him downstairs to the drawing room.

The Germans didn't notice them standing in the doorway, until Hans coughed. Werner, one of the older ones, was leaning over the console shaking his head. He fiddled with the dial until the radio crackled again and an American voice filled the room. One or two others acknowledged them with vague nods.

Astrid leaned against the wall and gazed across the room at an antique Brussels tapestry hanging above the radio. A pastoral scene of silky hens in the woods reminded her of the early years of her marriage. Jan was eager to refurbish the castle with ostentatious sculptures and gaudy oil paintings bought at French auction houses. She'd fought to preserve the muted, tranquil décor that grounded the castle in history. As much as she loved her black and white hens, she was alone in her appreciation for the faded beauty of the past. Everyone else in the room was engrossed in the horrors of the present.

She strained to make out what had happened. The officers, too, were struggling to piece together the dramatic news reports, but their rudimentary English was frustrating their efforts to understand. She looked at Benjamin. Over the past few weeks, she'd noticed that when he was in the presence of the Germans, he held his arms together tightly to control a slight tremor. Tonight his hands were shoved deep in his pockets while he listened intently. He looked so vulnerable—a wave of affection washed over her. He wanted to be invisible but also desperately needed to know what was happening.

The radio briefing ended abruptly, giving way to static.

"Come along," Astrid said to the children. She wanted to get out of the room and back to the safety of her quarters. She'd paid the exorbitant listening fee for the elegant, wood-paneled radio in the drawing room, which was mostly tuned to concerts in German since the ban on American and English music, but now she wanted to retire and quietly tune into *Radio Oranje*. Gebrandy or the queen might say more, but to listen she needed the small wireless she kept hidden in her wardrobe and the quiet of her own chambers.

"Wait!" Werner spoke in a low voice to his fellow officers. He pointed at Benjamin.

"Van Laar," the officer called after him. "You understand English better than us, *ja*? What did the news report say?"

Benjamin blinked like a trapped animal, glancing at the door and back at the men. Slowly he exhaled and sat down on the closest chair. After a moment, in a loud, confident voice, he explained how the Japanese had levelled a surprise attack on Hawaii early that morning.

"Four American ships have been sunk, perhaps more," he said, his voice calm. He looked at Astrid. Was it her imagination or were his eyes brighter than usual? She couldn't look away from them.

"What now?" one officer asked. "Will the Americans declare war?"

"On the Japanese of course!" another answered.

"We wait for orders." Werner spoke to his men, his voice full of assurance. He looked past his officers towards Benjamin. "What do you make of this news, teacher?"

"I don't know, sir," he replied.

He looked down at the floor and Astrid knew then he was lying. When they finally managed to excuse themselves from the volley of speculations and made their way back to the library, he paced the floor in front of the fireplace, cracking his knuckles over and over.

"Children, go to bed, please. Tomorrow's another busy day," Astrid said.

Hans and Katrine disappeared down the hallway and Astrid and Benjamin turned down the lanterns in the library. They sat together in companionable silence. Astrid took her hair from its bun and combed it out with her fingers. Benjamin watched her, a curious smile on his face.

He surprised her by reaching towards her and taking her hands in his. "Mark my words. By tomorrow, the Americans will be drawn into the fight."

"They've already been battling the U-boats for months," she said.

Benjamin nodded.

"How long until they arrive?"

At this he sighed heavily. "They were surprised by the attack…they may not be ready for war. Besides, they'll want to protect their interests in the Philippines. It might be a while before we see Americans on European soil."

"Until then?"

"See what Queen Wilhelmina has to say," he said with a smile. "And maybe work on your card game. What were you thinking when you gave up our winning streak?"

"My mind is on the trip to The Hague this week," she answered lightly. "I don't want to go."

Benjamin nodded. "You're worried about the children? I'll watch out for them. It's only a few days."

In all her years of marriage, Jan had never once promised to take care of Katrine and Hans. He sent money from abroad, but he always made a point of lording his benevolence over her, like a debt she owed.

"I appreciate that." She spread out her hands in a helpless gesture, indicating the castle and everything in it. "This war…"

He shook his head, smiled wistfully and got up to leave. He headed towards the door, then, changing his mind, turned back and leaned in close to Astrid, so close she could smell the aftershave on his collar.

"For someone who wanted to put their head in the sand, you've really failed. Between your Nazi guests and your card partner…" He touched her shoulder, but she twisted away. As if she'd wanted either. She'd only wanted to hold onto her home and give her children a future.

He looked hurt. "You must think I sound like Schueller."

"At least you didn't call me Madame Ostrich."

He raised his eyebrows and his bright eyes held her gaze.

"Kurt usually gives me some helpful advice on how to placate the Germans. Not exactly how I'd hoped to ignore them."

She hated Benjamin for a moment, for pulling her into his suffering when she had enough problems of her own. She hated the way his eyes unsettled her, when her mind was already made up.

"It's harder than I thought," she confessed. "Ignoring."

He was at a loss for words. But Astrid guessed what he might have answered if she let him linger any longer.

Benjamin Van Laar was simply trying to survive.

SHABBAT AGAIN, but Benjamin could not rest. In the quiet of the stablemaster's cottage, he prayed the familiar verses and went outside to enjoy the stillness of the garden at night. Schueller and Astrid would take the train west in the morning, but given all that was happening, he suspected no one was sleeping. He laid a blanket on a wooden bench and sat down to contemplate the moon. It glowed bright behind a curtain of fast-moving clouds, covering the garden in shifting shadows. A twig snapped, and he jerked his head around to see who else was outside. A lanky figure moved in the dark.

"Hallo! Nice night, *ja*?"

Frid.

Benjamin exhaled. "Yes. It's beautiful."

This young soldier with the white-blond hair was decent. He helped Hans carry the firewood and clear the pathways in the mornings before he left for the day. Katrine said he had a girlfriend in town, which would explain his evening rides towards the village. The motorcycle roared to life and he sped off down the lane.

While Frid may have been calm and solicitous, on the whole, the Germans seemed agitated. They were meant to be on patrol, but like the civilians, they were glued to the radio for news from Washington.

"Meneer Van Laar?"

Benjamin turned to see Hans leaning on the gate. Relieved it wasn't the captain, he waved him over.

"What are you doing out here?" Hans asked.

"Thinking about Hawaii," Benjamin replied.

"The Germans spoke of nothing else over dinner."

The boy could now understand almost everything the uninvited boarders said, though few suspected him of eavesdropping. Most wondered if he was very bright at all. He broke eye-contact almost immediately and never answered questions beyond a simple yes or no. But Benjamin knew better. The boy was not only intelligent, he was wise.

"What does the captain say?" Benjamin asked.

"He absolutely forbids speculation, but as soon as he's out of the room they start up again. They say the Japanese have shot themselves in the foot attacking the Americans."

"The Japanese Navy rivals the British. For now, perhaps they have the upper hand."

"I wonder sometimes…" Hans' voice trailed off.

"What?"

"If the Germans, Italians and Japanese are fighting battles on so many fronts, when will they run out of men?"

"God willing, before you turn eighteen," Benjamin said.

Hans' face fell. "In Germany they're taking boys out of school and sending them to the eastern front."

"That's suicidal." Benjamin looked at the boy's worried expression and instantly regretted his candour. It was easy to forget how young Hans was.

"Mother doesn't want to leave right now because the captain has been so irritable since the Germans declared war on the United States."

"Has he threatened her?" And if he had, what could he do? Shoot him? Benjamin scowled at his own impotence.

Hans shook his head. "No, but she's asked me to sleep in Katrine's room while she's gone. She used to say, 'Goodnight, I love you.' Now she says, 'Goodnight, lock your doors.'"

It amounts to the same thing, Benjamin thought.

"I'm sure your sister will love sharing a room."

Hans rolled his eyes. "Do you have siblings, Meneer Van Laar?"

Benjamin shook his head. "No. I was an only child. My mother wanted at least a half a dozen but my parents died young in an accident. I was raised by my uncle."

Benjamin pictured the small flat above the shop on *Roetersstraar*, near the *Prinsengracht*. His uncle would prepare precious stones for the high-end jewelers near the Hoofdstraat. Twice a week they strolled down the *Plantage Middenlaan* to a cafeteria where the waitresses served them extra-large portions of schnitzel and creamy potatoes. Benjamin looked forward to those outings. He wasn't sure what to study or what kind of work he wanted to do in the future, but he knew he'd continue eating in the cafeterias on the Plantage forever.

"Where is your uncle now?" Hans asked.

Benjamin closed his eyes. "I pray he's somehow still safe in our flat on the Prinsengracht."

Hans looked quizzical. "There's a canal Prinsengracht in Rotterdam, too?"

Benjamin rested his head in his hands. He'd been so careful to avoid talking about himself. Hans' innocence made him drop the thread of his lie. He looked at the shy boy and wondered if he could handle the truth. Benjamin had no way of knowing if Nathan had left the Jewish Quarter or not. He imagined his uncle would stay in the flat as long as possible. He was a rule follower. By now he would have a red *J* stamped over his name, like blood. Benjamin knew it without seeing it. His uncle believed in the goodness of people. Benjamin had reason to think otherwise. But something stirred him to confession anyway.

"The Prinsengracht *is* in Amsterdam. I'm sure you're intelligent enough to figure out why certain citizens have used the destruction of Rotterdam to create their own origin stories."

They stared at one another through the darkness.

"When I help Mayor Schueller with the transports, the men and women we bring back in the horse trailer are very scared," Hans said quietly. "You don't seem quite as terrified."

Benjamin sighed and looked up at the stars. "There's this man, an economics professor... his name's Benjamin Rosenblum."

"What's he like?"

"Skinny, green-eyed, curly hair...scared shitless."

"But?"

"Well, this other fellow, Meneer Van Laar, he appears and tells Rosenblum to just shut up. He's not mean about it—it's self-preservation."

Benjamin looked at Hans, whose eyes glistened.

Hans whispered, "It must be very hard."

Benjamin swallowed a lump in his throat. "We'll see your mother off, and afterwards continue our lessons."

"You can trust me, Meneer Van Laar."

Benjamin nodded and watched the boy lope back towards the castle. A few days earlier Schueller had casually tried to tell the captain there were no Jews in Brummelo. "Just Protestants and Catholics living peacefully together, sir," he'd said. He was trying to get the local shoemakers out of town, so far with no luck. "Trust me," Schueller had said, and Benjamin wanted to.

The night was quiet all around him again. He glanced up towards Astrid's balcony. The castle windows were tightly sealed with blackout paint, so there was no way of knowing whether she was still awake or not. She'd confided that she didn't want to go, and he realized with a start that he'd miss her. He'd grown accustomed to their daily conversation about the news. At first, when he sought her out, he told himself he just wanted an update on the broadcasts from America—but as the days passed, he admitted there was something else. He told himself he was imagining things, the way her face seemed to light up a little when he came into the room. For reasons he couldn't explain, he redoubled his efforts to make her laugh. When she smiled, the austere aristocrat disappeared, and he saw a flash of who she might have been before.

He stood up and made his way to the cottage, shaking his head.

Only a fool thinks the smile of a beautiful woman can save him.

16

"He's here!" I called out from my perch beside the kitchen window.

Carl emerged from the cold morning mist, his overcoat shimmering under a film of condensation. He parked the *Bakfiets* in front of our cottage and secured his load before knocking on the door.

"Who is it?" Papa looked up from the newspaper. Carl stepped inside.

"Oh," Papa said, "It's you."

I wondered if he thought *it's just the baker's son*. I could have told Papa that Carl was my boyfriend, but I felt bad enough stealing food from the pantry and risking everything to deliver Rosaura's leaflets. I tried to imagine his reaction to our relationship, tried to imagine his approval, but I couldn't. And then I thought of Loti, and how easy things had been for her. How a German Lutheran, a *Nazi*, was preferable to a Catholic Dutchman made no sense. But Papa had his logic and I had my secrets. I winked at Carl. His quick smile calmed my guilty conscience.

"Cup of tea before you go?" Papa asked.

"Kind of you to offer, sir, but I've got a schedule to keep."

Papa nodded. "Nice of you to give Hilde a lift."

"I'm heading that way anyway," Carl said.

Papa looked out the window towards the *Bakfiets,* and scratched his chin. He was about to ask Carl something, and then changed his mind and returned to his newspaper.

"Well, we're off then. Goodbye, Papa."

"I hope the lady likes the dress, Muisje." He blew me a kiss.

My face reddened. I would be sixteen in the spring, no longer a *little mouse*. I settled Lady Astrid's gown atop the tarp, safe in its case, and sat behind Carl on the metal rail over the back wheel.

"Nice outfit," he teased.

I'd finally convinced Papa to let me convert my skirts into wide-legged pants when it became impossible to buy hosiery or repair the woolen stockings I'd outgrown. I made a pair for Loti, with slim pockets and jaunty cuffs, and had begun taking orders from several of the wealthier women at church. After all, women were doing the work their husbands used to do, and skirts just got in the way. When the choir director's wife ordered a pair, it was the high-water mark—Papa agreed we could wear them in public, and save our dresses for Sundays. I liked to think he didn't mind the extra money, either, but Loti said not to wait around for a thank you. *Don't embarrass him,* she advised. *Just quietly put your money in the pot.*

We rode along the frozen path in silence, until we arrived at a checkpoint barring the way towards Soelenkasteel. I'd never get used to this. My hands turned clammy.

"Don't worry," Carl muttered under his breath. "We'll be fine."

A stocky soldier walked over to us, glanced at the cargo and asked for our papers. I wore a thin purse around my neck with my identification, Carl carried his in his wallet. The soldier inspected the papers, squinted at our faces and tossed them back.

He pointed at the suitcase. "What's in there?"

I rose from my seat and opened it for the man. The yellow silk was folded delicately, the fur-trimmed bolero framing an elegant neckline.

The soldier looked at me and then lifted the tarp from underneath the suitcase, revealing the loaves of bread Carl had neatly stacked. He inhaled the scent of the golden crusts and for a moment closed his eyes. We waited. The soldier seemed very far away, perhaps in his own town, remembering his own bakery.

"Are you hungry?" Carl asked.

The soldier tried to look insulted. He shook his head and approached me, examining my trousers, running his hand along the seam. I froze.

Carl cleared his throat loudly. "Captain Von Hahn doesn't like to wait for his bread, sir."

The soldier withdrew his hand as though it were on fire. A moment later, he waved us past.

Neither of us said anything until we rounded a bend, and the checkpoint was out of sight.

"Friendly guy," Carl said. The muscles on his back were tight.

"Thank goodness you were there."

"Mostly they just take the bread," he said. "But maybe you could dress a little plainer?"

"Maybe they could keep their paws to themselves," I snapped. My trousers were not the problem here.

Carl cycled on another kilometre without saying a word. We turned down a laneway, marked by an elaborate wrought iron cross, that led to a well-appointed brick farmhouse with an attached barn. I held the bicycle steady while Carl assembled his order. A lanky farmer met him on the lawn and stared at me. I waved politely and waited for Carl's return. When he came back, he slipped a heavy brown bag into the carrier.

"What's in there?" I asked.

"Meneer DeVries' potato and tulip flour blend."

Tulips? He must be joking. I made a face.

"We're experimenting. Grain's sparse. We'll have to get used to some new flavours."

"Was that all that was in the bag?" I asked quietly.

Carl didn't reply for a long moment.

"Do you ever wonder if perhaps you're too nosy for your own good?" he said, still staring straight ahead at the road. Mayor Schueller had all kinds of rules for our cell. The first was that we didn't ask one another questions. I put a gloved hand on Carl's back and left it there. I was bone-tired from late nights hunched over my sewing machine. Although it was still early in the day, I could have curled into a ball and taken a quick nap on the roadside. Wouldn't that be nice? To lie down with Carl for a moment and rest. We reached a grove of gnarly beech trees, and Carl slowed again and stopped in front of a stone cottage. Chickens pecked at the gravel in the yard, unperturbed by our arrival.

"Someday I'd like to live in the country in a little house like this," I said absentmindedly.

"When the war is over." Carl kissed me lightly on the forehead and went to knock on the door.

The mist had dissipated only to be replaced by a cold, bitter wind. I leaned into the shelter of the beech trunk. Soon we'd be enjoying a cup of tea in a fancy drawing room, and I'd collect my ten guilders for the gown. I closed my eyes and remembered the lavish interior of the castle, the dark wood, the polished marble and the beautiful tapestries gracing the walls. Elegant as it was, I preferred something simpler. Besides, how could anyone really feel at home with Germans stomping about?

Carl knocked again and peered in the windows. The curtains were drawn. Hesitatingly he tried the door handle. A moment later, he disappeared inside. I shivered. What was taking him so long? Maybe these customers didn't have money today. I stood up and explored the yard. I couldn't shake the feeling that despite the privacy of this rural cottage, we were being watched. I brushed my leg where the soldier from the checkpoint had grazed his hand.

"Hilde!"

I jumped. Carl's face was ashen.

"What is it?"

"The house has been ransacked. There's no sign of anyone."

"What should we do?"

Carl paced back and forth for a minute, his limp more obvious after our long ride. "Can you run across the fields to the farm we just came from? Tell Meneer DeVries what we've discovered."

"What about you?"

"I'm going to head straight to Soelenkasteel and find Schueller. He'll be loading up the horses. Hopefully he hasn't left yet."

"And after I've spoken to DeVries?"

"Ask him for a lift, but take the backroads to avoid the checkpoint. Meet me back at Soelenkasteel."

"Be careful."

"See you soon." His jaw was set in a tight line. He rode off quickly, leaning forward against the wind towards the castle in the woods. I took one last look at the chickens and was about to start across the frozen field, when something moved in the coop. I pulled my coat tighter and studied the low clapboard walls. My imagination was playing tricks on me.

I'm not sure what compelled me to move towards the small outbuilding instead of running to the DeVries farm as I'd promised to do. I took one tentative step and my fear turned into adrenaline. Striding towards the hatch, I heaved the door open in one quick motion. In a corner under the roost crouched a small boy whose dark eyes were filled with fear.

I stretched out my hand. "Hello, little one."

He shook his head.

I couldn't tell if he was trembling, shivering or both. I reached into the pockets of my trousers and produced a piece of kruidnoten I'd been saving for Carl.

The boy opened one eye and stared hungrily at my offering. But he still didn't move.

"I'm not sure where everyone else is, but I can take you somewhere safe."

I squeezed into the tiny coop and sat down beside the boy. The stench of chicken shit was making me dizzy. I propped the door open but still found it unbearable. Making a face, I pinched my nose shut. The little boy giggled.

"Come on. Let's get out of here," I said in a nasally voice.

I slipped out and waited. After a minute, the boy peeked out and looked longingly at the cottage.

"Mama?" he squeaked.

His dirty cheeks were streaked with tears.

"Meneer DeVries can help us," I assured him.

At the name DeVries, the boy began to tremble again and shook his head vehemently. "No," he whispered. "DeVries is a grumpy man."

"A grumpy man?" I said, confused. Who could I really trust?

I stood in the yard and looked west to the DeVries's brick farmhouse. And then slowly I turned east, to the forest—towards Soelenkasteel's turrets. Taking his little hand in mine, we set off, forging a path through the birch and pines while I tried to think of an explanation for the presence of my small companion, who at least was no longer crying. His silent trust scared me more than anything.

———

BENJAMIN ENJOYED the early morning hours, alone at his small pine desk in the stablemaster's cottage. As he prepared the day's lessons, he lost himself reading a well-loved, leather-bound edition of Darwin's memoir *The Voyage of The Beagle*. If he closed his eyes, he could almost hear the finches along the shoreline and smell the briny sea air. It was selfish to spend so much time on subjects that would be of no practical use to either Hans or Katrine, but he needed the distraction from his insomniac nights. He rubbed his eyes and opened the curtains. To his surprise, the gardener's daughter, Hilde, and a young boy were skirting the forest at a fast clip. The familiar knot in his stomach contracted. Even from this distance, from the slump of the child's shoulders, he could see the boy was terrified.

He lit a cigarette and inhaled deeply, watching as Hilde considered the castle for a moment before striding towards the barn. The child was practically running beside her. He guessed she wanted

Schueller, but she was headed towards trouble. The captain was due to inspect the horses in the barn before Astrid travelled to The Hague. The cigarette was now only a tiny stub in his trembling hand. He wanted to stay in his cottage, far from the Germans' scrutiny.

That girl, that boy—they're not your concern. Take care of yourself.

Turning back to his desk, he glimpsed the worn Darwin tome, open to a lithograph of a finch. After the week's reading, Hans had asked, *if we can adapt, can we survive?*

Yes, Benjamin imagined. Adaptation was key. But he was sick of adapting. He was tired of pretending to be someone else, learning new skills, shutting his mouth when he had an opinion. By trying to be invisible, he was being erased, his thoughts lost to the shadows and the cold and the loneliness. Yet to survive...

Against his better instincts he bolted out the door. "Hilde!"

She couldn't hear him. As they continued towards the stables, the wind whipped her hair around as though trying to force her back to where she'd come from. He put his fingers between his lips and blew a high, loud whistle. She stopped and looked around. He waved his arms, and she squinted towards the cottage.

"Hilde!" He motioned her towards him. It was no use. She waved tentatively and quickened her pace, stubbornly headed towards Schueller's automobile, parked outside the barn.

"*Verdorie!*" he cursed.

Benjamin ran towards them. He wasn't a natural athlete, and his breathing was laboured as he crossed the frozen ground. The child saw him first. He let out a strangled cry and Hilde stopped abruptly, pushing the child behind her.

"Meneer Van Laar?" Her expression was questioning but not fearful.

Benjamin thought fast. "Follow me. The captain is in the stables."

Hilde nodded.

Benjamin led them through the thicket to a path leading back to the stablemaster's cottage. Even in winter, the pines hid it from view of the castle. He opened the door and they followed him inside. Hilde sat down and immediately they began speaking at the same time, their breath visible in the cold air.

"Who's this?" Benjamin asked.

"Have you seen Carl?" Hilde said. "The young man who delivers the bread?"

Benjamin stared at the child who'd now embedded himself on Hilde's lap. His hair was a strange reddish blond and curled behind his ears. He hid his face in her shoulders.

"Go ahead," Benjamin said.

Hilde explained how she'd intended to deliver Lady Astrid's gown, but had met the boy upon the way.

"And where does this, uh, special parcel, need to be delivered to?"

Hilde shook her head. "I don't know, Meneer Van Laar. I came here looking for Mayor Schueller…"

There was a loud, insistent knock on the door.

Benjamin put his finger to his lips. "Hide in the bedroom," he whispered. Counting to ten, he hurried to the stove and began banging pots together to drown out the sounds of furniture being dragged. When the knocking started up again, he made a show of slowly drawing back the curtains and peering out to the landing.

He opened the door with trepidation. "Katrine? Our lessons don't begin again for another hour."

Her eyes darted around the room though she remained planted by the entrance.

"Meneer Van Laar, are you getting a coat altered?"

Benjamin shook his head.

"Buying seeds, vegetables?"

"Nothing of the sort, Katrine," he answered. And then he dared to ask, "Why?"

Now she fixed her eyes on his bedroom. "I went to retrieve my pencils from the library and saw you hurrying outside. I decided to follow you and see what all the excitement was about."

Benjamin began to prepare tea as though Katrine's story bored him terribly. He was grateful her back was turned, so that she didn't notice him fumble with the kettle's lid.

"I can't figure out why the village seamstress is here, while her handsome companion impatiently waits for her in the parlour."

Benjamin opened his mouth but Katrine put her hand up and stopped him.

"And before you say another word, I want to know about the boy, too."

THE GOWN FIT PERFECTLY.

Astrid turned in front of her mirror as Katrine and the young seamstress looked on from the couch.

"I took the dress down almost a full two sizes, Mevrouw. You have a lovely figure, if you don't mind me saying so," Hilde said softly.

"Mother danced with princes during her first season," Katrine bragged.

"Russian refugees—" Astrid said.

"I think the Russians are very elegant," Katrine said dreamily.

Astrid put her hands on her hips and admired Hilde's handiwork on the bodice. The fabric fell in soft folds, the pleats more delicate and measured than the original design. She stole a glance in the mirror and suppressed a satisfied smile. Silk-wrapped boning held her spine straight, giving her the appearance of strength. She felt beautiful again.

"The Czar's relatives had two left feet. In any case, to my parents' dismay, no match came from the extravagant balls of my youth," Astrid said.

"My mother doesn't believe in arranged marriages. She chose my father of her own accord." Katrine sighed. "For love."

Astrid smiled tightly. She'd married for the love of Soelenkasteel, not for the love of Jan Stenger. Hilde was watching her closely. The poor girl, she probably wanted to get back to the village. She was twisting her hands nervously and looking at the door. There was no need for Astrid to keep her.

"Thank you for the dress." Astrid opened her purse, counted out the bank notes and lowered her voice. "Trade these as soon as possible. I'm sorry they're not worth what they were when we agreed upon a price. On your way out, stop in the kitchen and Eva will send you home with some food to make up the difference. It's the best I can do, under the circumstances."

"My pleasure, Mevrouw. If you have any friends in need—"

Astrid laughed ruefully. "Friends! All the king's horses and all the king's men have left the country, jongedame."

"Why didn't you leave?" Hilde asked, her sweet face devoid of malice.

Astrid's eyes widened. Why didn't she leave? She didn't have another castle to retreat to. Astrid hadn't married an earl with cousins in neutral countries where she could wait out the war. If only!

"I apologize, Mevrouw. My father says I can be overly curious. I didn't mean to pry."

Astrid settled her face into something she hoped resembled a gracious smile. "It's quite alright. The fact is, I wanted to ensure my staff wouldn't suffer, and I had hoped the war would be over by now. Perhaps I was foolish, but here we are."

The girl nodded, curtsied and said goodbye.

"Mother, I'll show her out," Katrine suggested.

Astrid frowned. "That won't be necessary, darling. Stay and help me out of this dress."

"I'll only be a moment."

Katrine practically shoved Hilde out of the room, and before Astrid could protest, they were gone.

———

INSTEAD OF PUTTING the money into the pouch that held my identity card, I slipped the precious guilders into my brassiere, where they'd be safe from greedy inspectors. Carl was in the parlour, dark circles under his eyes. He looked up when I entered, frowning when he saw Katrine trailing behind.

"I'm so glad to have people my age in the house!" Katrine plopped down beside Carl on the brocade sofa. "It's so boring all alone here with only my tongue-tied brother and our tutor!"

"I suppose you don't talk much with your…guests?" Carl asked.

"The moffen? We can't stand them!" Katrine's voice was shrill. "But what choice do we have? Frid's alright, I guess—"

"Yeah. We know him pretty well," I said wryly.

Katrine quieted. "How's that?"

Carl looked at his watch. "We should really be going."

"Wait!" Katrine lowered her voice and shut the parlour door. "What's going to happen to that little boy?"

Carl put his hands on Katrine's shoulders. The gesture was so intimate I winced.

"Katrine," he said slowly, his deep voice low and calm. "While Mayor Schueller and your mother are gone, we'll find a safe place."

Katrine's face softened. "But no one can know he's there?"

Carl nodded. "That's right."

"Do you want to see the library before you go?" Katrine asked, looking directly at me. "My brother's probably up there rereading the papers. Thanks to Meneer Van Laar, he's a little obsessed with war news."

I tried to shake my head no. I just wanted to get home, but Carl followed Katrine and I followed him. I checked the time on the ornate grandfather clock in the hall. Papa was going to have a fit.

Hans looked up at us as we entered. He didn't smile, but he didn't frown, either. I felt compelled to apologize for the intrusion, but Carl spoke first.

"Hello, I'm Carl De Boer." He looked around the room appraisingly and whistled. "This place sure beats the parlour at the bakery."

Hans smiled, and I saw he resembled his mother. Reserved, but handsome.

Katrine began pulling volumes off the shelves and piling them on the table. "The Van Soelens have always been privately educated here in the library at Soelenkasteel."

I couldn't resist leafing through the books on the table. History, ancient Greek, literature and theology. The books were beautiful, but the subjects didn't intrigue me particularly. Hans smiled over his newspaper as though reading my mind.

"Something you'd like to read?"

I shrugged. "School has been haphazard this year." Did I need to explain that I found every excuse possible to avoid my Nazi teacher? "I always liked mathematics, though. Science, too."

"Meneer Van Laar loves science, too." Hans abandoned his newspaper and walked over to a desk beside the window. "Why don't you borrow these? You can bring them back later—"

Katrine spoke in a rush, her eyes glistening. "Yes. You must both take some books. That way, we can see one another again."

I winced as Katrine pressed books into Carl's arms. Even if Papa allowed it, I wasn't sure I wanted to return to Soelenkasteel anytime soon. The amused look on Carl's face irked me.

"Can we go, please? Papa will be worried."

Katrine clapped her hands together. "*Mama needs me, Papa will be worried.* Oh, to be a normal teenager in the village, eh Hans?" Katrine sighed dramatically. "Off you go, but remember..." She dropped her voice to a whisper and glanced over her shoulder. "I want to help with *whatever* it is you two are doing. I've been watching Mayor Schueller. I know he's up to something, too."

I swallowed. "We..."

"Oh, I know. Everything's a *secret*. But I can help..."

Carl clasped Katrine's hand. "We'll be in touch. Thank you for the books, and for everything else."

We said goodbye and walked out to retrieve the *Bakfiets*, propped against the fountain.

"Would you like me to pedal? Your leg has been bothering you."

Carl was proud, but I could see he was in pain, too. "Maybe for the first bit."

He settled himself in the front, balancing the flour and the books at his feet. I set off, veering sharply to the left and overcorrecting to the right before somehow managing to keep the bicycle straight.

Neither of us said anything at first. When we passed the chicken farm, I pedaled faster, wishing there was an alternate way back to the village.

"Will he be okay?" I said at last, my voice sounding loud against the quiet of the road.

Carl was silent. "I'm not sure he'll see his parents again, thanks to all these traitors working with the SS. It makes me sick."

He spoke each word with disgust, turning his head and looking back at the empty farm. "They're worse than the Germans."

I was scared. Long shadows covered the road, hiding the potholes and chilling me through my sweater. I wondered how many orphans the war would produce. Carl changed the subject. We talked about the canals, would they freeze or not, and the gas restrictions, how to get more, and what I would do with my earnings.

"Add it to the pot, of course."

Carl nodded but said nothing. When we arrived at the outskirts of the village, we switched spots. Carl hugged me close for a moment.

"You don't have to do this, you know. I'll understand if you change your mind about the group. If you want out." His brown eyes searched my face. Why was he doubting me now?

Of course I was scared of checkpoints, traitors and missing curfew, not to mention Papa's inevitable questions when I got home. But...

"Why did you squeeze her hands when we left?" I asked, my face reddening.

Carl scowled. "It meant nothing. I just wanted to get us out of there."

"But what if she thinks you were flirting?"

"I don't flirt with girls like that," he said.

"Like what? Girls from the upper class?"

"No...girls who laugh like hyenas."

I giggled, relief spilling out. He wasn't interested in Katrine. Maybe he'd even agree that Lady Astrid's daughter seemed a little crazy. I was making things more complicated than they already were.

"Carl," I said. "I don't want out. Of anything."

He lifted my chin and kissed me. "I have a feeling your father may not let you out of the house for a while."

I looked at the sky. It was already getting dark and I wasn't certain my excuses would pass muster.

"Then you'd better give me a week's worth of goodbye kisses, just in case."

17

DECEMBER 13TH 1941

THE HAGUE

As the chauffeur pulled up to the lane of Clingendael, Astrid noticed that the lovely old vines crawling up the casement windows had been clipped back, giving the manor house a more austere appearance than in years past, a reflection perhaps of its latest Austrian tenants. A tall, glowing valet stood waiting to take their luggage.

"The place has been renovated, apparently," Schueller muttered.

"It almost seems improved by the war," she said, thinking of the tiles that had recently blown off Soelenkasteel's roof and the cracks in the fountain.

The valet opened the doors, and Astrid and Schueller stepped out onto the lane to take in the fine seventeenth-century architecture and the Japanese gardens.

"There used to be a racetrack here, you know," Schueller said.

She remembered. Were all the best things in the past? What a terrible, dark thought. "Let's go inside."

"Lead the way, Mevrouw."

The smell of fresh paint greeted them as they entered the spacious hall. Chandeliers cast soft light onto sparkling floors below. Maids rushed past in crisp uniforms, buckles and buttons shiny and new, shoes polished to perfection.

"These people are lucky to work here," Astrid observed.

Schueller shrugged. "Lucky is perhaps going too far. Remember who they're working for."

They continued up a flight of marble stairs, their voices hushed.

"At least they're well fed. It could be worse," she said, thinking of the poor souls on the eastern front.

"The Germans like continuity," Schueller said. "Why do you think I'm still the mayor of Brummelo?"

The valet dropped Astrid's luggage and unlocked an enormous door. "Your suite, Mevrouw."

"Thank you." She peeked inside. It looked heavenly. The damask silk brought her back to the lush parties of her first season, travelling from one manor house to another to take in party after party. She could flop onto the bed and forget for a moment they were at war. There was a stillness in her room that made Germany's declaration of war on the United States seem very far away.

"I'm going to have a coffee downstairs. Will you join me once you've settled in?" Schueller asked.

Astrid shook her head. "Later."

The valet led Schueller to another wing and a young maid appeared. She unpacked Astrid's trunk, smoothed her evening gown, and hung it on an antique dress form. Before joining Schueller and going through the required formalities and introductions, Astrid wanted to sneak off to the stables and ensure that the groom assigned to Philomena knew what he was doing. She dismissed the maid, found her riding attire and was getting changed when a knock sounded at the door.

"May I come in?" A woman with soft blond curls neatly pinned in an elegant twist stepped into the room. "I'm Gertrud."

"Good afternoon." Astrid extended her hand towards the Reichskomissar's wife.

She'd been expecting an aristocrat; after all, this was once the home of a baroness. But Gertrud smiled shyly and surveyed the suite the way a child might contemplate a museum display. When she spoke again, her accent was decidedly provincial. "Goodness! What a lovely gown."

The woman in Astrid's boudoir was simply dressed in a black skirt and pressed blouse. Perhaps Astrid had wasted her money on the young seamstress' creation.

Gertrud glanced towards the hall and closed the door. "Mussert and his aides are gathering here tomorrow, but no one's in a festive mood. I'm afraid you may find our soirée a little dull, Lady Astrid."

Astrid struggled for words. It was so tiring to talk endlessly about the war, about Japan, the threat of gas restrictions, her personal losses. It had been a long time since she'd conversed with another woman who wasn't a servant or a shopkeeper.

"I suppose you might be feeling rather stiff from the train. Perhaps you'd like to tour the grounds?" Gertrud suggested.

Astrid looked into her eyes and saw her own loneliness reflected back. Gertrud led her through the mansion, pointing out the small changes she was making, and soon they were in the garden, walking over the frozen grounds. Behind the hedgerow, shiny black Horch town cars lined the gravel lane.

"Arthur will be busy in meetings for hours. Shall we say hello to the horses?"

A CLOCK TOWER dominated the entrance to the stables. Built in a semi-circle around a central courtyard, the stalls were bright and spacious. Each horse had fresh straw and water. Astrid found Philomena quietly munching on oats. Gertrud offered a lump of sugar from her pocket to the mare, but Astrid could have sworn her favourite mount eyed her before accepting the treat from a stranger's hands.

"Who was her dam?" asked Gertrud.

"Her name was Butterscotch. We brought her from a stable across the Channel. Do you know her?" Astrid asked.

Gertrud nodded. "Such a lovely horse. You take her, I'll ride this grey one."

She chose Stella, a strong, quick-tempered Arabian that Philomena adored. Keeping them together had been an easy decision. Astrid silently promised them both she'd be back someday.

An older stablemaster helped Astrid saddle up. She watched Gertrud from the corner of her eye. Gertrud was a confident rider, thankfully. She spoke softly to Stella, and led her towards the woods. They followed a path that opened onto a meadow and before long Astrid glimpsed the sea. Philomena cantered along the sand, relishing the familiar texture beneath her feet.

"She likes it," Astrid said. "It's like the heath at home."

"I've never been to the Veluwe, but I imagine it's a bit like the Fohrenberge, the woods outside Vienna." Gertrud had a faraway look in her eyes. Astrid wondered if Gertrud had trained in one of the fancy riding schools in Vienna. Somehow she doubted it. The woman struck her as very rural, possibly a self-taught horsewoman.

Gertrud shook off her reverie and began to gallop, testing Stella, and Astrid too. Philomena kept pace with the Arabian and they raced along the water's edge until the horses' coats glistened. She had to laugh. When was the last time she'd ridden with such abandon? They walked the horses slowly through the long grasses, nodding as they passed a handful of fishermen along the way.

"It's so quiet," Astrid remarked.

"The village has been abandoned," Gertrud said. "Hitler's defense program requires this land. But what can you do?"

You could go back to Austria where you belong.

She looked over her shoulder at the fishermen and the boarded-up houses beyond. She'd assumed the windows were shuttered for the blackout, but looking closer it was clear there was no one about, and it was Gertrud's husband, the despised turncoat, who was responsible for the ghostly silence.

. . .

THAT NIGHT at supper Astrid had her first glimpse of the Reichskomissar himself. He walked into the dining room, his awkward gait only slightly perceptible, shook hands with Schueller and Astrid, and casually asked his wife about her day. Gertrud smiled at him adoringly, but he was brief with her, and Astrid's German was insufficient to follow their entire conversation.

Eventually, Gertrud turned back to her guests.

"When Arthur's friends are here, it's economics all night long." She sighed and looked at Astrid. "What does your husband do, Lady Astrid?"

Schueller shot her a look across the table. She wasn't sure what he'd told them, if anything, of her private life. Of Jan, who might be halfway between Indonesia and Australia on who knew what kind of vessel, while the Japanese circled the ocean with their powerful navy.

"He's a textile importer," Astrid began. "But the factories have clo—"

"The factories have a long history of weaving the finest cloth." Schueller's face gave nothing away, but Astrid took his cue and offered no details. Gertrud, she supposed, was just being polite.

"How lovely for you. That explains the beautiful gown. Arthur is allergic to excess." She dropped her voice, not that her husband was remotely interested in their conversation. "I apologize for the food; I know it's quite bland. He prefers simple things and is adamant about not buying from the black market."

Schueller laughed. "You must be homesick for Vienna."

Gertrud moved the few tasteless potatoes around her plate. "You have no idea."

THE NIGHT OF THE BALL, Astrid waited for Schueller on a settee in the hallway outside her chambers. He whistled at the sight of her.

"Stunning!"

She swatted him away with an elegant beaded purse.

He held up his hands in mock protest. "I mean no harm. If I had a camera, I'd take your photograph."

She searched for a way to return the compliment, but Kurt Schueller would never be called attractive. Endearing, yes. He had the face of someone who was forever plotting mischief. Yet after all these years, when she needed a hand, he'd shown up, and for that she was grateful. There were more important things than a handsome face.

"We should get going."

Listening to the music drifting from the ballroom, she recalled the balls of the twenties, when her parents had been desperate to make an advantageous match to save the estate from ruin. And now, here she was, dressing up once again to make the right connections and maintain Soelenkasteel for as long as possible. Schueller offered his arm and escorted her into the great hall. She scanned the guests, looking for Gertrud. The perimeter was lined with men in black SS uniforms. Astrid shivered at the sight of them. She turned back, and a man greeted Schueller with a stiff embrace.

"Nephew! Good of you to come. Gertrud is ecstatic about the new horses."

"Lady Astrid, allow me to introduce my uncle, Gustav Schueller," Schueller said.

Astrid took in the badges on the man's jacket. He had a barrel chest and a shiny bald head. But there was something—perhaps the quick intelligence in his eyes—that confirmed his kinship with Schueller.

"Delighted to meet you, Mevrouw." The man bowed slightly.

Astrid shook his warm and sweaty hand and released it as soon as possible. She accepted a glass of champagne from a waiter and found a spot to sit within earshot of the rotund Nazi and Schueller.

"Are they keeping you busy, Uncle?" Schueller asked.

"Indeed, although not so much here in the Netherlands. Men like you are gathering horses from private estates while we continue to find the specimens we need for transportation." He wiped his glistening forehead and dropped his voice, his excitement palpable. "We're going to create a new breed of horse, a war horse like no other."

"Surely in the age of tanks the cavalry is becoming redundant?"

"Military vehicles are expensive, but Poland has millions of horses."

Astrid made a face. Millions of disposable horses, likely to be discarded after a couple years of service, their hooves raw from overwork, their legs pushed beyond their capabilities.

Gustav Schueller spoke again. "We aim to create a perfect bloodline from the Polish Lipizzaner stallions and English thoroughbreds."

The man was bursting with self-importance.

Schueller spoke again. "Interesting. I've read that the Americans aren't so concerned with purebreds; they look for specific qualities—obedience, docility etc.—and search for those horses—"

"The Americans are degenerates," Schueller's uncle scoffed. "As a race, they are so contaminated with every kind of blood, it's not surprising they use such unscientific methods in their equine breeding practices."

Schueller's too-tight smile twitched as it always did when he disagreed. She felt compelled to rescue him. Before she could change her mind, Astrid rose, abandoned her champagne flute and pulled him towards the dance floor.

"Please excuse us, the waltzes are my favourite," she said.

Dancing with a short man made for an awkward kind of intimacy, Astrid suddenly remembered. Schueller's head, though held at a polite distance, was level with her bosom. Thankfully, he knew the steps and his strong arms guided them along with confidence. After a few minutes, she relaxed.

"Your uncle is—"

"—a wind bag. I know. But perhaps he can be useful."

"Useful?" She wanted less association with the Nazis, not more.

"Astrid. They're coming to Gelderland."

"Who?"

"The SS is going to establish a training school in the Veluwe. My uncle told me this morning."

Her mind was racing. Why should she care where the Dutch traitors set up their training grounds? The music stopped and Schueller led her towards a banquette. Sitting down, she could look him in the eye again. But she didn't like what she saw.

"Where in the Veluwe?"

"Remember the old tennis courts? Apparently the captain mentioned to General Rauter that no one plays anymore."

Astrid was quiet for a moment. "I didn't realize the German military and the Dutch SS had much to do with one another."

Schueller sighed. "It's hard to know who's worse, frankly."

"The National Socialists don't have that much support in Gelderland, do they? I mean what about the arson in the storehouse last year?"

"Astrid, be careful."

She stared across the room at the officers—their champagne flutes brimming with bubbles, while rumours of atrocities swirled beyond the gates of Clingendael.

Astrid waved her gloved hand around the room angrily. "I don't want anything to do with these people, Kurt. I want my home back. I don't want to leave my horses here."

"Patience." Schueller leaned in close. "If we act too soon, Benjamin's life will be in danger. The Germans treat horses much better than humans, trust me."

Astrid stared at her friend. She didn't know who she was any longer. What was she doing here? She wasn't a guest amongst the upper class; she was nothing more than a well-dressed prisoner playing nice with the jailer, hoping for better scraps. Schueller however, could put on a pin or a uniform and become one of them whenever it was convenient. She realized he was born to be a chameleon, and that his changing colours might save her, too.

"Alright. You've warned me."

He looked at his uncle and grimaced. "Doesn't mean you should give up target practice."

She didn't have the stomach for violence, but she couldn't protect anyone standing around in a pretty dress.

"Kurt?"

"Yes?"

"Madame Ostrich may need more bullets."

18

WINTER 1942

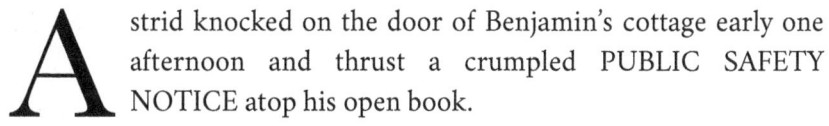

Astrid knocked on the door of Benjamin's cottage early one afternoon and thrust a crumpled PUBLIC SAFETY NOTICE atop his open book.

"Another one?" Benjamin sighed.

"Read it," Astrid said. "You're not going to like this."

Benjamin raised an eyebrow and began to read aloud.

"Eighty-two Tinderstraat is now under the authority of commander Alphons Brendel. One hundred and twenty-eight prisoners have been relocated from Amersfoort and will commence construction of the new training facility of the SS regiment. Citizens of Brummelo are hereby advised that between 7:00am and 8:00am no one shall be present on the streets, and likewise between the hours of 6:00pm and 7:00pm. Failure to comply with these requirements will result in detention. A complete blackout curfew remains in effect after 8:00pm..."

"Eighty-two Tinderstraat is the old mill near the railway station," Astrid said.

"Sounds like Brummelo's about to get a lot more Nazis."

"You need to leave, Benjamin. It's too dangerous here for you now."

Benjamin folded up the notice, feigning calm. "The Germans don't pay much attention to me."

"These aren't Germans, though."

"What do you know about the Dutch SS?" he asked.

"I'm ashamed of them," she said.

"Can't we just ignore this?"

She shook her head. "One of us can."

Benjamin's shoulders slumped.

"Let's go for a ride so you can see what you're up against."

THEY SADDLED two older mares and rode off into the forest. Benjamin would have preferred to spend his afternoon in the safety of the cottage, but once Astrid set her mind to something, there was no persuading her to do otherwise. If he weren't so terrified, he might have found her stubbornness charming.

"The tennis courts have been in Brummelo for years," Astrid remarked. "Did you ever play, Benjamin?"

"My parents tried to get me to love sports, but I preferred books, theatre…" He stopped. Dogs barked in the distance.

"Are we getting close?"

"Yes. Look through the trees. You can see a sand track—that's the foundation."

Benjamin squinted in the distance. As far as he could see, it was a regular construction site.

He looked closer. "Who are they?"

Haggard labourers huddled around crude barrel fires, yellow stars on their coats. While a few soldiers smoked and ate their lunches, others pounded posts into the frozen ground and wound a long piece of cord around them, forming a pen of sorts. He wanted to turn around and leave. He would have if it weren't for the damn dogs.

They'd smelled the horses and come running. Astrid had a soft spot for animals and often saved them treats. Soon they were sniffing their ankles.

"Let's go," Benjamin said.

"Too late," Astrid answered. "I'm sorry. This was a bad idea. I didn't know he was here, too."

From across the field, the captain came striding towards them.

"What brings you out this afternoon, Mevrouw?" he asked.

"I wondered what was going on here," Astrid answered, her head held high.

Benjamin would have made up some excuse, as though their arrival was an accident. But then, his whole life was a lie right then.

"Ah, I see. One needn't be too curious," the captain began.

"But now that I've seen it, we must be off. " Astrid lifted the reins and was about to turn when the captain stopped her.

"Wait a moment, Mevrouw. I'd like a word with the teacher," he said. "You like boxing, Van Laar?"

There was a hint of a sneer in his voice—a dare perhaps? A hammer dangled from his hand, slowly swinging back and forth.

"Not especially," Benjamin answered, his gaze flitting towards the pen across the field.

"That's too bad. You see, we need some entertainment. The sand delivery has been delayed. There will be no more cement mixing today. Tomorrow, they'll work a double shift."

"Captain, what's this about? My horses need to be fed and watered."

The captain glared at Astrid. "Then by all means, go home Mevrouw. But leave Van Laar with us. We need a referee, and teachers are fair." He turned to Benjamin. "Isn't that right, Meneer Van Laar? A teacher must always be fair."

Benjamin's stomach knotted with something other than hunger. He dismounted his horse and handed the reins to Astrid.

"Don't stick around on account of me," he said quietly. Why had he let her talk him into this stupid ride through the woods? His uncle's familiar admonishment echoed back to him: *a beautiful woman will be the death of you.*

She gazed down at him and back towards the captain. "I'll wait for you in the clearing," she whispered. And then she was gone. He followed the captain towards the pen, his heart thumping wildly in his chest. He couldn't do this.

The captain handed him a whistle. "Choose a man from over by the fires."

If he lived to be an old man, even if he only lived to see the end of this war, he was sure he wouldn't ever feel such profound shame and betrayal as at that moment. He closed his eyes briefly and saw himself in the cafeteria with his uncle Nathan, surrounded by brothers and uncles such as these men. When he opened them, hopeless gazes stared back at him.

The captain cleared his throat impatiently. "Get on with it, Van Laar."

He chose an older man. His hands were big and calloused. He wasn't wearing the star like the others. Benjamin led him to the captain and the SS men, but they shook their heads.

"No."

Benjamin trudged back to the group, and the husky man whispered under his breath, "Send Jacob."

He locked eyes with the man and followed his gaze towards a boy who couldn't have been much older than Hans, judging by his skinny arms. He looked up, his dark eyes flashing, and Benjamin nodded. He led the young man towards the ring. Despite the frost, Benjamin broke into a sweat. The men behind him collectively tensed.

Near the fence, the SS guards stood up and sauntered over to examine the ring.

The captain spoke in a low voice to his colleague, who in turn summoned a heavy-set guard. "You. In the ring."

Benjamin raised an eyebrow. The boy would be murdered. He didn't dare risk the captain's wrath. And yet...he *had* to say something.

"Sir, if you want to be entertained, the contestants should be more evenly matched. This round will be over in a matter of seconds."

And the Dutch SS would be down one slave if this match went

ahead, Benjamin thought darkly. The whistle around his neck felt like a noose. What was he supposed to do? He was no referee.

"Meneer Van Laar, the men here have been chosen precisely because of their exemplary physique, their intelligence, their willingness to root out the impure and weak in society and build a stronger future…"

Benjamin stopped listening and took a second look at the guards. They were uniform in height and build, a regiment of Goliaths. His eyes rested upon a fellow sucking on the butt of a cigarette. His hands were small compared to the rest of him. Perhaps his nervous energy would be a liability.

"He's a better match."

The captain narrowed his eyes for the briefest moment, and then laughed, a hollow sound that reverberated off the stable and got lost in the woods. As he waved the smoker into the ring, civilization felt very far away.

The prisoner shed his coat and began to slowly stretch his neck back and forth. He made fists and shook out his wrists as though he did this all the time. A soldier found water for the boxers and two guards rolled an enormous bell into the yard on a wagon, evidently the spoils of the metal collection campaign they'd been waging in the surrounding villages. From here, according to Frid and Werner and the others, the bells would make their way to Germany and be turned into ammunition.

"Time for school!" one of them said with a laugh.

The captain nodded that he was ready, drew back his hammer and struck the bell to begin. The sound roused the crows from the trees and the prisoner took his first jab, missing the guard's jaw by a hair. The guard tensed and struck back but the boy was swift, able to bob and anticipate the blows. After several minutes of circling, both opponents blocking and ducking, the prisoner dodged a right straight-arm leaving himself vulnerable to a surprise left hand upper cut. He stumbled backwards but recovered to deliver a hard hit to the guard's side.

The SS men, who'd been shouting encouragement to their comrade, now hurled obscenities at the prisoner as he delivered a few surprising upsets. If he heard them, he showed no sign of focusing on anything other than his opponent. Where he found the energy, Benjamin didn't know, but the boy continued to fight as though victory were possible.

Benjamin blew the whistle. Each man retreated to a corner. One of the guards offered a towel to their man, who was sweating profusely, while the prisoners watched from a distance. The boy drank slowly, wiped his brow and nodded. He was ready. But Benjamin was not. The fight was stacked against the prisoner. To blow the whistle again was to condemn Jacob to certain injury. Benjamin loathed boxing. While the men around him clamoured for more, bile rose in his throat —the taste of fear. As he raised the whistle to his lips, he saw movement in the treeline. Astrid hadn't gone far. Benjamin wished he could hide, too.

The captain wasn't waiting for Benjamin. He struck the bell and the fight recommenced. The boy got a lucky punch to the guard's eyebrow and drew blood. The SS men roared in response, rattling the ropes of the ring. Benjamin's sweat cooled against his skin and he shivered, his breath coming out in cold puffs. Every now and then, the captain hollered "foul," but Benjamin ignored him. Whatever else this fight might be, the contestants had kept their blows above the belt.

The boy was breathing hard now, his movements were more defensive, as though he hoped he could get out of the ring biding his time until the bell tolled again. Benjamin knew he couldn't dance forever. The guard had set his jaw—something primitive and dangerous flashed across his face. An inhuman burst of aggression took hold of him as he lunged towards the boy. Benjamin froze in terror. He looked at the captain and the SS leader. Their eyes shone with excitement and something like reverence for their man's brute strength.

The guard delivered three blows in quick succession.

Benjamin heard the *snap*, like a branch underfoot in the woods. The others began to count—*eins, zwei, drei*...but Benjamin fell to his knees, beside the boy. The opponent slowly backed into his corner. The boy's eyes stared straight into the clouds, and saliva escaped from the side of his mouth. Benjamin placed his fingers on the boy's warm neck, but his pulse was fast fading.

"You killed him." His voice was hoarse. He glared at the beast hunched in the corner. Another officer gave him his shirt and coat, ignoring Benjamin as though he were invisible. The bile rose in his throat again, but this time he recognized it as anger, not fear. He retched.

Standing up straight, he finally looked at the prisoners. Their faces were aghast. Some cried silently, the older ones shook their heads sadly. But no one dared to speak. The SS leader conferred with the captain, gesturing towards the woods, and proceeded to lead his men and the prisoners back towards the dilapidated, unheated mill on the other side of the canal.

"Van Laar!" the captain shouted. "Bury that prisoner before you go." He tossed a shovel towards him, whistled for his dogs and drove off, leaving Benjamin completely alone.

Benjamin leaned over the boy and closed his eyes.

"Jacob," he whispered. At the sound of footsteps he turned.

Astrid was crying. "I know a spot where the ground is soft."

They put the young man's body on one horse, covering him with his coat and securing the load with the cord from the makeshift pen. Astrid rode the other mare and Benjamin slid up behind her. He held onto the shovel with one hand and Astrid's waist with the other, fighting to keep his composure. After they'd ridden for a while, she stopped in a clearing.

"There's a parachute buried here," she said. "By this fence post."

Benjamin didn't ask her how she knew that. He took the shovel, ignoring the ache in his arms as he loosened the frozen ground. It was almost dark before the grave was ready, and they were both frozen to the bone. Astrid wrapped the man's coat around him tightly, while Benjamin quietly recited the *Yizkor*, the prayers Nathan had taught him. He vowed to remember this child. Jacob. When they had each tossed a final fistful of dirt over the grave they stood silently side by side. Benjamin reached for her hand and held it.

In the forest, a hawk circled the treetops and dove for its prey.

19

In March of '42, the Nazis began constructing the Atlantic Wall, a band of fortifications along the North Sea. I remember seeing the bunkers after the war, and later reading about the evacuated villages, but what stays with me most is how a trickle of desperation became a flood. I remember how those coastal evacuees spilled into Brummelo's town square, looking about with wild eyes, searching for relatives. Who was I to help? I was still a girl, barely sixteen at the time. I'd just left school. And yet, in cellars and woodsheds, sneaking out and delivering food to dirty, abandoned children in chicken coops and barn lofts, I always found someone a little more frightened than me. Someone who needed me. And this remains one of the worst things about war—terror becomes ordinary. With each passing day I became less shocked by the sight of frightened strangers. It's possible that their fear fueled me. I'm still figuring out where fear led me. Where love led me. Even all these years later, it's not always clear.

A WHISTLE SOUNDED, shrill across the platform. I tried to stand tall as I held Loti's arm. The evacuees gathered together while Frid herded them towards the Stadhuis.

"Follow the young lady, please. Miss Zontag will organize the registration."

Loti smiled and Frid puffed up a bit.

"Arrangements will be made to bring you to the homes where you've been billeted."

He could have been a hotel concierge if his uniform were slightly altered and his gun hidden away. His friendly manner put them at ease, but I knew better. He was a Nazi, and Nazis demanded obedience. Everything had been taken from these people, and still he asked them to move along. What if they refused? What if they said they'd had enough of being treated like refuse? But no one ever did. They remembered the strikes, the arrests, the bodies. They'd become like cows, I thought, prodded along, unsure whether food or slaughter awaited them. Slowly the procession of strangers, heavy-laden with their worldly possessions, made their way towards the Stadhuis. I wished I was back in school, my head buried in a book. Meneer Paul's speeches were nothing compared to this quiet suffering.

Papa had forgiven me for coming home late after the gown-delivery debacle, but only because we needed Lady Astrid's ten guilders. Convincing him to let me work at the Stadhuis alongside Loti wasn't a hard sell either, because he liked the idea of the two of us together. I was happy to spend my days there—I'd missed my sister. Under Schueller's watch I could run errands without making up excuses, visit my charges while still making curfew. The coffee tin in the kitchen filled with our earnings. He silently counted the money and didn't insist I return to school. Papa didn't need to know I'd skipped my exams. I promised myself that when Miss Reinhart returned I'd finish my studies. For now, I wasn't the only one with an interrupted life.

The evacuees were older than I'd expected. Soldiers found chairs for them, and instead of queuing up in the usual way, they came forward as they were called. After a while, I realized there were hardly any men among the evacuees. This was a brigade of grandmothers—wrinkled, hunched over and most of all, alone. My curiosity was stronger than my good manners.

"Will the rest of your family be joining you?" I asked, stamping documents and issuing ration cards as quickly as I could. But these women would not be rushed. They wanted to share their grief with anyone who had a second to listen.

"My son is gone, he's in a factory."

"My husband's been taken away."

"My brother is fighting on the eastern front."

Some of them whispered, others cried. They were exhausted from their journey, with no one to console them for their losses. I looked at Loti helplessly.

"Our daughters have stayed behind," one woman lamented. "Doing the men's work."

"What about your belongings?" I inquired.

An old lady sighed. "Some tried to move wagonloads inland, but much of it has already been stolen from the warehouses."

A woman at Loti's desk turned towards me. "They came in the night and ripped the metal from the wall. We could have burned in our beds!"

"The soldiers wouldn't let me stay with my husband!" Another woman said. "Jasper has pneumonia. They said they'd send him along afterwards but they plan to transfer the infirm to a retirement home in Utrecht. Can you help me get back on another train? I don't want to be here. He needs me."

It took us the better part of the morning to process the evacuees. Villagers offered watery tea to the women to calm their fears. The sun came out and Loti announced she and Frid were heading back to the cottage for lunch with Papa, and did I want to come along? I did not. Carl would be waiting for me, sipping ersatz coffee at the café around the corner and I was already late.

After my sister left, I scanned the room to see if anyone was watching and slipped a small bundle of ration cards into my bag. Each evacuee was meant to receive rations to share with their host families, but our cell had more and more *onderduikers* each day, and those men and women hiding underground needed to eat, too. I wasn't stealing—I just had different ideas about how best to share. The Germans would not look kindly on my logic, so I was careful to never get caught. And so far, so good.

I was almost at the door when the captain's voice stopped me cold.

"Miss Zontag!"

I froze. Had someone seen what I'd done? My hands began to perspire around my purse straps.

"Captain?"

"Where are you headed in such a rush?"

I pointed towards the café. He nodded, looking off in the distance.

"Don't go near the train station this afternoon. *Ja?*"

"Yes, sir. I'll be back at my desk shortly," I said, as casually as I could. Were there more refugees arriving? Where would we put them all?

He waved me out the door and returned to his desk, behind which a new portrait of the Führer had been hung. I tried not to run, but I was breathless by the time I arrived at our usual table, where to my dismay, Katrine sat in my spot opposite Carl. He gave me an apologetic smile I couldn't quite decipher. I settled into an empty seat, clutching my purse protectively.

Katrine spoke first. "You look like you've seen a ghost! What's wrong?"

I quickly explained about the evacuees from Scheveningen and the mountain of paperwork to get them resettled.

"And you? What brings you into the village?" I asked lightly. While the rest of our group wore drab colours in case we needed to roll into a ditch and hide, Katrine sported a rose-coloured rain slicker and a matching headscarf, a parrot in a flock of sparrows. Why had we let her get her foot in the door of our cell?

"Everyone else was busy, so Mother sent Hans and I to buy a few things at the market. Not that there's much to buy."

Papa would return to his stall in a couple months with the first offerings from the spring garden. For now, the tiny sprouts grew under glass, waiting for the ground to thaw. I wondered for a moment if she were telling the truth. The market would be virtually empty.

"To be honest, I think Mother wanted information more than food." Katrine took a sip of the bitter ground acorn coffee and made a face.

"What kind of information?" Carl asked, casting a worried glance towards me.

Finally, she dropped her voice into a whisper. "Did you know the SS were using prisoners to build a training facility at the old tennis courts?"

"*Were?*" I said.

She nodded. "It's finished now, but we don't know what's happened to the prisoners."

"Why doesn't your mother just ask the captain?" I asked.

Katrine gripped her coffee cup tightly and looked down. "She's angry with him about something, but she won't say. The good news, according to Werner and Frid, is that the captain has been seconded to a base in Utrecht. He could be away for months."

"When does he leave?" I asked.

Katrine shrugged. "The sooner the better as far as I'm concerned. Mother makes me sleep in Hans' room half the time…"

"She's keeping you safe," Carl said.

I tried not to be irritated by his concern and kindness. He was right, but I'd be happy to send her back to her castle so Carl and I could slip down to the canal and hold hands for the rest of my break.

"In any case, I mean to find out where those poor men are—" Katrine said.

"You're going to the mill?" I asked.

She shrugged. "Hans is waiting for a parcel at the train station, so I'll meet him and suggest we take the canal route home."

"The captain warned me to stay away from the train station this afternoon," I said, remembering. "You could be walking into trouble."

"Then you should both come with me. Trouble's no fun on your own."

. . .

WE LEFT the café and followed Katrine, both of us reluctant yet curious. I slipped the stolen ration cards from my purse to Carl's pocket as we fell in step together.

"For later," I whispered. Together we were looking after four families, and the number of onderduikers we fed grew each week. The extra cards were essential. We passed them back and forth like love letters.

"Isn't that your brother?" Carl asked Katrine, pointing to a young man carrying a parcel.

Katrine squinted. "That's him."

Hans rushed towards his sister. "We need to go home right now."

"But I want to stay. It looks like something exciting is going to happen!"

A crowd gathered outside the station. Women carried small packages wrapped in cloth. Everything was strangely quiet.

"No. Mother needs this parcel right away," Hans said.

Katrine's chin jutted, but for once she didn't argue. Hans practically dragged her from the station to find their horses and head back to the castle. They left just in time.

"We should go, too," I said to Carl, an uneasy feeling coming over me.

"In a minute," Carl said, his eyes fixed on the women. We found a bench at the far end of the platform.

The mail train arrived and a few people came and went. I heard the roar of a Krupp engine as it pulled up alongside the station. Several SS guards jumped down and began to circle cattle cars on the far tracks. The women whispered amongst themselves, their anxious glances betraying indecision.

The prisoners appeared in the distance, a grey column of despair. Their shrunken faces stared straight ahead as soldiers hollered at them to walk towards the train cars. The closer they came, the more I wanted to run away. When they stopped, I could only stare across the tracks in horror at the sight of their skeletal frames. I was so transfixed I didn't notice the woman crossing the tracks towards the soldiers and prisoners, until the shouting began and Carl pulled me close.

Rosaura Reinhart, our former teacher, stood beside the men and argued with the soldiers. We couldn't hear what she said, but she held out parcels and gestured towards the prisoners.

A guard yelled, "Get away from here, crazy woman!"

She threw her bundle into the huddle of prisoners, and the other women began to cross the tracks and toss food towards them too. I wished I'd brought something. Now the station manager was on the platform, waving his arms.

"Get off the tracks!" he yelled.

Everything happened at once. A passenger train rumbled through the station, obscuring the view of the cargo cars. We heard a shot ring out, screams muffled by the screech of the wheels, and then silence. When the train had passed by, half the men had already been loaded into one of the cars. On the ground, a prisoner lay face down in the gravel, blood dripping from his head, a piece of bread in his hand. The women were ashen. Guards hurried the rest of the prisoners into cars meant for livestock. Rosaura knelt by the body of the man. It was then that I noticed she'd affixed a crude yellow star to her coat.

Several soldiers boarded the caboose and the others walked back to the Krupp. No one bothered with the women or the corpse, though one guard helped himself to a boiled egg lying on the ground.

"You're animals!" Rosaura screamed. "Animals!"

The crowd broke up. I couldn't tear my eyes away from the man on the ground. Carl stroked my hair.

"Carl," I said, choking back a sob. "We're not doing enough."

"Dry your tears, sweetheart. You're going back to work." He pointed to the Stadhuis, his jaw clenched, his eyes steely and determined. To anyone walking past we looked like a normal teenage couple returning from the koffiehaus. But what he whispered in my ear was anything but normal.

"We will *never* accept this as ordinary. You and me, Hilde, we keep going."

. . .

I SPENT the afternoon in a fog, filing papers, my mouth dry and my heart racing. Working alongside Carl made me brave. Imagining *our* bodies lying facedown by the railway tracks paralyzed me. When Frid and Loti came back from lunch, I managed to smile at their jokes, but my mind was far away. I wondered where those trains were headed. I wanted to ask Loti, but she spent her spare moments smoking in the alley with Frid, her laughter floating into the Stadhuis. It struck me then how different our afternoons had been, how different the last few years had been. When it was almost closing time, a policeman brought Rosaura in. She had a bloody lip and was holding her jaw, but stared straight ahead.

"What's this?" the captain asked.

"A troublemaker," the policeman replied, shoving Rosaura roughly. "A night in the cellar ought to smarten her up."

The captain narrowed his eyes and yanked the yellow star from her lapel. "Show me your papers."

He scanned them and looked up at her with scorn.

"You're not even one of them."

Rosaura shook her head.

"Why are you wearing this?" He shook the felt star in her face and tossed it on the floor.

"It's against our civil code to discriminate in this way. All citizens are equal under the law," she hissed.

No one spoke to the captain like that. The civil servants looked down at their typewriters, ignoring the commotion, but I couldn't take my eyes off my former teacher. She was fearless.

The captain turned to the policeman. "Officer, what do you think? Since this woman values solidarity so much, I wonder if we shouldn't send her to Westerbork with the others."

Westerbork. So that's where the prisoners were headed. Schueller had spoken of the new railway lines leading to the transit camp in the north. From the look in Rosaura's eyes, she knew all about the camp, too. Beside her, the arresting officer's posture softened.

"Sir, I'll make sure she's learned her lesson."

There was silence as the captain considered his options. I prayed for Rosaura to lower her face, to temper her defiance. Save yourself for goodness sake! I kept my head buried until I heard the captain utter his sentence.

"I've made enough decisions today. I'm headed to Utrecht and don't have time for this nonsense. Do what you will, but don't let me see this woman in here again. If she wears the star, she can expect to be treated like the rest of them."

I watched the officer push Rosaura down the hall towards the desolate cells at the back of the Stadhuis, and I shivered as I thought of the dead man left behind by the rail yard. What further suffering had he been spared? The idea that the prisoner was better off dead ignited a now familiar rage inside of me. I knew what I was about to do changed nothing, that compared to swiping ration cards, it wouldn't help anyone, but I couldn't stop myself. When no one was looking, I scooted out of my desk and pocketed the star off the floor. As my fingers closed around it, I had the distinct sensation it was all I'd have left to remember Rosaura by.

20

In the shadow of the stablemaster's cottage Benjamin chopped thick beech logs. The bark was fragrant and wet, the axe sticky from sap and for a moment the rhythm the work demanded made him forget his fear. The crack of the axe and his own heavy breathing masked the footsteps of a visitor approaching from the castle.

The man tapped him lightly on the shoulder.

"*Verdorie!*" Benjamin shouted. The axe tumbled to the ground.

"Sorry mate. Deep in thought are you? I was whistling all the way across the field," Schueller said.

Was he? Benjamin picked up the axe and held it jokingly towards his friend. Perhaps he was losing it. Schueller sat on a stump and nervously patted his pomade-slicked hair. Dark shadows hung under his usually bright eyes. "I saw more black vans today in town."

Benjamin froze. "Where?"

"Outside the homes of certain friends."

"Did they arrest anyone?"

"An older couple. The SS opened the back doors of the van and just pushed them in."

As though collecting stray dogs, Benjamin thought. "Where are they taking them?"

Schueller shook his head. "Some say they're headed north and others say they're headed to Den Bosch. Things have changed since the training centre opened. The SS are a different kind of soldier."

"Kurt. I think it's time."

Schueller's eyes widened. "But everyone accepts that you're a teacher from Rotterdam, no?"

Benjamin shook his head. "Before he left for Utrecht, the captain kept asking me questions about my past, why I didn't do military service, which doctors treated my childhood epilepsy, where I studied…" He ran his hands through his hair and exhaled. "Astrid says I'm being paranoid—"

Schueller swore. "Why are you talking to her about this? She knows?"

Benjamin reddened. "She guessed."

"I'll be damned. You sneaky charmer—" Schueller looked at Benjamin in wonder. "It's your curly hair. I always wanted curls. They say women like rich men, but I've never met a curly-haired bachelor, have you?"

Benjamin was exasperated. "How much will it cost to get to Switzerland?"

"The only way we can get people there is through Belgium…"

"Or Germany?"

Schueller shook his head vehemently. "Impossible."

"For the average citizen. What if I was a soldier going home on leave?"

"You've been thinking about this for a while," Schueller said.

"I have a lot of time on my hands. Either I'm thinking of ways to leave or worrying about being caught."

"Will you tell Astrid?" Schueller asked.

Benjamin shook his head. "The less she knows the better."

"Won't you miss her?" Schueller didn't meet his gaze.

In that moment Benjamin understood something he'd overlooked all along. Schueller wasn't helping Astrid because of some unresolved guilt; he was in love with her.

"Anyone would miss her," Benjamin said quickly. "But she's waiting for her husband to come home."

Schueller waved his hand in the air dismissively. He picked up the axe and set a log on the stump, slicing it clean in two. "Right. The husband she adores. The one she talks about all the time." He rolled his eyes. "She misses Philomena more than her husband, and you know it as well as I do."

Schueller was right, but Benjamin couldn't dwell on that now. Falling for a married aristocrat wasn't part of his plan.

"I'm trying to survive, Kurt. Can we focus on that?"

"I'll need at least 3000 guilders to get you to the Swiss border," Schueller said, tossing the log on the pile. "It takes time to orchestrate these...trips. You must be patient."

Benjamin was broke, more than broke. "I don't have that much..."

Schueller was pensive. "That's why I think you're better off keeping a low profile here. Especially while the captain's away—"

"What about an apartment?"

Schueller coughed. "I beg your pardon?"

"My apartment in Amsterdam. My uncle keeps the deed in a safe. I could give it to you..."

Schueller sat upright, his cigarette languishing in the ashtray. "You haven't had a letter from Amsterdam in months. How do you know he's still there?"

"I don't. But if he's alive he'll help me."

"What if he's sold everything already?"

It was possible. According to the Jewish Weekly News, most of the businesses in the Jewish Quarter had been shuttered since Benjamin had fled the city. But when he closed his eyes and remembered the prisoners, he knew he had no choice. Nathan might have been rounded up any number of times, but if he hadn't been...

"Let's find out."

"I WANT you to make me a pair of these," Astrid said to Hilde, holding out a newspaper clipping of a woman in denim work-pants.

The girl looked back at Astrid and raised one thin eyebrow. "Only the factory workers wear those, Mevrouw."

Astrid walked over to her balcony and gazed at the barren garden below. If they were to survive, she'd have to get down on her knees and work the land, and she couldn't very well do that in a skirt.

"Katrine mentioned you have already been making trousers for quite a few of the women in the village. Surely you can make something for me?"

"You shouldn't have to wear dungarees, Lady Astrid. It doesn't seem right," Hilde said.

Astrid turned and unzipped her skirt before Hilde could stop her. "Measure me. Right or not, I want them as soon as possible."

The girl just stood there with her tape in her hands for a moment. "Very well."

Astrid was down to her brassiere and slip when there was a knock at the door. "Yes?"

Schueller burst in with Benjamin on his heels, both of them deep in conversation. Hilde grabbed her coat and threw it over Astrid, but not before Benjamin looked up and turned crimson red.

"Whoa! Sorry! Thought you said 'yes' to come in!" Schueller sputtered, turning to go.

Benjamin stood frozen, then muttered an apology as he stared at Astrid's naked limbs.

Quietly, Hilde went to close the door before Astrid burst out laughing.

"And *that* is why I need new pants," she said.

Hilde finished her measurements. "I should have locked the door."

"Before my, er…houseguests arrived, I rarely locked the doors. My father always said it made the castle too gloomy. The light is meant to flow into the hallways, you see."

Hilde was quiet. "What was your father like?"

"My father? He loved this place. It was very important to keep the castle in the family." Astrid exhaled. More important than his daughter's freedom.

"Relax your shoulders, Mevrouw," Hilde instructed. "You're tense."

"My father always tried to make the best of things, especially during hard times, and I did what was needed to please him."

Hilde dropped her measuring tape on the floor.

"Everything alright?" The girl was very pale.

"My papa says the same thing…about adapting to the occupation. We must make the best of things." She sighed, and put her pins in her case.

Astrid walked to the fireplace and picked up an old family photograph. Her husband might have been a catch, but she'd always felt like she was the one who'd been caught.

"I trusted my father when I was young, but I wish I'd followed my own heart."

"Where would that have taken you?" Hilde asked.

Where indeed? Sometimes, when she rode through the woods and her horse galloped in a perfect rhythm she wondered if she could have made a life as a trainer, apart from Soelenkasteel.

"I wish I had more imagination. It seemed at the time the only option was to listen to my father. But later…I regretted not fighting harder for my freedom." Astrid smiled at the girl. She would never speak to Katrine like this. So why was her tongue so loose with this seamstress?

"Maybe you were just scared to go against his wishes because you loved him. I can understand that."

"Can you?"

Hilde nodded.

Astrid recalled Hilde's miserable face at the Sinterklaas parade. Perhaps this child did understand. And yet…

"Trust that voice inside you that tells you what to do. Don't let anyone else's voice get louder than your own intuition." Otherwise, you'll end up like me, Astrid thought.

"Thank you. I'll try to remember that."

Astrid smiled. "Go on and find Katrine. She's been eager to show you some new books."

"Thank you, Mevrouw. I'll bring you your order as soon as I can get my hands on the fabric."

Astrid walked her to the door of her suite. She changed into her dress and tied her favourite silk scarf around her neck. Schueller and Benjamin lingered on the mezzanine. "I'm decent now. You might as well come in."

The odd pair made their way up the stairs towards her. Schueller as lithe and nimble as ever, Benjamin moving cautiously as though he were being followed. They slipped into her suite and took up chairs opposite one another by the hearth, mumbling apologies for barging in earlier.

"Forget about it," she said.

It had been a long time since she'd been caught undressed, and she found it oddly comforting to know she could still spark a man's interest just by standing in her underwear.

"So…gentlemen," she said. "Something is up. What is it?"

"You know me too well," Schueller replied. "Do you mind if I smoke?"

She held a lighter towards him. That she received guests in her private quarters was still bizarre to her. Someday she would entertain in the parlour again. Someday.

"We're going to Amsterdam to pay a visit to Schueller's uncle," Benjamin began.

"Uncle Gustav? I pity you," Astrid said, remembering the pompous equerry she'd met in The Hague. "May I ask why?"

Benjamin shifted his weight, looking at Schueller before answering. "We were hoping that he—"

Schueller interrupted. "Benji needs help."

Astrid looked from Benjamin to Schueller and back again.

"Don't worry, we're not asking you to get involved," Schueller said. "Just letting you know that the children will have a few days' liberty from their lessons." He might as well have whispered, *Madame Ostrich*.

From across the room Benjamin caught her eye and something in his face implored her not to ask too many questions.

"Are you sure it's a good idea to go to the city?"

Neither man answered, preferring to smoke in silence. She sat down beside them and stole a cigarette from Schueller's silver box.

"Be careful," she said, exhaling. She fixed her gaze on the green-eyed teacher whose company she'd come to take for granted. If anything happened to him...what? She'd miss him? She shook her head.

How had she let that happen?

———

ON THE TRAIN a few days later, Benjamin did his best to act bored and nonchalant, though a quiet panic resided in his heart. Each time the doors between cars opened, he imagined the Gestapo demanding to see identification. They'd rehearsed their story—he knew the words to say, but he couldn't stop sweating. Surely anyone would know he was lying. He pulled his hat lower. As a young man, he'd been proud of his dark, curly hair. Now, he saw only fair-haired men.

Across the aisle, a young girl stared at him. At first, he thought he was imagining it. Children got bored and gawked at strangers. It was nothing to worry about. He buried his nose in his book again, angling his body ever closer to the window. He checked his wristwatch. Now *he* felt like a child. How much longer until they pulled into Central Station? It was hard to breathe in their cramped carriage. The train slowed and the suburbs came into view.

"Documents!"

Benjamin jumped.

Two uniformed soldiers made their way down the aisle.

Schueller squared his shoulders and calmly opened his wallet. He raised his eyebrow as though to say *get out your papers*. Trying to control the trembling in his hand, Benjamin obeyed. It was then that he noticed the little girl was no longer staring at him. A look of terror covered her face. Her mother smiled weakly. She wore a straw hat, but strands of orange hair fell loosely on her shoulders. Benjamin recognized a poorly executed peroxide rinse.

As the train rumbled on, the soldiers checked the identification papers and travel documents. The younger of the two barked instructions while the older one held out his hand and carefully verified the papers. They moved along until they arrived at the woman and her daughter.

"These papers have expired. We need to see a photograph and fingerprints."

"Pardon me, sir. We've been caring for my elderly parents in Nijkerk and haven't had a chance to get new documents."

"You need proper identification to use ration cards. How have you managed so far?"

Everyone in the carriage seemed to hold their breath. Benjamin couldn't stand it a moment longer.

"Excuse me, sir?"

The men turned to face Benjamin. "Yes?"

"We're coming from the same district, and it's true there's been a backlog at the Stadhuis because of the evacuees. They've made those entering Gelderland from South Holland a priority. We only had our identifications renewed last week, but it's no trouble to get the ration cards, once the girls at the Stadhuis know you." Benjamin winked. "*If they like you.*"

Schueller jumped in. "I starved of course, but as you can see, the secretary liked my companion."

The older officer squinted at Benjamin. "Hmmm. I'm not sure what the ladies see in you."

Benjamin felt his stomach contract.

Schueller punched him lightly on the arm. "He gets them with his jokes. They're terrible but everyone likes a good laugh."

"A joker, *ja*? Alright. Tell us a good one."

In a matter of minutes they'd be at the station and off the train. He thought back to his college days, the time before war, before worries of any kind.

"How do you knock out a marine drinking water?"

The officer shook his head.

"You slam the toilet lid on his head!"

The two uniformed men smiled. Schueller rolled his eyes.

"Alright, here's another one. Where do rabbits learn to fly?"

A shrug from the younger one.

"The hare force!"

A passenger behind them groaned. Benjamin felt the mood in the carriage lighten. He'd been good at this once.

"One more…but this one I'll have to whisper. It's not appropriate for the little ones." He winked at the mother gazing across the row from under the brim of her straw hat.

"Here goes. There's a junior lieutenant on his first night shift patrolling the seashore. The weather's the pits, cold and damp as all get-out. Just then, his superior, the captain, shows up walking his dog, and says, 'Nice evening, isn't it?' The lieutenant, though he's shivering, knows his place, and responds, 'Yessir.' The captain says, 'The fresh air does the body good, doesn't it?' and though the lieutenant could fall over he's so bone weary, he replies, 'Absolutely! Yessir.' The captain, indicating his dog, says, 'Alsatian. Best companion ever!' The lieutenant likes dogs and reaches down to pat the shepherd on the head. 'Yessir. No doubt about it, sir.' The captain looks out over the ocean and sighs. 'I got this dog for my wife.' To which the lieutenant replies, 'Good trade, sir?'"

The older officer burst out laughing. His younger, more serious companion chuckled. The wheels of the train screeched as they pulled into the station. Would they allow them to disembark? The officers themselves seemed conflicted.

"Where's a good place to buy a sandwich near the station?" Benjamin asked the man behind him.

And that was it. People gathered their belongings and the officers stepped off the train. Benjamin watched the woman and her daughter walk briskly across the square and disappear into the crowd. The city smelled of diesel fumes, stagnant canal water and cooking oil. The plane trees and poplars sheltered travelers and mothers with baby prams. Everything looked so ordinary.

"Slow down, Benjamin."

"Pardon?"

Schueller dropped his voice. "You're practically running."

"This is a familiar route."

"Tell that to the next German you meet. Though I'm not sure they'll all be so receptive to your jokes." Schueller made a face. "What were you *thinking* back there?"

Benjamin shrugged. He hadn't been thinking at all. A woman and her child were in trouble. They walked along the quieter streets of the Nieuwmarkt. Schueller grumbled and pushed his hands deep into his pockets.

"You're in no position to play the hero, Benjamin."

They stopped then. Benjamin stared at the barricade. A barbed wire fence of debris and wood surrounded the street access.

"How do we get in?"

Schueller shook his head. "Are you sure you want to?"

"The apartment is three blocks from here. We could try circling back to the park…" How far did the barricade run? He squinted, but there was no one walking around the streets on the other side.

"It's clear. Let's just go in here. We can leave another way." They were so close. They couldn't turn around now. He needed to know where his uncle was.

Schueller lifted the wire and Benjamin ducked under. Just like that, they were through. Though the streets felt empty, Benjamin looked at the windows and saw shadows moving behind the curtains. There were people in their apartments, watching them. The absence of sounds—bicycle wheels, market carts, laughter, children playing—lent the entire street a sinister air. Benjamin had the urge to be inside, hidden.

The windows of the shop were boarded up. The nails had been hammered in crookedly, as though someone had been in a rush. The elegant sign hung loosely on one hinge, the words "Rosenblum & Co." faded and worn. Benjamin looked over his shoulder, and seeing no one, tried the door.

"It's locked."

Schueller produced a small tool and picked the lock. "Give it a shove," he said, opening it up.

They quickly moved inside and Benjamin got his first look at the wreckage of his childhood home. No one lived here now. His eyes adjusted to the darkness. The only light filtered through an upper courtyard window. The display cases in the front room had been smashed and the dining room chairs turned over and broken. Benjamin followed the path of destruction into the kitchen and froze. He smelled something. Cabbage?

Schueller looked at him. "Someone's here."

Benjamin nodded. "Let's check upstairs."

They followed a narrow set of wooden stairs to the loft. A layer of dust covered the floor but there were footprints through the dirt. He put his fingers to his lips and turned to face Schueller. His heart raced. Despite the silence, he was certain they weren't alone. Benjamin circled the room, and Schueller began opening all the closets.

"There's no one here," Schueller said gently.

Benjamin crouched down in the doorframe of the tiny bedroom. Gently he wiggled the oak transom until it lifted. He felt around between the gaps until he touched a soft, velvet pouch. Clasping his fingers around it, he lifted it out. The bag was light. There were no longer gems inside.

"What's wrong?" Schueller asked.

Benjamin opened the sac and showed him. "He must have needed money, in the end."

"Why leave the bag?"

Why indeed? Benjamin closed his eyes. When he opened them, he noticed an access door onto the roof, and a sliver of light filtering down. He pulled himself up from the floor and pointed. Schueller scrambled up a ladder and gently pushed the door open. Immediately a pair of slender fingers clamped around his neck.

Benjamin rushed to the ladder. "It's alright. We mean no harm!"

The hands loosened. A tremulous voice whispered, "Benjamin?"

Schueller held out his hand to his assailant, and a frail woman followed him down the ladder.

"Benjamin, is it really you?" the woman asked.

"Freida? Where's my uncle?"

"You haven't heard?"

Benjamin shook his head. The gems were gone, his uncle was gone and the housekeeper was hiding on the roof.

Freida sighed. "The Reichskommissariat had a list of diamond cutters and polishers—" Benjamin felt his chest contract. "Was my uncle on that list?"

"He said it was the only way to avoid deportations." She paused. "For a while he went to work at a warehouse outside the city. Then, they came and took his tools...yet he figured as long as they needed him, he was safe."

"And then?" Schueller asked.

Freida took a deep breath. "They said they would extend special exemption passports to other family members, for a price."

Benjamin's heart sank. He knew his uncle. Nathan had traded his gems to save some other family.

"Didn't the diamond workers have to give up their stock in '41?" Schueller asked.

Freida nodded. "Most held some back."

"And the Germans suspected this, so they baited them with exemptions." Benjamin cursed.

Freida began to cry. "I haven't seen your uncle in over a month. He was waiting for you to make contact. Since you refused to register, he's been so worried about you."

Benjamin embraced Freida. "Don't worry, dear Freida. You can see for yourself I'm alright."

"But you need money. That's why you're here, isn't it?" She pointed to the empty bag in his hands. "Ever since they blocked Jews from the universities your uncle agonized about you. He half hoped you'd return, but when you didn't, he let himself believe you'd found a solution."

Not every solution lasts forever, Benjamin thought.

"He left something for you." She climbed back up the ladder and retrieved a small briefcase. "For what it's worth."

Benjamin opened the case and stared at the deed. "Freida, you're a gem. What do you know about this warehouse?"

Freida shook her head. "The Jewish Council—"

"To hell if I set foot in their office," Benjamin muttered. There must be another way to find out where his uncle was.

Schueller put his arm around his shoulders. "We'll investigate. Meanwhile, if you hear anything, could you send word?"

Freida nodded, but her eyes filled with tears. "I burned your letters, Benji. In case they came back. But I memorized the address in Gelderland."

Schueller nodded and Benjamin could see he was moved.

"You're not planning to stay long at that castle…are you?" she said.

Benjamin looked down at the floor. His plan was as thin as April ice.

"Don't you think he'd make a good alpinist, Mevrouw?" Schueller said.

The housekeeper looked confused.

"I think it's time our Benji made his way to the mountains."

Benjamin closed his eyes.

Switzerland.

Was there still a chance he'd make it?

PART III

WINTER 1943

Nine Months Later

21

When I was a girl, our family went to the Reformed Church. Sunday mornings we sat for hours on hard benches in an austere sanctuary. As a consolation, Papa would give me peppermints or salty licorice, but sometimes it wasn't enough to keep me from drifting off, especially when I took over Rosaura's deliveries. Our pastor used to go on and on in those wartime days, as though a longer sermon might encourage us. He was a good man, though. I don't want to say he wasn't. Even if my head would sometimes loll and snap back during prayers, I still miss the pastor of my childhood. Not because of his reassurance from the pulpit, but because he saw me. And later, because of his selflessness.

It was a cold February morning and Reverend Van Veen stumbled through the liturgy. He raced through his sermon and went straight to the congregational prayer.

> *"Heavenly Father,*
>   *In this season of cold and darkness, we cry out for your provision. We ask*

for strength and wisdom. Lord, provider of all goodness, we drink from your well and thirst no more. Even in our depraved condition, you've shown us by your holy word how to bring water to those in need."

Because I'd lost some of my faith when Mama died (why did God take *my* mother?), I always kept my eyes open—to see who else might have doubts. With each year of the occupation, our numbers grew. We were a secret club unto ourselves. I glanced around. Many of the elders were nodding. Depravity was one of their favourite catechism themes. But what I liked about the reverend's prayer was that *despite* the evil in the world, we can bring water. At least bring water. A few of the open-eyed congregants liked this idea, too. One man had tears in his eyes. But Van Veen wasn't done yet. What he'd missed in his sermon, he was making up for in his prayer.

"... Lord, give us courage to open our doors to the stranger. Quiet our fears of scarcity so that our only fear is of you. God, give us convictions when what is right and what is demanded are not the same thing. Let the world call us fools, that we may be righteous in your sight."

At this moment, a most unexpected thing happened. Reverend Van Veen opened his eyes and looked directly at me. He nodded ever so slightly and in his serious way, smiled at the rest of the skeptics before bowing his head to finish. I closed my eyes then too.

"...Hear us, in thy name we pray, not because we are worthy, but for Jesus' sake alone, Amen."

The congregation was silent. Papa rubbed his eyes. Others stirred uncomfortably, whispering amongst themselves. *He's gone too far! He's asking for trouble. Does he want them to arrest us all? They'll be watching him more than ever! If he's going to talk like that every week, we'd better stay home.*

"Papa?" I whispered. He never cried in public, but now his eyes watered.

As the organist began to play, we stood and sang together. Papa's voice was tremulous at first. By the fourth stanza, a couple of strong altos found their way in and the congregation's voices swelled in harmony. Some stood straighter, their hunger replaced with resolve. Today, unlike most Sundays, Papa stayed to chat with our elder and a few other men at the front of the sanctuary. For a moment everything was as it should have been. We were in this together.

What would Papa say if he knew that only a week earlier I'd dropped off ration cards at the elder's home for two boys who'd been hiding in his barn? Now we acted like strangers. So many of us were leading double lives. I glanced at a fresco of Jesus, the only art that adorned the sanctuary. At least *he* knew our true colours. That was reason enough to hold onto the remnant of faith I still had. I looked across the pews at Van Veen. Had he convinced these men one by one to take in *onderduikers*? Would he try to convince Papa, too?

On the way home, Papa walked slowly, lost in thought. "Go on, girls. I'll be along shortly."

"Where are you going?" Loti asked.

He smiled. "Don't be so nosy. Put the soup on."

My sister frowned. "What was that all about?"

I didn't know. It had been a tense weekend. Rumours swirled throughout the Stadhuis yesterday that a general had been assassinated in The Hague, presumably by the Communists, though no one knew for certain. The officers had been on edge and jumped each time the telephone rang, which was often. Even Frid, who I'd never seen without a smile, patrolled the square with a furrowed brow, his expression somewhere between worry and frustration.

We arrived home, and I made a fire while Loti prepared lunch. Although I sat as close as possible to the stove, I'd caught a chill. I hated wearing so many layers at once. Carl snuck into the forest at night to cut down trees, despite the posted warnings. I wondered if Papa wished he had sons, to help him chop wood or find fuel. I wanted to be more helpful so he wouldn't feel so desperate, so he wouldn't feel as though he had no choice but to obey every single German order.

Just as I was stewing on all this, the door flew open. Papa's face was flushed, and he had something hidden under his thick wool overcoat. His chest was heaving—no, it was wiggling!

"Papa?"

He unbuttoned the coat and out squirmed a pink piglet. Loti shrieked.

"Shhh!! Be quiet! Here's your new pet." His eyes gleamed with mischief. "Don't get too attached though. I brought her home to fatten my girls up. You're both skin and bones."

The little creature squealed as she ran around the living room and I couldn't help but laugh.

"Come here, little rosy one," I cooed.

The piglet stared at me, trembling. I reached out and brought it close to my chest. It nuzzled into my arms and relaxed. After a few minutes, I warmed up. But how would we hide something as noisy as a little pig from the neighbours?

"Where will we keep it?" Loti asked.

Papa looked over at me and smiled. "Muisje is always cold. We'll keep it in your room."

I nuzzled the little piglet. I was proud of Papa for this small act of defiance. If he saw how it was possible to quietly resist, perhaps he'd grow braver. Maybe there was a chance he could help feed the onderduikers. We could work together…

"Where did she come from?" Loti asked.

He shook his head. "Let's say it was divine inspiration. Now, how about some soup, *ja?*"

Two hours later there was a knock on the door. We'd been playing with the piglet, who we named Rosie, rubbing her tummy and letting her nibble on an old ball, when Loti remembered Frid.

"Quick! Hide her in your room!" Papa said.

I scooped up the piglet and settled her on top of an old blanket in the wardrobe. I heard Frid's low voice as he greeted Papa. Rosie nestled into her bed, exhausted, and fell asleep. I closed the door and went downstairs.

Usually Frid and Loti went for long walks along the canal on Sunday evenings. But tonight he didn't seem in a rush to leave. His eyes drooped with fatigue.

"Tea, Frid?" Loti asked. We had very little, but since Frid had given us extra rations, it felt like the tea was his anyway.

Papa tried to make polite conversation, but Frid noticed his distraction.

"Meneer Zontag? Is everything alright?"

I prayed Rosie wouldn't wake up. I wasn't sure if Frid would turn a blind eye to our illegal pig, even for Loti's sake.

Papa's eyes shifted towards my bedroom. "Ah, yes. Fine, fine. It's just frightfully cold out tonight. The damp is seeping through the walls."

Frid nodded.

I decided now would be a good time to play some background music, just in case. I chose one of Mama's Louis Armstrong records and set the needle upon it while *Savoy Blues* crackled to life.

"You've been away a lot lately. Long hours?" Papa said, keen to change the topic. "But the captain will return soon, won't he?"

Frid mumbled his reply, staring at the tea in front of him. "Did I ever tell you about the Dutch family that took care of me in the early twenties?"

"I didn't know you'd been sent to Holland," Papa said.

I sat down beside the fire and picked up the commission I was working on. Loti sat close to Frid.

"I arrived by train in '23 with hundreds of other orphans. The De Haan family took in my older sister and me." He paused and got a faraway look in his eye. "They lived just outside Apeldoorn. I was one of the youngest transports but they let me come because my sister promised to take care of me."

It was no secret that the Dutch had saved many Germans from starvation in the twenties and thirties, but this was the first I'd heard that Frid was among them.

"Have you been to visit them?" Papa asked.

His eyes were filled with sadness.

Loti reached out and gently stroked Frid's arm, forgetting about Papa and me in the room.

"I was called up this week to clear out a mental hospital in Apeldoorn."

Papa looked aghast. "Those poor people…"

"What do you mean 'clear out'?" I asked, casting my sewing aside.

He looked down at his lap and his teacup clattered against the saucer. "They were sent away."

A heavy silence hung in the air.

"Afterwards, I asked for permission to visit the De Haans. I went to their farm, but no one was there."

"They'd moved?" I asked.

Frid shook his head. "The local head of the *Landwachters* informed me that they'd been involved in illegal activities."

"Everything is illegal these days!" Papa roared. "What did they do? Grow their own tobacco? Forget to claim a hen?"

Frid looked taken aback by Papa's vehemence. I was thrilled to see a little fire in Papa's eyes.

"The Jewish children were being taken from the orphanages, so the De Haans collected as many as they could and hid them in the farmhouse."

Loti's shoulders were trembling. None of us wanted to hear the end of the story, but Frid wasn't done. He spoke as though in a trance.

"An informant went to the Lyceum, where a troop of SS men were lodged. They descended on the farm in the middle of the night with a caravan of black military cars and a truck. They separated the children from Mevrouw De Haan."

Loti gasped. "The poor woman."

"They beat her with their guns in front of her husband and when he went to defend her they shot him." Frid was sobbing now, his head in his hands. "He's gone and she's in prison."

I couldn't stay seated. I paced in the kitchen. What could I do? What could we do? We had to do something!

"There, there, son." Papa spoke in a soothing voice. With trembling hands, he offered Frid one of the precious cigars.

Frid waved it away, collecting himself. "They are sending us all over now. I want to thank you for the hospitality you've shown me."

"You're not leaving Brummelo, are you?" Loti asked.

Frid muttered under his breath, so softly I almost didn't hear him. "I want to go home."

At last we agree on something.

He shook his head and pulled himself together. "There will be crackdowns throughout the region in the coming weeks. I may not see you as often."

"Speak plainly, son. We've tried our best to adapt to the circumstances," Papa said. "Is there something we should do?"

"I was too late to protect the De Haans," Frid said. "They were kind people, doing what they have always done, opening their doors. I don't want you to get hurt, but you understand I have to follow orders."

"There was nothing you could have done, Frid," Papa said. "And don't worry about us. You know me, I'm just a simple gardener."

A simple gardener with an illegal pig. I folded my arms against my chest to keep my hands from shaking. There was plenty Frid could do, if he had a spine.

Frid looked at each of us before responding. "I'll do what I can to help your family, but you must promise not to take foolish risks."

Maybe I just imagined it, but I could have sworn he was looking at me when he said *foolish*. Too bad for Frid—I'd already chosen sides, and aligned myself with the fools. Which meant I'd have to figure out how to protect myself against cowards like him.

22

Ninety-seven lies. I added up the tally in my diary, sharp lines on a blank page that only I could interpret. I wasn't even counting the times I answered *yes* when I meant *no*, and I'd only begun the list on New Year's Day. It terrified me to imagine how many lines I would scribble down in the weeks to come. Would I lose track completely? What would happen if even I couldn't tell what was true anymore?

I slipped the small leather book under my mattress. Papa had cleaned up Rosie's waste and raked it into the garden beds early that morning. Now the little pig was ripping up newspaper and making a giant mess.

Loti came into our bedroom. "You're getting attached."

"No, I'm not." Lie number ninety-eight and I hadn't even had breakfast.

The Stadhuis was busy that morning. New ration cards had arrived and the queue ran around the corner. The captain had returned from Utrecht and was in a foul mood, barking at his officers and slamming doors as he came and went.

I feigned looking for a missing file so I could get closer to the table where the officers were arguing, pointing at a map of Brummelo. Red x's marked several locations. One of the officers ran his finger along the Nonnenstraat and muttered *shoemaker*. I froze.

Loti glanced up from her work. "Hilde?"

"I have to go..."

Her eyes widened in alarm. "You can't just leave."

"I feel sick. I don't want to vomit all over everything."

I grabbed my coat and headed towards the side door before anyone could question me. People grumbled in protest but I didn't turn around. I ran.

Normally I would have circled the bakery a few times before going around to the back, but today there was no time. I prayed someone was home, saw the Bakfiets and banged on the door. The curtain moved slightly, the door opened and Schueller hustled me into the dark kitchen.

"Why aren't you at the Stadhuis?" he demanded.

It took a moment for my eyes to adjust and then another to realize there were others in the kitchen. I blinked at his appearance. He was wearing a black SS uniform.

"I didn't know we had a meeting today," I said, hurt no one had told me.

Van Veen sighed. "We have to move people right away, Hilde."

"I know! That's why I'm here. I saw the Germans' map just now." I was short of breath. "They're coming for the Loewensteins!"

Van Veen shot a glance at Schueller. "You said the raid was tomorrow."

"They must have changed their minds." Schueller's forehead creased in worry.

"That explains why the captain took the dogs with him this morning," Katrine said.

I looked across the room. I wasn't expecting to see her there.

Mevrouw De Boer went to the wall and began to move the old cabinet, revealing the doorway to the Loewenstein's closet hideaway.

"Come, quickly!" she called.

They crawled out into the kitchen and stood looking fearfully at the small group around them.

"Meneer Loewenstein, it's time," said Reverend Van Veen.

Carl spoke up. "I'll hide Hannah and Ari in the Bakfiets and take them to our address in the countryside."

Mevrouw Loewenstein began to cry. "I want to stay with my babies. They need me."

"We will make sure you are reunited when it's safe," Schueller promised. "But right now, we must hurry."

Hannah and Ari hugged their parents tightly before folding themselves into the bread-cart. Mevrouw De Boer covered them with burlap and loaded bread on top of them. Minutes later, Carl biked down the street, away from the bakery. I don't know how he was able to keep himself from racing away. Mevrouw Loewenstein shook uncontrollably, her eyes fixed on Carl, while her husband rubbed her arm gently and spoke in hushed tones. Van Veen ushered them out to the back alley.

"We must leave one at a time. Everyone, take your loaves of bread," Schueller instructed.

"Hilde, go back to work now, otherwise they'll suspect," Mevrouw De Boer said. "You can take some bread, too."

I hesitated. "I told Loti I was sick. Maybe I should just go home."

"Very well."

"I'll be careful," I promised, making my way to the front door. I circled back to the *Kerkstraat* and began walking faster.

I heard them before I saw them.

Standing in front of the square, blowing a shrill whistle, the captain and his Alsatian stood beside Frid and several other officers, blocking Reverend Van Veen's wooden funeral cart. A green Krupp cast dark shadows onto the cobblestone. Van Veen was trapped. I ducked behind the shelter of the bookseller's shuttered stand, my stomach twisted in knots.

"Papers!" shouted the captain.

Van Veen slowly lowered the cart and presented his documents.

"Who died?" he asked, glancing casually towards the cart.

"We don't know, sir. Another measles victim left on the church steps."

The captain grunted. "Why didn't you toss the bugger into a grave beside the church? There's no need to parade a pauper through the streets, you could be spreading disease." He glared at Van Veen, and even from a distance I could see how cold his hooded eyes were.

The captain called Frid forward. "Have a look at this miserable corpse for a minute."

I wanted to believe Frid dragged his feet—that he hesitated before obeying his superior—but that didn't change what happened next. Frid went to the side of the cart, and in one swift motion lifted the heavy black canvas. A shadow of dismay fell over his face, and when he turned to the captain, his voice lacked conviction.

"There's no corpse here, sir."

The captain shoved past Van Veen.

"Well, well, well."

Soldiers quickly surrounded the cart. One of them grabbed Van Veen while the others hauled the Loewensteins out. Mevrouw Lowenstein looked around wildly, but her husband's face hardened as they were shoved towards the Krupp. An old woman sweeping her porch stopped to watch, but an officer shouted at her to get back inside. No one noticed me.

A gust of wind blew down the street and Mevrouw Loewenstein's hat tumbled to the ground. For a moment, time stopped. Frid bent down, retrieved the hat and offered it to her. Two seconds later, he lowered the back hatch of the Krupp and told them to get in. The captain looked on with a smug expression. The metal doors clanged shut and he turned his focus to Van Veen.

"Now that we've taken care of your corpse, we'd like a word with you, Reverend."

"This,"—VanVeen practically spat out the words—"...is illegal." I'd only ever heard him speak in a calm, gentle cadence. His gaze was too provocative. I prayed with a fierceness I didn't recognize in myself. There was nothing else I could do.

"We'll see about that," the captain said. "Shall I remind you that it was your government that built Kamp Westerbork in the first place?"

Frid drove off in the Krupp. The captain got into a black Horch and the other officers hustled Van Veen into the back seat. I unfurled myself from the shelter of the bookstand and watched, helpless as the vehicles departed.

My throat felt dry. I stood in the street beside the abandoned cart. This was my fault. They might have been safe in the closet. Maybe the dog wouldn't have found the hideaway. Trying to leave town in broad daylight was foolishness, and I'd provoked it. I ran my hand along the edge of the cart and the rough wood gave me a sliver. For a moment, I welcomed the sharp pain.

I had to let the others know what had happened. It wouldn't be safe to go back to the bakery just yet. I pulled my coat tight and walked along the canal, trying to think of what to do next. I arrived on the *Muiderstaat* and glanced up and down at the abandoned market gardens. Near a deep section of the canal where there was some open water, Katrine stood beside her horse, while the old mare took a drink.

She looked up as though she sensed she was being watched and I began to cry.

"What's happened?"

I told her everything in a rush. "We have to tell the others."

"Are you certain no one saw *you*?" Katrine asked.

I nodded. No one had spotted me. I was as drab as the stone buildings around us.

"Well, you are just a little twig. There's not much to notice," Katrine said.

I was too distraught to be offended. We needed a plan.

"I'll find Carl, you find Schueller," Katrine said. "He'll be having lunch at home."

"What about Van Veen's wife?"

"Let Schueller go. In uniform. If either of us goes, it will cause suspicion."

I agreed, even though part of me wanted to run home and have Papa comfort me, tell me everything would be alright. But of course, this wasn't something I could share with Papa. Not now. I couldn't tell him anything, and after what I'd seen Frid do, I was more convinced than ever that I needed to protect Loti, too.

Katrine rode off towards the forest and I turned and headed towards Schueller's. I'd never been inside before, and it was risky to show up unannounced, but I didn't see any other options. The street was empty. On the heavy oak door was a brass knocker in the shape of a racehorse. I rapped three times and waited. Footsteps approached. Schueller opened the door, still in his uniform. Ever so subtly he shook his head. Were people watching us from the neighbouring houses? A chill ran down my back.

He spoke in a loud voice. "No. I don't want to buy anything today. Thank you for coming!"

For the briefest moment, he stepped onto the threshold, so close to me I could smell his cologne. It was my only chance to tell him what had happened.

"The delivery was interrupted. VanVeen has been taken," I whispered. Louder, I said, "Thank you for considering, sir. I'm sorry to have bothered you."

"It's no bother. I'll take some next week." Schueller closed the door between us and left me standing on my own. Were it not for the flash of grief I saw pass over his face, I might have thought he didn't understand. But of course he did. He understood perfectly.

ASTRID SIGHED as she watched Schueller drive off, dust billowing out behind his Adler as he raced down the lane. How was she supposed to tell Benjamin the terrible news? She sat at the dining room table and stared at the silver candelabra. It hadn't been polished in months. She crossed the room and took it in her hands, cradling it tenderly. With the hem of her skirt, she rubbed it until it shone. Then she placed it in the centre of the table and started to cry.

"Astrid!"

She stiffened, and tried to wipe away her tears. Too late.

"What's the matter?" Benjamin put his hand on her shoulder. "You're upset. Is it the captain?"

"It's not me they want."

The colour drained from Benjamin's face and he began pacing the room.

"He knows?"

She shook her head. "No, but there were arrests in the village today."

Benjamin reached into the pocket of his wool blazer. "Wipe your tears."

Accepting his handkerchief, she inhaled the musky scent. "If you know your life is at risk, for God's sake, why are you still here?"

He stood by the window and said nothing.

"You know what he's capable of. Why haven't you moved on?" she whispered, joining him at the window.

He fixed his green eyes on her. "When the time comes, I'll go to Switzerland."

"Wouldn't you say the time is now?"

"I don't want to leave you alone with him."

"You think *I* need *you*?" she asked.

He looked hurt, but instead of answering, he reached down and took a lock of hair that had fallen from her bun and gently tucked it behind her ear. Then he turned and walked out. Moments later, she watched him head down to the cottage.

It would be better if he left. But she couldn't help touching her cheek where his fingers had brushed her skin. *So why do I still want him to stay?*

THREE WEEKS PASSED. I thought the worst of winter was over, and then the weather turned bitterly cold again. Papa and Loti both got sick, and I stayed home to care for them. Thanks to Field Marshall Paulus' surrender in Stalingrad, no one missed me at the Stadhuis. The newspapers reported that 90,000 soldiers surrendered to the Russians. I couldn't fathom such a number. When the Germans invaded, our professional army numbered a mere eight thousand. I looked at the map in Papa's bedroom. I'd never given the Russians much thought, but they must be a formidable people to defend their capital so valiantly. As I tried to get Papa to take some broth that night, I asked him how the Soviets outmaneuvered the Germans.

His breathing was laboured. "They went for the…weaker divisions. They picked the battles they could win and surprised them with small victories."

"And I suppose that the harsh weather did the rest," I added. Those were the rumours.

Papa closed his eyes and nodded. He'd been overcome with sadness from Reverend Van Veen's arrest. The entire congregation was at a loss as to how to respond, what to do without a leader. Papa sent food parcels to his wife, but I suspected that her anger scared him. He said if she took a more conciliatory approach, the Germans might tell her where her husband was being detained. After a while, Papa sent me to the parsonage on his behalf.

I leaned forward to listen to his chest. "Papa. We need a doctor."

He closed his eyes. "How's your sister?"

"She's resting. I'll go and fetch Dokter Freisen and he can examine both of you."

"But it's past curfew."

"I'll be careful," I promised.

I laced up my boots and put on my beautiful maroon coat from Carl's mother, my hat and gloves, and set off through the snowy streets. It was so dark I had to walk with my hands in front of me so I wouldn't bump into the decommissioned streetlights. Dokter Freisen lived on the other side of the canal in an old house with gaudy baroque arches. The family had a reputation for their friendliness towards the occupiers, but I didn't think of that then. The only thing on my mind was the gurgling sound in Papa's chest.

Dokter Freisen agreed to follow me back home. He couldn't drive his car because of the snow, so we walked together in silence.

"Why aren't you in school anymore?" he asked after a while.

"We needed the money, so I went to work." I didn't mention that I couldn't stand Meneer Paul, our Nazi teacher, or that the school wasn't properly heated. I wasn't sure which of my schoolmates still went. Certainly not the boys. If they were lucky, they were hiding. If not, they were working in Germany.

"How did you know I wasn't studying?" I asked, suddenly suspicious.

"There were so few pupils, they moved the remaining ones into our library."

For a moment I felt a pang of sadness. I missed Miss Reinhart, my beloved teacher whose memory I cherished in the felt star hidden in my wardrobe. Where was she now?

"You'd be welcome to resume your studies at any time, but I understand if you can't right now."

"Thank you." Maybe he was a bit too friendly with the Germans, but I saw in his face a concern that reminded me of the old days. He was still our doctor and we needed him.

We arrived back on the Nonnenstraat. The snow had already drifted against the door. I kicked it away and let Dokter Freisen inside, praying Rosie wouldn't wake up and reveal her presence with her grunting and squealing. The doctor went first to Papa, and then to Loti. I stoked the fire and made him a cup of tea.

"Hilde. Here are some sulfa pills…"

"Pneumonia?"

He nodded. "You must keep the house warm and have them gargle with salt water to clear the mucus. Try giving them this tea as well."

I reached for the bag of dried herbs. It smelled like peppermint and some kind of weed.

"How long will it take for them to recover?"

"It depends. They are both otherwise healthy, but the damp and the lack of vitamins takes its toll."

"Thank you for coming."

I saw him hesitate, as though he wanted to tell me something, but thought better of it.

"Dokter?"

"Hilde, I don't have any more sulfa pills. But you have some connections at the Stadhuis, *ja?*"

A long silence hung in the air between us, and I understood.

"Make me a list of what you need, and I'll see what I can do."

I WATCHED him trudge through the snow until he turned the corner, and then I went and sat at the desk in our room while Loti slept. *Forgive me sister*, I whispered. I took out a pen and lined up Loti's old school essays beside her lilac print stationary. I studied the looping letters and slowly traced her signature over and over. Then I began to write.

Dear Frid,

You must be wondering what's going on. The truth is, I've realized that we don't belong together. You'll always be German and I'll always be Dutch. I wish it didn't matter, but it does. I'm grateful for the care you've shown to our family. I love you. In another world, maybe this would be possible, but right now, it isn't. Please forget me and be happy. I'm already jealous of the German girl who will be your wife one day.

Love always,

Loti

I blew the ink dry and quickly put the letter in an envelope before I could change my mind. I'd deliver it tomorrow. It was another lie, and perhaps because I was lying to two people, I should have counted it as double, but I told myself I knew what was best for us. Maybe I was taking advantage of Papa and Loti's illness, or maybe I was healthy for such a moment as this. I slid the letter into my jacket pocket and crawled into bed.

Wrapping my arms around her fevered body, I whispered, "I'll always take care of you. Someday we'll both be happy. I promise."

23

SPRING 1943

I blamed the sunshine for my impulsive desire to visit Soelenkasteel. During the last weeks of winter, I wrestled with what I'd done. The puddles on the dirt paths dried up and the poplars dared to bud, but still I hesitated to tell Carl about the letter. He'd disapproved of Loti and Frid, but even he might think I'd gone too far, that my deception was cruel. And what if he was right? I reasoned that everyone had to lie at some point for the greater good, but sometimes when I saw Loti walking alone to choir practice, her thin shoulders hunched, guilt threatened to overwhelm me. I made a detour from my usual deliveries and called on Katrine, hoping to find an ally to reassure my conflicted heart.

"Let me get this straight." Katrine lit a cigarette, giving me a haughty glance as if to say, *don't bother giving me that look*. We sat high up in the hayloft, our legs dangling from a thick beam. The air smelled of tobacco, straw dust and horses.

"The entire time your sister was convalescing, you convinced Frid she didn't want to see him anymore?"

I nodded. "He came by with flowers and notes, but I insisted her illness had made her realize it would never work out."

"How romantic! I wish someone would pine over me like that!"

"Sure, but not one of *them*. When the war is over, you can go back to your old life and find a suitable boyfriend."

Katrine exhaled with an angry frown. "You don't get it, do you? All the 'suitable' boys have gone overseas or underground." Katrine took one last drag and squished her cigarette butt into a tin can ashtray, looking suddenly very vulnerable.

"Even if I wanted to find the right beau, without my father's textile factory, we can't afford the parties and balls I would have gone to before the war."

She rarely spoke of her father, but suspected he was in a POW camp, since they hadn't heard from him in years. At one time, they'd hoped he'd made it to Australia, but that dream was gradually fading away.

Katrine looked pensive. "What did you do with all of Frid's letters?"

"I burned them, of course." I *should* have burned them, but something held me back. Instead, I'd rolled them into a cigar box and hidden them under the dresser.

"Well, good riddance," Katrine said. "Except that now a whole new regiment has moved to town." She gestured towards the castle. "And here, too."

I nodded.

Frid had been lucky to be stationed so long in Brummelo, but the Germans needed more officers in North Africa. He'd believed my account of Loti's feelings and rejoined his battalion in Tunis. He left a final goodbye note in our mailbox, which I intercepted just in time. I almost gave in and handed the farewell letter to her. But then I remembered Mevrouw Loewenstein's panicked face, and Frid's hands pushing her into the Krupp. What choice did I have? Frid was dangerous, even if he truly loved her. His obedience gave me no choice—his orders were corrupt.

We sat in silence for a while, and the barn door opened. Two very young soldiers walked in and looked around furtively, then closed the door behind them. Katrine held a finger to her lips.

The soldiers walked from stall to stall, inspecting the horses, speaking in low voices.

What were they doing?

Katrine shrugged, as though guessing my thoughts. These new recruits couldn't have been more than a year older than we were. They pointed and gestured around the stables, as though making calculations. We listened as they opened cupboards, rummaged around some bottles and then marched back through the stalls. As abruptly as they'd come in, they left, apparently satisfied with whatever they'd been looking for.

"What was that all about?" I whispered.

"I really couldn't say," Katrine answered, a dreamy look on her face. "The young ones are cute, though, not scary like the older ones."

I rolled my eyes. "Not you, too."

"If I fell in love with a German, you'd be the last one I'd tell. Now that I know what you're capable of." Katrine punched me playfully on the arm.

She was strange, but I was beginning to enjoy her company. She was one of the few people who wasn't anxious all the time about the future. With her, I could pretend to be a regular seventeen-year-old girl taking a break with a friend.

"Anyway, don't tell a soul, but I have to tell you a secret." She paused dramatically. "I think I'm in love."

"Is it the fellow you mentioned who comes by and takes care of the horseshoes?"

She rolled her eyes. "No. Not him. I know you'll say he's too old, because you and Carl are more or less the same age…"

I stared at my friend. My mouth went dry for a moment. Surely not…

"His real name is Benjamin. I think he seems older because he lost his home, but he just turned thirty a couple of weeks ago. I mean, my father's fifteen years older than my mother, so what's the big deal?"

"Why do you think he's interested in you?" I asked.

"He's always dragging us back into the library to study. He could be going to the beer hall with Schueller but he seems to prefer being alone with us, and more often, it's just me, because Hans disappears most evenings, too."

"But has the conversation ever shifted from your studies to something more...personal?"

Katrine smiled mischievously. "He compliments me on my work. I'm becoming a better student every month, according to him."

"More desperate words were never spoken. He must be smitten."

Katrine tried to look offended. "You're so smug, just because you already have a boyfriend. I'll show you."

"Good luck," I said, laughing at her antics. "I really should get going but I wanted to ask Hans if he has any old toys I could take for you-know-who."

That afternoon I planned to check on Ari and Hannah. I'd made Hannah some doll clothes the night before but I had nothing to cheer up Ari.

"He's been with Schueller all morning. Who knows what they're doing now."

"Your mother doesn't complain?"

Katrine frowned. "Mother's main preoccupation is the stables. She hasn't the foggiest idea what we have been up to. Can you imagine what she'd say if she knew both Hans and I were doing our little bit for the underground resistance?"

I shook my head. Lady Astrid struck me as someone who was trying to forget there was a war happening. In some ways she was not unlike Papa.

We jumped down into the hayloft and made our way towards the castle. Several soldiers lingered by the fountain, smoking. I looked over my shoulder. They kept their eyes on us as we made our way inside. It was cooler in the halls of the castle, and I shivered. I followed Katrine upstairs but she stopped when we reached the landing. Voices drifted out from the library.

"Shhh!" Katrine motioned for me to tiptoe behind her.

Lady Astrid's voice rose above the others. "There's no way Gertrud Seyss-Inquart will listen to me. She's the Reichskommissar's wife for heaven's sake!"

"There's no way she'll listen or there's no way you'll do it?" Schueller challenged.

Katrine looked back at me and raised an eyebrow.

"There's got to be a special reason to petition Arthur Seyss-Inquart to get those people out of there," Lady Astrid said. "We're talking about a couple of shoemakers. It's not like it's Max Hirschfeld or something."

I leaned in closer. "Who's Max Hirschfeld?"

"Don't you ever read the newspapers?" Katrine whispered. "He's a Jewish economist the Germans seem to like. Apparently they make exceptions…"

Meneer Van Laar spoke up. "Could you write to her about the horses, remind her of your mutual affection for Philomena? Perhaps out of a sense of sorority she'll consider your request. Gertrud likes you—she admires you. They say Jews are being sent from Westerbork into Poland…"

"I know—to the work camps," Lady Astrid said, her voice a shade gentler.

Schueller spoke again. "There are rumours they're being murdered."

Katrine and I stared at one another, wide-eyed. *Murdered?*

"I'm sure that's an exaggeration. The work must be difficult, but it can't be as you say," Lady Astrid protested.

"Some say they execute Jews upon arrival at the camps," Schueller said evenly.

"They gas them," Benjamin said, so quietly they almost didn't hear him.

Schueller continued. "If you would just get your head out of the sand for a minute you could save their lives!"

"But you said they had concerts at Westerbork…" Lady Astrid stumbled over her words. "That there was a school, a workshop. You said it wasn't so bad."

We pushed the door open a crack. Schueller held a pen towards Lady Astrid. Meneer Van Laar's head was in his hands and his skin was very pale.

"If I didn't think they were in urgent danger, I wouldn't be asking you to do this." Schueller said.

"And if it works? Where will they go?" Lady Astrid asked.

"Depends," Meneer Van Laar answered, now sitting up straighter. "We'll try to get to the Alps, and if we can't, then maybe Portugal, maybe Spain."

At this I heard Katrine breathe in sharply. *We?*

"Anywhere but here, I suppose," Lady Astrid said.

Van Laar spoke. "Much depends on the safe houses Schueller can find…"

"This farce can't go on forever, Astrid. Benjamin's teacher-from-Rotterdam story has held up for a long time, but the captain is back to his old lines of inquiry," Schueller said quietly. "If his attention wasn't divided between Brummelo and his assignment in Utrecht…"

"I'd be on the next train east, just like the others," Meneer Van Laar said.

Beside me, Katrine was shaking her head.

It was quiet in the library.

"All right," Lady Astrid said. "Give me the pen. Let's see what kind of influence she has with her husband."

"You might ask if she has any news from Batavia," Mayor Schueller suggested.

I snuck a glance at Katrine. Her eyes were shining, and she closed the library door.

"Now we know the score," she muttered. "So let's get out of here."

The Hague
June 1st, 1943

Dear Lady Van Soelen,

How nice to receive a letter from you after all this time. You asked how the broodmares are doing and you'll be happy to know we have enjoyed many peaceful rides along the dunes. The horses are in splendid form.

As to your inquiries into the family from your village who have been sent to Drenthe, I am sorry to give you disappointing news. At the moment Arthur is preoccupied with another strike (as you've probably heard, there's been no milk for days!) and isn't able to attend to personal requests, which I do regret, given your previous kindness to me.

Nevertheless, although Arthur refuses to look into the Westerbork lists, I'll see whom else I might contact. If your friends are highly skilled artisans, there's a chance they can stay on working in one of the workshops, which I realize isn't the answer you were hoping for, but at least you might maintain contact with them.

Furthermore, I'm terribly sorry for the personal losses the war in the Pacific has caused you and your family. I have asked the Foreign Minister if he has a census of the population, and perhaps I can find some answers for you with regard to your husband. (I'm not sure the Japanese can be trusted. After all, when Hitler wanted their support in Russia, where were they?)

Sincerely,

Gertrud Seyss-Inquart

24

FALL 1943

Though all the radios had been rounded up, the captain allowed his men to listen to *Greetings from the Homeland* on Astrid's console in the parlour. The news on everyone's lips as summer turned to fall was that the Japanese had renamed Batavia "Jakarta" and Italy had switched sides. Schueller was giddy about the Italian about-face, but newspapers also reported decapitations of Dutch officials in the South Pacific. It was impossible to know what to believe.

Like Astrid, the young soldiers who were billeted at the castle seemed confused by conflicting reports. Was the war really turning? Something in their faces—not quite fear but not bravado either—unsettled her. She needed something solid to hold onto.

And then, without warning, she got it.

The dreaded, black-bordered telegram arrived without fanfare. Gertrud had kept her promise and forwarded a list of the deceased on to Soelenkasteel. Jan Stenger was never coming home from Indonesia.

At the basilica, they held a mass to honour her husband. Astrid dressed in mourning clothes and lit votive candles in her home, but without a corpse, it all seemed surreal. Hans wore an impassive expression during the funeral but Katrine broke down and wept.

Astrid's heart cracked open for her children who had never quite had the father they deserved. Back at the castle, her only escape from the suffocating sympathy of the soldiers and her staff was the stables.

The familiar smell of the barn and the horses' gentle grunts as she opened the paddock door reassured her that not everything was lost. Yet.

"There now, shall we get some exercise?" She leaned into a yearling's neck and tenderly stroked its glossy mane. For a moment she could pretend that life would carry on just the same. The horse whinnied and Astrid led her out into the yard. After a few circuits, Astrid judged her ready to mount. She was about to get into the saddle when Benjamin appeared at the fence.

"How are you?" His eyes searched her face for the truth.

Everyone treated her as though she were about to crack, but she felt numb. And ashamed. She didn't miss her husband the way a widow should. She preferred to be alone rather than pretend to feel something she didn't.

"I was just about to head into the woods. I need to clear my head." She looked at his serious expression. "What's wrong?"

"Why don't I saddle up another horse and come along with you?" Benjamin glanced behind his shoulder towards the castle, where a few officers were cleaning their guns on the lane.

"Take the grey spotted one over there. This string of yearlings hasn't been properly broken in. They can handle a light trail ride, but nothing more."

Benjamin wasn't a natural horseman; she'd known that from the start. Yet he knew how to put the animals at ease by talking gently to them. She looped the reins of her horse around a pole and checked Benjamin's straps.

"If she feels the saddle loose, she'll bolt and you'll be on the ground..."

Benjamin frowned. "I don't want to hurt her."

"If you don't tighten this, *you'll* be the one with the bruises." Astrid cinched the leather straps. "Three fingers underneath is all you need. Come on, let's go. I really must get out of here."

THEY RODE past the garden and quickly found the path that led into the woods. Benjamin glanced through the trees. He knew the SS men were just on the other side of the woods, training in their horrible facility. In the afternoons he could hear their drills, a sinister sound that made Benjamin's chest tighten. Only when they reached the heath would he relax.

Today, the air was crisp and the sky empty of planes. The gentle thud of horse hooves stirring up fallen leaves soothed his nerves. Astrid held the reins loosely, fully confident the yearling would bend to her will. Away from the castle, the ever-present furrow on her brow fell away, and she was radiant.

She slowed down, and he pulled up alongside her. "You're leaving, aren't you?"

Benjamin sighed. "I want to stay, but every time the Resistance cuts the power, or torches another military vehicle, the captain becomes more and more unpredictable." He didn't want to end up packed in a truck, and once the captain's attention shifted from the new recruits, his gaze would return to Benjamin. It was only a matter of time.

"Where will you go?"

"Geneva."

Astrid stared at him. "Hans and Katrine will miss you."

And you? Will you miss me?

"Let's talk about them."

"This isn't about their lessons, is it?"

Benjamin shook his head.

"I don't know what to do with Katrine. I'm worried Jan's death will only make her more volatile," Astrid said. "She idolized him."

"She's handling it differently from Hans," Benjamin said, and then added with a wry laugh, "Even stealing the young Germans' cigarettes has lost its appeal for her."

"What?" *Katrine did that? What else didn't she know?*

Benjamin nodded. "The child has no fear."

"I'm not sure that's a good thing." She sighed. "Hans accepts his father is dead, but Katrine doesn't believe it. She's been sleeping in my bed each night since the telegram arrived, waking with nightmares."

"And what about you? Did you believe your husband was coming home?"

Astrid shrugged. "I'm sure you've heard the rumours…"

Benjamin raised an eyebrow. "If they're true, then he was a fool."

"You're speaking ill of the dead now?"

He could swear he heard a smile in her voice. "Maybe."

They rode along through the sandy heath, quietly lost in their own thoughts, until they reached an old pine tree in the middle of a clearing. Astrid dismounted and tied her yearling up to graze on the wild grasses. Benjamin followed her lead. Standing side by side, they stared past the forest at the turrets of the castle peeking through the treetops.

"Look at that. Why did I ever believe that war would pass without affecting me? I thought I was special. I thought somehow I could ignore everything and hide."

"Madame Ostrich has pulled her head out from the sand." Benjamin put his arm around her shoulders and led her towards a fallen log. They sat down, and he kept his arm around her.

She leaned into him. "The roof is leaking in three places—"

"You'll repair it someday. You will," Benjamin said. "Now…back to your sad and impulsive daughter…"

"Katrine has talked about training as a nurse in Apeldoorn."

"That would suit her."

"No one in this family has *ever* trained at a vocational institute. She's supposed to be in finishing school in France."

"You are such a snob," Benjamin teased. "What's the use of knowing how to plan a dinner party if you can't afford to buy the food?"

"So, what are you saying?"

"Her recklessness could put us all in danger."

"You said she's just hiding their cigarettes."

Benjamin was quiet for a while. He inhaled the clean scent of her hair and skin.

"After the war, everything will be different."

"How so?"

"The social classes, the *verzuiling*, none of those old pillars will exist. Live your life now, instead of trying to preserve..."—he gestured towards the castle and the grounds around them—"...all of this."

"And let my daughter go?"

"Let her *be*." He paused. "It's not going well for the Germans, especially after Stalingrad. If you thought they were harsh before, it's only going to get worse."

"The city might be dangerous for a young girl," Astrid argued.

"She'll grow up."

Astrid nodded. "And what about Hans?"

Benjamin pulled her closer. "He needs to go underground, too. The *razzias* are starting up again. They're sending all the men to factories for the winter."

"He's not even sixteen!" She stood up and faced him.

"But he's on the list. Schueller confirmed it."

He watched her pace back and forth, her long, elegant fingers pressed against her temple, sunlight catching on her signet ring.

"Astrid."

She started to cry. "I wish I could just leave, too."

Benjamin stood in front of her and held her hands. "You're strong. Someday all this will be a memory."

Dreaming about the end of the war was something neither of them allowed themselves to do very often. If he could, he'd take her along. At night, he imagined starting over in a sleepy village in the Alps. How they would make a living, what they would do, he didn't know. The breeze would blow through the window of a small stone house tucked into the shadow of a cliff. He would be safe and she would be there in his arms. No one would ever ask their names. They would wander through the market arm in arm and people would offer them walnuts, blue cheese, apricots and honey.

She wiped her eyes. "How long until you go?"

"I need another thousand guilders."

"I have money," Astrid offered. She loosened the scarf around her neck.

Benjamin shook his head. "You've already done enough. If I can keep out of the captain's sights, I should be able to leave by the New Year."

She nodded. "Have you learned anything about your uncle?"

Benjamin kicked the dirt with his boot. "I should have dragged him here with me."

"Is he... in one of the camps?" she asked gently.

Benjamin shook his head. "The Nazis wanted five hundred skilled cutters in some military complex in Northern Germany—"

"I'm so sorry."

"It's not your fault."

They held hands, and the sounds of a woodpecker filled the silence.

"I wish you didn't have to go."

Benjamin turned towards her and pulled her close. He kissed her then, a deep full kiss. She ran her fingers through his curls and pressed her mouth against his. All of his senses came alive as he touched her. He felt her body relax into his embrace; she was soft, tender, inviting. She stroked his chest, his arms, his face.

"I can't protect you, Astrid," Benjamin whispered into her ear.

Astrid traced his face with her fingertips. She shook her head. None of the men in her life had ever been able to protect her. "That's not what I need."

He lifted her chin and looked into her eyes. "What do you need?"

"To forget this damn war for a while."

Benjamin pulled her down onto the grass and wrapped his arms around her.

"How much do you want to forget?"

25

Under the old stone bridge next to the market, there was a wooden bench where generations of Brummelo's lovers had carved their initials. I thought of this place as our one refuge from so much despair, and though our visits to the river were stolen moments between food deliveries and errands, for me it was enough to hope for something better when the war was over. I thought Carl felt the same, but something was wrong. He held his body rigidly and stared out at the water, instead of looking me in the eye, or trying to kiss me.

Finally, he spoke.

"You could have any boy in this village. Why me, with this?" He pointed to his weak leg.

I took his face in my hands and brushed my fingers tenderly over his jaw. "It's always been you. How many times do I have to say it?"

He reached for my hand and moved it away from his face. "But what if…what if you had to choose?"

I didn't understand. There wasn't a lineup of suitors at my door.

"Your father," he said quietly.

I groaned. "Now what?"

I'd told Carl about Rosie, hoping he'd see that Papa was refusing to follow all the rules, but it didn't seem to matter. The only secret I'd ever kept from Carl was the truth about Frid. I'd come close to confessing a hundred times, when I thought I might earn his trust. But I was tired. Tired of living a double life and having a boyfriend who second-guessed me all the time.

"The black market is hurting all of us," he said.

"The *war* is hurting all of us. Papa is just trying to survive, like everyone else."

He was a good father, a provider doing his best to adapt. If he had to do some trading with shady characters so we'd have a bit of butter, was that so terrible? He wasn't a Nazi for crying out loud. Besides, Papa wasn't hoarding. Just last week, a neighbour affectionately called him Sinterklaas when he produced a jar of wildflower honey as a birthday gift.

"I don't know what you want me to say. I can't change him."

Papa was fearful because he'd suffered loss, because of what happened to Mama. "He's scared," I added.

"We're all scared, Hilde. Open your eyes! Look at the way your father talks to the captain. The entire village was happy to see that mof off to Utrecht, but the day he returned, who was the first to go see him?"

"He sells them vegetables! And you know as well as I do that because of our crops I can glean food for the onderduikers. That's just how it is…"

He looked miserable, like he was biting his tongue. He couldn't quite manage it. "The only men left in the village are collaborators."

So that was it. His father was gone and mine was still here.

"He's adapting to the circumstances. There's a difference."

"Is there?"

We were like two bulls facing one another in a cold pen, the clouds of warm air between us proof of our fear and anger. Was there a difference? Yes. The difference was that he was my father. Did Carl really think Papa had been corrupted beyond saving? And if Papa was damaged, maybe I was, too.

I brushed invisible dirt from my skirt, got up and walked away. Carl didn't try to stop me.

WEEKS PASSED, and we didn't see one another. I wrote him letters that I ended up tossing in the fire. I tried to say 'sorry' but it didn't feel right. Carl should be writing to me, but he hadn't. I missed him.

In the first days of December, it was Katrine instead of Carl who came by the Stadhuis to walk with me to a meeting. Since Van Veen's arrest, we'd stopped gathering at the bakery and now met in the back of Colijn's hardware store. Schueller was holding court when we arrived, a bead of sweat running clear across his forehead, despite the chill in the room.

He tried to smile when he met my eyes, but exhaustion was etched into the lines on his face. His black jacket hung loosely on his small frame. He wore the "Department XI" uniform, an extension of his NSB membership, assuring him he'd never be called to the front lines. Once upon a time he'd joked, "there are advantages to being my height. I don't even qualify as a proper Nazi!" Today, his face was entirely humourless.

"They searched the De Jong's barn this afternoon," he told the group of us flatly. "With dogs and bayonets."

We inhaled sharply, one collective gasp. Katrine was the first to tentatively ask if the *onderduikers* survived.

"They took an injured English airman, and a young boy from the city was killed." Schueller's voice cracked.

"And the family? Have they arrested them, too?" Carl's mother wrung her hands.

Schueller shook his head. "They claimed they had no idea there was anyone in the barn. But now we've lost another safe house."

"And another traitor out there is cashing in his fifty guilders," Carl said.

"The *Heinneicke Column* is recruiting more opportunistic snitches all the time," Schueller said.

"If they torture the Englishman, who knows how long he'll be able to keep quiet?" Carl stood beside his mother, his hand resting gently on her back.

We locked eyes across the room. *I miss you.* He blinked and turned back to Schueller, who was talking about ways another group hoped to get the airman out of prison, a doctor who might be enticed to help. In North Brabant, a cell had made contact with a guard in the prison where Van Veen was being held—plans for his rescue were underway. The conversation continued, low voices punctuated with detailed contingency plans and new passwords.

"Either we deal with the traitors, or we make it harder for the SS to find the onderduikers," Schueller said.

Deal with the traitors. Take them into the woods and shoot them? How would we know for sure we had the right people? How would we get a hold of the Landwachter's lists of informants? So many questions swirled in my head; thankfully, Schueller suggested we go with the second option: make it harder to find the onderduikers. When he explained the details of the assignment that he'd planned for Katrine and me, I balked. I liked animals—I'd fallen in love with a pig for goodness' sake!

We were almost finished when a bell rang in the front room—the clerk's sign that a stranger or a soldier had entered the store. Without a word, Carl and his mother slipped out the back door; Katrine and I pretended to look at paint, a few scurried upstairs to the owner's apartment and Schueller waited in the bathroom.

"Just this today, sir," Katrine said to the clerk. "Must keep the windows dark."

The clerk smiled nervously at Katrine and took her money. I hardly dared to look at the soldier, who seemed preoccupied with the different kinds of wire at the back of the shop. He looked up just as we were leaving, smiled and wished us a good day. Katrine flashed him a smile in return and we were on our way. We walked through the village in silence carrying our paint cans containing poison pellets.

"Do you know why they've cancelled the parade this year?" Katrine asked, her face pensive.

I shook my head. "People don't feel like celebrating?"

"It's true. It doesn't feel like Christmas."

We walked along the Hoofdstraat, past the empty Stadhuis and the churchyards. Someone had hung an old garland along the cast iron fence, but it drooped in the wrong places, as though they'd lost interest decorating midway. The cobblestone streets were wet with cold rain that seeped through my bones and made my feet ache.

"Are you nervous about this?" We might as well have been carrying guns. Delivering pamphlets was one thing...

Katrine shook her head. "My father loved dogs. Did I ever tell you he used to have a poodle? I was very young, but I still remember that dog following him everywhere."

I put my arm around Katrine. Her eyes were moist, thinking of her father. I felt sorry for her then. Papa would never put an ocean between us. He'd do anything not to be separated from his girls. Anything? I pushed the thought away.

Katrine continued. "People smuggled letters out of a POW camp called *Struiswijk*, and I keep hoping maybe there was one last letter coming, some kind of goodbye. It's so hard when you can't say goodbye. Can you imagine?"

I could. When it was clear Mama wasn't coming home from the hospital, Papa had gone to her, but we'd stayed behind. Saying goodbye to a corpse isn't the same.

"The newspapers even talk of prisoners being sent to other countries because of overcrowding. Though I still can't believe he's gone, I couldn't picture him cutting sugar cane, either. My father...with his elegant silk ties and his round belly—"

I wanted to offer some words of comfort, but none of the things people had once said to me felt right. My friend's father sounded like someone from a novel, not an actual Papa. What could I say about a man who had abandoned his family? I squeezed her thin shoulders and she rambled on.

"...and lately, even if I'm eating some disgusting farm food, like mashed carrots and potatoes, I can't help but wonder if he was hungry..."

Katrine rested her head on my shoulder.

"And the strangest part is this: I don't think my mother even cares."

"Don't say that. I'm sure she was just as worried. You've seen the way she devours the newspapers."

She wasn't convinced. "You're going to say I'm being ridiculous, but lately I've been wondering…" Katrine shook her head. "I know. It sounds crazy, but there's something about the way Mother and Meneer Van Laar have been acting around each other."

I couldn't help it. I giggled. Lady Astrid falling for her children's tutor, a Jewish onderduiker? It was absurd. Despite the charming twinkle in his eyes, Meneer Van Laar was the opposite of Lady Astrid's elegance and reserve.

"Stop laughing. How would you feel if the man you've wanted to kiss fell for your mother instead?"

I said nothing. My mother had been dead for more than a decade so I had no way of imagining anything like this.

"Sometimes when he's going on and on about birds in South America or algebraic equations, I just watch his mouth and imagine him kissing me."

Katrine wasn't someone you reasoned with, I understood in that moment. And why would she take my advice? Especially now. What did I know about love?

"You have a lot on your mind…your father, a doomed affection for your teacher—"

"Who may be in love with my mother—"

"Who expresses his *gratitude* in a charismatic way," I said gently, hoping I was right. Schueller encouraged our friendship. *You can bring Katrine back down to earth, once in a while*, he'd said with his trademark wink. Could I though?

Katrine stopped abruptly in front of the Loewensteins' old shop. A new family, NSB supporters, had moved in and painted over the old sign, erasing the shoemaker's presence on the Nonnenstraat. I had to force myself to blink back tears and keep walking.

"What if this doesn't work?" Katrine pointed to the buckets. "I guess I am a little nervous."

The traitors were everywhere; it was up to us to intervene. We had to.

I thought of bayonets reaching through the hay and piercing Hannah or Ari or any of the other children living shadow lives in the countryside. I thought of the dogs that had sniffed until they found onderduikers—lunging at them, biting them, making them howl until they gave up their hiding places to be killed like rabbits. These weren't pets—they were weapons.

"We haven't messed up yet. Come on, Papa will worry if I'm not home before dark."

———

BENJAMIN SHOVELED THE COLD, hard ground and looked at the dead Alsatians lying in the grass. He suspected Schueller was behind this, though he hadn't made contact with his friend for days. A raccoon and two large rats had also fallen victim to the same poison the dogs had ingested, and the soldiers were trying to piece together how it all happened.

"That's deep enough, Meneer Van Laar," Hans said.

"What's going on in the house?" Benjamin asked.

Hans shook his head. "Mother is trying to calm the captain down. When the recruits reported this at dawn, he threw Mother's Limoges porcelain across the room in a fit of rage. He can't figure out what they ate."

Benjamin ran his hands through his hair. He hated that Astrid was in danger in her own home, even though she insisted she could handle the captain's volatility. Poisoning the dogs was brazen, foolish even. Of course, the captain would find a way to blame Astrid; the animals had died on her farm. He cursed under his breath as he cleared a few more shovelfuls of earth.

Footsteps on the gravel made them turn. Two soldiers gently picked up the dogs' remains and lowered them into the ground. They'd shared scraps from their meals with these dogs, treating them like children while they were far from their own homes.

Hans moved to add the raccoon and the rats atop the dogs, but one of the soldiers stopped him. He pointed to the shovel. The dogs would be buried separately. Benjamin watched Hans for a moment, saw him wrestle with the temptation to argue. Picking up his own shovel, Benjamin broke the ground for the second hole. He didn't look up again until it was finished, and by then the Germans were gone. If he remained useful and invisible, he'd survive.

As he contemplated the forest beyond where he'd buried the prisoner, Jacob, he wondered *how long until the grave calls my name?*

———

IT WAS the eve of Sinterklaas and Papa was making pea soup with pork hock. My stomach grumbled with hunger and anticipation. Loti's gift sat wrapped on the table. It had taken me weeks to find the materials to create it. Her grief over Frid's sudden departure in the spring had shrunk her. I had to adjust the size twice, but in the end, it turned out beautifully. I'd worked on the coat late at night, using precious kerosene to see my stitches. Once a man's wool overcoat, the remade garment was lined with silk and fitted with a matching belt. I'd fashioned a hood with burgundy trim and affixed brass buttons on the lapels. I'd sewn my guilt into every stitch, and in the end, created my finest piece so far.

"Loti! Come downstairs. It's dinnertime," Papa called, but there was no response.

"Muisje, please go get your sister. There's warm bread to go with the soup."

I took the stairs two at a time, the familiar excitement of Christmas taking over, helping me forget our present hardships. *She must be wrapping gifts.* I knocked, but there was no answer.

"Loti?"

I waited a moment and gently pushed the door open. Loti sat cross-legged on the floor, Frid's letters scattered around her, the cigar box cast aside. She slowly turned towards me, her face contorted in a mask of grief and confusion. Her beautiful features hardened.

Like a fool, I fumbled for excuses.

"I thought I was doing what was best."

Her eyes glinted with anger, tears streaming down her face. "You think *you* know what's best? How would you know? You're just a kid. You know nothing of love."

How could I explain I'd loved the same boy since kindergarten, and that he was a good man—a decent human being—not like the handsome monster who carted innocent people off to camps, leaving their children hiding in cold and dreary hovels. I wanted to tell her all this, but I couldn't defend myself without revealing secrets I'd promised to keep.

"I wanted better for you."

"Right! Because everything has been so much better for me now? Do you have any idea what it's like for me at the Stadhuis since he's been gone?"

"Loti?" I tried to put my arms around her, but she pushed me away.

"Don't touch me."

"You're my sister."

She glared at me and shook her head. "I don't know who you are anymore. My sister would have wanted me to be happy."

That was all I'd ever wanted—a happy family. Everything I was doing was to keep us together, to preserve the fragile joy we'd fought for so stubbornly ever since Mama had died. Why couldn't she see that a weak man like Frid would break everything we'd worked to build?

"How could you ever be happy with the enemy?"

"He was just Frid to me." Loti choked back a sob. "He protected me."

He *protected* her. Did he do what Papa couldn't? What if all of Europe became German, and I died an old spinster with only memories of what my country once was? Had I spoiled Loti's happiness for some foolish notion that freedom was possible? I was convinced our troubles were temporary. What if I was wrong?

Loti gathered up the letters, wrapped them in a ribbon and tenderly put them on her bedside table. She sat down at her desk and found a piece of paper from a drawer. I hesitated in the doorway and nervously cleared my throat.

"For Papa's sake, come downstairs and eat. He has done his best to prepare a feast—"

"And enjoy pea soup with bacon? From a pig we were able to hide because Frid turned a blind eye? No thank you. For some reason, I'm not hungry." Loti turned her back to me and began to write, but her tears blotted the ink before she'd finished the first sentence.

"What should I tell Papa?"

Loti crumpled the paper and laid her head on her arms. "You're the liar. Figure something out."

I wanted to switch sides then. None of the risks I'd taken seemed worth it anymore. I just wanted my family back. The secret life I'd been living weighed on me. Not freedom or safety or anything else was worth losing the people I loved most. I trudged downstairs.

Papa was smoking his cigar at the table, his eyebrow lifted in question. "Muisje, what's wrong? You're so pale."

I sat close to him, breathed in the scent of his homegrown, weedy tobacco, and, like a child, nestled into his shoulder and cried. He gently rubbed my back with his rough farmer hands. He knew me so well. My papa would never abandon me.

"There, there. Everything will be all right."

"Loti's not feeling well. I'll bring her up some soup later. She said to go ahead and eat without her."

He sighed. "Someday we'll have a proper Christmas again."

"Do you really think so?"

"Wars don't last forever. We do what we must…"

"Papa?"

"Yes, Muisje?"

How far will you go to survive? How much of yourself will you give up?

"I love you," I said.

Papa led me to a chair and poured me a bowl of steaming hot soup. "And I you. I'll do whatever it takes to provide for you and your sister."

I knew he was telling the truth; I didn't doubt for a moment that Papa would protect us no matter what. And it only made it harder to swallow his delicious meal.

26

WINTER 1944

"Before the war, the Officer's Club was the summer residence of a reclusive baron, a distant relative of Duke Henry," Schueller told Benjamin as they rode along the back roads with the headlights off. Schueller smoked one cigarette after another, filling the air with an acrid blue haze. They were nervous to be out after curfew, despite being dressed in enemy uniforms. Once they arrived, two young guards at the end of a long, tree-lined drive glanced briefly at their badges and waved them along.

"Where's this baron now?" Benjamin asked.

Schueller shrugged. "England? Germany? No idea. Astrid was friendly with him at one time." He paused. "Before the war, when his stables were profitable, too."

"Will all these families come back someday?" Benjamin asked.

"Old money always finds its way back on top." Schueller parked beside a Krupp with a flat tire, far from the officers' vehicles. The night was clear and crisp, and in the fields nearby, Benjamin could just make out the anti-aircraft artillery trained towards English planes that might brave the skies overhead.

"You sure you don't want to stay around for the weapons drops?

Within a few months it should get interesting around here," Schueller mused.

Benjamin shook his head. The policeman's uniform was tight around his shoulders and smelled like another's man's sweat.

"It's been interesting enough, thanks. This could be my last chance."

Schueller patted his briefcase where the bills were tucked inside. All of Benjamin's savings. "If you're sure."

Benjamin nodded. Any other fool would have been long gone.

They walked towards the mansion. No light escaped from within, but the moon illuminated the front entrance. Benjamin glanced upwards at the ornate stepped gable.

"We'll go around back," Schueller said. "Don't want to draw attention."

Benjamin didn't want to go in at all. The hairs on his neck prickled. He should have insisted Schueller go alone. He was the wily negotiator; his half-German blood and NSB party pin ensured that he could contort into whatever shape was most advantageous at any given moment. The best Benjamin could do was pull his hat a little lower and generally avoid people's questions.

Schueller nudged him. "There's our man."

Surrounded by uniformed officers, the lawyer looked utterly out of place yet completely at ease. He wore a heavy gold watch and a navy blue suit. His hair was slicked back with pomade, his moustache waxed into a droll twist. Benjamin scanned the room, and seeing no one he recognized from the castle, began to breathe a little easier.

"Gentlemen," the man murmured. "I'm just about to win this hand. I'll be right with you." He waved over a long-faced young waitress.

"Truus, a bottle of *oude jenever* and three glasses."

Benjamin laced his fingers together to stop his hands from shaking.

Schueller leaned over and whispered in his ear. "You're safe. No one is looking for trouble here."

A door opened behind them, and an officer slipped into a backroom with a woman in a lace camisole. Laughter wafted above the music from the band on stage. He'd never felt less like drinking.

The lawyer threw his cards down and stood up. "Mayor Schueller, nice to see you again. Come this way, I've reserved us a private table."

They followed the man to an alcove and sat down in a wood-paneled booth. The leather seats were cracked with age.

"You've brought the fee."

Schueller opened the case and the broker stroked the bundles of cash.

"Very well." The man lit a cigar and sent a puff of smoke over the table between them. "Unfortunately, it's not quite enough."

Schueller bristled. "I beg your pardon? What's changed since we last spoke?"

Benjamin shifted uncomfortably. He reached for his tumbler full of the amber liquid and downed it, hoping its warmth might calm him.

"The Swiss have compassion fatigue. Their airspace continues to be violated by both the Germans *and* the Allies. It's hard to find support on the ground for refugees. As they say," he said with a shrug, "the little ship's full."

"I'll survive in the Jura until the war's over," Benjamin insisted.

The man chuckled, but it was not a sympathetic sound.

"You assume that somehow Swiss trees offer better protection than Dutch ones? I'm an honest man. You wouldn't be the first miserable wretch to try his luck hiding out like Robin Hood. No, I won't take your money just to bring you from one frozen bush to another. I guarantee my clients a safe house and papers."

Benjamin thought about the thousands of police officers stationed in the Netherlands. The broker was wrong. The Swiss mountains were safer. He knew it. It was a numbers game, and Holland was too crowded, not just with desperate men like him, but with bounty hunters—the Landwachters and their cronies.

"What are you proposing?" Schueller asked.

"Lisbon," the man said, twisting his moustache.

Benjamin shook his head. Living at the castle he'd read all the papers, heard all the radio reports, bent his ear towards whispered rumours. He knew no boats were leaving the Portuguese coast any longer. It was too dangerous. Besides, it had been years since exit visas were issued by any of the embassies.

The man pressed his hands together and took a deep breath. "You'll be safe there."

"Lisbon is bursting with refugees too," Schueller protested.

"It's the safest option. We haven't had a single interruption to our transports these last few months. Besides, Lisbon is warm." The lawyer wiped his forehead. "Hell, I'm thinking of going there myself."

Benjamin couldn't stand it any longer. "How much to get to Lisbon?"

The man leaned forward, ignoring Benjamin. "I've always admired your car, Mayor Schueller."

Benjamin shook his head. No. They'd figure something out. He'd give Astrid the deed to the apartment in Amsterdam—if it was worth anything after the war.

Schueller's lower jaw worked back and forth, his irritation palpable. "You'd have to get it out of here. Everyone knows my Adler. Cash would be cleaner."

"I'll ensure it arrives in The Hague before morning."

And then, before Benjamin could stop him, Schueller tossed his keys across the table, stood up and walked out.

"Wait, you don't have to do this." Benjamin followed him out of the bar.

"It's just a car."

"Why are you doing this for me?"

"You got me out of a tight spot once," he said. "I haven't forgotten."

"It wasn't the same." Benjamin was a naïve student with connections. It had cost him nothing to make a telephone call.

With a wave, Schueller dismissed him. They stood outside, kicking the gravel mindlessly. Officers loitering around glanced up. Benjamin gave a feeble salute. He didn't want to engage with a couple of restless teenage soldiers. If someone were to peek out of the upper windows and see them standing there…

Schueller lowered his voice. "Start walking, Benji, it's a long way home."

27

The art of stealing, Katrine explained, was to ensure no one missed what you'd taken. I felt sorry for the governesses who'd spent hours looking for their favourite pen nibs and hairpins at Soelenkasteel. Katrine skated along the canal, unburdened by her past misdeeds, excited to put years of practice to good use.

We'd skated to *Swevezeele*, a tiny hamlet ten kilometres outside the village, and were sipping ersatz coffee at a stand along the canal. The owner kept apologizing that she didn't have any milk or cream, but we didn't care. We just needed to warm our toes before the return journey.

"You've been pilfering ration cards for years and have never been caught," Katrine pointed out.

"Yes, but this isn't the enemy—this is my own father."

"If you don't take a bit for the onderduikers, it'll end up in German bellies."

I knew she was right, but each time I went into the cellar, I hesitated. In the early days, I'd been able to put aside extra, adding more water to each jar of preserves. What had been easy in harvest season was becoming impossible as winter wore on. Papa had worked hard to keep the shelves full of preserves and dried food. If he noticed, how would he react?

"Think of what Doktor Freisen told Schueller. If the children don't get the vitamins they need soon, they'll get sick. You've been a lifeline for him."

I'd done what I could. Now that there was almost no medicine, illness meant death.

"So? Where's your father?"

"He'll be at the co-op for another couple of hours," I calculated.

"What are we waiting for? Loti's still at the Stadhuis, right? We'll go to your house and load up now."

What if Papa counted the jars tonight? What if we were questioned at the checkpoint on our way back to the countryside, and all the food discovered?

Katrine raised an eyebrow, waiting. She was swirling one way and then another, like the weights of a grandfather clock. I saw her then with clear eyes. She wasn't content to take orders; she needed to insert herself headfirst as the heroine, no matter the risks.

I stood up and took her hand, but as we skated home, a sense of foreboding settled upon me, like a quilt left out in the rain.

WE TOOK DRIED PEAS, potato flour, canned beans, cabbages, apples, onions and beets—then layered them all between old bolts of fabric in the *Bakfiets*. If we were stopped...I couldn't even think about it. Schueller told us to always take the back roads, and we did, but even then I worried. It seemed to me that the young recruits liked to explore, and I'd come upon them by accident more than once. Katrine pedaled alongside on an old bicycle with wooden wheels, chattering incessantly. I missed Carl, who could be silent for hours on end, not even whistling or humming.

The plan was to make three drops and return the *Bakfiets* to the bakery. The first delivery went smoothly. It was rumoured there were four airmen hiding in the small yellow cottage on the edge of town. I slipped some of Papa's own tobacco into the parcel just in case it was true.

The next stop took us more time to get to. It had begun to snow lightly, and the wheels didn't roll as well. After a while we pushed the bicycles through the slush and arrived at a cabinetmaker's workshop. Only instead of wardrobes and cupboards, the shop was filled with wooden crates—the kind used for moving people's belongings. A bespectacled man emerged from a backroom.

"Sir, I have some food for you," I said.

The man looked at the two of us and said nothing.

Katrine spoke up. "We bring greetings from the Stadhuis."

His face broke into a smile.

"Oh, thank God. I thought he'd forgotten us." He paused and whistled, "It's alright boys, come out."

Slowly, half a dozen bone-thin young men emerged from the cargo racks. They were so filthy they melted into the surroundings, with only the whites of their eyes shining brightly in the dimly lit space. Unlike the carpenter, they were too exhausted to even smile in our direction.

Sobered by their hopeless demeanour, we handed off our parcel and quietly headed out to our final destination, the chicken farm where Ari and Hannah were staying. We would have enough time to visit with them for a bit before curfew. My legs burned from the effort of manoeuvring the heavy bike and when at last we turned down the lane, I breathed a sigh of relief.

I knocked on the door of the back kitchen and waited. Smoke rose out of the chimney, promising warmth inside. Still, no one answered. I knocked again.

"Anybody home?" Katrine hollered.

We waited for what seemed like ages, and then we heard the heavy sound of the lock sliding open. The farmer's wife stood aside to let us in, but her eyes darted around us furtively.

"What's wrong?" I asked, the sweat on my back cooling rapidly and making me shiver.

"The children are gone," she croaked. "They left in the middle of the night."

"No…" My voice caught.

"That's impossible… they wouldn't have just left. They know how dangerous it is," Katrine said.

The woman shook her head. "That's the problem. They have no idea. All they know is that their parents are somewhere out there…"

"And they've gone to find them." I finished her thought.

She looked down and pulled at a string on her apron. "I don't know what direction they've gone because the snow has covered everything." The woman began to cry. "They're just children."

Schueller's voice came to me in a flash. *Trust no one.* I turned away from the threshold, out of earshot from the sorrowful farmer's wife.

"Katrine," I whispered. "Think. Where would they head first?"

Katrine looked over the fields. "Meneer Van Laar's cottage?"

Would they be able to find their way back there?

The Bakfiets wouldn't make it through the woods. I hated to leave it behind, but we had to find them before the Landwachters did. "Let's go."

WE DIDN'T BOTHER to knock. Our legs were tired from pumping the old bicycles and trekking through the woods on foot. My boots were wet, and Katrine's nose was red from the cold. Our exhaustion and worry made us forget our manners. We barged into Meneer Van Laar's cottage convinced we would find Ari and Hannah.

There are some silences that stretch on for so long it seems as though the first person to speak is shouting.

Instead of two small children, we found Lady Astrid and Meneer Van Laar, entwined together on the small settee. The cold rushed into the cottage, making the lovers turn in surprise, and quickly scramble to fasten their clothes.

When Katrine cleared her throat and said, "Mother?" it must have been a whisper, but it cut through the air like a field commander's whistle.

Lady Astrid stood up. We backed out onto the door step, Katrine moving as though her limbs were made of wood.

"I told you she'd fallen for him," she hissed.

I didn't know what to say. For a moment I almost forgot what we'd come for.

"Katrine." Lady Astrid stood outside, her arms folded tightly across her chest, her oxford blouse still unbuttoned. "He's leaving tomorrow. What you saw—"

"Never mind, Mother. I should have known he'd choose you." Katrine turned and began to walk away. No one would have guessed she was heartbroken, but I saw the slight trembling of her chin and her conspicuous swipe at the corners of her eyes.

"Wait…" Lady Astrid's tone was pleading.

I stood between mother and daughter and pulled Katrine back. "We're looking for the Loewenstein children. We thought they might have come to the cottage, but seeing as they're not here, we'll head back to the village."

"I don't understand," Lady Astrid said, confusion clouding her face.

Katrine's eyes were wild.

I grabbed her with both arms. "Katrine. Ari and Hannah need us." I wasn't sure she could hear me.

She looked at me finally and slowly nodded. "The bakery."

Of course! "Maybe they've gone back to their hiding place."

Katrine looked back at her mother. She shook her head and her eyes darkened. "I'll follow you, Hilde."

Astrid buried her face into Benjamin's shoulder. "She hates me."

He pulled her close and stroked her back. Katrine was spoiled and sheltered but he doubted she hated her mother. She'd calm down. He tried to find the words to reassure Astrid.

"Did I tell you about the man who owned a pickle factory?" he began.

She put a hand up. "Please. Not now…I think…the look she gave me…"

He ran his hands through her hair. "I'm sorry."

"Such a fool…"

He looked over at his suitcase, packed with a few personal belongings, including a new passport. Benjamin Van Laar would cease to exist tomorrow morning. Benjamin Numan, expert in aggregates, consultant in bunker construction, would begin a new life heading for the Belgian border in the broker's own convoy. Astrid didn't even know his real surname. He should tell her. He would tell her.

My name's Benjamin Rosenblum.

"Benjamin?" She touched his face. He wanted her to say his name, in case he forgot it. He should have felt relieved he was leaving, but he was filled with doubt. He'd managed this long. The Allies were making progress. What if there was a way he could stay?

"I should say goodbye," she said.

He wanted to carry her back to bed. "I'm sorry Katrine saw us… like that."

Astrid nodded.

"But I'm not sorry for falling in love with you. After the war, I'll—"

"Shhh." Tears formed in Astrid's eyes. "I have to go back up to the castle."

"I love you."

She shook her head. "That's impossible."

Benjamin kissed her deeply. "No, it's not. It's not."

"I'm afraid." Her eyes searched his face for reassurance he couldn't give her. He thought of Katrine's frozen stare when she entered the cottage. A sense of dread crept up his spine.

"I know," he whispered. "I know."

28

February 10th 1944 18:00h
De Boer's Bakery

"The farmer's wife said Mother and Father were dead…that there was no more money, so we couldn't stay." Ari spoke in a whisper. I guessed he didn't want his sister to know the truth. I thought of all Papa's food and the Bakfiets left behind at that miserable farm. Traitors! Carl came and sat close to me, near the fire. Katrine shivered uncontrollably; we were both soaked to the bone.

"Are you okay?" he asked me softly.

I nodded and he followed my gaze. Katrine was seated but tapped her foot on the ground incessantly. I couldn't explain everything that had happened right then. We needed a new safe house for the children and we'd already passed curfew. Carl's mother held Ari and Hannah close to her on the couch and fed them fresh bread. The rumble of motorcycles in the street interrupted the tender moment. The children's eyes grew enormous and their tiny bodies trembled in Mevrouw De Boer's arms.

Carl peeked through the curtains and swore. "*Verdorie*! It's the Landwachters with the SS right behind them!"

Mevrouw De Boer sprang into action. One moment the children were there, the next, they were gone. Carl, too. I pictured him curled into the tight space between the houses, trying to stay quiet and keep the children calm.

A minute later the farmer and the SS guards forced their way into the house, tracking snow and slush over the rugs.

"Where are they?" one of the SS men shouted. "It's no use pretending they're not here. Why are you hiding these troublemakers?"

The traitorous *landwachter*, an old farmer with bad teeth, leaned close to me. "We all need to eat my girl. With the money for these two, my family will have food for months. Come on, tell us where they are, and I'll buy you some meat. Eh, skinny? Tell them."

The SS officers stopped their search and came over to where I stood.

Mevrouw De Boer stepped into the fray. "Officers, the girls were just here to bring some school notes for my son. He's behind in his studies—"

"Thank you, Mevrouw. We'll see what these young ladies have to say for themselves." An officer grabbed my arm roughly and pushed me onto the street. Another took Katrine, whose face matched the snowy landscape. A car waited behind the motorcycles, and we were shoved into the back seat. The old man planted himself outside the front entrance, ensuring no one left the bakery; I watched him until the car turned off the Nonnenstraat and we headed into the night.

THE SS GUARDS parked the car far from the jail and told us to start walking. The path was covered in snow and we had to hold one another upright.

"Katrine," I whispered. "Do your best not to talk for as long as possible. Remember, every hour we resist gives the rest of the group time."

She looked at me and nodded, but the bravado was gone. She stopped walking. To our right a man was digging in the frozen ground. A man, no... a skeleton. He didn't look up or acknowledge us in any way.

"A saboteur," the SS guard said dismissively. "The Führer has made it clear that resistors must be executed, but someone must bury the scum, *ja*?" His laugh was chilling. We were being marched through some kind of graveyard.

I closed my eyes and tried to imagine the future. A fire crackled in the hearth while Papa stirred his salty pea soup. Carl was teaching a small child something—what was it? I decided he was showing our son a map of the world, showing him all the free countries. Loti was sewing in the corner, an embroidered dress like the smocks we wore as girls. And me? I wanted to put my hands on Carl's shoulder and feel his face turn towards mine. I imagined his smile as we looked at our son together. I could picture our child's little face, I could even count his freckles...

"Jongedame!"

I startled. We'd arrived at the jail. A clock on the wall indicated we'd been walking outside for over an hour; judging by the numbness in my feet it could have been longer. The guard shoved me into one cell and Katrine into another. The brick walls were thin. I heard her crying and waited until I thought we were alone.

"Katrine?"

"Hilde...I'm so cold."

"Don't panic. They'll hold us overnight, and with a bit of luck, we'll be back home in the morning." I sounded just like Schueller, optimistic in the worst circumstances. But I had to keep her quiet. Our lives depended on staying calm. "Try to get some sleep. Trust me, we'll be okay."

"I don't know what's true anymore," she whimpered.

I reached through the bars. "*Sterkte.*" Have a little courage my friend.

Her fingers found the tips of mine. "Hilde...There's blood on the floor in here."

I swallowed.

"Someone's coming!"

Footsteps stopped in the hallway. *Don't talk, don't talk, don't talk...*

A tall officer stepped inside my cell. I could hear Katrine's ragged breathing on the other side.

He sat down on a metal chair and lit a cigarette. "So, jongedame, tell me—who sent you to that farm today?"

"I don't know what you're talking about. Nobody sent me anywhere. I was trading," I said. "The usual stuff, vegetables for chicken."

"Black market stuff," he said.

I didn't reply.

"Are you taking orders from a man or a woman?" he asked again. "Don't be afraid. Nothing will happen to you. It can be dangerous out there for a young woman."

I was quite aware of where the danger lay, but I kept silent.

"How about your meetings? Sometimes in the church, sometimes in people's homes, *ja*?" His tone was cajoling but my stomach tightened. Soon my silence would frustrate him. He got up and came closer. He smelled stale—too many cigarettes and not enough water.

"Jongedame, look at me when I'm talking to you! We know you people are hiding weapons, even the girls. You don't want to end up digging with the men outside in the yard, do you?" He waited, and began circling me. "*Do you?*"

I felt a momentary sense of relief when he asked about guns, because I truly had no idea about weapons. My last silence was an honest one.

He stared at me and then grabbed both arms and pinned them behind my back, shoving me against the wall.

"Talk, you skinny little bitch!"

I began to tremble. He ripped off my coat and pressed his groin into my back. I froze. I tried to go back to the fireplace scene in my mind when a searing pain tore down my arm. He'd jabbed his cigarette into the flesh of my bicep. I screamed out in shock and agony. No sooner had the sound escaped from my mouth than I heard Katrine yelling from her cell.

"Stop! Stop it, please! She doesn't know anything. She's one of the mayor's assistants at the Stadhuis for God's sake!"

The man let go of my arms and a cruel smile crossed his face. "Maybe I owe you an apology, jongedame. We'll see."

I collapsed onto the cement floor. The flesh on my arm blistered. I took off my cold, wet sock and held it against the hot wound. The cell door closed again. Crouching down, I propped myself against the wall while the man disappeared to interrogate Katrine.

"We know you and your friend took care of these children, and believe me, I understand. Women are sensitive. I have a wife and two daughters…I can see how it happens. You didn't mean to disobey orders…women are inclined to follow their heart, even if at times those instincts are misguided…"

I shivered. *Be brave, Katrine.* Carl only needed a couple hours to get the children to safety. When would I see him again?

"*Sir*, the Zontags are an extremely generous family—their congregation shares any extra food they have from the neighbouring farms…"

"Are you suggesting that the chicken farmers invented this entire story?"

"I was just helping a friend deliver vegetables."

"And your sudden appearance at the De Boer bakery? A family with known Jewish sympathies?"

"As Mevrouw De Boer said, we were bringing school notes to her son."

"Classes have been cancelled for some time."

"At Soelenkasteel we have a private tutor. He encouraged us to loan our books out."

"I see."

Silence.

"*Had* a tutor, I suppose."

"I beg your pardon?"

"He's leaving tomorrow. Trouble with his papers, it seems."

I sat up and leaned against the wall. *No, Katrine, no! You are so close. This man is done with you. You've been so brave...*

"Would you like to tell me more, jongedame?"

My heart beat wildly. *Why wouldn't she just shut up?* Keys jangled next door and two sets of footsteps echoed down the hall. The guard's heavy footfall and the distinctive clack of Katrine's leather riding boots. I looked for a way to escape, to warn Lady Astrid and Meneer Van Laar, but I was trapped. I held onto my injured arm and imagined how worried Papa must be.

Curling into a ball on the floor I prayed as fervently as I ever had. *Oh God—help.*

Soelenkasteel
February 10th 1944 23:00h

BENJAMIN LOOKED in the mirror one last time and wished he could change his appearance. He looked like his father, his uncle, and all the Rosenblums before him. In Portugal, he might blend in. He took a breath and stepped outside into the darkness. From deep in the woods he heard crows cawing. He hated the sound. It penetrated the calm of the castle grounds like a warning from the underworld. *Nerves*, he told himself.

He picked up his suitcase, checked his watch and looked back towards the castle one last time before he headed down the road. A dark town car idled on the shoulder. His future awaited. The driver draped his hand from the window casually, as though this were a Sunday drive. In the crisp, frigid air Benjamin could see the white exhalation of his breath, beautiful proof he was still alive. He quickened his step towards the car, opened the back door and slid inside.

Benjamin smiled towards his companion. "Good evening, Sir..."

His voice caught. White fabric was wrapped tightly around the broker's mouth, and his hands were bound behind his back. His eyes were pleading. Was he asking for forgiveness? Slowly, the driver turned around. "Going somewhere, Meneer Van Laar? Or, do you prefer I address you by another name now?"

The German began to laugh. "It doesn't really matter. From now on, you'll have a number, and it won't change."

The car lurched forward. Benjamin looked at the door. Could he roll out and make a run for the forest? The driver watched Benjamin in the rearview mirror and a cruel smile crept across his face. Behind them, motorcycles roared to life. The broker eyed him sadly and ever so slightly shook his head. It was over.

Detention Centre No 2834, Veluwe Forest, NL
February 11th 1944 01:00h

A KEY TURNED in the cell and the barred door swung open. Schueller stood beside the guard, grey-faced and angry.

I rose to my feet. Schueller cast his eyes over me quickly and slipped the guard something—money?—and I followed him out of the jail into the darkness.

"Someone's waiting for you," he said, pointing to an unfamiliar truck.

I slipped into the passenger seat and there was Carl. He pulled me close but I winced from the burn on my arm. Schueller reversed out of the yard quickly, without turning on the headlights. The truck roared away.

"I'm so sorry," Carl whispered into my neck.

I laid my head on his shoulder, exhausted. "My Papa…"

"We told him Lady Astrid needed you, and because of the roadblocks, you had to spend the night at Soelenkasteel," Schueller said.

"And the children?"

Carl stroked my hair. "They're safe."

I had more questions—Katrine? Meneer Van Laar?—but my eyes would not stay open a moment longer. When I woke up, it was still dark and I was in a strange bedroom. It smelled of Mayor Schueller's cologne.

Carl sat in a wicker chair beside me, a lamp burning low on the table beside him. "Who did that to your arm?"

I looked and saw that someone had carefully bandaged it during the night.

"The SS officer who questioned me," I replied.

He rubbed his jaw. "They've taken Meneer Van Laar."

"I didn't say a word—"

"I know. They don't usually torture the ones who talk…" His voice broke. "I'm sorry for being such an idiot these past few months…for doubting you."

I patted the space on the bed beside me. "You are an idiot," I said, trying to smile. "*My* idiot."

He rose from his chair and lay down beside me. "The Bakfiets…"

I groaned. "I should have never left it behind. How will you get it back?"

"I won't."

I didn't understand. He needed it for deliveries.

"Hilde, we don't know who we can trust anymore. I have to go."

"It's that time of day. Your mother needs you at the bakery—"

He shook his head. "My mother's in danger. We all are as long as those traitors are still hunting for names. I have to go into hiding."

I sat up, now wide awake. "When?"

He looked at the door. A small leather suitcase leaned against the wall.

"Oh, Carl…"

"When the war's over, I'll make it up to you. I promise never to doubt you again…"

I kissed him hard, pulling him on top of me, pressing myself into him. He groaned, with desire or despair or some combination of both, and then reluctantly untangled my arms from his neck.

"I love you." He got up and waved, closing the door softly behind him. I fell back against the pillows and waited for daybreak. There was no point in crying. I made the bed, washed my face and went downstairs. Schueller was nowhere to be found, but he'd left a coat and shawl for me on the table beside a hastily scrawled note: *Don't walk along the Nonnenstraat.*

Hastily I layered his coat over my own and headed outside. The wind whipped past me as I put my head down and headed home. Where were the Landwatchers? How did I know they weren't going to find me and drag me right back to prison? What if they showed up at my house and started questioning Papa? Surely Schueller wouldn't leave me alone if I was in danger.

I began to sweat and picked up the pace. The canal road was empty except for a lone German truck parked near the bridge. As I approached, I saw cigarette smoke wafting out of the cab. My breathing became shallow. I couldn't face the soldiers right now but if I turned around I'd raise suspicion. Oh God, what was I doing?

"Hilde!"

I squinted past the truck towards the docks. Papa! He began running towards me.

"Muisje!"

I fell into his arms and immediately burst into tears. He stroked my back and we stood in the cold leaning against one another, not saying a word. After a moment, I thought I should offer up an apology, but the lie I'd memorized—Schueller's story about roadblocks and Soelenkasteel—didn't form into words the way I'd hoped. Papa held me at arm's length and studied my face. Suddenly, a door slammed behind us and I heard the unmistakable sound of soldiers' boots on the hard ground.

"What's the matter here?" the soldier asked.

I'd never seen this tall, slim officer before, thank goodness. The young Germans and the Dutch SS were like wolves and foxes...both dangerous but hunting in different packs. I stole a glance at his truck. Two men stared back at me, and a chill ran down my spine. I felt exposed even though I knew they couldn't possibly know where I'd been. Papa slipped his arm around me and pulled me close.

"Nothing's the matter. My daughter's been out on an errand and I brought her more thread." Papa unfolded my needle kit from his pocket. "She always forgets something."

The soldier nodded, bored by Papa's mundane answer, and returned to his companions in the truck.

They walked three blocks before Papa spoke. "Your sister was worried about you."

Could any good come of this? Maybe she would talk to me again. It began to snow, big flakes that melted on my cheeks. I shivered as I remembered the faces of the prisoners last night.

"You must stop now, Muisje." He looked at me straight, his jaw quivering. "I am doing what I can to take care of you. I promised your mother…" His voice caught. "But how can I feed my girls if you steal from our own cellar?"

I felt suffocated under the layers of fabric I'd tried to hide myself in. My face flushed with shame. "But Papa. There's so much need."

"It's not your responsibility!"

Why not? The Loewensteins were our neighbours. *Love thy neighbour. Obey thy father.* It was impossible to do both. My arm was burning with pain again. All of a sudden we were at the town square, and the Nazi flag clanged against the pole. I remembered Papa's warning from the early days: *there's no resistance without blood.*

"Have I made myself clear?"

I nodded, biting my lip, biting back the urge to say *I can't ignore them, Papa.* I might have apologized, but I couldn't stop now. I looked away from the hateful flag. Without Carl, there would be double the work. I thought of the freckled little boy I'd conjured the night before while trying to forget the faces of the prisoners. Someday I'd tell my child Papa's version. *I spent the war mending coats.*

And those marks on your arm, Mam?

Shhh, child. Nobody needs to know about that.

―――

Soelenkasteel
February 11th 1944 01:00h

WRAPPED IN A DUSTY FUR COAT, Astrid waited on the balcony for Katrine. Soldiers came and went throughout the night, undisciplined without the captain's supervision. Returning from the beer hall they fell asleep in the garden, almost like regular teenagers. She refused to look beyond the garden towards the stables and Benjamin's cottage. He was free now; she'd heard the car on the road hours earlier.

As she sat awake in the shadows, she replayed the scene from the previous afternoon in her mind. Alone in the stablemaster's cottage she'd given him a gold charm bracelet—her grandmother's—and without making any promises, he'd reached for her to say goodbye. If only they'd locked the door…

She's stayed out to punish me, Astrid thought, as a hawk screeched somewhere in the darkness of the woods. A car rolled into the laneway moments later. Katrine was home. Astrid ran down the stairs and onto the lane. Hans was there, too, but it seemed he wasn't relieved to see his sister home safe; he was distressed. Katrine's clothes were disheveled, but she appeared completely calm.

Hans stood in front of her, his body rigid. "Tell me you had nothing to do with it."

Astrid stared at her son. What was he talking about?

Katrine said nothing; she marched into the foyer and Astrid and Hans followed.

"Where have you been all night?" Astrid demanded.

Katrine faced her. "How dare you ask *me* what I've been up to?"

Hans looked at her curiously and turned back to his sister. "I followed Meneer Van Laar this evening—"

"What?" Astrid stared at her son, disbelieving. "Why?"

"He didn't get away, Mother. Someone betrayed him." Hans stared at his sister, his face frozen with anger.

Astrid felt the adrenaline of her night watch faded away. Katrine's expression was impossible to read. Astrid thought of all the governesses who'd left in frustration. *Mevrouw, your daughter's tantrums are unnatural…*

Katrine opened a bag and calmly placed coffee, chocolate and four books of ration cards on a side table. Hans stared at her, incredulous.

His voice cracked with emotion when he finally spoke. "You sold him for *coffee?*"

"A scoundrel who steals another man's wife deserves to go work in Poland. Maybe some hard labour will make him think twice…"

Katrine didn't have time to get her hands up. Hans struck her and she stumbled backwards. He lunged towards her again. Astrid pushed between her children, holding Hans back.

"You vain, stupid idiot! Labour camps? You believe that propaganda shit?" He grabbed the table and overturned it, sending coffee and chocolate all over the floor.

"Who are you calling stupid? You know *nothing* about what goes on around here!" Katrine was screaming now.

Astrid tried to shush her, whispering her name over and over, but she refused to calm down.

Hans was shaking. "They're going to kill him."

Katrine's shoulders sagged and the fight slowly went out of her. "No…No. I just wanted to teach him a lesson."

There wasn't enough oxygen in the room. Astrid felt her lungs constricting. She wanted Hans to be wrong. He had to be wrong.

"Hans. Does Mayor Schueller know?"

Hans nodded. "As soon as they drove away, I rode to town to find him."

She held her arms open to comfort her son. He stepped into her embrace and she rocked him gently, watching tears fall down his ruddy cheeks. She looked up and locked eyes with her daughter, who watched warily from across the room.

Katrine covered her mouth with her hand. She ran up the stairs and slammed the door to her bedroom.

Astrid needed fresh air. She led Hans to a bench near the fountain. Neither spoke. Everything was surreal.

"He must be terrified," she said. Oh, Benjamin, where are you now?

"What Katrine said… was Meneer Van Laar ever inappropriate towards you?" Hans asked uncertainly.

Astrid shook her head and stole a glance at Benjamin's cottage. "No, darling. Nothing like that."

"I see," he said.

How could he? How could anyone have predicted any of this? If she could have ignored him, shunned his friendship—and his love—Benjamin might still be safe. What a fool! She would not cry in front of Hans; it would only trouble him more.

"Mother," Hans said. "Could Katrine still apply to the nursing college in Apeldoorn?"

This surprised her. "You sound like Meneer Van Laar."

"She can't stay in Brummelo anymore."

Astrid stared at her son. How much had he seen in the past four years as he'd followed Schueller around? His dark, wise eyes told her he was a secret-keeper, though deep down she'd always known that.

"Katrine could hurt others."

Astrid stared at her son. He was holding something back. Would someone want to hurt Katrine?

"You know more than you should, too, don't you?"

He nodded. "But I can keep my mouth shut."

She could weep that this trustworthy, handsome young man belonged to her—as much as any child can ever belong to a parent.

"If she can't stay, neither can you. You're older than some of the young men sleeping in the garden right now."

He almost smiled. "There'll be hell to pay when the captain returns." He gazed out towards the stables. "But I don't want to leave you on your own."

She didn't want to be left alone, either. But it was becoming clear that she had no choice. Hans and Katrine were no longer safe at Soelenkasteel.

"They'll send you to Germany if you're still here by spring," Astrid said. "Even Schueller admits it would be better for you to go underground."

"The razzias," Hans said knowingly.

"I'll miss you. I'm sorry I haven't been able to give you the education you deserved."

"I've learned plenty, Mother," Hans said. "Enough to get by."

"Getting by wasn't what I had in mind for you, darling." She stared at her son's disheveled appearance, his old cotton button-down, his wool trousers stained from the stables. He should have been wearing a school blazer, an elegant cravat. She fingered the ever-present scarf around her throat.

He was quiet for a moment. "I'm sorry I hit her. Something came over me..."

"She feels very deeply."

Katrine had thought Benjamin's humour was flirtation. She was young, impressionable and—thanks to Astrid's stubborn belief her children should be raised like nobility—isolated. If Astrid hadn't been so taken by Benjamin too, she might have noticed. She might have saved him. She took a deep breath to control the rage and grief rising in her chest.

Resolve flashed across Hans' face. "Send her away."

Astrid hugged her son close, inhaling the scent of his skin, the last whiff of the boy he'd been. She missed him though he wasn't yet gone. She'd struggled to keep Soelenkasteel for her children and now they would leave it behind. This very afternoon she'd write to the head nurse and see what could be done. Whether the college would accept Katrine or whether she'd have to beg the nuns in the convent to take her, Astrid didn't know, but there was no one to educate the girl at Soelenkasteel anymore. She squeezed her eyes closed, terrified for Benjamin, ashamed of her daughter. She should have anticipated something like this. She should have tended to Katrine's broken heart, held her tighter as she cried for a father who would never return from Indonesia.

"You're right," she murmured, her voice full of regret.

Katrine had to go. And Astrid had to find Benjamin.

March 14th, 1944

Dear Hilde,

Today's your birthday and I'm not with you. You've probably put away your skates and are enjoying the sunshine. I wish we could go out walking along the canal together. One day...

Schueller told me you've moved on from coats and now make your own shoes! He tried to describe what you'd done, but I can't picture it—you've wired on the heel and somehow crocheted a wool tongue? Mevrouw Loewenstein would be proud of your resourcefulness, and I am, too.

When I talk about you here, the other fellows say I've gone soft, but they're jealous, because they can tell from my stories that you're brave. They don't know how smart you are, because I don't want to brag, but I promise you, when the war is over, you'll go back to school. (I will, too, but you definitely must. We both know you're the brighter one.)

Now that the captain has returned, how are things in the village? Please be careful, the Landwatchers are still active. Have you been able to borrow more books from the library at the castle? Is Lady Astrid lonely all by herself in that fortress? It's a good thing Hans got away when he did though, before the Germans dragged him across the border. Eisenhower will invest in more fighters this winter (at least that's what the boys here say!), and they're targeting the munitions factories. Mother is terrified they'll bomb Father before the war's over, but he insists he's safe and I want to believe him, but of course his letters are censored. He writes "the apples are ripe" when things are alright, which shows you how dumb the censors are—apples blossoms won't bloom until May.

With luck I'll be out of here in a few short months. I'd give anything to stretch out fully, especially my leg. Whenever I think my situation's bad, there's somebody who's got it worse. One of the guys who's hiding here with us was chased by the SS. When they couldn't find him, they took his girlfriend's father in his place. We have to convince him to stay put—he wants to run away all the time, and we have to hide our belts and rope. Things like that keep you up at night...

Sometimes I can go outside after dark and exercise, and when I do, I always think of how poorly I treated you. I know you've forgiven me, but I'll never forget the sight of your arm. When this war is over...how many times have I said that already? The days are long here, so I think it often: when the war is over.

Thank you for taking care of everyone—the children and my mother. Take care of yourself most of all. (I know I'm selfish to ask.) I love you.

Kisses,

Carl

29

I never told him how his mother had become so thin, or how Schueller had grown despondent. Now when I read those old letters (the ones I was meant to burn immediately), I think of my grandchildren—there's so much of the story that is missing! But I couldn't tell him then how afraid I felt. In those days, I prayed for Meneer Van Laar and all the others, what more could I do? After the war, people said families just disappeared into Hitler's Night and Fog, and that's how it felt. It was as though the sun had hidden itself. In those days, I pushed down my fear and reached for every scrap of hope I could find, and with that, stitched together my letters to Carl. They were the best lies I ever told.

"At least I can be of service to my favourite lovebirds," Schueller said with a sigh. "What does he write? Let me guess—he wishes you were there, he loves you, he—"

"Oh, stop." I swatted him with a newspaper.

"Ha! So I'm right. I knew he was the sentimental type. Lock up any man long enough and he'll write all manner of drivel."

We were sitting around his kitchen table. He'd refused to give me Carl's address, promising that when—*if*—it were ever safe to visit, he'd let me know. Reverend Van Veen's imprisonment in North Brabant weighed on him. He trusted no one now, not after Katrine's betrayal of Meneer Van Laar, and had no intentions of rebuilding our cell. When I eavesdropped on his private telephone conversations, I sensed he hadn't given up on either of the men, though if he was making plans, he didn't share them with me. I worried that the SS or the Landwatchers would come after me, but Mevrouw De Boer shuttered the bakery and the dangerous men disappeared into the shadows. Yet, for the moment I still looked over my shoulder wherever I went.

I was finishing the hem on a uniform jacket, but out of the corner of my eye I watched Schueller closely. The week before he'd been attacked by a band of young boys. They'd hurled insults at him, calling him a dirty half-blood. He'd tried to laugh it off, but I knew it hurt him that small children considered him the enemy, after everything he'd done to keep things as normal as possible in Brummelo.

Schueller lit a cigarette and paced the kitchen while I finished up.

"Why do you keep this single grey button separate from all the rest?" he asked, examining my kit.

I put down the officer's overcoat I'd been repairing and sighed. "Not much escapes your notice, does it?"

"It's been there a long time. I wondered why you haven't used it."

"It belonged to Carl," I replied.

"I see." He said nothing. I knew what he was thinking, though. Why wasn't the button back on Carl's shirt?

The truth was I wanted something of his to keep with me. As long as I had it, he'd be safe. I knew it was just superstitious, but I'd kept it anyway.

"He'll be back," he whispered.

Tears sprang to my eyes, and I wiped them away without missing a stitch.

"They're supposed to do their own repairs," he added, glaring at my handiwork.

I folded up the overcoat. If I was fixing their coats, I reasoned that they wouldn't arrest me, even as I knew buttons were no armour against brutality.

"All done. Be a gentleman and walk me back to the Stadhuis, will you?"

WE WALKED past a lineup of bundled up housewives holding pots of what I could only guess was watery soup. Meneer Frits' factory, the only remaining industry in the village, offered its ovens to the workers' families since they still had a bit of fuel.

Schueller nodded politely at the crowd, and a few reached out to shake his hand. Others eyed him warily. He was the mayor. If they didn't have fuel, he should do something about it. He held his head high, but I knew he didn't like to see Brummelo's citizens suffering. I shared his guilt. Neither Loti nor I ever had to stand in those lines or eat that watery soup. Papa disappeared once a week and came home with meat for the both of us, refusing to eat it himself. He told us he'd read about what happened to young women who were malnourished —their bones stopped growing, and later in life they suffered in childbirth. "I don't want either of you to die that way," he'd said. "I want healthy girls, and someday, healthy grandchildren. Eat up."

When we arrived at the Stadhuis I paused a moment in the doorway and watched Loti at her desk. Her brow was furrowed as she spoke with an older woman. She no longer had the face of a young girl. She went to work every day, to choir on Wednesdays and otherwise led the quiet life of a nun. Her hair had grown long and fell in soft waves over her shoulders, and her gaze put desperate strangers at ease for the few moments they spent with her.

"I wish I could make her smile again," I said.

Schueller followed my gaze. For a moment neither of us moved, transfixed by the everyday, ordinary beauty that drew out tentative smiles from the desperate crowd around her.

"Let it go. They used to see her as a Nazi and now they don't."

"So I did the right thing?"

"You did what was right in the moment. I don't think you can ask for more—"

"From a child? That's what you were going to say?"

He shrugged. "Why should you apologize for acting like a child? That's what you were when you sent that boy away. And now you're a woman, acting like a woman."

The world was so simple to Schueller. A clear-eyed perspective was refreshing, if you agreed with it.

"Uh-oh. Dark clouds ahead," Schueller said.

The captain strode across the vestibule, his boots heavy on the parquet. Spotting us, he gave a curt salute and disappeared into his office. Schueller had made sure none of the soldiers in Brummelo knew of my arrest, something I would wonder about years later as my sewing machine thrummed late into the night. Who did he have to pay to get me out of there? How much did it cost him for the jailers to forget me altogether? I never asked. He never told.

"I sure didn't miss him," I muttered.

"No one did, but never mind, you should get back to work. Look who just walked in…"

I turned towards the door to see Lady Astrid surveying the room. When her eyes landed on Schueller, she strode towards us.

"She looks determined," I whispered.

"Lady Astrid," Schueller said, bowing slightly. "To what do I owe this pleasure?"

She ignored him momentarily. "Hilde. You must come by and borrow some new books. The library is getting dusty these days."

"Thank you, Mevrouw. That's very kind." When the captain returned from Utrecht, he had confronted her about harbouring a Jew, but she'd feigned ignorance. She'd insisted he was a teacher and they had made a mistake. Yet dark circles under the aristocrat's sharp blue eyes hinted at her private distress.

"Kurt. Can I have a word with you?" Lady Astrid said.

Mayor Schueller cleared his throat. "Let's step outside. Hilde, your sister will be ready for a break."

I nodded, knowing I was being dismissed. As he led Lady Astrid towards the courtyard I strained to hear their words. Her face was contorted by worry. His eyes wouldn't meet her gaze. I only caught one word as I skirted by them towards my desk. *When?*

I took off my coat, sat down at my station and quickly nodded hello to Loti. As usual, she ignored me. I wouldn't give up on her though; I would never give up on my family. In a way, her silence made me fearless. God wasn't so cruel that he'd let me die before she forgave me. I don't know why I believed this, and unreasonable logic that it was, it gave me courage.

"Next, please!" I waved over the first family in line. The stream of human misery coming in each day kept getting worse. In the absence of men, women were left to manage on meagre savings or trade their valuables. When all their goods were gone, they came to see us. Some days, people were meek, grateful to receive a few extra coupons. Other days, frustrated and tired, they yelled and complained to anyone who would listen.

When Schueller was there, he'd try to calm them down. On occasion, I'd seen him take money from his own wallet and give it away. Other times, no matter what he did, people would spit on the floor and then on him. If the captain was in his private office, people stole angry glances at him though the glass partition. But since no one dared to openly challenge the captain, their frustration most often fell upon Schueller.

It was foolish to give out more ration coupons randomly. It would earn me unwanted attention, but I couldn't help myself. I wanted to see my neighbours' eyes light up again; I wanted to give them a bit of hope and dignity, to return what had been taken.

My last customer, an old woman with a braided crown of white hair, took her extra coupon, blinked twice and then quickly shoved a single tract back across the desk at me. *Trouw*. My eyes widened. I hadn't seen a copy of the underground newspaper in the village since Schueller's car mysteriously disappeared and our cell fell apart. I felt exposed, though everyone was busy with their own affairs. Slipping it into my vest, I nodded to the woman and briskly tidied my desk. I couldn't wait to show it to Schueller after work. My hands shook as I sorted documents, stamped letters and filed complaints.

Resistance is still alive, don't give up.

If only I knew for sure who was on my side.

PART IV

30

JUNE 1944

The rusty pickup truck sputtered and coughed as it pulled into the laneway, stopping with a jerk in front of the fountain. A strange hot air balloon contraption rested on the roof racks. Astrid had never seen anything like it.

Schueller slid out of the driver's seat. "Your carriage awaits, Mevrouw."

"What on earth is this now?" she asked. A few officers wandered up from the garden to inspect Schueller's inflated canvas apparatus. Astrid eyed them warily. She didn't need their questions right now. Why couldn't Kurt be more discreet?

"A mayor must travel in style," Schueller said.

"I'll say," she said.

He noticed the confusion on her face. "It's a coal by-product. I know it looks strange, but this street gas will get us fifty kilometres without stopping."

She felt as though she was stepping into a Jules Verne novel. Astrid laid her coat on the grease-stained seat and sat down, trying not to dirty her travel suit. She wanted to get going, even as she understood Schueller was trying desperately to act as casual as possible.

One of the officers stepped forward. "Mayor Schueller, we could offer you a lift if you're in a bind."

Schueller shook his head. "The mayor of Zwolle is expecting us and assures me we can refuel there. But thank you for the offer."

Astrid wondered what kind of story he'd invented to secure travel passes. Just when she hoped he'd answered all their questions and they could finally leave, the captain himself stepped onto the lane. He eyed the gasbag curiously and approached the driver-side window.

"Mayor Schueller. You're not looking for trouble, are you?"

"No, sir. My uncle Gustav asked me for a favour, perhaps you've made his acquaintance? He was named chief—"

The captain scowled. "*Ja, ja*. I know who he is."

Schueller cleared his throat. "Is there anything I can do for you, sir?"

The captain had a faraway look on his face. He seemed to want to ask something, but changed his mind, remembering where he was or who he was. Or maybe it was all Astrid's imagination. Ever since the children had gone—to the city, she'd told him—she'd avoided him, shielding herself in the shadow of the cook and the gardener.

"Good luck. Remember, no smoking," the captain said, pointing to the roof.

"Ha! No, sir. No death wish here. Goodbye!" Schueller said.

Astrid stared straight ahead while they pulled away from the castle.

"Aren't you going to wave adieu?" Schueller teased.

"No."

As they travelled the highway towards Zwolle, they passed clusters of men digging ditches, supervised by teenage soldiers with guns and grenades at their waists. They stopped working to stare at Schueller's strange vehicle. Astrid even caught a few wry smiles.

"Remind me why we're not taking the train," she said.

"The service is spotty and would take us only so far," Schueller said. "The tracks that lead to Westerbork are just for prisoners."

She swallowed nervously.

"The upper classes generally avoid the camp," he said.

Ignoring his insinuation, she asked, "How many people are at Westerbork?"

Schueller shrugged. "Thousands? I'm not sure. Word is Max Ehrlich is there. He's been directing a theatre troupe."

Astrid frowned. "So the camp is full of actors?"

"Besides the doctors, lawyers, artists, professors, cabbage-sellers, engineers and bakers, there are plenty of actors, yes. We've been invited to a cabaret performance."

"Maybe this is a mistake." She looked out the window, suddenly afraid to go any further.

Schueller glared at her. "You begged me to arrange this—"

"I know." She sat up straighter. But she didn't just want to see him, she wanted to get him out.

THE TRUCK CHUGGED along in spasms and miraculously delivered them to the gates of Kamp Westerbork just before dinner. Barbed-wire fences on ten-foot poles bordered long green wooden outbuildings. A watchtower loomed above the closest entrance.

As they pulled into the driveway beside the three-story residence of the Kommandant, a train trundled in. Schueller showed his I.D to the guards, and while he parked, Astrid stared out the window. Travellers in winter coats with yellow stars tumbled out onto the platform, haggard and bewildered. Even from a distance she could hear the shouting of police directing the flow of new arrivals.

"Come." Schueller took her elbow and led her towards the gloomy porch of the Kommandant's residence. "They're expecting us."

She was stiff from the long drive and her nerves frayed by the sounds of shouting. The smell of overcooked kale, potatoes and vinegar wafted from the house. Though she hadn't eaten in hours, she'd lost her appetite. How could she eat when all those people on the platform were clearly hungrier than she was? They knocked on the door and Schueller's uncle appeared. He had aged since the ball in The Hague a few years earlier. His rotund middle had thickened, and his triangular moustache had whitened, but his arrogant countenance remained the same. He led them into a dining room where the other guests rose at their arrival.

"Gentlemen, my nephew, Mayor of Brummelo, and his friend, Lady Astrid Van Soelen."

The officers murmured a collective hello and the Kommandant invited them to join their light supper. They ate bread with cheese and salami as well as some kind of potato mash that might have been palatable with butter, but there wasn't any in sight. Astrid saw that it would be rude to refuse to eat; she managed to swallow a few morsels, but her nerves had her stomach roiling. The Kommandant poured them each a glass of sherry and quietly discussed the Normandy landings with Schueller. From where Astrid sat, she could just see through a crack in the curtains towards the storage huts. She wondered why the windows weren't painted black and why the children were running around the yard without their parents.

"We have some time before the performance. Would you like a tour?" Schueller's uncle asked. "If the Kommandant has time?"

The Kommandant yawned. "You take them, Gustav. You know your way around. I must excuse myself." With that, he wiped his jowls with a linen serviette and left.

"I wouldn't mind stretching my legs," Astrid said.

Schueller shot her a warning look.

"You'll get dusty, Mevrouw," Gustav said. "Surely you'd be more comfortable in the parlour?"

Schueller tried to sound casual. "Before the war Lady Astrid spent many hours at the racetrack. She's used to a bit of dust in her eyes."

Gustav looked from Schueller to Astrid and shrugged. "Very well."

They set off walking towards a group of children playing soccer. The older ones on the sidelines balanced toddlers on their hips protectively. The players were so thin, their ribs were visible beneath their uniforms, and after running the length of the field they had to stop and rest. A handful of policemen lingered around the perimeter of the field. The police looked as ragged as the children, she thought, and whispered this to Schueller.

"Those are the Jewish police, the OD. Together with the Dutch forces, they keep order and make the selections. They decide who goes on the next transport." He sighed. "They're popular on Monday nights but keep a low profile on Tuesdays."

Schueller's uncle walked ahead of them to greet a couple of officers who were sharing a cigarette under the trees.

"What do you mean?" Astrid asked, horrified.

"Every Tuesday the train leaves for the East. The OD makes the transport lists, and in the morning everyone lines up on the roll-call ground to hear if their names will be called."

She considered Benjamin's letters to his uncle in Amsterdam, and his worry about the Jewish Council's cooperation with the German authorities. But this? The cruelty of using Jews to administer their own deportations was outrageous. But there was no time for her sorrow to find release; Schueller beckoned her to follow him.

She fell behind as his uncle pointed out the barracks. Astrid wanted to peek inside and see where Benjamin slept, but they were clearly in the women's part of the camp. Teenage girls hurried past, glancing curiously at them. Though it was summer, their feet were clad in worn out boots and long dresses. They continued along a dusty boulevard and arrived at a school. Long rows of planks stood for makeshift desks. Astrid imagined Benjamin here, and searched for signs of him. But all she saw was despair in the furtive glances of a few students who quickly buried their heads in books.

"Perhaps Mevrouw would like a coffee?" Gustav offered.

Astrid glanced across the way and saw men in suits milling around another shack. Music streamed out onto the dusty path, luring people towards the smell of roasted beans. She hadn't smelled coffee this rich in years, and yet here they'd found some!

They sat at a small table and several officers joined them. Just then two young men got up and began to sing in the corner of the café.

Schueller's uncle leaned towards Astrid and whispered, "This is the pre-show. Everyone loves this duo, except for the Kommandant. He allows them to perform here at the café because as you can see, it keeps everyone calm."

The men sang a tune called "The Westerbork Serenade," and the patrons clapped enthusiastically. Astrid found it strangely chilling. Beside her, couples held hands and a few souls even danced together to the upbeat melody.

I sing my Westerbork serenade,
   Along the little railway the tiny silver moon shines
   On the heath.
   I sing my Westerbork serenade
   With a pretty lady walking there together,
   Cheek to cheek.

The words brought tears to her eyes. The young men's rich voices and the thrum of the guitar rose above the din of chatter.

Schueller's smile was tight. Astrid knew she wasn't alone in her despair. Behind her, an extremely thin man whistled from the back row. Astrid's mouth gaped open. Willy Rosen. The celebrated jazz pianist. If Benjamin were here, he'd try to get his autograph. She excused herself and strode towards him.

"Excuse me, Meneer Rosen?"

He smiled gallantly and took the measure of her clothes. She felt rumpled from the trip, her silk scarf sticky with perspiration, but compared to all the other women, she looked like a queen and this made her suddenly self-conscious.

"What can I do for you, Mevrouw?"

She dug in her purse and found some paper and a pen. "May I have your autograph?"

"My pleasure. To whom shall I address it?"

"Please write: For Benjamin Van Laar…no, sorry. Benjamin Rosenblum." She twisted her fingers around her purse straps nervously. "A friend of mine. My children's tutor…"

Willy Rosen stood very still. The pen hovered above the paper.

"…He's a big fan of yours," she rushed to explain. When he didn't move, she thought he'd taken a spell. He was very, very thin. He probably needed a doctor.

"Meneer Rosenblum already has my autograph, sweetheart." His voice dropped to a whisper. "He runs the lights for the cabaret."

Her hands began to tremble. There must be some mistake. "I wish it were so. My friend is—"

Willy Rosen leaned in closer. "An economics professor from Amsterdam?"

She couldn't speak. The crush of bodies was suffocating. The pianist took her arm and led her to the back. Schueller caught her eye and nodded. She followed his gaze across the room and all the clatter and bustle of the café seemed to fade away until there was only silence in her head.

Benjamin.

His skin was sallow, his shoulders bony through his dress shirt, and yet he moved with ease, adjusting the spotlight on the famous jazz duo. He was so focused he didn't notice the people around him. Astrid remembered how he'd lean over the children intently, helping them with their work in the library, oblivious to her standing watch in the doorway.

She wanted to engrave this picture of him in her mind. She wanted to cross the floor and take him in her arms, but she stood there, untethered.

Willy Rosen led her to a table directly beside the lighting board and she sat down. And then he saw her. Looking past her face, he spoke in a low murmur.

"You found me," he said, his eyes on the switchboard. His fingers trembled as he moved his hands across the luminaire.

"I'm sorry it took so long," Astrid replied.

His voice was hoarse. "The fat Nazi with the moustache is watching. Order a drink and turn your back to me."

She did as he asked, though she couldn't stand it. "I don't know how to help," she whispered.

"You're here," he said.

"What good is that?" Astrid stared out at the room of terrified patrons, all trying to escape their reality for a moment under the spell of the music. Beneath their smiles was a palpable dread. "I'd hoped if I found you, we could figure a way out of here."

Astrid could feel his nearness behind her. She listened as he rotated the heavy lights and still said nothing. His knees cracked as he crouched down and stroked her ankle.

His touch lasted seconds and then across the room Schueller and his uncle stood up to leave. Willy Rosen had disappeared into the crowd.

"When did you discover I didn't make it to Switzerland?"

Astrid couldn't bring herself to tell him the truth, that her own daughter had betrayed him. Her mouth went dry. His face searched hers for an answer, and not getting one his expression hardened.

"Thank you for coming to say goodbye," he said, turning away.

Astrid hadn't come to say goodbye. She'd come get him *out*. She stared at him in profile. He wouldn't, or couldn't, look at her. Benjamin stared straight ahead at the stage, as if she wasn't there beside him.

Her feet wouldn't move.

"Please. You need to leave. The cabaret performance begins shortly and by the looks of things, you'll have a front row seat."

Astrid glanced over to where Schueller and his uncle chatted by the bar with the camp brass. Knowing this might be her last chance, she elbowed her purse onto the floor and let the contents roll across the planks. They crouched down together and slowly gathered the coins. When his hand brushed hers she shivered.

"After the first duelling piano set, there's an intermission. Go outside for some air, and I'll find you."

She swallowed the lump in her throat and nodded.

BENJAMIN WAS RIGHT. In the front row of the performance hall, three seats were reserved for them. The room was cramped, but a small orchestra occupied a corner, and dark velvet curtains decorated the stage. She could almost forget where she was. She closed her eyes, and for a moment she was a little girl joining her parents at the Music Hall in Apeldoorn. Here, there was no heady scent of perfume or shuffle of programs. She was in a room of mostly men. A gentleman in a tired tuxedo appeared on stage and gave the sign for the orchestra to begin. Only then did the music take over and distract her from the smell of exhaustion and sweat.

One after another, comedians and singers appeared on stage. They wore heavy makeup and smiled at the crowd as they sang in German. Their frenzied movements unsettled her. When the dancers emerged, she couldn't believe their costumes. Where did it all come from? From the tight bustiers to the high white heels, the entertainers moved in perfect harmony. Their performance was intense, as though they knew there were no rehearsals, no closing nights, no standing ovations—only this moment.

The Kommandant smiled in her direction. "I love to see a lady moved by a fine performance."

He couldn't know that Astrid's tears weren't for the music but for the musicians, who believed their art could save them.

Before long, Willy Rosen appeared and sat down at a piano opposite Erich Ziegler. With a nod of his head, they began to play. She barely registered the music swirling around her, though she could see from the smile on the Nazi officers' faces that they were enthralled. All Astrid could think was *Benjamin's outside*. When Ziegler hit the final note and the audience erupted in cheers, she quietly stood up, signalling she needed some air.

The night was cool and dark. It took a moment for her eyes to adjust to the shadows. She breathed deeply and waited alongside the barrack wall. When she finally made out his frame, leaning against a shed, her breath caught. She brushed away sudden tears, stepped down and reached for his hand.

"Why are you here?" he asked, his green eyes shining. "You could get arrested." He pulled his hands away and stuffed them into worn pockets.

"I had to see if there was any way—" She'd sold all of her pewter just to put gas in Schueller's ridiculous truck.

"Money doesn't work here, darling. Plenty of rich people here, but the same fate awaits us all."

"So what am I supposed to do? Go home and forget you?"

His eyes watered. "No. Don't forget me—"

How could she? Where her parents had sold her to the highest bidder, like a horse bred for show, Benjamin had seen her. He was seeing her now, and as much as he held himself away from her, his tired face was full of tenderness, though his dimple had disappeared.

"Stop. There must be some way. There's a fee—"

"The infamous *gegen Zahlungeiner Busse–*"

"You've heard of it?"

"Astrid. A hundred thousand Swiss francs and men ten times more connected than Schueller can't orchestrate ransoms anymore. Even if you sold the castle—"

"I would."

He stopped and shook his head. "You would?"

"Anything. I love you."

"It's no use. Even if you could, it would be too late for me."

"But Schueller says the Allies—"

He snorted. A bitter laugh caught in his throat.

"Have you no hope at all?"

"Look around you, woman!"

Astrid was taken aback by his harsh tone. She feared someone would come out of the music hall and see them together. "Don't yell."

He ran his hands through his thick curls. "I'm starting to lose it."

"You're lonely."

"Facing death is a lonely business."

So there it was.

"This is hell's waiting room." He gestured towards the rows of outbuildings, the dusty lanes. The first notes of a violin drifted out into the night. The second act had begun.

She shook her head. "You can't just give up."

He looked around warily. "I've stayed off the list for months, but I'm a nobody. Look at Rosen and Ziegler! They're hanging on by a thread, and you've seen how exhausted they are. I've got nothing to offer. It's only a matter of time."

Astrid stole a glance towards the camp perimeter, at the floodlights from the tower. "Has anyone tried?"

He nodded. "You don't want to know what they do to those who try to escape."

She shivered, desperately wanting him to be wrong. Who did she think she was that she could get him out? In a flash, she took off her signet ring with the Van Soelen coat of arms, and pushed it towards him.

"I know this won't get you out, but it might buy you time." Was it a fool's errand, coming here? Was she a fool loving him? She didn't care anymore.

He tried to refuse, but she dropped it into his pocket. They stood so close she could feel the warmth of his breath on her skin. He'd kiss her then, despite the risk, despite their surroundings. The heath was quiet, though the barracks were swollen with human desperation and a million stifled screams. She thought he'd draw her towards him like before, but instead he backed away slowly and began to sing the final verse of the haunting melody she'd heard earlier in the café.

> *Oh there's nothing you can do*
> > *But you'll feel a whole lot better*
> > *After you give her a kiss or two*
> > *But that...you mustn't do*

His voice caught on the last line before he turned and disappeared into the night, leaving Astrid alone.

She stood with her shoulders back until he was out of sight, and then crumpled onto the Music Hall steps and wept, her despair muffled by the cabaret.

The only free woman in Kamp Westerbork.

September 1st, 1944

Dear Carl,

How are you? The tips of the oak tree have begun to turn, and I've pulled out your mother's burgundy coat once more—another autumn and we're still at war. How is your leg? Have you been able to stretch it at all?

Are you keeping my letters? If it's dangerous, burn them. But if not, hide them so we can read them to one another when the war is over. Someday I'll fill in the details I don't have time to add right now...

You didn't tell me about Piet Van Noord! (Maybe you didn't know either. I assumed you were hiding together.) Last week, after I had finished up at the Stadhuis, I was walking home and who sidled up to me but this very strange woman—Piet! I'm sure my eyes almost popped out of my head. I didn't recognize him at all; he's very good with the make-up. The only give-away is his Adam's apple; with his scarf on he can pass as "Petra", but even then, he shouldn't open his mouth—no woman has a voice that low.

Piet told me he couldn't handle hiding any longer and that even his own parents don't know he's left the farm in Groningen. Do you think he's a fool? Are some people more inclined towards homesickness than others?

I've been to Soelenkasteel to see Lady Astrid. She puts on a good front, but she's terribly lonely and thin as a rail. I keep asking myself if I could have done something to stop Katrine; it hangs in the air between us. She'll lend me a book and say, "My daughter loved this story..." and get a look on her face, as though she's about to cry. The war has torn apart so many families, in one way or another. Papa says as long as we're safe, we'll be happy. You know what I think? I think Miss Reinhart knew better: we'll be happy when we're free.

For weeks your mother and I have been collecting the ingredients to make your birthday cake. I hope you like it. I wish I could deliver it myself, but you know how Schueller is—"the less you know"...

I miss you. I promise to send a picture once I've saved up enough money to visit the photographer's studio.

Kisses,
Hilde

31

SEPTEMBER 5TH 1944

It was foolishness, wanting to deliver it myself. You could hardly call it a cake, but with only dried potato flour and a teaspoon of molasses, it was the best Mevrouw De Boer and I could do. When Piet turned up on the doorstep of the bakery, I decided Carl and I had been apart long enough: today, I'd pester my old schoolmate into taking me to where Carl was hiding. It was his nineteenth birthday and I missed him. The Allies were coming, I felt it in my bones. If France could be freed, surely we would be rescued soon, too.

"Schueller says I should go alone," Piet said.

I walked along the Nonnenstraat beside him. I was getting tired of taking orders from men and boys. "Sure, but you'll be safer with me beside you. If we get stopped, I can do the talking."

"It won't be much longer, Hilde. He'll love the cake. How about another time?" Piet said.

I looked at my friend's earnest face, his green sundress and his women's loafers.

"Besides, what would your father say if you were caught in a room full of onderduikers?"

"He'd ask why I didn't bring some tobacco to sell them," I answered wryly.

Piet laughed, and then quickly covered his mouth with his hands. "Ha! I didn't realize you had a sense of humour."

I sighed. Papa had been roasting tobacco leaves in a barrel cooker for the past year, making a little money on the side. He taught Loti and I how to methodically turn the hand crank and keep an even heat on the pungent leaves. "People smoke to forget they're hungry," Papa said. He'd been smoking more than ever, while Loti and I continued to eat the meat he procured each week.

Piet and I kept walking, taking the back alleys because the streets were unusually crowded.

"What's all this?" he asked.

I shrugged. In the last week there had been a steady flow of families looking for houses to rent. The main street was clogged with cars, something we hadn't seen in years.

We rushed towards the dyke, where we could walk along a higher, less travelled path. Piet moved awkwardly in his dress and his broad shoulders stretched the seams. I really hoped nobody stopped us. Just the thought made me quicken my pace.

"This is against my better judgement to let you come along," he said, sweat running through the layers of powder he'd carefully applied to his face.

That's when we saw them approaching. There must have been about twenty people pulling large suitcases behind them. Some of the small children were crying, exhausted, and the parents tugged them along impatiently. Piet froze and pulled me in front of himself like a shield.

"Piet?"

"Shhh," he said. "I think they're NSB."

We crouched together in the shade of a scraggly bush. I prayed the branches would hide us and the travellers would pass us by. No such luck.

"Jongedames!" one of the men called out, spotting us. "Can you help us please?"

My heart sank. I'd have to do the talking. Piet nudged me roughly into the clearing.

"Yes?" I said. It looked as though there were three or four families travelling together.

"We're looking for the Stadhuis in Brummelo. We heard perhaps Mayor Schueller could help resettle us—"

"Where are you coming from?"

"The South. The Americans are advancing and it's not looking good." A man spoke for the group before being interrupted by another, younger fellow.

"They better let us into Germany, after everything we've done for them!"

"The windows of our homes have been smashed..." one woman cried.

A small child held up a single blue suitcase. "I had to leave my teddy behind."

Piet rose and came to stand beside me, taking the measure of the group. Before I could stop him, he uncovered Carl's cake and offered it to them.

They dropped their suitcases and sat down to enjoy the treat. I thought one of the women might cry, she looked so content to rest her legs.

"Thank you so much, this is so kind," she said.

I couldn't do more than nod curtly; inside I seethed at Piet's impulsiveness. My beautiful cake, devoured by traitors.

"We can take you to the Stadhuis and try to find you some accommodations," he said, his falsetto voice barely cracking. Still, I prayed for him to shut up before we got in trouble.

"Bless you, girls. The women and children are so tired."

Piet nodded, and linked his arm in mine as we turned around and led the travellers back to the village square.

"What are you doing?" I hissed.

Piet's eyes gleamed. "Did you see the earrings that fat woman was wearing? I think those are real pearls!"

I didn't understand. All I could feel was the crushing disappointment of not seeing Carl, and the crumbs of his gift on the ground behind us.

"We'll find a place for these people to stay alright, but not for free, no jongedame. Didn't you hear? One night's stay on the floor of Smits factory—that's a room with heat by the way—costs exactly one pair of pearl earrings. If you want to use the bathroom facilities, that's extra."

"Schueller won't squeeze the NSB, he'd lose his post," I argued.

Piet shook his head. "The National Socialists are done for in Holland. Now it's time for the rest of us to take back what's been stolen."

I thought this over. "Are these people really going to go to Germany?"

He shrugged. "Let's wait and see."

When we showed up later in the village square, there were hundreds of people milling around the Stadhuis.

"I better leave, Hilde. Too many soldiers for my comfort. Take this lot to Mayor Schueller and I'll find you later." Piet disappeared into the crowd.

"Wait…" What did he expect me to do with these people? I looked at the troupe behind me and reluctantly gestured for them to follow.

When Schueller saw me approaching, his face broke into a smile. His NSB pin was long gone.

"Thank goodness you're here. Listen, be polite but firm. Nothing's free for these traitors… but you didn't hear me say that."

We spent the afternoon directing the stream of families to various households in the village. Brummelo's citizens were not eager to help NSB families. We hated the German soldiers, but on some level we understood that many of them had no choice—they couldn't stay home and ignore the war either. These Dutch men and women had chosen to side with the Nazis, and that was unforgivable.

When Schueller cajoled the newcomers into offering their food, jewelry and other goods in exchange for a couple of nights' rest, villagers reluctantly opened their doors. Disappointment slowed me down when I finally trudged home that night. I looked up into the sky and heard a humming drone in the distance. Tonight, I'd sit with Papa and listen to the BBC on our hidden wireless. Maybe the war really was coming to an end. Was Carl outside now too? Had someone shared their tobacco with him and wished him a happy birthday? I hoped so.

I stood on the threshold of our cottage and listened for a moment. Unfamiliar voices drifted out from the living room. I opened the door and to my surprise, Papa and Loti sat around the table with a group of seven other people, all still wearing their hats.

"Oh, Muisje, you're home! Meet the Kellers. They're heading across the border and I've offered them shelter here tonight."

Papa had colour in his cheeks. He looked both nervous and jovial, and something in the pit of my stomach hardened. Tonight should have been a celebration of Carl. It wasn't easy to claim Papa was just *adapting*. Letting the NSB sleep under our roof was *cooperating* with the Nazis, wasn't it? No one was forcing us to extend hospitality. *I certainly didn't want to.*

I excused myself, begging off with a headache. As I made my way upstairs, I heard Papa offer Meneer Keller some of his personal tobacco. I wanted to run away, but there was nowhere to go.

THE KELLERS DIDN'T CROSS the border right away as planned. After hearing reports that some people had been turned back and there was nothing left in Germany, Meneer Keller balked. Papa traded Mevrouw Keller's Sunday shoes and for a while we all had meat again. It was crowded in the house, but it was the best we'd eaten in a long time. Meneer Keller wasn't a harsh man, like so many of the NSB I'd encountered. He was a pragmatist who judged it better to wait and see in our crowded cottage than to rush on to Germany with the others. We heard that thousands of NSB had fled, and the newspapers were calling the exodus madness; to me it seemed like cattle running towards a barn that was burning down.

A week later, while sitting around the radio, we heard the news that Maastricht had been liberated. I heard cheering in the streets, but Papa refused to let us join.

"It's a victory south of the Rhine, but here we must wait and see," Papa said.

I hadn't felt this claustrophobic since the beginning of the war. The Kellers had spread their belongings all over the cottage, and we were tripping over one another. Mevrouw Keller offered me my favourite salty licorice, but it didn't feel right to accept. I couldn't understand how someone could love something as quintessentially Dutch as *dropjes* and yet not be loyal to the Queen. I wanted these imposters gone.

"Papa. Can I talk to you in your room, please?" I whispered.

He followed me down the hallway and sat on his single bed. I sat beside him and took his weathered hands in mine.

"You don't think the war will be over so soon, do you, Papa?"

He shook his head. "If they'd been able to penetrate further north..." He sighed heavily. "...Without a foothold on the Waal river... no. You've heard the reports, Muisje. They may be dancing in the streets of Paris, but the Allies seem to have forgotten us."

The look of defeat on his face made me want to hold him as tightly as I could.

"But Papa. The railway workers have gone on strike again. This time, no one is backing down. Everyone is getting ready for liberation, no?" If the Allies didn't come, the Germans would launch their rockets from our shores towards England. The war would never end.

He shot me a pitying glance and I felt my insides churn.

"I wish it were as simple as that. A railway strike may paralyze the Germans, but it will cripple the rest of the country, too. If the trains don't start running again, and soon, we'll find ourselves under siege. No trains, no food."

Papa shook his head. "My job is to make sure you never go hungry. I'm doing the best I can."

I hugged Papa. His voice was shaky and I couldn't bear it if he cried. "I know, Papa. I know."

"How can you know? You're just a child, Hilde. But you need to believe..."

He shuddered, as though a ghost had brushed her fingers across his spine. "You need to trust I'm doing all this…" He gestured towards the living room, the space occupied by the Kellers. "To protect you and Loti. Everything I do is for my girls."

I leaned onto his shoulder. "I love you, Papa."

"I love you, too, Muisje."

LATER THAT EVENING, I served the Kellers dinner. They stayed with us until Gebrandy reported from London that, just as Papa predicted, the Allies were unable to gain a foothold at Arnhem. The orange pennants were ripped down from the streets as quickly as they'd been hung. The cars disappeared from the market square, yet a few families stayed on in Brummelo. The Kellers rented a house from Meneer Paul, the ill-tempered teacher, and Papa arranged to bring them produce every week. Meneer Keller invented a story about his home being bombed, that few believed, but he was affable in nature and generous with his tips at the café. Before long, people forgot about the murky origins of his arrival. *Some* people forgot, but I wrote to Carl every night, and even if I couldn't always send my letters, I wrote it all down. If I didn't, I worried I might also forget how things really happened.

I MIGHT FORGET THE TRUTH.

32

Eva yanked the turnips from the ground with such force Astrid thought she'd fall over.

"He's not himself, Mevrouw," the cook said. Though a grandmother many times over, Eva was strong and capable and never complained.

"I find it difficult to summon concern for an intruder," Astrid said, a scowl creasing her muddy forehead. These days, all she could think about was her exiled children. The young seamstress had stopped in to borrow more books, and the girl's youth cracked something wide open in Astrid. She missed her daughter. Sometimes she thought she heard Katrine's and Hans' footsteps in the castle halls. And when she looked out from her balcony to the cottage on the forest's edge, she remembered Benjamin, and an entirely different ache radiated through her body. She was surrounded by ghosts, or so it seemed.

"The tide has turned but he's in denial. I overheard some of the younger ones whispering about hanging up their uniforms and trying to head home." Eva was solemn.

After the liberation of the South, the captain had taken Astrid's beautiful wooden radio console and smashed it to pieces on the laneway. The young officers were stone-faced, but she suspected they mourned the loss of it as much as she did. The SS training facility on the other side of the forest had all but emptied of trainees in the past month, as collaborators began to waffle in their allegiance. As for the captain, he did not waver. He continued to drive to the Stadhuis every day and post new orders in the market square, as though the war could be won by plastering commands on posts.

"Don't know that they can escape, though. They're trapped here, aren't they?" Eva sighed.

The garden gate creaked.

"Shhh," Astrid said. "He's coming."

The captain stumbled across the rows of beans and potatoes and heaved his weight onto the old stone bench. His eyes were glassy. He opened his mouth and belched. Eva looked at Astrid warily. They could back away from him and scramble over the wall. But what did he want with them? Surely he had better things to do.

He sat back on the bench and studied the horizon for a minute. Reaching into his breast pocket he pulled out a silver flask and took a swig. Then, slowly, deliberately, he took out his revolver and played with the safety. The *click* echoed through the quiet of the garden, a small, terrifying sound.

"Oh, Mevrouw." The colour drained from the cook's ruddy face.

Astrid bent low to the ground and began yanking out the turnips faster than she'd worked all morning. The smaller ones she should have left another week or so, but she would not look up. She refused to give into her fear, focusing on the soil between her fingers. Eva crouched down and followed her lead.

When her bushel was full, Astrid raised her head to meet his gaze.

He was crying, the revolver back in its holster.

His ugly face was red and blotchy. He passed his flask from one hand to another, then rose abruptly and launched it against the castle wall. Eva was shaking, but Astrid straightened up and stared at his back until he ambled back into the castle.

"What are you going to do, Mevrouw?"

Do? She was standing in mud holding turnips while a Nazi tried to intimidate her in her own home, a home emptied of family. Reaching for her pinkie finger, she massaged the empty space where her signet ring had marked her flesh. She loved Soelenkasteel down to her marrow, but perhaps there was more for her and her children than the English stables, marbles floors and magnificent library. Was her imagination so small that she just couldn't conjure anything beyond the familiar walls that had kept her safe—or maybe trapped—all these years? If it was bombed tomorrow, and turned to rubble and dust, is that what she would be also?

Surprising herself, she reached out and hugged her cook.

"*I'm* going be alright, and *you* are taking the train to your niece's in the North until the war is over."

"Oh, Mevrouw. I couldn't leave you."

"You can and you must. It's an order." She pointed over her shoulder. "After all, I still have the stables to look after."

Eva got up. "Mayor Schueller can look after you."

Astrid smiled wanly. *I can look after myself.*

"Go pack. You've endured enough. I never imagined this circus would go on this long."

The old cook seemed relieved, but afraid, too. "When the war is really over, everything will go back to normal."

Astrid nodded, and waved her off.

Normal? Gazing at the four turrets, their tiles broken in pieces and the vines on the stone walls overgrown, she wanted to believe Soelenkasteel could be restored again, but she was forgetting the way the garden bloomed before everything became so untamed. She took in the vegetable garden, the iron gate, the graceful balconies. Seven generations of Van Soelens were buried beside the wild thickets of this garden. But dead bones belonged to the past.

Astrid closed her eyes and tried to imagine the future, but all she saw was a pair of green eyes. The eyes of a man she'd been helpless to save.

"You mustn't despair, Lady Astrid," I said, pushing the tract towards her.

She shoved it into her desk as though it were on fire. "You're foolish to deliver these, Hilde. Do you want to get yourself killed? Stick with what can help you survive." She pointed to the dungarees. "These, for example, are the best trousers I've ever owned."

Lady Astrid was as thin as a willow branch these days. It would take time to properly adjust the pants I'd made for her. No one else would bother, but she had the money, while in the village people simply added another hole to their belts. I wondered if Katrine and Hans had lost weight, too.

"How are Katrine and Hans, Mevrouw?" I asked.

"The captain is furious my son left 'without saying goodbye,'" she said. Her face brightened. "I send him packages with our friend the mayor." She dropped her voice. "But Hans can't write back, and not knowing how he's managing is terrible."

"Cheer up. Even at the Stadhuis people whisper that the war is turning. He'll return before you know it." And Carl, too, I hoped.

Lady Astrid just shook her head. "The new soldiers that they've moved into the castle are younger than you, Hilde. One of them, a boy named Otto, apologized to me in the kitchen the other day. *I'm sorry about all this, Mevrouw.* Can you imagine? That gave me some hope, I'll confess. You can't win a war with a soft heart like that, can you?"

A conflicted enemy might be weak, but my mind was on the villagers, whose desperation grew more palpable every day.

"All I know is that you can't win a war if you're starving. Did you know in Amsterdam they're eating the canal swans?"

Lady Astrid shuddered. "You must think it's silly to have my clothes taken in when people are starving."

I wasn't sure if it was a question, but I needed her guilders so I changed the subject. "Have you heard the Mosquito planes flying at night?"

She nodded. "Schueller says it's the sound of rescue, but I'm not so sure. One thing is certain—it terrifies the Germans. The officers have whispered about men abandoning their regiments, and I can tell you for a fact it is happening, even here. Each time one of them leaves, some of the silverware goes missing!"

"And the captain?"

"He swears he'll kill them if he finds them," Lady Astrid said, her voice cracking. "But these new recruits are just boys."

I wanted to give her a hug, but the flash of vulnerability disappeared and she straightened her back. "As if we needed more corpses. Now then. You must take more books. Meneer Van Laar always said you were a bright creature."

"He did?" This was news to me. I'd hardly exchanged more than pleasantries with Katrine and Hans' tutor.

Lady Astrid nodded wistfully. "You were good for my daughter, Hilde."

I winced. My arm was scarred because of Katrine. Lady Astrid was all alone in this drafty castle. Meneer Van Laar…I couldn't think about it.

"I should go. I have more of these to deliver," I said, patting my bag.

"It's foolishness you know. I thought you were smarter than that."

"You just said Meneer Van Laar found me clever."

Lady Astrid inhaled deeply and shook her head. "Please be careful," she said finally.

"Always," I promised.

I HEADED SOUTH towards the Van Popta farm. A wiser person would have quit. We heard the Allied planes every night; soon we would be free. I could have gone home and looked after Papa, mended things with Loti and forgotten about the Resistance. Of all the terrible things I saw during those war years, I wish I could have kept walking that day, delivered Trouw later. But the Van Poptas looked forward to the news bulletin, and instead of heading home, I turned up their lane. That's when I saw him.

He stepped out from behind the barn, his back to me, the same Landwachter who had led the SS to the De Boer's bakery in the spring. I froze. I looked around for a place to hide. In the middle of the yard was a lone oak tree, but all the lower branches had been hacked off for fuel. I'd never be able to climb it.

Bang!

A scream lodged in my throat, choking me. Throwing my bag into the brambles, I scaled the trunk, grasping the bark until it ripped through my skin, gasping when I finally reached a branch to hoist myself higher. As more shots rang out behind the barn, I climbed higher, hidden behind the leaves. A man cried out. Oh God. I couldn't make out his words. It could have been a defiant cry of allegiance to the Netherlands. He could have been crying for his mother. It was his last breath on earth.

When the shouting stopped, I heard car doors slam. A black Horch roared out of the lane and for the longest time, all was quiet. I stayed in the tree for hours until a woman began to wail. Slowly neighbours trickled down the lane to the farmhouse, and then the priest. When darkness fell, I finally shimmied down, my legs shaky.

I gathered my bag from the hedge and ran home as though I were being chased. When I finally arrived on the Nonnenstraat, the cottage was empty. Papa? Had he gone out to look for me? Where was Loti? What would I tell them? I washed my scraped hands and hid the tracts between bolts of denim. My teeth chattered. Curling up on the sofa I squeezed my eyes shut. Who had they killed in Van Popta's barn? Fathers, brothers, sons. Could Carl have been hiding at that farm? A headache pounded behind my eyes, pulsing with a ferocity that made me think I was going blind.

It was close to ten o'clock before Papa, Loti and Schueller burst through the door.

"Where were you?" Papa cried.

Schueller shook his head almost imperceptibly.

Loti scowled and put on the kettle. "Visiting your boyfriend again?"

Papa stared at me, confused. "Hilde?"

I couldn't tell him what I'd seen. I couldn't tell anyone.

"Not that fool Otto, the new young officer staying at Soelenkasteel?" Schueller said.

Something in his gaze willed me to nod. Loti turned and stared at me, her eyes narrowing. Papa slumped into a chair at the table.

"I thought you didn't like the Germans," Papa said.

"It was just a walk in the woods, but then we heard gunfire, and it wasn't safe." I began to cry.

Papa got up and put his arms around me. "Why would you sneak around like that?"

Because I wanted the war to end.

Because I wanted to help.

Where was Carl? I needed to know if he was still alive or if he'd been murdered in a pig barn. I leaned my head on Papa's shoulder and he placed his coat over my shoulders. Tears streamed down my face. I wiped a fist against my eyes.

Papa held a hand to my cheek. "You're feverish."

Schueller was staring at me, his eyes impossible to read. There was no way to tell him what I'd seen.

"I'll take my leave," he said. "Get well soon, Hilde."

I nodded and pulled Papa's coat tight around me.

How could anything ever be well again?

33

SEPTEMBER 1944

A thousand Jews a week, every Tuesday at eleven. They called out numbers, then names, sometimes both. It took a long time, this gathering on the roll-call ground. "Silence!" the police shouted, but prisoners still whispered, "Oh, it's them. God have mercy." Benjamin watched as families left the gathering platform, clutching one another tightly. "They've passed the *F's, G's* and *H's*—we're safe for another day."

Astrid's ring had bought him six weeks, but each time he lined up he wondered if today was his day. Already he'd remained at Westerbork longer than he'd thought possible. He'd watch the trains depart and sometimes feel a strange curiosity to leave the sandy heath, just to know for certain what his fate would be. He'd paid one of the Jewish police officers to search the records for Nathan's name, only to discover his uncle had been sent to Bergen-Belsen almost immediately after he'd arrived.

At first, he wanted to get onto the next train east to find him, but Willy and the others said he must stay as long as he could in Westerbork. "No one who's gone east has ever written to us here." So Benjamin made himself useful, hoping to survive, pushing down the guilt of living when his uncle was surely already dead.

At one o'clock in the morning, in early September, he heard the names of the orchestra, the dancers and the pianists called out from his barrack leader, who then turned to him.

"Rosenblum!"

He looked at the barracks, where he'd slept with about three hundred other men for the past six months. The top bunk had been his private oasis amidst the misery, and already someone else was moving into his place. Probably the straw pillow and mattress had already been stolen.

He followed the other men from number sixty-three towards the train, thinking of all the lives he'd already lived. He remembered an old family portrait his father had taken at a picnic by the sea, just before his parents died. He thought of his uncle at the cafeteria on the Plantage, spoiled by the friendly waitress who always gave them extra gravy. "Too skinny," she'd say. *If she could see me now.* Lastly, he closed his eyes for the briefest moment and thought of Astrid. He pictured her the day they'd sat pressed close together watching the Sinterklaas parade, the day he decided he'd win her over. How he'd loved watching her face transform as she tried to maintain her composure, only to burst out laughing. He'd always remember her that way—the moment her lips twitched and the real Astrid emerged—beautiful, reserved, vulnerable.

As he was jostled along, men and women stopped to examine the train.

"This train's not going to Auschwitz!"

"The Goldblatts were sent to Sobibor last week, where is this transport going?"

"Is this a trick?"

Rumours swirled around Benjamin. Maybe it was a covert American rescue, maybe the artists were going to another camp to perform. Nobody knew anything, and the police weren't giving them any information. They pushed and shoved those with suitcases onto the trains, their faces expressionless as ever. Those who'd come to say goodbye shouted encouragement.

"Safe travels! Save a good bunk for me when it's my turn!"

"Don't eat everything at once!"

"May God go with you!"

Benjamin found a place to stand on the train and surveyed the men around him. There wasn't a soul he knew by name in the cramped carriage; he'd lost track of the men from his barrack. The engine whistle blew and the carriage trundled backwards, leaving the camp. The wooden windows had been sealed shut, though light seeped through the cracks. Benjamin strained against the walls to see where the train was headed, but he couldn't get his bearings once they'd passed through the first villages. The men began to argue about which way they were headed. Some thought it was certain they were en route to Poland, but others suggested the train had turned slightly north, and perhaps they were headed to one of the rumoured work camps within Germany.

The men took turns standing and sitting, each one trying to rest a little despite their worry. When it was Benjamin's turn to sit, he noticed a man furiously writing on a small card.

"What are you doing?" he asked.

"Letting my friends know we've left Westerbork," the man replied. "We're approaching a town. If you listen, you can hear the sound of other trains in the distance."

The man stood, kissed his note, and pushed it out between the slats of the carriage. "Someone will pick it up and mail it. They do that, you know. The villagers walk the rails and mail our last letters."

Our last letters.

Benjamin closed his eyes. Men and women had been running around the camp frantically filling containers with water and making food parcels. When should they eat? He was hungry now, or perhaps it was his nerves. He felt the boiled egg in his pocket being crushed against his leg by the swell of bodies. How long would they be travelling? Staring at the bucket in the middle of the carriage, he wondered how long until it filled with piss and vomit, or worse?

"What time is it?" a burly man inquired.

"We traded our watches in long ago," replied a bald man with a smart blazer and well-worn trousers.

"Come on. One of you has a watch! I'm sure of it." The man surveyed the group, challenging them.

Finally, an older gentleman sighed and took out a gold pocket watch. The other men's eyes widened. "It's only three o'clock in the afternoon."

The men groaned. The watch-keeper had weary eyes. "We'll be on this train another day or more, unless one of you young fellows can open that hatch and climb out."

Benjamin looked up at the roof.

It was suicidal.

The train was travelling fast. There were whispers all around him now, a palpable excitement. Could they do it? The burly man summoned another fellow and crouched beneath the hatch. A third man braced himself above them. Finally, a fourth man, a skinny lithe teenager, balanced himself on the trio and set to work forcing the hatch open. Benjamin marvelled at the suitcases of stolen or bartered items. If they could make themselves useful wherever they were headed, they had a chance. They had more tools than food: corkscrews, pocketknives, pens and even a dull screwdriver appeared on the carriage floor. The teenager grabbed the screwdriver and jabbed it under the hatch.

There was a great creaking sound, and then miraculously it opened.

They began to laugh as the fresh, crisp autumn air swirled around, filling their lungs with hope.

The watch-keeper, the elder of their group, spoke. "We must wait until dark."

"The young ones must go first," another added.

"We need a ladder," the screwdriver owner suggested.

The next hours were filled braiding a rough ladder from their undershirts and securing it to the hatch. Benjamin was energized by the vigour of these thin and haggard men. He felt proud to be among them. They told one another stories as they worked, where they'd lived and loved, and even, what they hoped for in the future. He imagined himself running through a forest, eating mushrooms and wild apples and finally, making his way back to Astrid.

As night fell and the train continued on, an orthodox man offered up prayers on behalf of the entire transport. Then it was time. The first up was the teenager, Johan. He climbed the rope quickly and looked about to survey the land, and assess whether the guards could see what they were doing.

"The train is moving too quickly," he concluded. "We have to wait until it slows down for a bridge or a tunnel."

"We haven't got all night!" another man protested.

Now that the chance of escape was there, the men were anxious to get out, despite having no idea where they were.

The watch-keeper asked for calm. He instructed Johan to keep a lookout and for the rest of the men to be patient. It made sense to Benjamin to wait until the train slowed, but he was terrified of heights. What was the sense of escape if he broke his leg and ended up dying alone in a field? If the others had the same fears, they said nothing.

At ten minutes to midnight, the train slowed. The moon shone brightly and Benjamin and another man used the screwdriver to pry open the window and survey the landscape. Gentle, sloping mountains surrounded a village, or what he imagined was a village. He thought he could make out a church steeple. There were no lights on in Germany, either. Only moonlit shadows outlined the world outside.

"There's an aqueduct or something coming up," Benjamin reported.

"The train is slowing," another man said. "Let's do it now."

The watch-keeper nodded.

Johan climbed the ladder once again, hoisted himself up and was gone. Benjamin watched his dark figure roll onto the grass, get up and run towards the forest.

"He made it! Keep going!" Benjamin encouraged.

A dozen men, one after the other, scurried up the ladder, jumped into the fields and ran off.

"The aqueduct is right up ahead, wait until we're past." Benjamin looked at the fifty odd men surrounding him. None of them looked patient.

He and a few others waited by the window and scanned the darkness for the next opportunity. The shadow of the mountains promised sanctuary. The train couldn't go much faster if it was headed into the hills. When they cleared the aqueduct, he gave the go ahead. Another five men climbed out the hatch and escaped. They might have all escaped were it not for the coat.

His name was Jaap. They learned later that he was a teacher who had volunteered for the transport in place of his wife and son. He climbed the ladder without hesitation, but when he jumped, his coat caught on the metal rails and he fell upside down and screamed. Through the cracks in the boarded-up window, the men saw his body swing past and heard the thud of his skull against the side of the carriage.

Though he was already dead, his cries garnered attention. An instant later they felt bullets fire past their carriage.

The old watch-keeper bravely climbed up the ladder. He took a knife and without a moment's hesitation cut the dangling man free. They listened as soldiers yelled obscenities from the rear wagon into the darkness. The watch-keeper closed the hatch and took down the ladder.

The burly man who'd asked the time a day earlier was the first to speak.

"Are we going to try again?"

Another man nodded. He looked longingly at the hatch. "My wife is Dutch. She's still in our home. I promised I would return to her."

"You'll sooner meet her in heaven," another said. "Forget it. It's suicide. The soldiers will pick you off like rabbits if you jump now."

They sat together in silence again, the sounds of Jaap's terrified screams still ringing in their ears.

Very quietly, the watch-keeper untied the rope and laid out the shirts. A few men wept openly, but most could only silently claim their shirts and wait for what came next.

A half-day passed. The carriage smelled of shit, sweat and fear. The train pulled to a stop.

"Where are we?" a man asked.

Benjamin squinted through the slats. Low brick walls stood in the distance. This was an old building, some kind of fortress.

"This is where they held Gavrilo Princip," said the watch-keeper. "The man who killed Franz Ferdinand."

"So, if we're not in Poland…" Benjamin said.

The man shook his head. "Czechoslovakia. This is Terezin…though the Germans call it Theresienstadt."

How many people were here? Would they survive?

The old man's eyes grew watery, as though he knew Benjamin's fears. His shoulders began to tremble and then he reached into his pocket and took out the piece of Jaap's coat he'd cut from the roof. He rubbed it between his fingers, whispering a prayer. *Be'ezrat hashem.*

With God's help.

Benjamin took the old man by the arm and led him towards the entrance, towards the sounds of Yiddish, Czech and German. Painted on the arch were the words *Arbeit Macht Frei*. Work Makes You Free.

"To the Sluice!" someone yelled.

Sluice? He looked at the old man.

"Now they sort us, Benjamin."

"Again?"

"They will never be done sorting us, my son."

34

At the end of my shift, the old woman with the braided crown of white hair returned to the Stadhuis and approached my desk. Before I could begin the charade of asking how I could help her, she slipped me a heavy envelope. Inside, I knew there were more than a hundred copies of Trouw. She didn't have to warn me what would happen if I were caught. Every soul in Brummelo had learned of the massacre at Van Popta's farm. When Papa found out, he'd gone into the greenhouse and stayed there all night. Van Popta was a good man. He sat four rows ahead of us in church. And now his pew was empty.

When I left the Stadhuis, it took a minute for my eyes to adjust to the darkness—how I missed the streetlights. I found my way through the village's cobblestone streets. *Post them wherever you can*, the old woman advised. *But always be on the lookout.* A light drizzle began to fall, chilling me to my bones, but the fog made it easier to slip the tracts into postboxes and onto telephone poles.

I'd circled back to the market square and was ready to head home when I spotted Piet through the mist. For some reason, he'd abandoned his disguise. He strode quickly along the sidewalk two blocks away. I didn't want to frighten him, so I quickened my pace and followed to see where he was going. He pulled his cap down low and disappeared down an alley. Though I hurried, I lost him in the fog and darkness. Disappointed, I turned to head home when a pair of hands seized me, covered my mouth and pulled me into a dark room.

"Shhh. Don't say a word."

I struggled to break free but now there were two of them. I thought of Papa and Loti. I wondered where they'd leave my body when they were finished with me.

"*Bitte*," I pleaded. *Have mercy*. My shoulder bag fell to the ground and the tracts scattered onto the cement floor. It was so cold.

"Hilde."

I froze.

"Carl?"

He lit a candle and then other faces emerged in the darkness. Piet, Carl and four other men stood around the bare room. He gathered me into his arms and apologized.

"You shouldn't be here," he whispered. "Why on earth are you wandering the streets now?"

I showed him the nieuwsbriefs and pointed to Piet. "I spotted him darting out from the market and followed him."

"Sorry. I didn't know she was behind me," Piet said sheepishly.

"Good thing it wasn't one of the SS night watchmen," another man replied. The men started arguing in low, terse voices, pointing at Piet. "You could have got us killed, idiot!"

I stared at Carl in the semi-darkness. His cheeks were sunken but his eyes were warm.

"Can I sit down for a moment?"

Carl and I crouched on the floor together with our backs against a cement wall.

"Where do you sleep?"

He pointed to a mat a few feet away and smiled wryly. "It's a bit close to the pot, but we're safe and dry so we try not to complain."

I followed his gaze to a porcelain bowl just as a mouse scurried around it.

"Who is taking care of you?" *Why wasn't it me?* He'd changed in the months we'd been apart. He no longer had the face of a boy. I missed him more than ever.

He shook his head. I could feel the other men staring at me, willing me to leave, or at least to stop asking questions.

"It's late." He took my hand and held it. Leaning close to my ear he whispered, "It's good to see you again. I like your hair. It looks like—"

"Lana Turner?" I asked hopefully. All the girls wanted to look like the beautiful American actress now.

He looked at me blankly. "Who?"

I laughed. "Are you kidding me?"

"I haven't been out much," he said.

"Of course," I said, feeling dumb. "Can I come back?"

He shook his head. "The more people who come down this alley, the riskier it is for all of us."

"I know." *There's no resistance without blood.* "I know about the risks. I was there."

He stared at me blankly. "Where?"

"Van Popta's."

His eyes widened. "No..."

Tears spilled onto my cheeks. "I thought maybe you were hiding there. Schueller told me you weren't but I couldn't help but imagine..."

Carl was quiet. The other men were pretending not to eavesdrop, but I knew by their silence they'd heard everything.

He stood up abruptly, taking my arm to help me to my feet. "You have to go."

Pulling me close, he kissed me hard. I backed towards the door and, when it was all clear, let myself out. The streets were empty. I quickened my pace, resisting the urge to break into a sprint all the way home. I rehearsed my excuses for Papa as I walked across the square but my thoughts were interrupted by a loud droning sound. I looked up into the sky and saw vapour trails for miles around. An explosion rang out, and then another, and pieces of a plane—or perhaps two?—spiralled down towards the canal. A window from the convent opened above me and a nun peeked out.

"Get off the street!"

Metal debris rained down onto the cobblestone in front of the basilica and carved a hole into the three-hundred-year-old lane.

I ran and tripped, landing hard against the ground. I touched my forehead. It was wet and sticky. I wiped my hands on my skirt and pushed a handkerchief against the pulsing gash. I had to get to the Nonnenstraat. The stench of burning metal in my nose made me sick to my stomach. Finally, after who knows how long, I pulled myself up and limped home.

When I finally arrived at Number Eleven, Papa was in a state.

"Muisje! Where have you been?" Papa looked at my bloody skirts and the wound on my head. "Oh God, what's happened?"

I burst into tears.

Loti's face turned ash white. She ran to get a towel to wash my cut. When she placed it on my head, she began to cry. "Oh, Hilde. Was it one of the soldiers from the Stadhuis?"

I shook my head, confused. What was she talking about?

"There was a plane crash," I answered. I tried to tell them about the craters on the street, but my head was pounding, and the words came out jumbled.

"Why didn't you wait to walk home with your little sister?" Papa turned to Loti, accusing.

Loti stammered. "She stays late to help Mayor Schueller—"

"Run Hilde a bath," Papa instructed. "No more unnecessary errands on your own, either of you. The man is risking your lives sending you here and there, and especially after dark—"

"But Papa, the money—"

Sirens blared into the night. The fire brigade and an ambulance wailed down the Hoofdstraat. The tail of a damaged plane had rained down on me, but where had the pilots landed?

He waved his hand. "We'll find it somewhere else. I won't lose you."

Papa.

He was the one drinking jenever with Meneer Keller at the table, offering vegetables to the captain, disappearing late at night.

I'm not the one who's lost.

35

"They're perfect!" Astrid declared, running her hands down the seams of her denim pants. "Kurt, you must admit, the girl is a genius."

They were once again in Astrid's chambers, Schueller smoking contraband cigarettes while Astrid admired herself in front of the mirror.

"Why couldn't she deliver this to me herself?"

"Hilde's father has forbidden his daughters from running errands without his permission. They had a scare with that downed airplane and now they're only allowed to go to work and straight home again."

Astrid shook her head. Life was strange. She'd wanted to keep her children close, and they'd gone. The seamstress roamed the countryside and now…

"Who will deliver her tracts?" she asked.

Schueller's eyes widened.

"Don't look so shocked. I haven't been living under a rock."

"No, just *in* one," Schueller muttered.

"Well?" she persisted. She would not admit that she'd come to look forward to the young girl's visits. Maybe she could have a word with her father…

"I need to ask you a favour," Schueller said.

"That makes two of us," she said, patting her apron. "I have another parcel I was hoping you could get to Hans. So, what is it that *you* want?"

"I need food, Mevrouw, and you have a cellar full."

"How much?"

"A little bit here and there. Hilde did more than just deliver tracts, and her charges are getting hungry."

"Oh," she said. No wonder the girl was always in a rush to leave. Astrid looked out the window towards the east tower. "I'll show you what I have stored up for the winter, but we must be careful the captain doesn't see us."

"I wouldn't worry about him today," Schueller said. "There's an important general in town touring the training centre and I have it on good authority the captain has gone to meet him."

"Fine. Follow me." She grabbed her coat and the heavy iron keys and they made their way to the tower at the edge of the garden.

The stone stairs to the cellar were covered in a thin layer of ice. They trod carefully towards the door before she noticed the lock had been severed. They looked at one another in confusion.

"Astrid?" Schueller whispered, pushing open the door.

The shelves were bare. The floor was cleared. Every last bushel of potato, rutabaga, carrot and cabbage was gone. Even the apple barrel had been emptied. Astrid slid to her knees and put her forehead against the wooden drum.

"Tell me this wasn't you," she said.

Schueller paced the floor. "It looks like I wasn't the only one who knew you had food."

She stood up and brushed the dirt from her knees, pointing to a message etched in coal on the wall. *Oranje zal overwinnen.* Orange shall overcome. The Resistance motto she'd seen scrawled across the propaganda posters of the occupiers.

"Who did this?" she asked.

"I don't know."

"Come on, you know everything that's going on."

Schueller grew agitated. "All the small resistance groups—the OD, the LKP and the RVV—they've all joined forces under Prince Bernard to overthrow the Germans. They call themselves the *Binnenlandse Strijkrachten*, the Interior Forces—"

"And are you working with them?" she asked.

Schueller shook his head. "I do my own thing, Astrid. It's not always easy to know whom one can trust and, as you know, my efforts haven't always been successful."

She thought of Benjamin, alone at the camp. Schueller had done his best and it wasn't enough. So there were other groups. For a moment she let herself be pulled into a fantasy where brave citizens would storm Westerbork and rescue the prisoners. But she shook off the thought.

"Will the Queen send potatoes along with weapons?"

Finally a little smile. "Wouldn't that be nice?" He ran his hands through his hair. She could see it had shaken him to have to revise his plans. He was not someone who liked surprises. "Astrid, if things get desperate, I could find you a few ration—"

She waved him off. "The soldiers are bringing me dead animals they've hunted in the woods. I suppose I'm to spend the winter skinning rodents..." She shivered at the thought.

Schueller reached for her arm. "*Kalm*, Mevrouw. The end is in sight. Those dirty moffen will be gone from here before spring."

"I hope you're right," she said. "What am I supposed to tell the captain when he arrives?"

"Tell the young soldiers about this and *they* can tell him."

Astrid thought of young Otto and his apologies. He was liable to get a beating if he broke the news to the captain that there was no food. No, she would tell him herself. The teenage soldiers were making her soft. It was their unshaven faces. She couldn't look at them without feeling an unnatural desire to give them a horse and send them on their way back to their mothers.

They closed the cellar door and walked side by side towards the laneway.

"I need to return to the Stadhuis," Schueller said. "Will you be alright? The captain knows where he can get food. Your lovely seamstress' father has a garden…"

The last thing Astrid would wish upon Hilde would be more contact with the Germans. "Maybe the captain will be too drunk to notice the shortages…"

Schueller frowned. "I have a guest room if you feel—"

Astrid shook her head. "I can take care of myself."

"So you've told me once or twice," he said wryly.

She held out her parcel. "For Hans."

He hesitated, looking over his shoulder, though they were alone. "I really can't do this anymore…yesterday someone was following me all afternoon."

"What did you do?"

"I went for a very long walk, and returned home."

"You'll manage."

"Has anyone ever told you you're not the centre of the universe?"

She smiled. "I think you just did."

He sighed.

"I trust you." She pushed the parcel towards him and he stashed it under his jacket.

"More the fool you!" He got into his truck and closed the door.

"I do appreciate the risks you're taking."

"Risk! I plan on lining my pockets with the profits from Soelenkasteel someday."

"The eternal optimist."

"A good businessman always takes the long view. There's no reward without risk."

"How much longer can you placate everyone?" she asked. *Especially when it's clear you don't even know who all the players are?*

"They haven't got me yet, have they?"

His insouciance was genuine, but Astrid was left haunted by one single word.

Yet.

36

OCTOBER 1944

"The water's *brown*." The man at the pump looked at the trickle coming from the spout. He kicked the dirt and cursed. Another man yelled at him to hurry along.

"It always is. Bit of rust. Keep moving!"

Benjamin stood in line with hundreds of men behind him, waiting to fill their buckets at the single pump in the centre of the yard. Dark circles ringed his eyes. For a month he'd been sleeping in the Sudeten men's barracks, under the eaves. The bunks were stacked three high, his mattress a bed of straw covered in flea-infested rags. Though the barracks had been disinfected, lice and bedbugs crawled over his flesh, and despite his fatigue, he often woke in the night unable to fall back asleep.

It went on like this every day. Benjamin would fill his canister with the stale water that came from the marsh surrounding the village and bring it back to his room. He ate watery soup and coffee for breakfast and then reported for work. At one hundred and thirty pounds, he was still in relatively good health, so he'd been assigned to pull a cart through the streets and clear the paths with a broom and a shovel. His partner Filip, a teenager from Prague who spoke German, taught him some words in Czech. Most of the prisoners were Czech, but he felt less lonely if he could manage "good morning" and "thank you" in their language.

One day, as they swept the streets around the *Brunnepark*, Filip said, "Professor, did you know this town was built for soldiers and their families?"

Benjamin nodded. "How many people do you think are here now?"

"The leader of the *Ghettowache* says we're up to ten times the original population…" Filip heaved a shovelful of dirt into the cart. "But that will change soon."

"What do you mean?"

"They are going to send people east again," he said, dropping his voice. "A thousand at a time."

Benjamin straightened up. "How do we stay off the transports?"

He couldn't be sent east, not after getting this far. He was sure the war was almost over and he needed to get back to Astrid. He regretted that he hadn't kissed her goodbye one last time.

Filip was full of useful information. "The Germans are terrified of disease. Stay healthy, stay useful. Nobody needs a professor of economics here, but since you speak German you might be able to find another job that's less backbreaking."

"What kind of job?"

"From what I can see, they never send the craftsmen, work crews, policemen or firemen onto the transports." Filip looked towards the *Central Markplatz*. "The men in the records department, mostly those with connections to the Jewish Council, are also safe for now." The teenager sighed like a much older man. "But they thought they were safe in Prague too, and here they are."

"Don't you have any good news?" he asked Filip.

Filip knit his eyebrows together and shrugged.

"Well, I do," Benjamin said. "Didn't you hear the announcement from the camp commander?"

"No…"

"Tomorrow's our lucky day. Everyone gets to change their underwear! You'll give me yours, and I'll give you mine—" Benjamin barely had time to duck before the dirt flew from Filip's shovel over his head.

"You're an imbecile," Filip said, but Benjamin could see he'd made him smile, and the kid was handsome when he wasn't so serious. Without some kind of distraction, their own fear would be the end of them.

Benjamin thought about the artists and musicians who'd been sent here from Westerbork. He hadn't seen them at all since he'd arrived. Here, there was no cabaret, but the men whispered about a pianist—a woman who played for the sick and elderly in the Council Hall. When he asked Filip about her, the boy was adamant.

"Don't go there," Filip advised.

"Why not?" Benjamin asked.

"Some people think they can be saved because they're special. But no talent or bar of gold will save you here. It's better to be a nobody. Keep your head down and stay out of the way."

Benjamin wondered if his new friend was right. They steered their cart around the bodies that had been laid out in the night. If the corpses belonged to the elderly, Benjamin said a prayer for their souls and continued down the street. But more and more the dead were children. Filip would shovel faster when they passed them, not looking at their uncovered faces for even a second in case he passed a friend. It horrified Benjamin how quickly he'd learned to close his eyes to the realities of garrison life. Even the youngsters were matter-of-fact as they blessed their friends, leaving flowers on their bodies as though they were saying goodbye to a beloved pet.

A WEEK LATER, the *Zimmeralteste*, the dorm elder, told Filip he was on the next transport to the East. He packed and repacked his bag many times, pulling his cap down over his eyes so Benjamin couldn't read his expression. He promised he'd stand with him in the line, but Filip told him, no: keep working. Nevertheless, Benjamin snuck down to the crowd and watched as the Jewish Police counted out the passengers. Filip was at the very end of the line, and no guards stood nearby to keep order.

Run! Benjamin thought.

As though he could sense his presence, Filip pulled his fedora low one last time, looked over his shoulder and slipped out of the line into the crowd. The police continued counting, and when they arrived at the end of the line, they discovered they hadn't met quota. The engine was going and there was no time to waste. A huddle of young girls waved to their friends on the train, scarves and handkerchiefs blowing in the wind. Two minutes later, the police grabbed them and shoved them on as well. A mother screamed out for her daughter.

"You can't take her! She's not on the list!"

"She doesn't have her suitcase!" said another.

But the police ignored the protests and the train rolled out of Theresienstadt, the day's transport complete.

Benjamin walked away from the crowds and found his cart. He was shaking. The prisoners returned to their barracks in a daze, more stunned now than ever. When the dorm elder saw Filip that evening, he said nothing, but he took both Filip and Benjamin off the cleaning crew. Benjamin thought he'd seen misery before, until the next morning, when they were re-assigned—to the crematorium.

37

DECEMBER 1944

Papa's work clothes were caked in dirt, but he no longer bothered to brush it off. He would come in from the garden, forget to take off his clogs, and sit at the table staring off into space.

"Papa, eat something," we pleaded, but his once healthy appetite was gone.

"Take a bath, Papa," Loti cajoled him. When she succeeded, I would do his laundry, iron his pyjamas and send him to bed with a warm brick. We tried our best, but he wasn't sleeping. He sighed in the darkness long into the night—I never thought I would miss his snoring, but I did.

One morning, Loti and I sat down together on the wooden bench in the garden. He'd managed to start a winter crop, and spent long hours raking the elevated beds in the humidity of the greenhouse. He puffed away on his pipe, pungent tobacco smoke coiling under the glass. While outside the earth had hardened once again, Papa stayed warm in the silence of his garden, planting the precious seeds he'd saved from previous harvests.

"We have to help him," I said, massaging the scar on my forehead.

The cut from the night of the plane crash had healed, leaving pink skin over my left eyebrow. When Loti was changing the bandages, I begged her again to forgive me. I knew she heard me, but she said nothing, only biting her lip and carefully cleaning my wound. The next day, she checked on it again, though it had already begun to scab over and heal. I began to hope we might become close again. After all, there was one thing we both agreed on: something had to be done about Papa.

She squeezed my hand and pulled me into the greenhouse. "You do the talking."

He looked up from the soil when we walked in.

"Papa," I began. "There's a small Christmas market in the square this afternoon. Would you like to take a stroll with us?"

He put down his tools and blinked hard, as though trying to remember what day of the week it was.

"Perhaps that would be nice." He removed his cap and scratched his head. His hair needed a good wash. "I suppose we could do that."

Loti beamed as though we'd been awarded a ribbon at the fair. "Let's go."

HALF AN HOUR later we strolled into the village, our arms hooked through his, to admire the Christmas booths. There wasn't much to see, and we had no money to purchase any of the second-hand trinkets anyway, but Papa's spirits seemed to lift with each step along the way.

"Hello there, Meneer Zontag!" boomed Mayor Schueller from across the square.

Papa started, jolting my arm, and when he turned to greet Schueller his smile was pinched. "Good morning, Mayor."

"I suppose the girls are trying to convince you to buy them some sweets—"

Papa untwined himself from us and took Mayor Schueller by the shoulders, drawing him aside, his face pale.

"I can't stop thinking about those poor men…"

Schueller shot a worried glance in my direction.

Loti put her arms around Papa. "Shhh, Papa. It's alright now."

"Which men, Meneer Zontag?" Mayor Schueller asked, his voice low.

"Even if you weren't from that town, if you were walking nearby, they put you on the train with the rest of them. *Six hundred men*, Mayor. Six hundred."

"Putten," I whispered. "They rounded up all the men and boys and sent them to the camps. Only the women are left."

Schueller lowered his head. "The Resistance shot a German Lieutenant and the reprisals were meant to send a strong message."

Papa's breathing grew faster. "They burned down one hundred homes!"

I looked from Papa's face to Schueller's. We'd been hearing about the events in Putten for weeks. On the rare nights Papa slept, he'd awake yelling, confused and terrified. His fear was written in the deep lines across his forehead.

"Mayor Schueller, the Chief of Police was asked for ten hostages, and he refused."

Schueller stared at Papa. "What are you getting at, Meneer Zontag?"

"The Germans went to the Stadhuis and asked the clerk for thirty names—"

"And the clerk did his duty, and gave up *nothing*," Schueller said tersely. "Just as I would do, if such a thing were ever to happen here in Brummelo."

"But you are an NSB mayor, the NSB supports the Nazis—"

"Every mayor in this country threw their lot in with them. It was the price I paid to keep working." He lowered his voice, just in case. "If I've had to wear a new badge or uniform to perform my duties, I've done so out of obligation. The day I can no longer serve the citizens of Brummelo, I see no purpose in belonging to any party." Mayor Schueller's smile disappeared. "We're living in exceptional times. We have had our share of tragedy here, too. Look at what happened at Van Poptas—"

"But these men were innocent!"

"Surely you don't believe the men in Van Popta's barn were criminals?" Schueller said.

"I don't know. I don't know." Papa rubbed his forehead. "But those women need their men. Who will take care of them now? Homeless? Fatherless? Promise me this won't happen here, sir. Promise me!"

Mayor Schueller took a deep breath. "I will always look out for your girls, Meneer Zontag."

Papa shook his head violently. "No! That is *my* duty. There are troublemakers here in the village... secret newspapers, onderduikers, railway workers... who knows what else? What if they burn Brummelo to the ground because of these agitators? We must protect our homes and families."

A few shoppers had stopped to stare at Papa. He spoke so passionately tears streamed down his cheeks. He wanted Mayor Schueller to assure him *our* village was safe from the pot of Nazi rage poised to boil over and scald us all. I felt suddenly very lonely. He was supposed to be brave and comfort us. Why couldn't Papa be stronger?

"Papa," Loti gently whispered. "Let's go home now."

"See you later, Mayor Schueller." If I could manage to get out of the house.

"Gone, gone, gone..." he mumbled.

Once we arrived back at Number Eleven, Loti poured him a glass of oude jenever, the good stuff. He gulped it down and announced he had more work to do. We watched him trudge back out to the greenhouse, lost to us again.

I picked up the liquor. "Where did you get this?"

My sister hesitated. "Kaspar."

I stared at her blankly.

"One of the guards at the Stadhuis. You've passed him a hundred times, Hilde."

"This is an expensive bottle."

She shrugged. "It might help Papa relax. You see how bad he's gotten."

I felt sick to my stomach. "Why did Kaspar give you this?"

Loti scowled. "It was a trade, Hilde. Let it go. You're not the only one with secrets around here."

"Is he your new boyfriend or something?"

Loti let out a bitter laugh. "Ha! As if I'd tell you."

My sister stormed out of the kitchen and went upstairs. I was all alone in the kitchen. The fire in the small stove had gone out. I found some wood and rebuilt it. I began to make soup to keep myself busy. Had I been wrong to lie to Frid? I thought the worst thing that could happen was for my sister to fall in love with a Nazi, but at least Frid would have assured Papa we were safe.

Watching him through the window, bent over his trays in the greenhouse, I saw his back was still strong, the body of a younger man. But though his muscles were taut, his mind was fraying. For Papa, everything outside of his glass box was terrifying. On Sundays, he sat nervously in our pew, but no longer socialized after the service. Instead, he was eager to get back to his seedlings and plants. Few people talked to him, knowing he wouldn't consider hiding their sons and nephews, and Papa sought out no one. The community that had held us up since Mama's death now kept their distance, mistrust clouding their wary gazes.

I selected a large potato for the soup stock and cut it into tiny pieces. The kitchen filled with the scent of bay leaves. My stomach grumbled. I wished Papa could believe that help was on the way. I wanted to tell him about the rumours of weapon drops, the orange armbands and the plans for more sabotage, but what would he do with such knowledge? Would he keep us locked up forever? I wished he could feel the hope I felt when I read the nieuwsbriefs. The only promise Papa clung to was the green shoots of his winter crop.

I sat down at the table and chopped turnip and onions while the soup simmered. I was warm. I was safe. I should be grateful, but instead my insides churned. I looked at the jenever. What *had* my sister traded for this nerve tonic?

In the beginning, it had all seemed so clear: Right and wrong. Dutch and German. Occupiers and Resistors.

Now, everything was murky. In trying to protect Loti, I'd hurt her.

In trying to protect us, Papa had rolled a stone between himself and the world, between our home and the village, waiting until the predator passed by. My brave and wonderful Papa, who could reassure me in the early days of aerial bombardments with a hug and a story, was now a frightened recluse who refused to bathe. This is what 'making the best of things' looked like. And yet, who was I to judge him? I'd heard with my own ears the woman's screams at Van Popta's. I knew what resistance sounded like. Who was I to say he didn't have every right to be terrified? Maybe I was the one who needed to feel more fear.

I was so focused on chopping the onions I didn't hear Loti slip back into the kitchen. She was standing right beside me before I realized she was back, and by then tears were streaming down my face.

"Don't try to tell me it's the onions," she said softly.

I wiped my cheek with my sleeve. "I'm so worried about Papa."

Loti nodded. "He needs us. Both of us."

"He thinks he has to sleep outside so thieves don't steal the plants in the night," I sniffed. "When the Germans first arrived, he was scared, but he figured out what to do to get by." To get ahead, even.

"And now?"

"The war will be over soon, but Papa still believes everything the Nazis shout from their blasted loudspeakers. He thinks they are going to be here forever."

"He's confused. He's mixing up his delivery schedules." Loti rubbed her forehead with her fingertips. "So…what should we do?"

I put down my paring knife and turned to my sister. We were now the same height, but Loti would always be prettier.

"Please stop hating me."

Now it was Loti's turn to cry. She sat down at the kitchen table and buried her head in her hands. "I miss him."

I placed my hand tentatively on her shoulder. "Maybe we could go to the captain and try to track him down?"

Loti shook her head. "Do you even know where Tunis is, Hilde?"

Somewhere warm and sandy? I admitted I wasn't sure.

"I haven't received word from Frid in two years…"

"The Allies took back the French colonies on the Mediterranean."

Loti stared at me. "Good for the French."

I didn't start the war. I was sorry for hurting her, but he hurt people I loved. Ari and Hannah hadn't seen their parents in two years thanks to Frid. *Hold your tongue, Hilde.*

Loti sighed. "How's *your* boyfriend?"

"What?"

"Oh, come on. I know that somewhere in all your sneaking around you're still seeing polio boy."

"Don't call him that."

Loti smiled. "So you admit it? You're still seeing him?"

I wouldn't bite.

"After dinner, I'll cover for you…if you want to take him a Sinterklaas treat."

"That's nice of you."

Loti nodded. "He's not dead, you know."

"Pardon?"

"Frid. He's still alive." Loti put her hand over her heart. "I feel it."

Could she forgive me if he *was* still alive? I turned my back and concentrated on the soup once again. My chest felt tight. I remembered one of the headlines from a *nieuwsbrief* about a year earlier. The Luftwaffe had lost almost half their aircraft in the North African sorties, and a quarter million men had surrendered to the Allies. Maybe Frid was one of the lucky ones. I didn't wish him dead—I didn't—but I still hoped to God Loti could forget him.

It was dark when I snuck out of the cottage. Papa and Loti were sleeping and the street was covered in a thin layer of snow. I made my way through the alleyways back to the granary where Carl was now hiding, checking behind me to see if my footprints were obvious and hoping the *Landwachters* were in bed for the night. I buried deep in my mind the thought of six hundred dead men. I would be careful.

Gently I pried open the storage door and slipped into the loading dock of the warehouse. High windows let a sliver of moonlight into the large room. I walked towards the canvas bags of seed and looked around for signs of life. The granary was full of striking railroad workers and others who were on the run. I sat down and waited for him to come to me.

My head grew heavy after twenty minutes. I leaned against the wall and decided to wait another half hour before leaving.

"Hilde."

Carl smiled at me in the semi-darkness. His handsome face was lined with fatigue and pain.

"I brought you a few candies," I said. "But you look like you need medicine."

"Just a bit of muscle pain." He shrugged. "I haven't been moving around as much as I should. Tight quarters this week."

I was getting better at finding him. Even Schueller didn't try to stop me anymore. If I was going to risk everything running flyers around town late at night, this would be my reward.

Carl looked at me sympathetically and sat down. "I missed you."

I massaged his leg where the muscles had seized up and told him about Papa's worries.

"Mayor Schueller told him Seyss-Inquart won't back down on the blockades. Papa's convinced we'll remain under German control even if other countries are liberated. He can't find even a scrap of hope to cling to."

Carl listened intently and pulled me closer. "Close your eyes."

I did as he asked. "Where am I?"

"We're sitting beside a river on a wool blanket. It's spring."

I began to relax. "I can hear the birds. The sun is shining on my face."

"I brought a picnic basket. Would you like a sandwich?"

I could almost taste the croquettes and mayonnaise between two thick slices of bread. "Mmmm. Can we go for a swim afterwards?"

He smiled. "I would love to see your bathing suit."

I opened my eyes and swatted him. "All our picnics end the same way."

"Why else do men go on picnics?" He laughed and I did, too.

It was cold and I could see my breath, but I didn't want to leave his side. He took my hand in his. From his pocket he took a piece of rough string, the kind used to secure bundles of wheat.

"What's this?"

"This is me asking you about our future," he said.

I blinked.

"Hilde," he said, tying the string around my ring finger. "Will you wait for me? I want to marry you when this is over."

I wrapped my arms around his neck and buried my face in his shoulder. "Yes. Of course. Yes."

He held my face in his hands and looked at me seriously.

"Listen to me. I'm so proud of you. You are brave and beautiful and the only girl I ever want to picnic with…"

"But?" My stomach clenched.

"Don't come looking for me anymore."

I stared at him in disbelief.

"Even if Piet tells you where I am, I want you to trust me that it's better for everyone here if you don't keep trying to find me."

"How can you ask me to be your wife and make me promise to stay away? That's cruel!"

Carl shook his head. "You can't marry a corpse, love. The Nazis are losing and their cruelty is unpredictable. Everything your father fears, from the Putten raids to on-the-spot executions, can happen."

"Don't talk like that!" I cried.

"Shhh. If you can find a way to take care of Ari and Hannah, do that. Visit my mother. Take care of yourself and I promise to come back to you when this is over."

"Are you leaving Brummelo?"

I understood his hesitation as a yes.

"All of these people living underground need food."

"I miss seeing your face."

He was quiet for a moment, and then his eyes lit up. "I have something for you." With some difficulty he rose and limped into the shadows, rummaged around in a suitcase and came back with a passport. I opened it and saw Carl's picture with a different name typed inside.

"Not a bad looking fellow," I said.

"Not a very good forgery though. I was too afraid to use it because the stamp isn't as crisp as it should be. Here." He took a knife and cut the photograph from the passport. "Keep it. That way you'll have a picture of me."

I had an idea. "Give me that knife."

Confusion crossed his face. I took it from his hands and cut a lock of hair from underneath my ear.

He leaned in close to my head and whispered. "By the time your hair grows back, we'll be sharing a bed together."

I closed my eyes to keep from crying. "I love you."

"And I, you. Remember—"

"I know… I can't marry a corpse."

"Nor I."

We kissed goodbye and I pulled my jacket tight against the cold. When I rounded the first corner, I looked behind me and all was quiet. I exhaled and quickened my pace. When I arrived on the Nonnenstraat, the stars were out and I thought to myself, *I'm going to be Carl's wife*. I began to hum under my breath and as Number Eleven came into view, I skipped up the front steps and quietly let myself into the kitchen.

His pipe smoke stopped me in my tracks. Papa turned from his chair and looked me up and down.

"Where have you been?" he roared.

I stood still. "Papa…you'll wake the neighbours!"

"If it weren't for the neighbours I'd have no idea my daughter wasn't in bed." Papa began patting my coat and purse. "What have you got? What kind of activities are you up to, Hilde?"

I shook my head. "Nothing, Papa. I just wanted to get some—"

He wrested my purse from my hands and dumped it onto the kitchen table. Carl's photograph lay atop all my personal effects. Slowly, he picked it up and examined it. His lower jaw began to tremble. When he looked up at me his eyes were red-rimmed and watery, the exhausted eyes of a man at the end of his rope. A man who believed they would burn down his house.

"Do you know what they do to those who shelter onderduikers, Muisje?"

It would have been useless to plead ignorance. He wasn't the only one with nightmares. Phantom gunshots woke me more often than I would ever admit. I would hear them for the rest of my life.

"They bring them to the churchyard, tie them to the iron fence and shoot them."

I shivered.

"And then, in case people don't get the message, they leave the bodies bleeding into the pavement for days as a warning to others who might be inspired to help."

"Papa, I'm not trying to get anyone in trouble…"

"Enough! Girls who don't want to get into trouble stay home!" With that, he opened the stove door and tossed my only picture of Carl into the embers. I watched the tiny paper fold, melt and turn to ash.

"I'm sorry, Papa."

I went to embrace him but he stood stiffly and stared at the fire, unmoving. After a while, I left him alone and went upstairs to sleep. I dreamt of large ovens where men tossed black and white photographs into the flames and the smoke swirled into the night sky, a vapour that rose upward and disappeared into the darkness.

38

The warnings were posted everywhere throughout the streets of Theresienstadt. On the doors of the Magdeburg and Dresden women's barracks, the Sudeten men's barracks, the children's homes—the typhus notices filled Benjamin with dread. Day after day, more victims of the epidemic arrived at the crematorium. The supervisor, a cold SS man called Heindl, went to the Council of Jewish Elders and demanded more workers to keep the oil-fuelled ovens operating day and night. The small, hot crematorium swelled from four workers to almost twenty.

One day at shift change, Benjamin was able to pause for a moment with a Slovak doctor who spoke German.

"It's the overcrowding," the doctor said, rubbing his eyes. "Doesn't help that there's not enough water of course."

"Are there treatments?" Benjamin asked.

"We've nothing stronger than the aspirin that's been pilfered from the new arrivals." The doctor paused, backing away ever so slightly. "Why, are you feeling unwell?"

"No. I'm fine. Just tired. Good evening, doctor."

He'd trade a day's meals for just one aspirin to ease the aching muscles in his back, but if he stopped moving, he'd be the next one laid out on a wooden gurney. He put his head down and kept going. He imagined the purple heath of the Veluwe, and Astrid riding ahead on the sandy path. He tried to remember the smell of her skin while the stench of death threatened to overwhelm him. Sometimes he could escape into his memories. Other times, Filip's urgent questions brought him back to earth.

"Do you think we can catch it from the bodies?" Filip asked one day, his brow creased with worry as he gazed upon a young man about his age. By now, they'd lost count of how many corpses they'd handled since they'd been sent here.

Benjamin could see that just the thought of contagion was making Filip a little crazy, even with their masks. His gaze wandered over to the Slovak doctor in the adjacent autopsy room.

"We need the powder he's got, whatever it is."

"I'll get some," Filip promised. "When the guards aren't looking."

"Be careful. If they catch you—"

"You should know by now I don't get caught."

Benjamin didn't think it was kind to remind him that he was no longer a courier for the Resistance in Prague, but an undertaker in hell, also known as Theresienstadt.

A stroke of luck gave them a chance. The Germans suddenly began to make bonfires in the meadow outside the crematorium and the guards were called in to help, allowing Filip to slip unnoticed into the infirmary and pocket a tin of powder.

"What are they doing out there?" Benjamin asked.

Filip shrugged. "Burning papers. Who cares? Look at this stuff." He spread some of the talc on his scalp and lice jumped out.

"Oh—" Benjamin was revolted, but he also wanted to try some. His head was crawling.

"It kills the buggers. It kills *everything*."

That night they spread it sparingly on their bunks. While their days remained the stuff of nightmares, sleep was once again possible. If the Slovak doctor noticed that his supply of insecticide was dwindling, he turned a blind eye, earning him Filip's devotion.

. . .

"I THINK I'd rather be digging graves," Benjamin said one evening. Sweat from the heat of the ovens poured down his back.

"The ground is too marshy," Filip informed him, as he painstakingly printed individual tags for each corpse.

They lowered their voices as the guards passed by to inspect their work. Transferring the ashes to the urns, they plucked out any gold and gave it to the guards. Benjamin hoped Filip wouldn't try to keep some for himself. The end was in sight, and if he could keep the boy out of trouble, they would both survive to see it.

IN THE EARLY days of February, a train arrived in Theresienstadt. Benjamin heard it pull in while he was loading an elderly man into the oven. He made it a habit to never look at the victims' faces, but this time he did. His heart sank. It was the watch-keeper from Kamp Westerbork. He felt a rush of tenderness for the old man, and thought then of his uncle Nathan, who'd been taken three years earlier.

"Rest in peace," he murmured.

A sudden commotion in the annex made him stand up straight. The other workers put down the makeshift coffins and went outside.

"What's happening?" Benjamin asked.

The Czechs ignored him and instead gestured excitedly at the train and the passengers in the distance.

Where was Filip?

Finally, he caught a word he understood. *Die Scweiz*. Switzerland. Switzerland! He couldn't believe it. Could the rumour be true? Some people were leaving for Switzerland? He felt hopeful, jealous, angry, doubtful.

They stood outside watching the procession until the police returned and forced them back inside.

"Was it true? Was the train headed to Switzerland?" a man asked one of the policemen.

The policeman shrugged. "What does it matter to you? Your work is here."

Benjamin stole a last look outside and spotted Filip. He trudged behind the guards leading a procession of children across the field. They marched towards the back of the crematorium. The other workers wore puzzled expressions on their faces. Why were the children being brought out of the ghetto? Filip stood at the door of the columbarium where the urns were kept. The children formed a line from Filip towards a waiting truck. They passed cardboard boxes down the line, one after the other.

They're going to empty out all the ashes, Benjamin realized. Though he should have known by now, every new revelation of treachery injured him. Why bother with the artifice? Why make people believe their dead would be given dignity, only to cart their ashes somewhere else? And then, his despair turned to anger. Why make the children suffer?

He left his post, and without thinking stormed towards the lineup. The children looked up. One of the little girls was crying. He went to her and knelt down on the cold ground.

She held out the box and read the tag. "It's *Muti*," she said in German.

Benjamin pulled her into an embrace. He looked up and saw that Filip's face was pale. Maybe today would be the day they shot him. He didn't care anymore. If he died holding this child, so be it. He could be a father for one moment. Benjamin didn't believe in freedom anymore. The train to Switzerland was probably another cruel trick, just like the rows of labelled urns. What a fool he'd been to believe he could survive this.

"You! Back to your post!" a policeman yelled.

The girl shivered and Benjamin gently pushed her back into the line, nodding encouragement. After a moment, she passed her mother's ashes to the next child and the procession resumed.

Benjamin slowly rose from his knee to face the policeman. "I suppose now you're going to throw me in prison?"

The guard hesitated, and Benjamin thought for moment the man sympathized with him. But then his face twisted into a snarl.

"The jail's full," he said. "Get moving."

Benjamin turned and began to walk. When they rounded the corner of the building, the guard raised his rifle and brought it down hard against Benjamin's skull. He tumbled to the ground. For a moment he felt the taste blood of blood in his mouth, and then blackness.

39

I felt so old towards the end of the war, and later, after the children were born, I'd look at them and wonder, was I ever so young? I can't remember. I felt such heaviness on the mornings I spent at the Stadhuis in the winter of '45. Mothers would file in to receive food vouchers and I'd send them on to the soup kitchen in the empty factory. The children were so gaunt; they walked as though in pain. Dokter Freisen taught me a word that still haunts me: oedema. Children whose limbs were swollen at the joints walked with stilted steps, their skinny arms listless at their sides. With so many people dying, we sometimes forgot to mourn the other losses. Youth was a luxury the war stole from us, and like a thief in the night, it seized what was most precious, leaving a trail of broken dreams behind.

At the Stadhuis, housewives tossed rumours back and forth while waiting patiently in the queue. Their haggard faces and fragile hopes broke my heart.

"Soon the Red Cross will deliver bread and margarine," they whispered.

"Just a bit longer and the Swedes will help us out," one woman said, cradling a jaundiced baby boy. I couldn't look at him; he didn't cry like a normal child and his face was as weary as an old man's. Like Papa's, I realized with a start.

When the vestibule emptied, Mayor Schueller came over and offered me a cigarette. He knew I didn't smoke, but the break gave us an excuse to share a bit of news. A week earlier a general had survived an attack outside of Apeldoorn, pretending to be dead. The mayor was fascinated with this story and spoke of it whenever the Germans were out of earshot.

"He just lies there in his own blood, in his BMW, and survives! It's something out of a novel."

"But it's not a novel. They've hauled out over a hundred people from the prisons in retaliation, and there could be more." The story reminded me Papa was right, we were all vulnerable.

Schueller grew somber. "I know. I know. And I still haven't managed to get Van Veen out of Amersfoort."

"He's been there for so long I've forgotten the sound of his voice," I said, remembering my own night in prison. "His wife wishes he'd been sent to Germany. At least there they don't haul you out when the Resistance starts shooting people."

He winced. "I know, believe me. I'm trying my best."

We smoked in silence. He knew the risks, especially the risks of charming the Germans by day and conspiring against them after dark.

He got up and put out his cigarette. "Let me know if you hear any hacking coughs. Doktor Freisen worries tuberculosis has come to the village."

"People sneeze in here all the time!"

"I know. Wash your hands immediately and advise them to go to the free clinic. People can't fight off illness living like this."

For women, war was one lineup after another, and I was the one telling them where to stand next. I wasn't sure I could take it much longer. "Have you been to the factory lately?"

His eyebrows knit together. "Not a happy place, is it?"

"Yesterday a woman dropped her soup on the ground and scraped it back into her pan." I shivered. "She *licked* the floor in front of all her neighbours!"

He wiped his forehead with a handkerchief and sighed. "What upsets you most? That she licked the floor or that her neighbours saw her do it?" He smiled at me in his crooked way. I could never be sure if he was teasing or reprimanding.

"The Allies are coming," I said, as if I knew what generals were planning any more than the next person.

"I hope you're right," Schueller said. "Otherwise there won't be anyone left standing to run the country."

I showed him the list of people who'd applied for assistance. Some had travelled from as far as The Hague. "Every day there are more and more people pouring in from the West looking for help."

He grimaced. "No one will admit how many civilians are dying."

"What, you mean the Germans won't admit it? Why would they?" I caught sight of the jaundiced baby again and rage coursed through me. I was so angry I forgot the gnawing sensation in my own stomach.

"Not just that…families are burying their loved ones in their yards under the snow to keep the ration coupons," Schueller said.

My hand flew to my mouth. "You're joking."

He shook his head. "Saw it with my own eyes. Did you ever go to school with any of the Colijn children?"

"Not Gert?" Please, not sweet little Gert.

Schueller nodded sadly. "His mother came in for ration coupons but she couldn't stop crying. Finally I got the truth out of her."

"How did he die?"

Schueller shrugged. "Weak lungs. I guess that's what starvation is called now."

I fought back tears. "Those ration cards are almost worthless. There's nothing to buy anywhere!"

He looked out the window towards the large farms on the edge of town. "These people from the cities have prams and wooden carts full of belongings they'll try to trade." He sighed. "But you can't eat linens."

I laughed bitterly. "Speaking of people coming from the city… Katrine is back."

He seemed surprised. "Why?"

I shrugged. "I think she needs a job, but I haven't spoken to her. Lady Astrid sent word."

Schueller's furrowed brow turned into a deeper frown as the captain walked into the Stadhuis. He hadn't spoken to anyone in days, preferring to smoke non-stop, pacing in his office and listening to the radio reports from Berlin. The younger soldiers whispered amongst themselves that he was agitated by the Allied bombings. His belligerence inspired his men to patrol the outskirts of the village, far from the Stadhuis.

The clock struck two and I tidied up my desk and grabbed my coat. Just then, Papa appeared. Ever since the night he'd burned Carl's passport, he often dropped in to check on Loti and me. I tried not to feel suffocated by his attention. He cares for us, Loti said. He doesn't trust us, I thought.

"Hello, Muisje. Is your sister here?"

I glanced behind me towards the door that led to the small holding cell. There weren't any prisoners today, only Kasper the guard and a small table set up for playing cards. Papa couldn't see her with him.

"I'll get her. Wait right there."

I found Loti sitting on Kasper's knee. She jumped when I opened the door to the tiny cell and quickly buttoned up her shirt. Kasper said nothing but seemed hesitant to let her go.

"Papa's here to take us home. Get your things." I refused to make eye contact with the German.

Loti followed me out to the bright reception area and looked around for our father.

"Where is he?"

I turned and saw Papa shaking hands with the captain. My skin grew cold.

He drew himself a little taller and walked towards us, leaving the German rocking on his heels in front of his office.

By the time we got outside, I could no longer contain myself. "Papa. What were you discussing with the captain just now?"

He shook his head. "I was checking to see if he needed more vegetables at the castle this week—"

"But didn't you do your rounds yesterday?" I asked.

He shrugged and kept walking.

Loti frowned. "Let it go, Hilde."

But I couldn't. We arrived at home and Papa retreated to the greenhouse. Loti prepared lunch and I stood in the doorway sick to my stomach. I leaned against the wall to steady myself and noticed Papa's wool overcoat had a jagged tear along the side that wasn't there before.

Lifting the hem, I examined the damage. The scent of him—soil, tobacco, sweat and worry—were soaked into the rough fibres. I'd clean and repair it, and try to mend things between us, too.

I was filling the washbasin with cold water and vinegar when Loti walked in and asked what I was doing.

"Don't forget to check the pockets," she suggested.

I slid my hand into the silky folds of Papa's wool coat and found a handful of blackened zinc coins, a handkerchief, a pack of seeds and a page ripped from the ledger book. I laid everything on the front hall table and carefully unfolded the paper, assuming it was the weekly orders.

Except the people on the list weren't customers.

In Papa's elegant, old-fashioned handwriting were the names of twenty-three males, including Carl De Boer. In the peacock blue ink he favoured, Papa had identified the *onderduikers* and an address: 65 Tingen. Smits' factory! At the bottom of the sheet, as though he'd written a grocery list, were his calculations: 23 x 50G = 1150G.

I ran out onto the street and threw up.

I tried to think fast. What if I was already too late? What if the captain had already sent his men?

"Loti?" I called back into the kitchen.

"What's wrong, Hilde? You're as pale as a ghost."

"I'll be right back. Don't wash the coat; I'll mend it first. I just need to borrow some heavier thread."

Before my sister could protest, I grabbed two turnips and took off running towards Smits factory. When I got there, breathless, the matron scowled at the sight of me.

"My father wanted to send a couple turnips to add to the soup," I panted.

"Oh, he did, eh? He's decided *now* is a good time to help feed his fellow citizens and not just the moffen?"

A few by-standers shot dirty looks in my direction but I ignored them. I was trying to find a door to a backroom, a staircase... anywhere that would lead me to Carl. I glanced around, panic closing in on my chest. Desperate, I leaned close to the matron.

"I'm looking for Carl De Boer. It's urgent."

After what seemed like an eternity, the matron's eyes darted towards a landing on the far side of the factory. I followed her gaze and nodded. If that's all she could give me, I had to hope it was enough.

"You can leave those turnips over there," she said, breaking her gaze and turning back to her watery soup.

I slipped into a hallway and crept towards the back of the building. It was dark and eerily quiet, but I kept going. A creaky iron stairwell curled up two stories. Looking over my shoulder, I made sure no one was following me. It was freezing. If the furnace didn't heat this part of the factory how did the onderduikers keep warm? At last I spotted a large metal door with the word 'storage' crudely painted across it and I knew I'd found them.

The door was locked tight. There was just enough room to slip my identity card underneath. I waited. The silence dragged on. And then, finally, someone pulled my card from the other side and it was gone.

"Hilde!" Carl opened the door a crack and beckoned me inside.

Once again, we were together amidst a crowd of men in hiding. In storage, I thought bleakly, for life after the war. Piet looked up from a chess match. His opponent was Hans Stenger, Lady Astrid's son. I began to sob uncontrollably.

"Shhh, love. What's wrong?"

"I can't take this anymore. He's changed so much," I cried.

He waited. "Your father?"

I told him about the list and watched his face lose all colour. I understood that he wanted to hold me, his eyes told me so. But there was no time. The captain's men could arrive any minute.

"Thank you," he said.

I looked down at my finger where he'd once tied a string engagement ring and swallowed a sob. But I could not bring myself to say *you're welcome.*

40

Late one afternoon, a bleeding carcass greeted Astrid when she stepped into the kitchen to light a fire under the cauldron. The young officer Otto emerged from the scullery.

"Can you prepare this, Mevrouw?"

She looked at the animal and her stomach tightened. Eva would have known what to do. If only she hadn't sent her away.

"I would take care of it but we have to go." He dropped his voice. "The captain has a special assignment and needs us all at Smits' factory, so we probably won't be back until late. But I sure would love some rabbit stew…"

A gnawing hunger in the pit of her stomach matched her longing for her own son. Where was Hans? Did he have food? "Go on," she said, gently. "I'll see what I can do."

He waved and ran off. She looked out the window and saw him jump into a jeep full of young soldiers. Otto was barely inside before it took off down the lane towards the village.

An hour later, Katrine appeared in the kitchen and spotted the carcass. "What are you doing?"

Astrid was at a loss as to where to begin. "Making rabbit soup."

"You?"

Astrid didn't answer. It was strange having her daughter back after six months of separation, six months of silence. No letters, no telegrams. And now here she was looking for work. She'd been polite; like a stranger, like a guest.

"I might be able to help," Katrine said tentatively. "I assisted quite a bit on the surgical ward in Apeldoorn…"

"I think this one's beyond saving."

"Ha."

Katrine picked up a sharp knife and with a swiftness that surprised Astrid, cut off the feet, head and tail and proceeded to pinch the creature's neck to make a clean horizontal cut. Astrid was fascinated.

Deftly she peeled away the fur, showing greater care than Astrid would have. "If you pierce the stomach, the meat is ruined," Katrine said.

Astrid nodded.

"Same goes for the bladder and colon," she added, methodically gutting the rabbit, naming its organs one by one. She wasn't talking to Astrid so much as to herself, as though she were under examination.

"Do you enjoy nursing?" Astrid asked.

"I do, but I miss it here."

Katrine had hurt her once, but she had nothing to hide anymore.

"I missed you, Mother," Katrine continued, not looking up from her work.

Astrid blinked. "I'll throw this in the pot and head out to the stables. Thanks for…"—she pointed to the rabbit—"…your help."

"I'll get changed and meet you there." Katrine headed upstairs.

Astrid had her back to the door and was rinsing out a bloodied rag, her nose filled with the primitive odour of rust and guts, when she heard movement near the oven.

"Did you forget something…?" She looked up. The captain rocked on his heels in front of the hearth. "Oh. I didn't hear your car."

He stumbled across the kitchen and stood close to her. "I was at the factory."

Astrid tried to ignore him. She didn't want to know what for. But he was determined she take an interest.

"My men and I were looking for troublemakers, and I found this." He held out a distinctive hardwood rook.

Astrid's eyes widened. It was from Hans' Indonesian set.

"Where's my son?" she whispered.

"That's what I'd like to know," the captain said. "I think it's time you stopped keeping secrets from me, Mevrouw. I've had a very disappointing afternoon."

He circled the kitchen and paused to pick up an onion. He tossed it back and forth and then laid it gently on the table.

"My wife liked to cook onions slowly. She'd add a bit of sherry and pour them over homemade bread…"

She didn't trust a nostalgic captain. Arrogant, abrasive and cruel she was familiar with. He gazed at Astrid and took a step towards her. The expression on his face was cold. The flash of gunmetal at his side made her grip the counter.

Astrid swallowed. "I'm sure she'll make you that when you return."

He exhaled. "My entire family lived in the centre of Dresden, which, perhaps you've heard, is in ruins."

She'd forgotten where he was from, until now.

The captain lunged towards her, his breath sour. "Ruins! The perfect little house I bought for them. And all this time I've been playing the fool."

She sidestepped him and backed around the counter as he chased her clumsily, ducking left, then right.

"You upper class women think you're so special. In your castles…"

"You're upset—"

"But underneath those fancy clothes, you're all the same."

Astrid's body tensed. She dashed towards the ovens. He followed her, closing the distance between them.

"Why don't you admit you're dying to feel a real man? Now that your dirty little Jewish lover is long gone."

Astrid looked into his wild eyes and froze. If he knew about the botched Portugal plan, what else did he know? Her skin grew cold despite the heat from the fire.

"You think I didn't see? I see *everything*. I knew since the day we arrived here your good-for-nothing husband wasn't coming back—not because of the Japanese, but because of his Indonesian mistress, which by all accounts at the Hunt Club, is an open secret…"

Her fear evaporated and was replaced by anger and humiliation. How dare he taunt her? Before she could stop herself, she slapped him across the face.

It took a second for him to react.

"*Kalm,* Mevrouw. We don't want our first time to be like that, do we?" he sneered.

"There isn't going to be a first time, captain." She whirled around and grabbed the boiling cauldron's long arm and held it between them.

"If you take a step closer, I'll make your face uglier than it already is," she warned.

He stopped and rubbed his holster. "I've always liked feistiness, but if you throw that stock, you'll waste good soup, and the boys will be upset their dinner was ruined."

It was all the provocation she needed. With a deep breath, she heaved the contents of the cauldron towards the captain's head. The hot liquid arced across the space between them, but he darted out of its path and the soup landed on the floor. They both stood still, Astrid shocked that she'd missed, the captain shocked that she'd tried.

"Tsk, tsk. It's more pleasant if you relax, I assure you."

"*Hilfe!*" Astrid cried out.

He seized her by the arm.

"Do you think my men would barge in here to help *you*? I am their commander. They do as *I* say, and men must have their small pleasures, *ja?*"

His fingers bruised her arm as he pushed her against a wall. Astrid was all alone in the castle; she heard her cries echo against the bare walls. He tore at her apron and skirt. He was stronger, but she pushed him away.

"That's enough!" He held her by the throat with one hand and loosened his belt with the other.

"Yes, that is enough." Katrine appeared at the door with Astrid's pistol aimed at the captain. "Let her go," she said, her voice cold and steady.

He froze, and slowly reached for his own weapon. "Is your aim as lousy as your mother's?"

"I've never shot anyone before. Let's find out."

A bullet sailed past the captain's head and ricocheted off the wall. Both Astrid and the captain ducked for cover.

"I've only got a few more bullets, so next time I won't miss," she said.

The captain recovered and lifted his gun towards Katrine. In a split second, Astrid dove on him. His eyes widened, and he threw her backwards towards the stone fireplace. Pain seared through her head, and she was aware of warm blood in her hair. *This is it.*

A second shot rang out.

A body dropped onto the ground.

Astrid's vision blurred and the room faded to black.

41

An official summons, sealed with a Nazi stamp, arrived that evening while Loti was at choir practice.

"I'm wanted at the docks," Papa said, casually retrieving his coat from the hook and examining my stitches closely.

"You're a good seamstress, Muisje." Papa kissed the top of my head tenderly. "Save some meat for me. I'll be back later."

Mother!"

Cold water hit Astrid in the face. She opened her eyes. Katrine knelt in front of her and held out a clean rag.

"Hold this on your head."

Astrid looked around the kitchen. What had happened? The floor was covered in soup. She glanced towards the island and inhaled sharply.

"Did he...?" Astrid braced against the wall and pulled herself up.

"No," Katrine answered quickly. "He dropped his gun when you attacked him and I picked it up. When they find his body, they'll think it was a suicide."

Astrid stood over him and shook her head. Katrine had shot him in the chest. "I doubt that." She shivered. Now what?

Katrine spoke up. "We've got to get rid of the body before the others return. We'll tell them he went back to Germany to find his family."

"The captain a deserter? Even if we convinced them, how would we explain why his car is still here?"

They leaned against the wall, shoulder to shoulder.

"You saved me," Astrid said.

"I saw him pull up when I was on my way to the stables. He seemed agitated, so I followed him."

Astrid nodded.

"How did you know where to find my pistol?"

"Hans showed me once... before...," she stumbled. "Before I let you down."

She put her arm around her daughter. "Shhh. Listen carefully. Go upstairs and pack a suitcase, and quickly."

"But Mother, we need to stitch your cut..."

Astrid waved dismissively. "Put on as many clothes as possible and if there's anything at all you would like, just take it."

Katrine shook her head. "I don't understand."

"Trust me for once!"

Katrine backed out of the kitchen and ran up the stairs. Astrid wrapped her apron tightly around her head. She walked towards the black Horch town car and opened the gas nozzle. With an old rubber garden hose she siphoned petrol into a soup tureen. She stumbled back into the castle and poured it over the captain, the entire kitchen floor and the old wood cabinets. Then she ran upstairs.

Astrid's suitcase had a broken latch, so she pulled down the silk curtains from her bedroom window and laid them on the bed. She swaddled up her best clothes and the photographs from the mantelpiece. What remained of her jewellery was buried beneath the stables; she'd come back for it someday, perhaps. She closed the door to her bedroom and turned to find Katrine coming out of the captain's room.

"What are you doing?"

"Checking to see if he had any money," her daughter replied.

"I don't want his money."

"Me neither, but we have to eat."

Astrid relented. "Are you ready?"

"I'm scared."

"Go and saddle up two horses. Let the others free—whip them if they don't want to leave the stable. I'll join you shortly."

"I don't understand what you're doing, Mother."

"I'm taking care of what's mine," Astrid answered. She drew herself up and held her daughter by the chin, pausing for a moment to look into her eyes. "Go."

Katrine ran down the stairs. Astrid heaved her improvised sack over her shoulders and laid it on the bench in the front hall. She then returned to the kitchen, but refused to look at his body. Instead, she walked along the far wall towards the fireplace and with a pair of heavy iron tongs, retrieved a glowing log. With care, she placed the log on the floor next to an antique cabinet full of china. Eva had polished the old wood religiously, and the layers of oil caught fire quickly, spreading to the floor and licking the cabinets. The room filled with smoke, but Astrid was transfixed. She didn't want to leave until she was sure it didn't burn out.

When the flames touched the ceiling she grabbed her sack, ran out and found Katrine.

"Mother?" Katrine looked at the castle, anguished.

"Let's go," Astrid said, gingerly mounting a young gelding. A trickle of warm liquid escaped from her turban. She wiped at her head and her hands were red.

They galloped towards the forest and only looked back once they reached the heath. At first Astrid thought she heard the thundering of a German tank rolling down the road, but it was the castle snapping and crackling. The smoke clouds coming out of Soelenkasteel were dark and dense, with flames bursting through the windows and reaching the roof of the east wing. The fire roared like a beast. The horses edged closer to the woods, skittish.

After an eternity, they heard the sirens of fire brigade.

42

I SAVED HIS DINNER, but Papa never returned.

As soon as the door closed behind him, I ran and got my own coat. After a moment's hesitation, I pulled on Papa's wide-brimmed hat. Sneaking out through the garden, I bolted down the alley and headed towards the dockyards. There was no one in sight.

The German barge had been anchored in the canal all winter, its massive berth hiding the dockyard from view. An old windmill stood at the eastern edge of the canal, abutting the docks. I climbed the ladder to keep watch from the stage.

No sooner had I hidden myself from sight when Papa appeared, striding down the Hoofdstraat. He headed towards the docks.

From the shadows of the barge, another figure emerged. I couldn't see his face, but even from where I crouched, I could tell he was uneasy. He didn't have the ramrod-straight back typical of the soldiers in town. Narrowing my gaze, it was obvious his uniform didn't fit right—too short on the legs, too broad across the shoulders. The uniformed man saw Papa approaching.

"Heil Hitler!" Papa saluted.

"Heil Hitler!" The man coughed. "You have brought something, *ja?*"

My stomach clenched. Surely Papa would notice the soldier's accent was off.

Papa unfolded a piece of paper from his pocket and handed it over.

The soldier quietly scanned the list before tucking it away. He handed Papa an envelope.

My heart contracted. Suddenly, I couldn't breathe.

Adapt? Acquiesce? Cooperate? Collaborate.

Papa had watched Carl grow up in the market square, he'd brought vegetables to the bakery when Meneer De Boer was sent to Germany. And now, he'd sold him, and the others, for just over a thousand guilders. Carl's life, a life I couldn't possibly appraise, had been valued on a scrap of paper—by my own father.

As Papa reached to accept the envelope and turned to leave, the soldier brought a small hammer from his belt and hit Papa hard on the back of the head.

I screamed.

The attacker looked around but didn't see me. He quickly retrieved the envelope from the ground. Moving swiftly, he checked over his shoulder again before unclasping Papa's watch, twisting off his wedding ring and tucking both items into his pockets. For a moment he stared at Papa. His body lay still. The soldier swore in Dutch and then apologized before rolling Papa towards the edge of the dock and into canal.

I wanted to cry out again, but my voice caught in my throat. Every part of me seemed frozen in place, as though if I stayed hidden, none of this could be happening. Suddenly, there were sirens blaring.

The man tore off the uniform and took off running towards the train station. From the deck of the mill, I peered down at the water, listening.

I don't know how many minutes passed as I crouched near the sawing floor, hugging my knees to my chest and trying to breathe. Finally, I forced myself to climb down the ladder and approach the edge of the canal. The water was dark, like a clear, black mirror.

"Papa?"

I scanned the dockyards for a rope, anything I could toss into the canal. It was a four-foot drop from the dock to the surface of the water, but in the darkness, I couldn't make anything out. For a moment, I thought I'd dreamt it. There was no sign that he'd been there, not even a drop of blood on the pavement. Pulling his hat down to cover my face, my shoulders began to heave.

Papa, where are you?
Papa, can you hear me?
Papa...I'm sorry.

IN THE DISTANCE, the sirens blared. I looked up, and the forest was on fire.

43

They rode through the woods until they reached a back road that led towards Apeldoorn. Astrid hoped they could trade clothing for supper. But her hands grew stiff and cold, and her head throbbed. Katrine was strangely quiet. Darkness was falling and many of the farms had posted signs at the end of the laneway: No Food.

"We need help," Astrid said. "Let's shelter in that barn overnight. In the morning we can make our way back towards Brummelo and find Schueller."

"And tell him what?" Katrine asked.

"We went to trade our belongings for food, like everyone else…" And came back to find the castle in ruins?

Astrid looked across the field shrouded in fog. All was quiet. They had nothing to lose. They encouraged the horses forward and surveyed the brick barn up close. Katrine hopped down and led her horse towards the large open door. A jersey cow eyed them cautiously. Astrid dismounted and tied her horse to a fence post. The inside of the barn was pitch black, but there was livestock, and it was warm.

As soon as they sat down on a bushel of straw, they realized they were not alone. From the shadows, young men stepped out of the stalls and stood in front of them.

"Hello," Astrid said nervously, her head throbbing. "We've had a bit of bad luck and needed a place to stay…"

The men were quiet. Astrid squinted in the darkness and saw they wore uniforms. But not German uniforms. Thin uniforms poorly suited to the freezing cold outside.

"Douglas, you speak a bit of Dutch, say something!" said a man with a strange English accent.

"Ben je voor de koningin?" the man asked.

Were they for the Queen? Of course they were. But Astrid was too confused to answer. Katrine understood quickly. She knelt down in the darkness and unlatched her suitcase. Under a layer of dresses, she unveiled the captain's pistol, and gave it to the soldiers.

"Yes," Katrine said. "We support the Allies! Orange Shall Overcome!"

Immediately animated, they began chattering excitedly, wondering how Astrid and Katrine had got their hands on such a prize weapon.

Then Katrine unearthed a little white box from her suitcase, a first aid kit. She opened it and showed them her scissors, her thread. Then she pointed to Astrid's head, touching the sticky fabric of her improvised bandage.

Douglas inhaled sharply. He gave instructions to two other men, and they ran towards the farmhouse.

Astrid lay down. She felt an overwhelming desire to sleep right where she was. And she would have if the soldiers hadn't returned with hot water and some towels. The farmer appeared with a lantern.

"Mevrouw. What happened?"

Astrid couldn't answer. Katrine untied the improvised apron-tourniquet and washed the wound with the hot water.

"The horses," she whispered.

"Don't worry, Mother. This kind farmer has watered and fed them. We can stay here with the Canadians tonight." Katrine spoke softly as she pulled Astrid's skin back together and began to stitch her injury closed.

Astrid refused to cry, and though Katrine worked quickly, the pain was searing. In her mind's eye she saw black smoke coming through Soelenkasteel's roof.

What had she done?

She laid her head down on the silk bundle she'd hastily assembled and closed her eyes as Katrine curled up beside her. That night Astrid dreamt that her string of horses ran through the forest all the way to the North Sea, where they found their mother running wild along the dunes.

PART V

44

By April the ground had thawed and the buds on the poplars were bursting into defiant green leaves. I took long walks along the canal, letting my toes sink into the soft grass. I was barefoot like a child, but I couldn't relish innocent pleasure like before. Would I ever feel carefree again?

Sometimes I'd trek all the way to Soelenkasteel to see the destruction for myself and to listen to the sounds of birdsong in the trees. On the roadways, the Germans, erratic and jumpy, commandeered groups of old men and farmers to dig foxholes. Across the skies, the RAF flew boldly and bombed any German military vehicles in sight. Carl's mother discouraged me from wandering, but sometimes it was easier to walk past burned-out armoured cars than to go home, where the smell of Papa's pipe still lingered in the corners of our kitchen.

At the market square I saw the empty space where his stall should have been; at church, I missed the weight of him beside me in the pew. I looked for Papa everywhere, and instead met wary glances. The whispered comments of fellow parishioners tortured me long after the church services were over.

Look what a bit of extra meat cost Nico Zontag.
I heard he never gave up his radio.

The poor man died years ago, when he lost his wife.

ONE AFTERNOON I was having tea with Carl's mother. She took one sip, set down her china cup, and looked at me seriously.

"There's something bothering you."

"People are saying—"

"We could spend our whole lives worrying about what other people say. Ignore them."

"But Papa—" I looked at a portrait of Saint Peter on the wall calendar. "Do you think he's in hell?"

"Not anymore."

And suddenly I understood. The last five years in Brummelo were Papa's hell. His fears, his desperation, his choices. Would a German surrender have ended his torment? How would he have lived with himself if the frozen canal hadn't taken him?

THE FOLLOWING WEEK, Loti and I walked past the Reformed church, where we'd been baptized, studied Calvin's catechism and buried Papa. We continued on to the Saint Martin's Basilica and sat down in the De Boer's pew.

The interior of the church was dark and ornate, cozy compared to the stiff benches and austere white walls of protestant churches. As I admired the stained-glass portrait of a man cutting his robe in two, I thought about Hannah and Ari, and how after the service I would take them food at the Bouwman farm. Ari was ten now, and wanted news of the war, news of his parents. But with each week that passed, I worried my small charges would become orphans like me. The priest said the Americans had liberated concentration camps in the East, and the utter depravity they uncovered was more horrific than anyone could have imagined. He implored his congregants that though the war was ending, there would be many in need of care. How was I supposed to tell innocent children that their suffering wasn't over?

When Mass finished we made our way into the churchyard. I

spotted Lady Astrid, and beside her, Katrine. Lady Astrid raised a hand in a tentative wave. Her Sunday dress was threadbare and her hair was gathered in a loose bun at the nape of her neck. Around her shoulders she wore a cape that did nothing to disguise how thin she'd become. Her familiar silk scarf was the last vestige of her once elegant attire.

"Good morning," I said. Why had I thought we could hide?

"Lovely to see you, Hilde. This must be your sister."

I made the proper introductions, and then we stood awkwardly together.

"How are you? Your beautiful home..."

Rumours that the captain started it on purpose swirled throughout Brummelo, and without a proper investigation, the story held.

"We're making do," Lady Astrid replied.

Katrine seemed to be at a loss for words. We hadn't spoken at all since she'd reached for my hand in prison and then walked out with the guard. Like her mother, she'd grown thinner, and whether from hunger or regret, the spark in her eyes had dimmed a little.

"Would you like to come for lunch?" Katrine asked.

"We're staying at Mayor Schueller's for now," Lady Astrid said. "Though he's rarely there."

I looked at Loti, who shrugged. "Sure," I said. There would still be time to visit Ari and Hannah afterwards.

We walked in silence along the *Neustraat*, past the Central Square and the Stadhuis and headed toward Schueller's home, located across the canal from the factory and the endless food lines. I hadn't seen him lately. Loti had gone back to work at the Stadhuis, but I preferred to tend to the greenhouse, wearing Papa's old coveralls and gathering food for the onderduikers. If I couldn't be with Carl—I stole a glance at the large brick building—at least I could feed him.

A small army tank was parked near the delivery doors and Schueller stood beside it. *This is strange.* Everybody knew the German artillery was kept in sheds by the railway tracks to avoid the Spitfires. I lingered for a moment, staring at the tank, when out of nowhere a bullet whizzed by.

We froze.

Suddenly a German patrol unit ran into the street and threw us down onto the pavement.

"Into the dugout, Mevrouw!" one of them yelled. He was just a boy.

He held out his hand to guide them into a muddy hole. Our shoes were instantly soaked and we huddled together against the earthen wall, trembling.

The Germans lost no time firing back across the canal towards the factory. Villagers ran in all directions, screaming in terror. I desperately wanted to see who they were shooting at, but Loti held me down beside her.

"Come on out Boche! It's over for you!" a man shouted from the opposite bank.

Lady Astrid looked up and locked eyes with me.

"Canadians," Katrine whispered.

And then another voice, a more familiar one, came from a loudspeaker. "Hengelo, Almelo and now Brummelo. Soon all of Gelderland will be free from Nazi tyranny. Surrender and go back to your families!" Mayor Schueller called out in German.

Was this the end? Another round of shots rang out above our heads, and one of the soldiers swore. His rifle had jammed. The others reloaded and took aim once again at the factory, where the Allies were now positioned on the roof. The Germans stopped firing and pulled out a small radio transmitter. The leader spoke quickly. His voice was shaking.

"*Nimm die fabrik*," he yelled into the receiver.

Take the factory.

My breath quickened. The Germans quickly reloaded and moved back into position. Carl was still hiding in the factory, with who knew how many others.

"Oh God," I whispered. "They have no intention of surrendering."

Loti was pale beside me. She closed her eyes and sank to the ground.

We heard nothing for an hour. The sky grew dark and it began to rain. A thick fog settled over us. It was our moment to escape.

"Please," I begged the soldiers. "We're almost at our destination. Now that the fighting has stopped, can we continue?"

Lady Astrid spoke up, too. "Officer, we're leaving now."

The young soldier was surprised, but nodded. He helped her out and then shook her hand gravely.

"Take care, Mevrouw."

"You too, Otto," Lady Astrid whispered.

We hurried along the sidewalk, but we didn't make it to Mayor Schueller's home. Tanks thundered towards the factory. Unless the Canadians had a back-up plan, they were in trouble. The Germans' plea for reinforcements had been heard. I clung to my sister in an alleyway and watched as the Germans circled the factory, trapping the Canadians and anyone else who'd hidden along the road in front.

Lady Astrid began to count aloud. "Six, seven, eight...almost there."

I stared at her, perplexed.

She closed her eyes and pointed to the sky. "It's a trap. The Allies have lured the Germans to the factory."

I heard a loud, mosquito-like buzz and looked up to see bombers overhead. They flew in formation, dipping low and dropping their bombs in unison into the ring the enemy had made around the factory.

"No!" I cried out.

Lady Astrid, Katrine and Loti stared at me in confusion.

"Carl's in that factory!" I broke free from Loti's grip and ran back into the street, but Katrine grabbed my arm and hauled me back to safety.

"You can't do anything." She pinned me against the wall. "You'll be killed."

"So now you care about who gets killed?" I yelled.

Katrine bit her lip and held my arm tighter. "I made a mistake—"

"I don't believe you! Just let me go...I can't lose him, too..."

Katrine grabbed me and threw me back down into the alley.

Loti caught me as I collapsed. We stared at one another, both of us shaking, and only partly because of the bombs.

One of Schueller's neighbours called out to us frantically. "Get off the streets. Come and hide in the cellar!"

We scrambled from the alleyway into the woman's home and huddled under musty rugs against the damp walls of the old home. The woman had boiled eggs and pickles she encouraged us to eat, but I couldn't. With every tremor and explosion, I imagined Carl crushed beneath the thick cement factory walls. The thought of him pinned underneath rebar and dust made me claustrophobic.

Every so often, Lady Astrid tiptoed upstairs. "The sky is orange with fire," she reported.

We felt the trembling of the bombs through the ground, and the sound of gunfire rang in our ears. After that, we endured an eerie silence until hours later, when ambulance sirens punctuated our anxious waiting.

In the early morning, after a sleepless night, we stretched out our cold, wet legs and left to see what was left of Brummelo.

"Mother, look!" Katrine cried.

The bridge hung like a broken arm, its frame badly twisted, the wood planks splintered like matchsticks. We continued walking towards the square, detouring around shelled walls and broken fences. We passed the large foxhole where we'd spent the first hours of the battle and there was nothing in the pit but dirty water. I stared across the canal at the smouldering factory and the charred tanks.

"Listen!" Katrine said.

We stopped. The sound of the organ drifted over from the Basilica. Someone was playing *Het Wilhelmus*, the national anthem. Lady Astrid leaned against a boarded up storefront and held her hand to her heart. Tears streamed down her face.

The four of us locked arms and sang together, at first softly, and then louder as people wandered through the streets and joined in. In the shade of the plane trees a sombre crowd gathered where bodies were lined up, covered in blankets.

My stomach roiled. What about those caught in the factory? I searched the crowd in vain for someone who might know their fate and spotted a large man with a bushy moustache and an orange armband. He was trying to control the crowd while the Canadian general stood behind him. He smiled as children milled around asking the soldiers for chocolates. His name was Arnie.

"Sir," Lady Astrid said. "We're looking for Mayor Schueller."

His smile disappeared. "What for?"

"We saw the battle last night at the factory and we're worried for his safety," Katrine explained.

There was something unnerving about this man. He obviously knew who Mayor Schueller was but didn't appear to have the same concern we did.

"He's been detained," the man named Arnie said. "Your query will have to wait."

We exchanged a quick glance and took off running. A stranger, bearing the orange armband of his comrade, opened the Stadhuis door to us.

"We'd like to speak with the Mayor," I said.

"That's not possible right now," the man replied.

"Who are you?" Lady Astrid demanded.

"I'm a Dutch loyalist—" he started.

"Great," I said. "We are, too."

Lady Astrid raised her eyebrows. "What she means is, we're grateful for what you—what The Resistance—has done..."

The man puffed his chest. "We're guiding the Canadians to German targets to rout the Boche from the entire country!"

"We're sincerely grateful." Lady Astrid shook his hand. "But, why is Mayor Schueller locked up when he should be at his desk?" She spoke with such forcefulness the man took a step backwards.

"If he's such a good friend, Mevrouw, you'd also know that he's an active member of the NSB."

This man obviously didn't know Schueller.

Lady Astrid interjected. "I believe you've been misinformed. Mayor Schueller is only NSB in name. He has served this municipality well—"

The man furrowed his brow. "That may be, but in the eyes of the *Binnenlandse Strijdkrachten*, he's a collaborator."

A man who'd been eavesdropping stepped into the room. "Don't listen to these women. Those are the chatelaines the Germans lived with, and those other two are the daughters of a man who kept the Germans fat all through the war; the older one kept them happy in other ways too…"

Katrine's and Lady Astrid's eyes widened.

"You don't know anything about my father! And as for me…" Loti's voice rose above the crowd and I reached for her arm, pulling her away.

"Loti!" I whispered. "Leave it. Let's get out of here."

My hands shook. Running away from bullets was one thing, but who could say what would happen now? The vestibule of the Stadhuis felt like a boxing ring, the crowd surrounding us like rabid spectators reaching through the ropes.

"Go home girls, I'll find you later," Lady Astrid muttered. The look on her face told me she wasn't going to leave the Stadhuis until she got what she wanted. Katrine stood silently behind her mother. I grabbed Loti by the wrist and pulled her through the crowds until we were running. We made it to Number Eleven.

For five years I'd lived in fear of the Germans. Now my fear of them had been replaced with something else. I slumped onto a chair and cried. Now what? The people of Brummelo were tired of feeling impotent. They'd suffered. The Germans would go home and there would be no one left to blame for the mess they'd left behind. Unless…

Loti sat on the steps of the garden and brushed out her beautiful, thick hair. I listened as she hummed an old folk tune and combed her long mane into one thick braid.

Unless they found someone else to blame.

I bolted the door shut and checked it twice.

Just in case.

45

I spent that night tossing and turning. Every half hour I awoke drenched in sweat, while visions of a burning factory took my breath away. When day broke my head was pounding; a gnawing pain pulsed behind my eyes so intensely I had to stay on the sofa. Loti quietly swept the floor until a loud banging on the front door paralyzed us both.

"Should we answer?" Loti whispered.

I dragged myself to the porch, my robe wrapped tight against myself, and opened the door a crack.

Mevrouw De Boer stood on the threshold, her face flushed. "The onderduikers...they escaped to an underground bunker!"

I shook my head. Surely I was still sleeping. My heart had grown dull to any hope, my mind paralyzed by fear. The pain in my head spread towards my ears, my neck. I felt warm all over, and then my knees buckled.

"Hilde!" Loti rushed to help me stand.

"I...I don't understand."

"Meneer Smits built a bunker under the factory after the first war, and that's where all the men hid. Once the fires were put out, they were pulled to safety."

"Carl is alive?"

Mevrouw De Boer tried to speak but the words kept getting caught in her throat.

"Smoke seeped into the bunker. The men are being treated for smoke inhalation and…poisoning."

My hand flew to mouth. "No…"

"There are five men at the bakery. Dokter Freisen says only time will tell how much soot has entered their bodies. Carl's been drifting in and out, but when he opened his eyes…he whispered your name."

"I have to see him." I pulled myself up, lurching towards my coat.

"Hilde, you're not well," Loti protested.

"I have to go," I said. "Stay here."

I leaned against Mevrouw De Boer and walked down the Nonnenstraat as fast as my feet would carry me, ignoring the waves of nausea from the pain in my right temple.

When we arrived, the parlour was quiet. All the furniture had been moved to make room for cots. Carl was laid out near the stove. His skin was bluish and his breathing ragged. An extremely thin man with hollow eyes sat beside him, holding his hand. It took me a moment to realize it was Carl's father.

"Meneer De Boer!" I hugged him gently, trying not to stare.

"Hello, child. Come sit here beside Carl. He's been calling for you."

I sat. "Carl? It's me, Hilde."

I crouched down to his ear and brushed it gently with my lips, willing his eyelids to flutter open. "I'm here now."

I held my breath, and he reached for me and squeezed my hand.

Dokter Freisen came and stood with us. "I'd like to give the patients more oxygen, but I'm still waiting on supplies. The less they talk, the better."

"Will he recover?"

He glanced warily at Meneer De Boer. "God willing…I must go now and check on the others at the clinic."

Mevrouw De Boer walked him to the front door and as she opened it wide, the sound of shouting drifted into the bakery. Carl's body tensed and I gave his hand a gentle squeeze.

"Don't worry. It's probably just hooligans returning from the beer hall. They must have raided the Germans' supplies."

Mevrouw De Boer scanned the street. Suddenly, above the din, I heard a familiar voice cry out. My heart stopped.

"Carl, I need to go…" It pained me to leave his side, but I had to see what was going on.

Outside in the street, a mob of people shoved several men and women towards the market square. A knot formed in the pit of my stomach. I needed a closer look. Peering into the melee, I saw her long braid.

The angry crowd pushed Loti forward, jeering and pumping their fists in the air. I chased after them, Mevrouw De Boer calling my name. The mob stopped in front of the flagpole, where the Dutch tricolor flew once again. Two men held my sister, and a third brandished a pair of scissors. She was trembling, but she'd stopped crying. Someone produced a wooden chair and they shoved her down roughly, like macabre circus performers. I elbowed my way towards her, but before I could reach her, they'd lopped off her beautiful blond tresses.

"Stop!" I cried. My head was going to explode. I could hardly see straight.

My protests were drowned out by the shouts of onlookers. Someone took a piece of coal and etched a swastika on her forehead. Another spat at her feet. I moved to get closer but strangers held me back. Their angry glares challenged me to defy them.

"See who wants you now, you mof slut!"

"Whore!"

The insults rose in volume, though a few melted back when Loti began to cry.

The pain behind my eyes exploded and something inside me snapped. A raw anger that I'd pushed down rose in my chest.

"ENOUGH!"

The men holding me back released me. Loti's eyes met mine. I burst through and began kicking and hitting the men who'd held her, never once stopping for a breath. I'm not sure how long it went on, the time it took to overturn the chair, grab the scissors and hurl them across the cobblestone. I was panting, my throat raw. Gradually I became aware of another voice yelling into the crowd, full of righteous indignation, and at once my breathing slowed back down.

Mayor Schueller broke through the onlookers with two Canadian soldiers at his side. He stepped up onto the chair they'd been using. Lady Astrid appeared and gently steered Loti and me towards a private garden. Turning to those assembled, Mayor Schueller contemplated them darkly. He met my gaze and lifted his chin ever so slightly.

"Citizens of Brummelo. You pretend to know the hearts of your neighbours? Do you know the secrets kept all these years? You judge one another by what you can see, but we've been living in darkness, the windows of our homes as black as the cruelties committed amongst us."

The crowd grew silent.

"You judge blindly, but in your hearts you know that what happens on the streets isn't what happens inside our homes. You've been brave. And for some of you, it has come at a cost. How many people found shelter in Brummelo because of your courage?"

The mob was silent.

"You don't know! Be careful. Your need to punish has you treading on angels' wings." Schueller seemed to stand taller at that moment.

He was unshaven and bedraggled from his night in prison, but in that moment, in the shadow of Germany's surrender, he truly became our mayor.

"Who among you remembers the Loewensteins, whose shop used to be beside the De Boer's bakery? Perhaps you are still wearing boots they made that have lasted you through the entire war? What about the Goldblatts, who crafted the simple wedding bands on your fingers? Or the Rosens?"

The crowd murmured. They remembered Brummelo's Jews.

"Who has fed their children?"

Silence again.

Schueller turned to me. "Miss Zontag, where are the Loewenstein children right now?"

My head cleared and I found my voice, though it cracked when I spoke. "At the Bouwman farm, Sir."

Schueller feigned surprise. "Hmm. Yet people say Meneer Bouwman was a Nazi sympathizer."

"No sir. He was a very good actor, though, and his farm was one of the safest."

The men who'd shorn Loti's head stood with defiant faces, desperate for a scapegoat for their heavy losses.

"No doubt Brummelo has seen its share of collaborators. The Landwachters and all those who sought to profit and extort will be punished, but the wheels of justice move slowly. If we take revenge, if we take things into our own hands, we risk making tragic mistakes. Civilization will only be a memory."

"So, what do we do?" an old woman asked. "What now?"

Mayor Schueller took a deep breath, and I held my trembling sister closer to me. He pointed to the blond braid trampled on the cobblestone.

"We are better than this."

Lady Astrid left us to stand beside Mayor Schueller while he continued speaking. "If you want to rebuild, come to the Stadhuis tomorrow at seven o'clock. We will restore Brummelo. Brick by brick."

Slowly, the mob dispersed. The men walked past us as though we were invisible. No one apologized; they refused to meet our eyes. I was numb, but Loti was shaking, her forehead hot to the touch.

"Take her home," Lady Astrid said gently.

Loti's scalp had small nicks where the scissors had cut into her skin, but as we made our way home, I wondered about the wounds no one would ever see. How easy would it be to rip them open? How would we ever heal?

If I wanted to protect her, we had to leave.

46

Though the sun was setting behind the east tower of Soelenkasteel Astrid could stay in the garden as long as she wanted. Curfew was over. The Germans were gone and soon, she hoped, the war would truly be over. She surveyed the charred outline of the castle while Schueller tied the horses to a fence post. They'd ridden here from the village for some peace and quiet.

"What now?" Astrid asked, gazing at the home where she'd loved and lost so much. An owl perched on the windowsill of the highest gable.

"More people are making their way home from the East every day now. Men forced to work for the Germans, POW's..."

"Jews?"

Schueller sighed. "Not yet."

She bit her lip. "Is it true people are driving to Kamp Westerbork to retrieve their loved ones?"

"If they can find fuel. But until the entire country is liberated the roads aren't safe." Schueller looked over at Astrid. "If Benjamin's alive, he'll find you."

Astrid wasn't so sure. She thought she'd know if he was alive or dead by a change in the wind or some other kind of sign. It was a silly notion, something out of a romance novel, and yet she found herself looking for him in the crowds, for his black curly hair to appear in a sea of pale, bald heads. Perhaps Benjamin's hair had been shaved off, too. His eyes then. She'd keep looking for his clear, green eyes.

"They hardly look like men now," Astrid said, remembering the skeletal frame of the baker she'd spied crossing the town square.

"I know." Schueller cleared his throat. "Which brings me to something I want to discuss with you."

"Please tell me you've had word from Hans."

"Don't worry about him, he's in good hands. No, it's something else. It's the clinic in the village."

"Go on."

"The Red Cross needs more space. They've taken over the SS training facility but they still need more beds. I've been thinking…if we could repair Soelenkasteel, we could convert it into a convalescent home."

Astrid gazed at the grounds and tried to imagine it. Perhaps the patients could be accommodated in the castle. Besides the factory, it was the largest structure in the village, but it would require a massive effort to restore.

"I want to help, but I have nothing left. A handful of horses, some buried jewels and silverware and this shell of a castle."

"These stone walls were built for medieval enemy raids. It could be repaired—"

"But how? I haven't any money."

"For a treasure like Soelenkasteel, I could gather funds. We could work together—"

"I can't take the town's money."

Schueller nodded. "True. But you could *gift* the town the deed to your home."

Astrid's eyes widened.

He explained hurriedly. "I'll write a provision that allows you to keep a small apartment above the stables, and the property and castle will become Brummelo's new hospital."

"You've thought it all out," Astrid said.

"I don't want to see Brummelo's crown jewel fall into ruin," he admitted.

"*Further* ruin, you mean." She closed her eyes and tried to picture the castle full of people again. Not the elegant gentry or the uniformed Germans, but the citizens of Brummelo, the future of the country.

Schueller got up and stood beside his horse. "I understand if you need time to think it over. I know I'm being bold to ask this from you…"

She took a deep breath and smiled mischievously at this man she'd once been so wary of, a man she now trusted more than a brother.

"Race you," Astrid said, turning towards the horses. "To the heath and back, no short cuts."

Schueller's face broke into an enormous smile. He'd waited twenty years for this. "You're on."

AS THEIR HORSES tore down the hill and into the open meadow, they whooped with excitement. She pushed herself up, feet firmly planted in the stirrups, and shook the reins, but Schueller pulled ahead, his lithe body becoming one with his horse's.

"Come on!" she encouraged her horse, but it was no use.

Schueller had already made the half turn and was headed back towards the castle when Astrid's horse snorted and seemed to shift into another gear. She went from cantering to galloping and Astrid was left hanging on, barely controlling the horse. The filly panted and stretched its legs, closing the gap. Another hundred metres and they would be at the fountain and the race would be done. Fifty metres, twenty-five.

Schueller reined in his mount, and Astrid blew past him, struggling to slow down her horse.

"Whoa!" Both horse and rider were breathless. She began to laugh so hard her belly hurt.

"You know, with a good partner and a horse like that, you could rebuild."

"Maybe." She wondered if she could still get Philomena back after all these years. Gertrud Seyss-Inquart had fled the Netherlands, leaving Clingendael and everything they'd stolen behind.

"Do you miss the tracks?" she asked.

"People will bet on a jockey sooner than a mayor."

Astrid reached for his arm. "I'd put my money on you. You kept this village going." She swallowed, thinking of all the young men buried across Europe. "You kept my son safe."

"I did what I could."

"I'm sorry if I haven't always trusted you."

Schueller looked at Astrid. "They let me out of jail, thanks to you."

Astrid scoffed. "Those men are so ignorant. Prancing around in their armbands…it's so presumptuous. I bet a few of them put those outfits on yesterday, while you've been working for the people for five long years. Someday everyone will see you for who you are."

She thought of her children again.

Wiping away sudden tears, she pictured Hans coming home and walking through the stables with a bucket of oats, greeting the horses. When the Germans had begun to suspect there were men in the factory, Schueller had moved the youngest ones to Amsterdam. How long until they would be together again? Katrine had found a purpose caring for the wounded. She had the energy for the punishing hours at the clinic and never complained, despite the devastating injuries she'd witnessed. The war had taken so much, but somehow, they were still here. The only thing left to do was to move forward.

"Kurt, I see you dressed in your mayoral robes, standing where we are right now, cutting the ribbon to open the Brummelo Convalescent Home."

His eyes widened. "What are you saying?"

In the beginning Astrid remembered Schueller musing that the war was a game—there would be winners and losers. She'd lost what she meant to keep. And yet, even as she looked at the blackened stone and broken glass, she thought, I haven't lost *everything*.

"Soelenkasteel is yours."

47

APRIL 1945

Filip told him several times what had happened, but whenever new prisoners arrived in their barracks and asked about the bright pink scar over Benjamin's eye, he was amused by his friends' recounting of the story. He would tell it himself, but he couldn't remember the details, thanks to the butt end of the German's rifle.

"Two months ago now, there he was, lying face down in the snow, blood seeping from his brain," Filip began. "Karel and I dragged him into the morgue and bandaged his head."

Benjamin smiled; the new prisoners loved the next part of the story best. They'd arrived from Austria and Camp Sered, and whatever they'd seen there had left them with a sense of humour far darker than his own. Still, from their eyes he could tell that they stubbornly held onto some kind of hope.

"And then what happened?" a man asked.

"Karel told the guards we'd thrown Benjamin into the ovens!"

The new arrivals laughed, holding their sides, though it seemed to take all their energy. The dorm elder wouldn't assign them heavy jobs; they were too weak. The Hungarians and Slovaks helped clean the barracks and kill bedbugs; the heavy lifting was left up to the prisoners who'd been in Theresienstadt the longest. Filip and the Slovak doctor, Karel, returned to the crematorium, but Benjamin stayed behind to help prepare for thousands of new arrivals.

"Where are all these people coming from?" Benjamin asked.

"They don't tell me anything," the elder answered. "But," he said, lowering his voice. "The Danes are all leaving tomorrow."

"What?" Benjamin stopped working. No one had left the camp since February. Could this be it?

"Red Cross trucks are arriving in the morning, and every Danish Jew will go home."

Benjamin stared out the window at the fields beyond the garrison walls. He wondered if the Dutch would send relief. Would his government find trucks to repatriate the Jews, too? Filip and Karel said they would walk home as soon as they could; they wanted Benjamin to come to Prague with them. Sometimes at night, he imagined they could do it. Yet every morning the streets of Theresienstadt were once again lined with the dead. People were too sick and hungry—rumours of the end couldn't save even the most hopeful if their bellies were empty. He could always spot the new arrivals by the way they stayed close to their loved ones in the streets, refusing to leave their bodies alone on the sidewalk. For those who'd been in Theresienstadt for months or even years, the dead had become as normal a sight as clouds in the sky.

TWO WEEKS LATER, a frenzied crowd gathered in the *Markplatz*.

"Hitler is dead!" someone cried out.

Filip grabbed a girl and began to dance in the streets, but others eyed the Germans warily. The Red Cross was setting up inside Theresienstadt, alongside the German Lieutenant Colonel. Some kind of deal had been made, but most prisoners were too scared to believe the end was in sight.

"Who the hell is in charge?" Karel asked Benjamin.

"I'm not sure. Why don't you talk to him?" Benjamin pointed to the Red Cross administrator.

Karel shook his head. "If they find out I'm a doctor, they'll force me to stay. I've been here long enough. I need to find my family. As soon as I see American tanks, I'm running back to Prague."

BUT NO AMERICANS came to liberate Theresienstadt.

Filip shook him awake early one morning. "Benjamin, it's over!"

Benjamin ran to the windows. "Where are the Germans?"

"They've gone. Look what I've brought you!" Filip held out cigarettes for him. Benjamin's eyes widened.

"Come and see," Filip said.

In a daze, Benjamin followed his young friend out to the streets. Hundreds of people walked around, but no one was brave enough to laugh or dance down the sidewalks. It all seemed too good to be true. Filip stopped suddenly, and Benjamin almost tripped over him.

"What the…?"

On the pavement lay a dead German officer. Filip knelt down to check for a pulse, and then relieved the man of his belt.

"What are you doing?" Benjamin asked.

Filip shrugged. "Someone else got his watch."

Shots rang out from the buildings above them.

"Take cover!"

They ran back to the barracks. From the window, Benjamin saw a few soldiers give up their weapons and leave, but he didn't trust the streets yet. For every soldier who surrendered, there might be a vengeful sniper in the wings. They spent the day indoors listening to the sound of gunfire. Benjamin was thirsty, and the heat and smell of so many people in one building was suffocating. Still, they stayed where they were safe until nightfall, when a woman's voice called out: "Red flag! Red flag!"

The gates of Theresienstadt opened and Russian tanks rolled in. Along with the others, Benjamin ran outside the garrison walls and for the first time walked along the forbidden streets.

Karel and Filip looked at Benjamin. "Are you coming with us?"

"What? Now?" He hadn't eaten all day. All he had were the clothes on his back.

"If we stay, we'll be quarantined," Karel said.

Benjamin hesitated. People were panicking. It was dangerous. "The roads are full of Nazis."

"When that guy hit you on the head, he sure knocked out more than your memory! Where's your courage, man?"

He didn't want to answer truthfully: he had doubts about courage. It might be brave to run, it might be brave to wait; he didn't have time for a philosophical debate. The Germans had lobbed grenades over the walls, and at any moment the ground around them might explode.

"Don't you want to see her again?" Filip asked quietly.

He looked over his shoulder at Theresienstadt, *Terezin*, and listened to the jubilant cries of prisoners. Someone began to sing, and soon thousands had joined in. It brought tears to his eyes. It was over. He was alive. What was a couple of more weeks of lineups and watery soup? Between the Russian army and the Red Cross, he'd get new papers and find his way home. Sometimes courage was running. Sometimes courage was staying put...

"You can only save a fool so many times," Karel grumbled. "Let's go."

Filip gave Benjamin one last hug. "I will miss your stupid jokes."

He watched his Czech friends until they disappeared into the night. Instead of turning back towards the barracks, he walked to the top of the meadow and lay down on the grass. In the distance he heard a violin, and hopeful melodies rose into the night. Under a sky of a thousand stars, he fell into a deep sleep.

THREE HUNDRED KILOMETRES NORTH, with the stroke of a pen, the Armistice was signed.

48

MAY 1945

One morning, as I pushed our old cart towards our stall in the market square, a soldier greeted me with such a hearty grin I couldn't help but smile back. The soldiers were so healthy looking. I remember thinking it had been so long since I'd spied such ingenuous expressions. Immediately I felt unsteady, guilty. When would I be happy again?

A rusty pick-up truck pulled into the square and Mayor Schueller and Lady Astrid stepped out.

"Good morning, Hilde," Mayor Schueller said, tipping his hat.

Lady Astrid admired the seedlings, a sympathetic gaze crossing her fine features.

"Where are you off to?" I asked. Today was a day for celebration. All around the square flags were flying; music played loudly from the coffee house and people worked to dismantle the signs of five years of occupation. They washed their blackened windows and dug up their buried pewter. The village thrummed with freedom.

"We're going to Amsterdam to bring Hans home," Lady Astrid said.

"*If* we can find enough petrol," Mayor Schueller added.

"You'll be glad to see him," I said. Brummelo teemed with men and boys returning from hiding. The reunited families stirred both hope and despair in me. I only cried when I was alone in Papa's garden. In the market, at mass or anywhere else, my eyes remained dry.

"How is your sister?" Mayor Schueller inquired. He was glancing towards the De Boer bakery where she now spent her days learning to make bread. Hiding in the shadows until her hair grew in.

"Have you tasted her delicious rye cake—"

Lady Astrid interrupted. "We don't care about her bread. How is *she* doing?"

I hesitated. They wanted to hear good news. Like the children who surrounded the soldiers, their hands out for chocolate or chewing gum, they wanted something sweet. Carl was improving, even his father was gaining weight. But there was no denying the truth: Loti was shrinking. Still...

"She's agreed to be my maid of honour," I said.

Lady Astrid's face relaxed into a smile. "When's the big day?"

"Next month, once the renovations are done."

Lady Astrid's eyebrows arched. "Oh?"

Schueller jumped in. "The De Boers have taken over the old shoemaker's shop until the Loewensteins return. Ari and Hannah are back in their old bedrooms."

"And where is the family that moved in when the Loewensteins were taken?"

I wondered the same thing. Mayor Schueller shifted uncomfortably. "They have been sent to Kamp Westerbork with the rest of the Dutch Nazis."

"Oh dear God," Lady Astrid said.

I wanted to change the subject. "With so much going on, the wedding will be small."

"And you will make a beautiful bride," Mayor Schueller said. "Truly."

We locked eyes for a moment, and for a few moments they were silent until Lady Astrid murmured goodbye. They had to get going.

"Safe travels," I whispered to their backs.

Moments later, the truck pulled out of town and they were gone.

HER GRANDMOTHER'S silver spoons for a tank of gasoline. She must be mad. At least she still had her silk curtains. They were packed away safely in the trunk—she'd trade them for information about the horses in The Hague when the moment came. Now, she stared out the window and imagined rebuilding her stables. Along the highway a line of travellers in rags pushed carts along the bicycle path. She looked for Benjamin among the refugees, but saw no green eyes amongst the throng.

"Do you suppose we could inquire at the Red Cross?" she asked Schueller.

"About Benji?" He frowned. "The Red Cross helped Hitler all the way."

"That can't be right," she said.

He shrugged. "They obeyed every order. Without question."

Was that neutrality? No. He was right. Obedience to cruelty could never be called neutrality.

"So, you don't believe they can help us?"

"Let's get your boy home first. If Benjamin's alive, he'll find you."

If. Astrid's heart sunk. She hated that Schueller kept saying *if*.

Schueller slowed the truck as a column of Canadians marched behind a German battalion, blankets and kits thrown over their shoulders. He rolled down his window. "Excuse me, officer?"

A Canadian brigadier walked over.

"Where are you headed?" Schueller asked.

The officer sighed. "Back to Germany. Their commander negotiated a good deal for them."

"What do you mean?"

"The Commander-in-Chief would sign off on anything so long as it meant their men weren't sent to the Reds."

"So, you'll hand these men over to the Americans?" Schueller asked.

"Those are more or less our orders, sir."

"I wish you well. God bless." Schueller saluted the officer and they continued down the highway, careful to avoid the craters that dotted the roadway.

Astrid stared at the backs of the soldiers. They all looked alike, in formation. She thought about how arbitrary it all was. Born on one side of a river, the uniform bore enemy patches. Born on the other side of the water, the victor's.

"I have an idea to help those who have suffered the most. I'll need your help," Schueller said.

"Oh?"

"I want to try using horses therapeutically." Schueller told her about a Swede who'd been experimenting with animal companionship to calm patients with nervous disorders.

"I didn't know you were so fascinated with modern medicine," she said.

"We have a lot of healing ahead if we're going to build a modern country again."

"Why do your grandiose plans always involve my stables?"

Schueller lit a cigarette and smiled.

They drove on in silence towards Amsterdam, over narrow bridges until they found a spot to park along the Singel. People crowded aid booths, holding photographs of their missing friends and family. Lampposts were covered in crude missing persons placards, desperate pleas for information about those the war had swallowed up. Astrid said a prayer for the anonymous lost ones whose eyes stared at her from the flimsy posters. Could a piece of paper possibly bring families back together?

Schueller pointed to a tall black house. "Here we are."

Astrid adjusted her silk scarf and followed Schueller down the street. Her heart was racing. She looked around and saw the crowds moving towards the Dam Square. Instead of knocking on the door, Schueller stood in the middle of the street and whistled. A window on the third floor opened and Hans appeared. Overcome with relief, she had to hold onto Schueller to steady herself.

"Mother!"

Moments later, he burst through the door onto the street. "You got my letter! I wrote as soon as I could, but since they blew up the tracks—"

"It doesn't matter, son. We're together now."

He'd grown since she last saw him. She'd wanted to find him, to warn him about Soelenkasteel. "Hans, there's something I need to tell—"

Schueller cleared his throat. "Let's go sit in a restaurant and talk. You have a lot of catching up to do."

"Mayor Schueller is right, Mother. Right now, the best thing to do is join the party. Listen…You can hear the singing from here. How about some croquettes?"

They joined the crowd and walked along the *Kalverstraat* towards the Royal Palace where the streets were littered with flags and flowers. Here and there houses were missing their wooden shutters and trees had been crudely chopped down, evidence of a harsh winter and an urban population under duress. Finally, they arrived.

"You should have seen the crowds here two days ago, Mother. Grown men weeping at the sight of the Allied…" Hans stopped, practically bumping into two men with orange armbands standing on the corner, facing off with a couple of Germans.

"Give us your guns," one of the men ordered.

The German soldiers scowled. "The Canadians are in charge of disarmament, not you lot. Get lost!"

One of the Dutch Interior Forces men, a stout figure with close-set eyes, refused to budge. "Give us your gun or I'll shoot."

Astrid gasped. Surely, he wouldn't—

Bang!

From the Grote Club behind them, shots were fired towards the Interior Forces men. One of them fell, and then more of their comrades appeared and shot back at the snipers. The crowd dispersed in a mad panic.

"Run!" Hans pulled Astrid towards the meagre shelter of a street organ.

"Hans!" Astrid screamed. The Germans inside the club returned a hail of bullets into the Dam Square. They were trapped. All around them people were lying on the ground, bleeding.

"Oh my God." Schueller pointed to a balcony where a machine gun was trained on the square below. "Shit!"

Astrid looked around in desperation. People were searching for cover behind lampposts. Adults shielded children with their bodies. A pregnant woman tripped and fell onto the streetcar tracks. Hans looked wide-eyed at his mother. They were going to die if they didn't make a run for it.

Schueller spotted an open beer cellar in front of the Café Oranje. "We've got to get over to that bar!"

It was no more than twenty metres, but Astrid's legs felt like they were made of lead.

"Take your mother," Schueller said, looking across the square at the Royal Palace. "I'll be right there."

Hans grabbed her hand and they ran. Astrid covered her ears to drown out the sounds of the bullets whizzing past, and they clambered into the cellar. Righting herself, she had a clear view of Schueller scaling the palace wall across the square. He reached the top of the tower and crouched down on the roof. Drawing his pistol, he aimed towards the German manning the machine gun. His first shot missed. His second shot crippled the gunner and attracted the attention of the snipers.

He didn't get a third shot.

Astrid screamed as his body crumpled and disappeared from sight.

"He's been shot!" she cried. "I have to go to him."

Hans crouched beside her and scanned the square. "We can't…we have to wait."

After what seemed like ages, the guns were silent. A Resistance leader and a German officer entered the club together.

"Now is our chance," Hans said.

"How will we get into the palace?"

"Follow me."

They ran. Astrid flew behind her son while the sounds of ambulances rang in her ears. Hans banged on a door. No one answered.

"Adrian, it's me! Hans Stenger!"

The door opened a crack, and a portly guard looked out warily.

Hans was breathless. "A man climbed into the tower to stop the gunner but now he's been shot."

The guard shook his head in disbelief. "Follow me. Quickly."

They crossed through the marble halls and ran up a winding staircase to the top floor. The guard opened door after door from a set of keys that jingled around his waist.

"Please, sir. Hurry. Our friend..." Astrid's voice cracked.

Finally, they reached the tower. Schueller's small frame was curled in a ball. His pistol lay on the ground beside him. Astrid ran to his side and knelt down. She turned him over and saw the blood seeping through his shirt. She held his wrist, anguished to feel only a faint pulse.

"Kurt, it's me. It's going to be alright." Astrid choked on promises that he'd be okay, while life flowed out of him before her eyes. This wasn't how it was supposed to end.

Schueller opened his eyes briefly, and they fluttered closed again.

"No. No... The war is over! You can't die now!" Her words escaped in desperate, staccato bursts. How could he have been so careless?

Hans knelt down and put his arms around her.

She glanced at him. Schueller's breathing grew ragged.

"Ever since that day at the tracks..." Schueller rasped. "I've wanted to be better...for you."

A furious lump rose in Astrid's throat. She kissed Schueller's head and listened as he breathed his last. Hans held her close, and the guard gently closed the dead man's eyes. On the street below, hundreds lay wounded.

The unfairness of it all washed over her. She unwrapped her silk scarf from her neck and gently covered her friend's face. When the sirens below were silent, the guard and Hans carried him out of the palace, through the streets, towards Schueller's rusty truck.

"Who was this man?" the guard asked. He took off his hat and held it over his heart. "The newspapers will want to know."

Astrid looked at her son. Who *was* Kurt?

Hans' voice trembled with emotion. "Meneer Schueller, mayor of Brummelo and leader of the Resistance in the Veluwe."

Astrid and Hans squeezed one another's hands. Finally, Hans started the engine. He glanced backwards at the body, now wrapped in an old silk curtain, and drove east towards a home that no longer existed.

49

SEPTEMBER 1945

I'd inherited two things from my mother—her Singer sewing machine and her flat chest. I'd hoped to improve on what nature had given me with a few well placed darts, but in the end it wasn't fabric that changed my profile. We'd only just married, and I was newly pregnant.

So many children were conceived in those early weeks and months after the Germans left. In our little attic bedroom with the leaky roof, it felt as though the entire household resting below us had willed the conception. As if one child could make up for all the death.

When I told Carl the news, that was the end of my gardening days. He must have thought the baby would fall out of me. The next afternoon he hauled the Singer up to the attic, along with scraps of fabric, back issues of Vogue magazine and a carefully folded parachute.

"You'll be needing some new clothes," he said, eyeing my belly.

I didn't want to sew anymore, not after everything. The machine had sat idle, but Dokter Freisen agreed with Carl that I shouldn't exert myself in Papa's greenhouse. I wanted to resist them both, to carry on tending the garden, but morning sickness held me back, and eventually I relented and began sorting the fabric. My mother-in-law brought old coats and dresses, and I ripped everything apart until I had a fresh canvas.

One afternoon Loti knocked on the door and let herself in. In her hands she held a pair of baby booties. I burst into tears. There would be no more school for me, maybe not for Carl either. Loti misunderstood the source of my grief.

"It's going to be all right," she murmured.

It had been years since she'd comforted me. I took a deep breath. She was right. I flipped through the magazines and showed her a dress I'd marked up with pencil.

"I have a new design," I said.

She raised an eyebrow. "For you?"

I shook my head. "For you. I need a model."

THE FIRST SHIRTWAIST dress I made in the De Boer's attic wasn't my best creation, but Loti wore it well. After she finally went out in public to see the Queen, who was travelling through Brummelo on her victory tour, I could hardly keep up with the orders. And then, once I'd perfected the cut, I was ready to try the silk parachute. Loti called it a "victory gown." The summer of 1945 flew by as orders for the most coveted bridal fashion in Gelderland piled up.

ONE SUNNY SEPTEMBER AFTERNOON, Carl turned the sign on the bakery door to 'closed' and the entire family set off together towards the square. The whole town stopped working and headed towards the ceremony at the Stadhuis, following the sound of a brass band tuning up in the distance.

I scanned the crowd, but my friend was nowhere in sight. A group of engineers from the rail yard fell in step alongside us.

"I reckoned old Smits would have wanted the job," one man said.

"Nay, he's an entrepreneur. No time for politics. He wants to rebuild the factory and focus on the future," another said, hopping gingerly over a gaping hole in the cobblestone.

"We're entering a new age, gentlemen," my father-in-law said, in his calm manner. They took in the measure of his frail body and nodded politely. I could tell they were sceptical; the conversation in the coffee houses was the same everywhere. Could anyone replace Mayor Schueller?

Katrine spotted us from the dais set up in front of the Stadhuis. "Hilde! Mother needs you. Can you come with me?"

Without waiting for an answer, she grabbed my arm and dragged me towards the Stadhuis, promising Carl we'd be right back.

Katrine led me to the mayor's office, where her mother stood frowning at her reflection in the mirror.

"Lady Astrid, what's the matter? The ceremony is about to begin. Why are you still in here?" I asked.

"She's nervous," Katrine said.

"How can I help, Mevrouw?"

"Something is missing," Lady Astrid said.

I stood back and looked her over. She wore a long dark skirt, a blouse and an emerald green jacket I'd altered for her the week before. But she was right. The outfit was too subdued for someone used to making an entrance. I had an idea.

I whispered in her ear and a smile spread across her face.

I turned to leave, but thought of something else. "One more thing. Where's your silk scarf?"

Lady Astrid's face tightened. "I gave it away."

I opened my purse and pulled out a silk square sample from the last of my parachute stock. Gently I secured it around her neck, letting it flow over her jacket.

She fingered the fabric. "How clever," she said, turning to slip out the back door.

Katrine and I made our way out to the square. We found the De Boers and settled onto a bench beneath the shade of a sycamore maple. Dignitaries jostled one another on the stage as the master of ceremonies cleared his throat and spoke into the microphone. The crowd stilled as he introduced the Minister of Home Affairs. An old man with a tuft of snow-white hair looked out at the crowd and began to speak.

"In my line of work," he began, his voice the crackly timbre of an elder statesman, "one must be careful what one promises, especially if one puts it in writing."

Around me the crowd chuckled.

"When I wrote to Lady Astrid to express my sorrow that her home had been destroyed, I penned these fateful words: *if there's anything I can do, count on me.* As you can see, we're gathered here today because Lady Astrid, a woman whose ancestors established this village in the fourteenth century, called me up to make good on those words."

I leaned into Carl. "Mayor Schueller would be so proud."

He pulled me closer, his eyes shining.

The Minister continued. "And so, it is my privilege to officiate the swearing in of Lady Astrid Van Soelen, the new mayor of Brummelo."

The band started to play and the crowd waited for her to emerge from backstage. Instead, she entered the square from behind the Stadhuis, riding a handsome golden palomino and tossing sweets to the children. She radiated beauty and confidence.

Lady Astrid gracefully dismounted, and Hans took the reins. She walked up the steps to the podium and accepted the wreath the Minister placed around her neck. Resting her hand on the Bible, she swore an oath to the town and its citizens. As she gazed out at the crowd and beyond it to the graveyard, I imagined she was making a promise to Mayor Schueller, too.

ASTRID HAD POLITELY DECLINED the jenever she was offered at the council celebrations in the Stadhuis. She wanted a clear head. The endorsement of the town's wealthiest businessman ensured that the new councillors accepted her leadership, however grudgingly, and by the end of the evening, she felt she'd made inroads with the doubters. Astrid looked forward to the challenge of steering the town into the future. She'd sleep well in her apartment tonight, but before she rode home, there was someone she wanted to talk to.

She opened the creaky iron gate of the graveyard and let herself in. The grass was damp so she spread out her jacket before sitting down. Reaching into her pocket, she retrieved a silver flask.

"I hate to drink alone, but I hope under the circumstances you'll forgive me."

She took a swig and let the amber liquid warm her.

"I missed you today," she said with a sigh. "How do I know whom to trust? *You're* the one who knows everyone's true colours."

The jail behind the Stadhuis was still full of collaborators awaiting trial, but someday—perhaps sooner than later—they'd be released and the town would have to learn to live together again.

She kicked a stone with her boot. "I feel so alone."

It was quiet in the graveyard. The trees created an intimate dome, and moonlight shone through the branches. Shadows that once might have frightened her tonight did not. Tonight, she was the mayor. At least, that's what she told herself until a cool breeze rustled the dry leaves around the headstones, and the hairs on the back of her neck pricked. She took another swig of jenever to shore up her courage.

"Kurt…tell me it's just the two of us here."

She glanced behind her. The bar across the street cast a yellow glow onto the pavement. A man leaned on the iron gate, as though hesitating whether to step forward. From his clothes she guessed he was another vagrant looking for a quiet place to sleep. She eyed the high stone walls around her, feeling suddenly hemmed in.

Astrid rose. The intruder's face was hidden in the shadows but when he opened his palm, she saw he carried a single, smooth stone.

"I was hoping to pay my respects," he said, placing the pebble on Schueller's headstone.

She'd know his voice anywhere.

"Are you a ghost?" she asked, her voice barely a whisper.

Benjamin stepped into the moonlight. "I've wondered the same thing myself." He reached for her hand and squeezed it lightly. "If you can feel this…maybe that means we're both still alive."

He held out his arms and Astrid fell into them. He was so thin, so very, very thin. She reached up and touched the scar above his eyes.

"What happened?"

He gave her a sad smile. "It will take me a lifetime to tell you."

Astrid began to cry.

"Shhh," he said. "We have...a lifetime."

She tilted her head towards his to meet his lips. He pressed against her and ran his hands through her hair. When they finally pulled apart, she asked him, "Where have you been?"

He closed his eyes and his jaw began to tremble. He couldn't speak.

A jazz melody floated into the street from the bar, and a saxophone solo echoed off the alley walls. Slowly they danced, their hearts beating against one another's.

"I will never let go of you again," she said, brushing her fingers lightly along his cheek.

He picked up Astrid's jacket from the lawn.

"Have you seen the castle?" she asked.

He nodded. "A young nurse cleaned me up a bit and told me where I might find you."

Katrine? "What did she say?"

Benjamin shook his head. "She couldn't stop crying. I told her the salt from her tears was stinging my skin, and she finally got on with the job. She's not half bad at dressing blisters..."

"Don't joke. Please."

He began to cry.

Astrid put her arms around him and stroked his back.

"Everyone thinks the work will be rebuilding roads and bridges and dykes." He sighed. "But what about living beside the same people who wanted us dead? Doctors turned in by their patients, shopkeepers by their customers..."

"...Teachers by their students."

Benjamin was quiet. "She was just a child."

Her child. She'd raised her.

Astrid untied her horse from the pole outside the graveyard. "You ride, I'll walk."

He didn't protest.

"I always liked the look on your face when you wanted something." Benjamin put his foot in the stirrups and hauled himself into the saddle. "I fell in love with that determination."

"Some would call it stubbornness."

"Or the snobbish gaze?"

He was teasing again. He was still Benjamin. "Underneath all that you saw something you liked," Astrid whispered.

"Loved." He leaned down and caressed her hair. "From the beginning."

They travelled the streets in silence, along the canal and past the burned-out factory until they arrived at a darkened home, large and modern, with a stable out back where they settled the horse.

"He left it all to me," Astrid said, pointing at the house. "But whenever I step inside…I can only move his stuff from one pile to another."

Benjamin put his arms around her. "We'll put things back together."

She ran her hands along his jawline, as though a map to the future could be traced on the contours of another's body, and slowly led him upstairs to bed.

50

EPILOGUE

Volendam 1947

The ship cuts white lines that instantly disappear across an endless black expanse, nautical miles erased in seconds. I close my eyes against a swell of nausea and clutch the railing. The roiling dark waters below make me shiver, and I pull my coat tighter across my chest.

Tonight is a full moon, and here at the stern I can breathe. Atop a storage bench for life preservers, I tuck myself against the cool, steel wall and listen to the exhalations of the ocean liner. The tears come when I'm alone; I don't even try to stop them. I wish I could choose what to remember and what to forget, but I can't. I miss the weight of his arm around my shoulder, assuring me we'd be alright.

Behind me, the steamer's whistle blasts. A sailor strolls past with a mop and a bucket. He doesn't see me and sloshes the deck with bleach. I close my eyes and it is a spring day, years ago, and the market smelled just like this. I'd taken out my braids and was skipping past the stalls. Instead of tulips, the air stank of grease. The flower seller held a gun.

Another whistle blast. The sailor hums while he drags the mop across the deck. I watch him until my legs ache, then I get up and take one last look at the inky black waters, as I've done night after night since leaving Rotterdam. There are days when I imagine that his body sank peacefully below the waves, that the waters welcomed him expectantly as a mother embraces her long lost son. But other times I remember how he crumpled to the ground when he was struck. My confession is barely a whisper, but I say it anyway.

I'm sorry.

"Hilde?" Carl rounds the corner, a worried expression on his face.

"I'm right here, sweetheart." I take his hand and we walk towards the dining room where Loti and Hendrik wait for us on the deck chairs. Our toddler is snuggled against his auntie and doesn't see us approaching. He has Papa's serious gaze. No one knows where his freckles came from.

"Shall we go in? I think I smelled roast beef."

We leave the quiet of the deck and head into the bright dining hall. I glance around the room at the laughing faces gathered under twinkling chandeliers. I try to be happy; after all, this was my idea. Leaving Carl's family, and Ari and Hannah, for the chance to start over.

An elegant older woman beckons us to join her. She's made friends with Loti at the card table. We sit down and make introductions. The woman insists we call her Ro.

"You're the famous seamstress I've heard so much about. Your sister told me that the ballerina Audrey Hepburn is wearing one of your parachute silk neckties. Well done!"

The praise makes me blush. "Thank you."

Carl and Loti proceed to brag about the Montreal atelier that has hired me, and for a moment I'm pulled into the dream, back into the present.

The waiters serve dinner, and between courses we share stories from the war.

"We lost so many, didn't we?" Ro remarks, her cloudy eyes brimming.

I nod. I think about my parents, buried side by side. Who will visit their graves now that we're gone?

Loti pushes away her dessert and wipes away an errant tear. "Our father was killed during the war. He was just a gardener, but he wasn't afraid to bend the rules, either."

Ro raises an eyebrow. "Ah?"

Loti rushes on. "He once kept a pig so we'd have meat and hid his radio until the very end…he couldn't resist the BBC."

I feel the nausea returning. Carl reaches for my hand.

"…One night he went out on an errand. Thieves robbed him and threw him into the canal."

I struggle to control my breathing. Ro comforts Loti, offering her some water.

"Hendrik," I call out. "Come snuggle Mam for a minute."

He leaves Loti's lap and crawls onto mine. I stroke his cheeks and kiss his sweaty head. When we packed up our wooden shipping container, I made sure to save Papa's stationary. Sometimes when I look at the horizon I imagine him at the kitchen table at Number Eleven, writing me a letter. *Dear daughter…* it reads… *I've always wanted the best for you.* I swallow hard.

Hendrik falls asleep on my chest, so we lay him down on Carl's coat and cover him with a shawl. We stay in the dining room, and someone pulls out a deck of cards. Sipping jenever we quietly trade anecdotes from the war. Though only two years have passed, I sense we've edited much. Underneath the bravado—the daring tales, improbable encounters, glorified accounts of heroism and survival—I wonder about people's private regrets, their moments of cowardice, the shameful submission we endured. How will we curate our memories on the ocean so that we can live with them on land?

Carl squeezes my leg under the tablecloth. A wave of understanding passes between us, a promise we make without words. I reach for his hand and hold it tightly, as though touch is enough to cradle our secret. To the world, we're united by our rings, our vows, Hendrik. But from the day I reached into the smooth folds of Papa's coat and found the list, we've been bound together by a story we'll never tell.

After the final round of Klaverjassen, Loti takes Hendrik down to our cabin, and Carl and I do another lap around the deck. This time we head to the bow. I gaze at the water below and reach into my pockets, fingering a wedding ring and gold watch I never wanted in my possession. The evidence of a choice I never wanted to make.

"Are you sure about this?" Carl asks.

I wasn't. I wasn't. I wasn't…and then, I can almost hear Papa's voice as he banged his fist on the table, sending teacups clattering to the floor. *We won't speak of this anymore!*

And then, another voice reaches up to me. I close my eyes and see Mama's yellow dress, her easy smile from where she stood by the sink. *Well now, Muisje. Are you going to just stand there?*

In one swift motion I heave the jewelry as far as possible into the sea.

The gold sparkles in the moonlight for the briefest moment and disappears. I cling to the echo of their voices, knowing they will speak to me for the rest of my life. By morning our ship will dock in Halifax and in the new country our children will grow old with an origin story formed out of the ashes of the war. They'll tell their children stories of resistance.

ALL BUT ONE.

THE END

ACKNOWLEDGMENTS

A little boy spent the war years hiding in a bakery. A young girl sat on the floor of her dining room once a week so that the Jewish guests could have a chair. Hanging from the trees over the gravestones another girl played in the shadows of the cemetery, safe from the Germans who patrolled the streets and stole their food. In a photograph of rail thin men with armbands at the end of the war, a familiar face smiles uncertainly into the camera. To my grandparents—Sake Dijkstra, Tjaltje Hilverda, Jannetje Vreugdenhil and Jake Timmerman—thank you for your stories. Thank you for sharing them with my generation, in bits and pieces, and for passing on the desire to discover the layers that lie beneath.

I was probably only nine or ten years old when my grandmother put *Journey Through the Night* in my hands. Though Anne De Vries' children's book has been criticized by contemporary readers for oversimplifying the moral dilemma of Dutch citizens during the Nazi occupation, it opened a window for my grandparents to share painful stories that they hadn't been able to speak aloud in their first decades in Canada. Though arguably a propaganda piece—curated memories, shall we say—the book gave me a frame of reference, a vernacular to contrast the ways of the old country with the experience of the new country.

This novel started in my imagination with the shred of a tragic anecdote about a father and daughter and the chasm between them. The snippets of stories from the war years that stayed with me the longest were the betrayals and divisions within families. Throughout the years researching this novel I often felt the eeriness of history repeating itself. As I read about the Dutch constructing Camp Westerbork using Jewish assets, the news was filled with clips of children in cages, a border wall and the former president's call to make the Mexicans pay. Suddenly, learning the lessons of the past seemed not only interesting but urgent.

In 2018 I visited the Resistance Museum in Amsterdam where on the wall in the entryway in bold font are the stark choices that citizens faced. *Resist? Collaborate? Cooperate? Strike? Inform?* I wondered what would lead a gentle farmer to make the choices he made. What path would you take if you had nothing to lose? If you were wealthy? If you were Jewish? I realized I couldn't imagine a person's worldview in 1939 unless I went further back in time to understand the open wound that was WWI. I am grateful for the introduction to Elisabeth Van der Jagt, a teenager herself during WWII, and the invaluable personal experience she shared with me. For a love of history, I thank my parents, Sid and Jane Dykstra. Our home was always filled with books, and I learned that you can't truly know people or places unless you investigate their backstory.

In the same way that *Between Silk and Wool* is the story of unlikely allies becoming friends, so too is the writing life. I owe a debt of gratitude to the brilliant writers whose stories have intersected with mine, and who have encouraged me to tell the truth. To the original Loving-Ass-Kicking Society members gathered at Brian Henry's Wednesday writing group, thank you for the push to take a short story and turn it into a novel. To Mary, who always asked for *MORE*—here you go.

To Sally Basmajian, Inge Christensen, Nancy De Guerre and Catherine Skinner—thank you for being my constant companions from creation to completion of this novel. For your faithful reading of each draft, for brainstorming solutions to plot holes and character flaws, for the big *what if* ideas and the copy edits, I couldn't ask for a better dream team of talented, funny, and beautiful women. Thanks for the gift of your presence each week at Station One.

I am thankful for my readers, family and friends along the way who have often asked *how's the writing going?* Whether through my short stories, my blog or at a live storytelling event, I've been encouraged by every single person who has ever tapped me on the shoulder, or emailed to say, *I enjoy your writing.* Thank you to Victoria McMurchy for reading an early draft. Thanks to you, this novel has one less POV, and is the better for it.

To my hometown friends, thanks for reminding me where I come from, and the annual *what are you reading?* chats at Memorial Park. Thanks for believing in the authors among us. For this one-of-a-kind cover, deep gratitude to my longtime friend and talented artist, Kim Collins of 4x5 design.

To my New Hope family, thanks for making space for creative retelling of the stories that shape us. Thank you to my friends gathered each week at Main and Kenilworth who remind me what's real and what's only hubris and dust. I thank God for putting our lives on a collision course. Thank you for sharpening me and softening my rough edges.

To my brothers and their families, I love you all. To the entire Dykstra family, my aunts and uncles and cousins, thanks for being a family who keeps stories alive by staying connected to one another. To the Scholman and Karsten families from Niagara to Iowa and back to Markelo, NL, thank you for sharing your life stories with me, and for your love. Special thanks to my family in the Netherlands, the Dijkstras and the Van Holtens, and to the Tingen sisters, for filling in many of the gaps.

Special thanks to dear friends Pat H, Alison S, Sylvia A, Trish D and Sarah L. I'm thankful for the friendship of the Dinner Club crew, the SCS community, Martha and Mario T, Martha and Thomas R, Magali B, the Nagtegaals, the Goodrows, the Libedinskys, the VanRijns and many branches of the Buys family. Thank you for the unique ways you have nurtured this dream and shared your personal histories with me.

To the local writing community in Hamilton Ontario—what a vibrant, encouraging group of authors reside here! I want to thank the LitLive reading series, Steel City Stories and GritLit for the robust army of volunteers who have given new writers a platform to share their work.

Lastly, to my family. For the better part of a decade, I have been curled up with autobiographies, memoirs, history books and novels about WWII. And the three of you have often been right beside me, buried in your own books. I'm so grateful you share a love of story with me, and grateful to live life off the page with you. Maria and Peter, thanks for reading my sticky note on the bedroom door—*author at work*—and giving me space to write. Wayne, even my best words won't come close to being enough. I'm grateful that you've been here every step of the way. I love you.

Because of each of you, this novel is finally out in the world.

And now, on to the next book.

GLOSSARY

DUTCH WORDS AND ABBREVIATIONS

Appleflappen: apple fritters
Bakfiets: a specialized delivery bicycle cart
Binnenlandse Strijdkrachten: Interior Forces; Dutch armed resistance group combined into an army under the command of Prince Bernard
Dropjes: quintessential black salty licorice candy
Heinnecke Column: civilian snitches who took Nazi money to betray those who harboured Jews and other individuals in hiding
Hoofdstraat: Main Street or High Street
Jenever: Dutch gin similar to an unaged whisky. Popular in Holland and Belgium. There are two main types, *oude* and *jonge,* which refers to distillation techniques
Jeugstorm: a Nazi counterpart to Scouting and Guiding in the Netherlands
Jongedame: a young lady
Jongen: a boy
Kasteel: castle, as in Soelenkasteel "Soelen Castle"

GLOSSARY

Kerk: church
Klaverjassen: typical Dutch card game popular amongst the working class
Kruidnoten: round, bite-sized spiced cookies that are popular at Christmastime
Landwachters: Dutch citizens who worked for the SS betraying their fellow countrymen for various offences against the German regime
Luftwaffe: German air force
Meneer: mister
Mevrouw: ma'am, Missus, Milady
Mof *(plural:Moffen):* Dutch slur directed at Germans; similar to the Anglo "Jerry", "Boche" or "Kraut"
Muisje: nickname — "little mouse"
Nieuwsbrief: news bulletin; proper name of one of the underground illegal tracts in the 1940s
National Socialist Bond (NSB): the Dutch political party that supported the Nazis
Onderduikers: divers, those who had gone underground into hiding
Pepernoten: honey-anise Sinterklaas cookies
Persoonsbewijs: the Nazi-issued photo identity cards Dutch citizens were mandated to present at checkpoints
Razzia: a raid; most commonly used to describe the round-ups of Jews in the cities
Schatje: sweetie
Sinterklaas: Father Christmas
Stadhuis: City Hall
Straat: street
Trouw: Dutch Protestant newspaper circulated by the Resistance in the later war years
Verdorie: damn
Verzuiling: pillarization; the social spheres of Dutch society before WWII
Werkdorp: experimental farm in Holland to train urban Jews in agriculture so they could leave Holland and re-settle in Palestine

GLOSSARY

Zwarte Piet: Black Peter; clown figure in blackface who accompanies Father Christmas

GERMAN WORDS AND ABBREVIATIONS

Fallschirm: parachute
Herr: mister
Reichskommissar: Imperial Commissioner; the top Nazi leader in the Netherlands, appointed by Hitler (Arthur Seyss-Inquart filled this role in the Netherlands from 1040-1945)
Scheisse: shit
Schutzstaffel or SS: security and surveillance arm of the Nazis throughout occupied Europe
Vaterland: Fatherland, a.k.a Germany
Wehrmacht: war machine

SUGGESTIONS FOR FURTHER READING

The following books provide a further lens into life in WWII Europe, whether in Holland or other occupied countries. I focused most of my research in Holland, but also dove into survivor accounts from Terezin, the garrison town in Czechoslovakia that appears in Between Silk and Wool.

Fiction

- All the Light We Cannot See by Anthony Doerr
- Journey Through the Night by Anne De Vries (yes, that's the book that started it all)
- Girl in the Blue Coat by Monica Hesse
- Salt to the Sea by Ruta Sepetys
- Stones from the River by Ursula Hegi
- Suite Française by Irène Nemirovsky
- The Baker's Secret by Stephen P Kiernan
- The Book Thief by Marcus Zusak
- The German Girl by Armando Lucas Correa
- The Nightingale by Kristin Hannah
- The Orphan's Tale by Pam Jenoff

SUGGESTIONS FOR FURTHER READING

- The Tiger Claw by Shauna Singh Baldwin
- Winter in Wartime by Jan Terlouw

Non-Fiction

- A Boy in War by Jan de Groot
- Helga's Diary: A Young Girl's Account of Life in a Concentration Camp by Helga Weiss
- Last Hope Island by Lynne Olson
- Terezin: Voices from the Holocaust by Ruth Thompson
- The Ambiguity of Virtue: Gertrude Van Tijn and the Fate of the Dutch Jews by Bernard Wasserstein
- The Diary of a Young Girl by Anne Frank
- The Dutch in Wartime: Survivors Remember Series edited by Anne van Arragon Hutten
- The Girls of Room 28: Friendship, Hope, and Survival in Theresienstadt by Hannelore Brenner-Wonschick
- The Hiding Place: The Triumphant True Story of Corrie ten Boom by Corrie ten Boom, John Sherrill, Elizabeth Sherrill
- The Nazi Officer's Wife: How One Jewish Woman Survived the Holocaust by Edith Hahn Beer and Susan Dworkin
- The Occupied Garden: Recovering the Story of a Family in War-torn Netherlands by Kristen Den Hartog and Tracy Kasaboski
- The Perfect Horse: The Daring US Mission to Rescue the Priceless Stallions Kidnapped by the Nazis by Elizabeth Letts
- The War in the Corner: Chronicle of a Village in Wartime Netherlands by Jan Braakman

ABOUT THE AUTHOR

Born and raised in Grey County (with a few fantastic detours), Lena Scholman now draws inspiration from the proud, local writing community of the Golden Horseshoe. She holds a bachelor's degree in French and Spanish from the University of British Columbia and an education degree from the University of Toronto. Her writing has appeared in the Hamilton Spectator, the Toronto Star and the Globe and Mail. She lives with her husband and children in Hamilton, Ontario. In addition to writing, she is the Spiritual Life Facilitator for a gap year program that encourages young people to explore the stories of home and land and wonder about their place in the world. She enjoys hiking and skiing along the Niagara Escarpment, long meals around a big table and curling up with a good book.

www.lenascholman.com

CPSIA information can be obtained
at www.ICGtesting.com
Printed in the USA
JSHW052011060422
24600JS00004B/9

9 781778 018800